NEMESIS.
A Novel of the Battle for Syracuse and the Spartan Gylippos
By Jon Edward Martin

Acknowledgements

I would like to thank Ms. Jennifer Coonan for her expert assistance in the final editing of this manuscript. Thanks, also, to an indispensable friend on my trips to Greece, Mr. Spiros Halkides who has driven me all over his beautiful country to view firsthand the many locations in my novels.

Jon Edward Martin

Historical Note

Approximately a half century after the Greek victory over the Persian Empire, one time allies, Sparta and Athens, became engaged in a protracted struggle for supremacy of the Greek world. Called the Peloponnesian War by modern scholars, the first half of the conflict ended after a Spartan victory at Amphipolis led by Brasidas. A fragile peace treaty was enacted, but this was quickly undermined by the ambitious Athenian aristocrat Alkibiades. Once again the two major powers of ancient Greece would collide.

Nemesis

Throughout time people did not send requests to Sparta for ships, or money, or soldiers, but for a single Spartan commander... - Plutarch

Jon Edward Martin

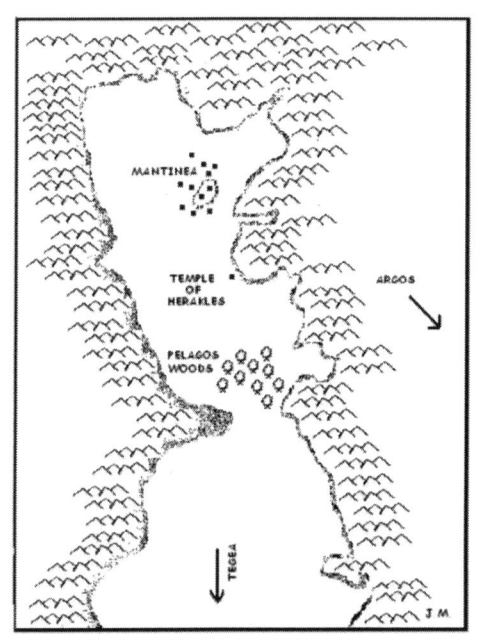

BATTLE OF MANTINEA

Chapter One
Mantinea, North of Sparta – 418 BC

Gylippos swiped his face with his cloak before tossing it to his armor-bearer. "Shield," he softly commanded, extending a linen wrapped forearm. Kanthos slipped the armband of the shield over Gylippos' clenched fist, shoving it to his elbow. The Spartan grabbed the rim-strap, swinging the aspis shield smartly to his shoulder, looking up, squinting, while measuring the height of the sun and calculating with what potency and duration it would continue to pour down its swelter. The Spartan army formed on the flat bottom of a valley, ringed by mountains, with the town of Mantinea ahead, spreading out from the single isolated hill of the acropolis, so conspicuous in the plain. Like two dogs thrown into a pen, the opposing armies faced off, confined, with no exit except through victory. Though most often the Spartans welcomed combat, they had not expected to find the enemy battle line spread before them and so close to the Pelagos Woods from where they had emerged. Days earlier, when Agis, the Spartan king had foolhardily ordered an attack, their enemy, the Argives, Mantineans and others had deployed on the slopes leading to Mantinea town, an amphitheater-like high ground and protected by javelineers and archers

5

Nemesis

bristling atop the slopes . Only the words of old Pharax—or his threats to be more precise—had aborted Agis' folly. Now in the plain stood the enemy, vague forms of men, shimmering in the heat, armor glinting as they jostled about with battle unavoidable.

Xenias, lokhagos of the Brasideioi, jogged up to Gylippos. "Agis got them off their ridge. Look!" He spiked his eight-foot spear into the sun-scorched turf of Mantinea.

"More accident than plan, I would say," replied Gylippos. "I do not think he expected to see them so close to the woods." He stared across the valley floor, over the fields that the Spartans had trampled and the river Sarandopotamos that the engineers and sappers had diverted from Mantinean land. They had emerged from the Pelagos Woods, blind to the location of the enemy, but Spartan discipline brought them quickly into battle line. "This will be interesting," Gylippos said out of the side of his mouth as he continued to face forward, studying the enemy, the field, and the sun. He turned around now, looking back to the thick swath of trees that blocked any quick withdrawal, and to the pair of ridges that cinched the valley tightly like the embroidered girdle-belt of a voluptuous maiden. *No retreat,* he thought. *Not today.*

Gylippos, commander of the fourth pentecostys, second lokhos of the Sarinas mora, held the end formation of Spartiates. To his right, extending far to the flank formed the bulk of the Spartan army. To his left the freed helots of Brasidas' campaign in Thrake, the Brasideioi, covered his other flank. Far off to the extreme left, the Skiritai held their traditional position. Arrayed across from them, beyond the baking earth and parched, grain stripped fields of Mantinea lie the army of white-shielded Argives, the Mantineans with the trident of Poseidon emblazoned on their aspides, variously adorned shields of the Orkhomenians, and a band of rogue Athenians.

Xenias continued to stare out, studying the enemy lines. "Hoplitodromos?" he quipped, making reference to the athletic race in armor.

"Run, no, but we may jog a bit," said Gylippos before he sucked up some phlegm. He spit, his target a brown striped lizard sunning itself on the stump of an olive tree. It flew into the trampled stalks of wheat. He shook his head.

Xenias frowned. "You look a bit unsettled."

"It's not the fight, my friend. If anything a little exercise will dust off the cobwebs. But I have never been in one like this though," admitted Gylippos. "Never."

His vision bored into the enemy formation like a drill, through it and to sights beyond—sights manufactured in his imagination. *If we lose this one, it will be over. If we lose this one, the Argives, Athenians and the rest will march into Sparta.* He shook his head again. *And we have an imbecile leading us.*

Two quick blasts from a salphinx trumpet silenced all talk. From the center of the phalanx heads turned left in a cascade, passing the order along the front ranks, officer to officer, then down each file. "Next one, step off," yelled Likhas, his order rolling along the front rank until it fell upon Gylippos. Now the phalanx exhaled the light troopers, archers, slingers and javelin-men, all scurrying forward, halting barely in range of their counterparts. Arrows shredded the air. Sling bullets clattered and thumped into the men and the bone-dry earth like hail. For minutes this long distance exchange between the two forces continued, with no side gaining advantage. Beneath this shower of missiles, some men dropped, while others sustained wounds but held their place. In the long run though, this furious scramble inflicted little damage, and only served to churn up sight-obscuring dust, from where disembodied insults emanated. Finally sling-stone pouches and quivers were emptied. Only words could be launched now in anger.

Xenias grinned. "Time to dance." He plucked up his spear and tugged on the leather tie-down to ensure his bronze pilos helmet stayed snug to his head.

Moments later, after a calculated interval that allowed the order of the king to reach the far flanks, the salphinx blared again. At once and to the sound of Lakonian flutes the front rankers stepped off in unison, rank after rank spilling in perfect order behind the officers. No cheering. No war-cries. Only the determined, measured stride of

six morai of Spartans advancing; a storm of muffled thunder marched to the resonant tune of the flute.

Gylippos peered ahead, focusing on the settling dust, straining to pick out the detail of men. The light troopers streamed away from the center, toward both flanks, sprinting for the cover of the heavy infantry. Soon the front ranks of the enemy crystallized into view. He surveyed their line as a whole before scrutinizing individual hoplites, picking out the officers, mentally demarcating the files of the Argives from the Mantineans by their wavering battle pennants, searching for the small band of rogue Athenians, the real instigators of this battle. Their foes had begun to slide their phalanx to the right, either by design or the instinctive shuffle of hoplites in battle to edge right, into the protection of their neighbor's shield. The far left, anchored by the Skiritai, had its flank overlapped by the best troops of the enemy—the Mantineans.

They marched forward, flutes keeping time, men to the right and to the left talking in casual fashion, suppressing fear and imparting the routine with confident conversation. Now from the center of the phalanx where King Agis stood, a runner sprinted along the front rank, yelling new orders to each polemarkhos. Gylippos kept calmly to his advance, checking the progress of the messenger now and then. "*Why a runner?*" he thought to himself. "*And why now!*"

Men in the front ranks of his pentecostys glanced to him, eyes full of concern. His face reflected cool confidence. The runner blew by the last files of the adjacent mora, slowing as he approached the polemarkhos Likhas. "The Skiritai and Brasideioi are moving left." He heaved out the words, punctuating each phrase with a deeply drawn breath. "Two companies… from the right will fill in… next to you." He stared for a long moment down the line at Likhas, to be certain he had heard each word. This was an order,
unplanned, and no abbreviated trumpet blast or flurry of battle flutes could convey it. Gylippos watched out of the corner of his eye as the two divisions on his left moved

Nemesis

off, disconnecting from his mora and opening a deadly gap in the phalanx.

Likhas yelled, "Is he mad!"

The gap widened. No two companies appeared from the right to fill it. Across the diminishing interval of no-man's land he could see the Argives seething toward the breach, not quite running but hardly walking, anxious to pour into the vulnerable, ever widening fracture.

"Double files!" barked Gylippos. Like a perfectly choreographed dance his pentecostys transformed from eight men deep to sixteen, halving their front, shields rippling in synchronization as they hefted them to the front sliding smartly into their new positions. The breach yawned invitingly to the Argives. Gylippos knew he increased the exposure of the Brasideio and also knew that if he did not strengthen his left flank, the enemy might roll up the Spartan line and take them in the rear. The gap, he hoped, would invite them deep into the baggage train and away from his own troops. Separated by less than fifty meters now, the enemy burst into a sprint, slamming into the exposed flank of the Brasideioi, with the thunder of shield on shield, bellowing war-cries. They hit Gylippos' left flank hard. Even at double depth the impact reeled them back, his men leaning hard into their shields, trying to absorb the mass and collision of the numerically superior formation. Like a hammer pounding a slab of red-hot bronze, his company bent at a right angle to the line of march. Still, like red-hot bronze they bent, but did not shatter. The two divisions to his left disappeared into a swirl of dust, metal ringing, men howling; it all melding into an indistinct but deafening roar. Shadows faded. The dust hung so thick and heavy now it seemed to him as though night had descended upon them all. Or had the most despised of all gods, Ares, flung his fearful cloak over the battlefield, stealing vision and courage from them all? This had never happened to him before. Now the Argives smacked into his front ranks, crashing hard at a jog while the Spartans stepped forward at a measured, almost mechanical pace. Bronze-faced shields squealed and thudded under impact, followed by the staccato of spearheads pumping into helmets and armor. He did not see men before him, but targets: the flash of glistening skin beneath a helmet cheek-piece; the thick, exposed thigh as a shield dropped for a moment. At each one he thrust—burying and quickly withdrawing his bloodied spearhead, checking his feet as he stepped over the fallen. Once more he glanced left. The gap was thick with Argives.

The pressure—from both the fury of combat and sheer weight of men—had always hit him head-on and in the front, but here today, it squeezed him from both front and left, confusing the usual rhythmic Spartan advance, jostling them from their ordered, confident files. He could feel them slipping from army to mob.

*****

Endymion's company, due to the chaos and misfortune of battle, pressed toward the Sparta left, its front ranks scraping along the enemy shield line as the bulk of them and the allied Mantineans plummeted into the breach. He found himself carried forward, inexorably, like a storm-wrecked vessel, driven by wild swells toward a rocky shore. Ahead and unavoidable, the polished lambda embellished shields of the Spartans filled his field of vision. Finally he crashed hard into one of the enemy front-rankers. He tucked his shoulder deep into his shield and barreled forward, hoping to drive his adversary off his feet, but it was as though he rammed into a deep rooted oak or olive tree. He rebounded off, recovered and stepped forward, but before he could take aim with his spear he felt a rapid succession of blows rattling off his shield and every so often his helmet, the rhythm and cadence of the strikes sounding almost musical. By the very volume of the impacts, he was certain he contended with several Spartan infantrymen, but when he lifted his eyes above the shield rim he saw a solitary Spartan officer marked out by his transverse horse-hair crest staring straight into his eyes with a blank, stony expression.

Endymion, now recovered from the initial shock, cocked his arm and thrust forward, attempting to plunge his spear into the Spartan's seemingly exposed neck, but before penetration the man flicked up his shield, snapping Endymion's shaft below the spear socket. Almost in a panic, he reached across his chest, trying to free his sword from its scabbard. The Spartan, anticipating this, drove his shield into Endymion's, ejecting the sword from his grip while propelling his helmet into the bloody muck at his feet.

Now, coolly, the Spartan began to draw back his own spear, preparing to deliver one fatal plunge into Endymion's exposed side, but paused, staring eye to eye, then while shaking his head, he sent the Argive toppling backwards with another swat of his shield.

Endymion scrambled to his feet and with blind instinct, followed the man in front as he and his Argives streamed into the fractured Lakedaimonian phalanx, avoiding the Spartan shield wall that had sealed off the flank. At any moment he expected to crash into another Spartan, but he stumbled forward into the dust and clamor. With each step the air began to clear—to his left he saw the still intact Spartan morai rolling by and forward, ranks tight and trimmed, spears sloped high, war-flutes trilling. To his right the cloud of battle lingered, but ahead he saw his men running now, pouring through the rent enemy phalanx, hell-bent on looting the baggage train. "Stop!" he yelled. Men streamed by him.
"Stop! The battle is over there!" He plucked up an abandoned spear from the battlefield then pointed with it at the Spartan rear ranks as they rumbled away. He grabbed one of his men as he ran past. "We must strike them from behind."

The man laughed at him. "The fight is over. Now is when we turn battle into profit."

Endymion smacked the man with his shield, ringing his helmet like a bell; he wanted to grab him, and any others he could lay hands on, and drag them all back into formation and bring them to bear where the battle, still raging, might be contested. For a moment his hand loosened from the antilabe shield grip, but he thought better of dropping his shield to snag these looters. The man snarled at Endymion through the narrow eye-slits of his helmet before running into the wreckage of the Spartan camp,

Nemesis

the over-turned carts and the torn and bloody corpses of helpless old men and beardless boys, kicking aside ox-hides and blankets, hoping to uncover some valuable bauble, some bulging purse of coin, or casket of jewels. All they lay bare consisted of shattered pottery, spear shafts and carpenters' tools.

"Fools," barked Endymion. He stopped where he stood and planted his spear into the ravaged turf. He could keen voices, distinct cries and pitiful moans of individual men, no longer spun together to create the roar of combat. He heard the wounded—and the dying. The battle had swept by like a storm. He turned around. The Spartan phalanx, now over two stades off, began to swing in a great arc, trampling the Athenians, Mantineans and the picked One-Thousand Argives—the very ones thought by many to be the equals of the Spartans—into the blood soaked plain. Soon dust engulfed it all. They had their chance, their one fleeting chance, to end Spartan domination of the Peloponessos, but had tossed it all away for a wagon full of rough-hewn poles and broken pots. *Fools*, he
repeated to himself as he looked at his men quarreling over an adze, tattered hide, or surplus shield.

Finally the sun broke through the haze of battle dust, revealing the now far off Spartan scythe cutting down his friends, neighbors and allies in the fields before Mantinea, swinging around the valley in a great, murderous arc. As the air cleared, he could see the hundreds of fallen littering the trampled croplands. Well beyond the melee, plumes of dust poked the sky, marking the retreating column of Athenian cavalry, heading for a cleft in the ring of mountains that cinched the valley. Suddenly the Spartan phalanx slowed, finally halting, the harvest of battle seemingly complete. Far off, he could see people fleeing from the low city, huts and dwellings, scrambling up the discrete hill of the acropolis. Even the towns-folk knew the outcome and prepared to withstand the final Spartan assault.

*****

Xenias trudged through the mud, a mixture of churned soil, blood and viscera, looking for any that still lived amongst his lokhos of Brasidieio. The Mantineans had crushed both their flanks, netting his division and the Skiritai adjacent, like tunny. For more than an hour they stood against this onslaught, isolated, out-numbered and evidently forgotten until finally the wheeling Spartan phalanx slammed into the Mantineans from behind, pulverizing them.

He came upon one of his platoon leaders, face down in the mire the only color evident a swatch of his cloak that had not been trampled by the advancing Mantineans. A bubble formed in the mud near the man's chin. Xenias frantically pulled at him, clearing his head from the puddle. He coughed then launched a stream of vomit followed by a fit of hacking that brought a smile to Xenias. His eyes blinked open, wide and white against

face caked with muck. He spit.

"Hiding?" quipped Xenias as he wiped the mud from Bryas' face.

"All I remember is pushing and slashing at the enemy ranks ahead, then suddenly, like Patrokles at Troy, someone or something whacked me from behind."

Bryas licked the dirt from his teeth and spit again. "The battle?"

"Won, but barely," answered Xenias. "Agis ordered us to the left, but never filled the gap. The Spartans rolled up the enemy line—finally!"

"Barely soon enough for me," added Bryas, "but certainly not for him." He tugged on the limp arm of one of his companions in the mud. "What's going on now?"

A hundred meters or so nearer the city the full portion of the Spartan phalanx stood motionless and silent, except for the incongruous duel of two men in argument. Xenias began to jog toward the main body. No longer in close order, their ranks became spaced by a meter between each file. He found it easy to shoulder through to the front. The Spartans had formed a massive ring, penning in about a thousand of the enemy, cutting them off from the mountains to the right and their town and acropolis behind.

"What are you doing here?"

Xenias turned quickly. There stood Gylippos. He said nothing in return. They both refocused on the two men in front of the Spartan phalanx.

"Let them go!" barked Pharax.

Agis' head shook violently. "I promised the Gerousia a great victory. I owe it to them. I owe it to Sparta." He turned toward the ranks and the files of Hippieis, the Royal Knights, about to raise his spear to order the final attack. Pharax grabbed the king's arm, lowering the spear. He whispered words only Agis could hear. After a few minutes of motionless silence, orders rippled across the phalanx. The ring of Spartans parted.

Pharax, not waiting for Agis to give the order, sent a herald forward to speak with the surrounded Argives. Gylippos trotted just behind, halting when the herald did, wanting to appear as the herald's escort.

The Argive survivors had huddled together into a fractured cluster, a few standing with shields held on the ready while others sprawled in the blood and muck—most collapsed to one knee, clutching their spears, heads hanging, waiting for the Spartans to finish their work.

The herald planted his staff directly in front of him. Gylippos stared at it and its twin snakes that wrapped around the shaft, facing each other like mirror images at the top. "The Spartans," he announced as he searched amongst the battered Argives for who would appear to be in command, "have decided on mercy today."

Amongst the Argives, heads slowly raised up, these few words having breathed life into men resigned to death. Faces emerged as helmets dropped to the ground. Men of flesh and blood began to bloom like spring flowers amongst the bronze and iron of defeated warriors.

The herald announced, "There is only one thing Sparta asks in return." Now grumbling bubbled up throughout the Argives, gaining in volume. The Knights, still ringing the perimeter, leveled their spears. The muttering ceased. "Sparta wants no ransoms, nor tribute, no hostages. Sparta wishes only that you remember where your

Nemesis

Athenian allies were when the outcome of this battle hung undecided. Remember where the Athenians are now, and look around you and remember who remains on the field of battle." The herald turned on his heel and headed back to the center of the Spartan
phalanx. The ring of Knights reeled back into the Spartan lines. In moments the Argive survivors shuffled through the gap, away from the Spartans and toward the town of Mantinea.

*****

"Wait here!" Likhas ordered as he brushed past Gylippos, snapping back the flap to the tent of Agis. "You are lucky he is not calling for you."

Gylippos edged closer, trying to sift through the barrage of rambunctious shouts within. Only the king and the six polemarkoi entered the tent, but it sounded like the entire Spartan army argued within.

"My orders were clear!" boomed the voice of Agis. "You, Aristokles and you, Hipponoidas, failed to redeploy."

"Thanks the gods we did not, or we'd be carrying your body from that field." It was Aristokles who answered the king's charge—Gylippos could never mistake his gravelly voice for anyone else's.

Now more voices boomed out, one shouting over another, reminding him of a sorely contested vote in the Apella, but it was Agis, loudest of all, that punctuated the argument. "Arrest them both!"

Likhas whipped open the tent flap and motioned for a squad of Hippieis to come forward. The eight Spartan hoplites, fully armed, bracketed the entrance to the tent. Agis stepped out to join Likhas, squinting as the afternoon sun struck him in the face. "Take these two to Sparta—now!" Hipponoidas and Aristokles emerged from the tent, still in battle armor but without sword, shield or spear. Aristokles, in particular, glared at Agis as they marched past, squeezing between the twin-sided escort of royal Knights. Agis
snorted out a contemptible laugh before charging back into his tent. Likhas did not follow.

Gylippos stepped toward Likhas, but before his mouth could form a single word Likhas answered him. "Cowardice. That is what they are charged with." Likhas shook his head. "Walk with me," he said, almost in a whisper, as he draped an arm around Gylippos', leading him away from the King's tent and the fanatical gaze of the Hippieis guards. Their stroll took them to the small shrine of Herakles, tucked into foothills just south of Mantinea. Here the grove of sacred olive shaded them from the sun. Here they sat.

"They are no cowards," blurted out Gylippos. He looked now to the acropolis of Manitinea, its crest smudged with puffs from the sacred fires of thank-offerings —not the conqueror's smoke of arson.

"Of course they aren't." Likhas stuck a finger into his mouth, swirling it around, probing. "Lost a damned tooth today." He stared off, back toward the battlefield and the swarms of helots that had been detailed to recover the Spartan dead. "Do you know why we don't strip them?" He referred to the often seen practice of victorious armies looting the bodies of their enemies for armor, weapons and coin. Not waiting for Gylippos he continued, "because what value is there in the armor of one who has been defeated? Certainly didn't stir them to bravery—or victory."

Likhas eased himself to a seat upon the steps of the shrine. He laughed, spit, and laughed a bit more. "Why did you spare him?"

"What?" replied Gylippos, somewhat confused.

"That Argive. You snapped his spear-shaft, swatted away his shield, helmet and sword. You had him fighting naked. Why did you not finish him?"

"By Kastor and Polydeukes, I do not know." He shrugged his shoulders. "I looked into the man's eyes, and—."

"Gentleness and mercy are fine things after the battle, but could prove fatal during it." Likhas grinned. "But not with that one. You appeared as though you were at the training ground, disgusted with poor effort by a pupil. You tossed him away like a broken pot."

Gylippos nodded, waiting for minutes to pass before posing a question. "What will happen to them?"

"They will be brought before the ephors and the council of the Gerousia, and they will be found guilty," Likhas said dryly. "Then, I would expect they will be exiled."

This suddenly brought back memories of his father Kleandridas to him, a man exiled for nothing more than patriotism, a victim of the Eurypontids' ambitions. Gylippos' lips tightened into a grin of resignation. "But surely the ephors will see that it was Aristokles and Hipponoidas and their clear heads that won this battle. They won it by refusing to carry out an fool's command. They should receive the prize of victory, not Agis."

"It is all simple arithmetic. Those two, like you and I, owe our allegiance to king Pleistoanax. By the gods, poor Aristokles is his brother, a bitter enemy of Agis and the Eurypontid house. Unfortunately Agis' relatives hold majority with the ephors and the old men of the Gerousia. After all, it was his father Arkhidamos that planted eighteen of the twenty-eight of the old ones there. He surely made it cozy for his son. They will vote for the memory of Arkhidamos—and Agis—not for justice." He explained now how Sparta had become cleaved by the politics of the two royal houses. The Eurypontids, Arkhidamos, Agis, and his clan, vied for ultimate sway in the governing of the city with the more prestigious house of the Agiads, the family of Leonidas, the clan of heroes "They will kill our city. They will kill it from within." Gylippos rubbed the crusted splashes of blood from this arms, blood not his but the foe's.

"You, my friend, are luckier than most, I would say." Likhas smiled broadly now as he summoned the memory of his dearest friend. "Brasidas was your Inspirer. He taught you. I saw you in the battle today. He taught you well. There was no greater champion of Sparta."

Nemesis

"And he is dead because of them." Now Gylippos' face burned red. "If they had only sent the reinforcements he asked for—."

Likhas cut him off, "—and he would still be dead. The gods took him at his time, as they will with me and with you. His was a beautiful death. His name will live forever in Sparta." He struggled to rise, his stiff legs and battered knees causing him to wince until a few long strides restored flexibility and chased away the pain. "I'm sure they already have their eye on you. Give them no excuse. Do what they say, but do it in your own way. That is what Brasidas would counsel you to do."

Gylippos laughed a bit. "I know. He already did."

"I think it is a good and proper time for you to pray to him again. Agis wants your hide too. He's ranting that you purposely deepened your files to widen the gap that he created."

Gylippos could feel the heat rise in his face. "Any fool knows I had no choice. If I spanned the gap with my lokhos, the enemy surely would have broken through. "

Likhas grinned. "But Agis is not any fool. He is a royal one and still exerts much influence on the ephors. I would think your punishment, if any, would be slight."

"We surely are a unique and amazing people. Our soldiers carry out orders and are blamed for failure while our king enjoys acclaim. When we disobey, and deliver victory, we are still punished and again our king enjoys acclaim."

"This state of things is not so unique. Everywhere justice is dispensed by the powerful. So, of course, they receive the larger portion."

Jon Edward Martin

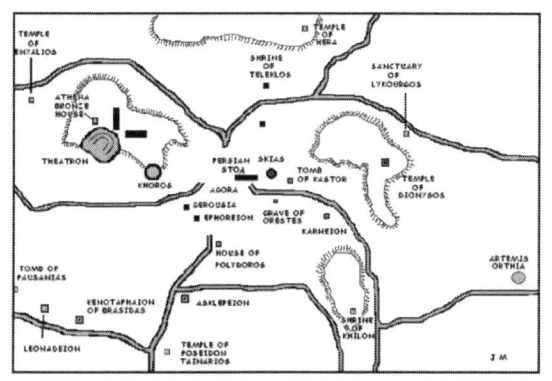

ACROPOLIS AND AGORA OF SPARTA

Chapter Two
Sparta – 418 BC

The northern ridge fell away suddenly revealing the lush Eurotas valley and the formidable stone curtain of the Taygetos mountain range beyond. An ancient helot shepherd stood on a nearby slope, his flock swirling around him as he shaded his eyes to view the vast column of Spartan infantry as they trudged past. Poking up from the flat valley, Gylippos easily spotted the hill of the acropolis and the orange tiled roofs fanning out from it in every direction. Snakes of smoke twirled skyward. It all seem so routine, so undisturbed, so inured to news of war that none of them really knew how close their beloved Sparta came to extinction. As they gradually descended into the valley, through the groves thick with olive, mulberry and plane, herds of boys from the Agoge bracketed the road, and as the column passed them they cheered and then began to sing the poems of Tyrtaios in tribute to the returning warriors. With each step and each stride they all seemed to gain in strength, as though the very air of their valley restored life. Now he could spot the gleaming ribbon of the Eurotas itself, its banks bristling with tall reeds, and the stony Babyx Bridge that spanned it.

Helots, here and there, lifted their heads up, ceasing toil, and leaned on hoes, rakes, or the handles of their ploughs, most exhibiting the blank stare of resignation—resignation at another triumphant return of the army that held them all in check. They crossed the bridge, following the road past the shrine of Artemis Orthia and between two low hills that funneled them towards the agora. Suddenly, silently, crowds of Spartans edged to line the road. There were no cheers, or songs of Tyrtaios, but only cool stares and restrained grins. The rolls of the dead had been tallied, but Agis did not send them ahead of the army. He would personally deliver them to the ephors.

Once it had entered the agora the army began to disperse, the drab clothed relatives and friends melded with eddies of crimson garbed hoplites. Gylippos turned

Nemesis

around. The surviving Brasideioi had not followed. They had abandoned the column at the head of the valley, their smartly dressed files dissolving quickly as they made their way to their homes in Lepreon. They would share in no Spartan celebration.

Gylippos watched as fathers and mothers greeted their sons, wives embraced husbands, and young sons and daughters screeched out the names of their fathers on sighting them. His own father, now in exile and in far off Thurii, would not be greeting him.

"Good to see you alive," bellowed Tellis as he stepped in front of Gylippos. Tellis, father to Brasidas, had become his sponsor in years past, having provided his dues to attend the Agoge in place of his true father Kleandridas.

"It is an honor to see you, sir," responded Gylippos, with a reverent dip of his head.

"Will you be at the phidition tonight?" Although posed as a question Tellis undoubtedly tossed it out as a command, expecting only confirmation.

Gylippos hesitated a bit before answering. He knew he must attend the mess of his dining mates, but all he wanted to do now was sleep, and not endure the grilling he was sure to face regarding the battle and particularly the conduct of Hipponoidas and Aristokles. "Why of course," he finally answered with a manufactured smile.

"Good. Likhas has invited me to attend. I am anxious to hear, first hand, of the battle."

*****

Tellis wrapped the table with his kothon, sending a splash of wine out of the cup and onto an empty platter, silencing the grumbling of fifteen men in argument. "So you say the order came down after the army commenced its advance?"

Gylippos, his eyes heavy from lack of sleep, his head pounding from the incessant questions, stood up squeezing the bridge of his nose between his thumb and forefinger. "Yes, yes," he answered impatiently.

"And our shield line was longer?" Again Tellis went over the battle's recounting.

"Yes, by more than a hundred shields." Gylippos began to stalk the phidition, hoping to stave off drowsiness. All eyes followed him as he paced back and forth. Finally he reached for his kothon and drowned his parched tongue in wine.

Kallikratidas bobbed his head knowingly. "And why was the left flank uncovered?"

Gylippos laughed while shaking his head. "Because our king and commander marched out of the Pelagos Woods blind. He sent no day-watchers ahead. We traipsed out not knowing what lie in front and discovered the enemy arrayed before us. By the Holy Twins, it was a miracle we pulled our formation together as quickly as we did."

The door to the phidition creaked open. In strode Likhas. He extended his open hands as he apologized for his tardiness then sat, pulling himself close to the table as he reached for a flap of bread. A helot quickly slid a bowl of black zomos broth in front of him. Likhas, to the amazement of all, proceeded to tear his bread casually, dipping portions into the broth before slowly dropping pieces, bit by bit, into his mouth. His eye brows arched. "What? Can't a man eat?" He motioned for a tankard of well-watered wine. "I'm sure Gylippos has already regaled you with the courageous escapades of our

king." He took two long gulps of wine before slamming the kothon atop the table. "Ahh. That is the most delicious of any wine. The first cup drained after a victorious campaign."

Gylippos almost collapsed with relief into his chair. Another to quiz. Someone else to cross-examine. He leaned back, arms crossed, burying his chin in his chest as he waited for the assault to be unleashed upon Likhas.

Likhas chewed deliberately. Being a senior of the mess, the others did not press him with questions immediately, but allowed him whatever time he required to instigate the session. "The official account of the battle is this, my friends. Agis, having duped the enemy from their unassailable ridge, deliberately presented a gap, a lure to the Argives and Mantineans. Hipponoidas and Aristokles received clear and timely orders to dispatch the rear half files from two of their lokhoi to fill it. They refused. It was the leadership and valor of our king that enabled the Spartan army to crush the enemy ahead then wheel to the left, providing relief to the detached and battered wing of our dear, loyal, and slightly less populous allies, the Skiritai."

Now the entire mess broke into laughter. The helot servants stood by, their faces twisting in perplexity at the uproar. Gylippos laughed quietly, not lifting his chin from his chest.

Likhas banged his cup hard, demanding quiet. His face reddened. His temples throbbed. "But the real truth, my friends, and you will only hear it in whispers, is that our king almost destroyed Sparta on that battlefield, and it was Aristokles and Hipponoidas, and our mess-mate Gylippos here," he said acknowledging him with a wink, "that pulled our balls out of the grinder. Agis is a witless dolt, and two men will suffer because they disobeyed him and saved our city."

"Cannot Pleistoanax help them?" Kallikratidas pleaded.

Likhas shook his head. "It is precisely because Pleistoanax is both friend and brother to them that they will suffer, at the very least, banishment. Agis and the Eurypontids hold the numbers in the Gerousia. The first story is the only one you will hear of the battle at Mantinea."

The room emptied of talk. All present stared ruefully at their cups swirling the wine, or blankly at the mud-brick walls, absorbing the poignant truth. Gylippos, slumped in his chair, began to snore, inciting a mild bout of laughter. With each breath in, he opened his mouth, so Likhas walked around the table, kothon in hand, approaching his friend quietly. Gylippos' mouth opened again and Likhas filled it with wine. He exploded into a fit of coughing.

"Your throat sounded a bit dry," quipped Likhas.

Gylippos coughed and sucked up both phlegm and wine, finally spitting it out. "Is it a crime to nap?"

Nemesis

Likhas placed both his hands upon his friend's shoulders and shook him affectionately. "You need your rest." Now he strode to the front of the table, like an actor crossing the orchestra. "Gylippos' quick thinking sealed our open flank. He doubled his files to sixteen shields deep, strengthening our line. The Mantineans got funneled by us and into the baggage train. He and his men took a beating, exposed as they were, but they allowed our army to pivot and roll up the line." He leaned upon the table, palms down, his arms flexing under tension, sweat seeping from his forehead. "Our king nearly ruined us in defeat and then almost succeeded doing so in victory. The fool let the Athenians escape then ordered the annihilation of the picked Argives."

Kallikratidas, always one to see things in only two colors barked out, "Why not destroy our enemy? Why not finally put an end to the Argives?"

Likhas' arms twitched as he answered, hands still planted upon the table. "By Zeus, they are the only ones in Argos we can trust, the only men of substance." Likhas, the proxenos to Argos knew them all well. "Men who own land, and whose families have been upon that land since before the war with Ilion. Kill them and what is left but rabble, a rabble with more in common with the Athenians than any Peloponnesians. They will return to their city as men acquitted by battle and will wield, if only for a short time, great influence. This influence will benefit Sparta, but only, of course, if they are alive to exercise it. We should have bound Agis up and left him in his tent, fought the battle, and delivered victory in his name."

Gylippos, eyes still heavy with fatigue, lifted his head up and spoke. "Likhas, since you are the proxenos for Argos, and know most all their important citizens, I yield to your knowledge of their politics. But I must ask this: Why did the escape of so few Athenians irritate you so?"

Likhas finally lifted himself upright and away from the table, crossing his arms. "The Athenians, although their numbers at the battle were small, included their most ambitious men, and the most ambitious of these seen running from the field was Alkibiades. He would make his fame upon the destruction of our city."

"He is correct," barked out Tellis. "I know, for when both Athenians and Spartans met to sign the treaty of peace, this Alkibiades was barely into manhood, but wanted to be treated as an equal—no, more than an equal—during the negotiations. I ignored him to the favor of Nikias, an older and therefore more able statesman. This impetuous man-child Alkibiades threatened us all. We would regret the insult cast at him, he warned. Likhas is most certainly correct. We had our opportunity to eliminate Alkibiades, and indeed save many a Spartan life. I pray that we have this chance once again. He is a dangerous man."

A rapping on the door compelled one of the servants to open it, revealing a nervous messenger. In silence everyone drilled him with their gaze. "The ephors command Gylippos son of Kleandridas to appear before them now." Certain his message was heard, he turned on his heel and sprinted off.

"Damn them," muttered Gylippos, as he pushed himself free of his chair.

"Most likely you are a witness." Tellis said, trying to reassure him.

Likhas knew better. "I'm sure by now Agis knows what you did. He will twist your actions into insubordination also." He stepped next to Gylippos. "Polyakes will be there. He will keep them honest."

Gylippos exited the silent phidition, hustling onto the Amylkaian Way northwards toward the acropolis and the agora.

"Wait!"

Gylippos looked back over his shoulder to find Kallikratidas jogging after him. "They want only me, my friend."

"And so they shall have you. I'm just bringing along your wine. You know how difficult it can be to speak with a dry tongue." Kallilkratidas shook the wine-skin at his friend.

Gylippos, truly thankful of this gesture could offer no words, his mind spinning with the dire prospects of this summons. No one is called to the Ephorion after a battle for a commendation. He hustled along the empty road, coming first to the village of Mesoa at the southern fringe of the city. Houses bracketed the road now, but he found no one about, the evening steeped in silence broken occasionally by a dog barking as he passed by a cottage. As he neared the agora he caught sight of the Agoge youths prowling

the colonnades and porticoes, dutifully carrying out their nightly assignment as guards of all the public buildings. Torches blazed in front of the Ephorion, and a few Peers loitered outside its single bronze door, engaged in frantic argument. They all went silent as he approached. One of the men, old Pharax smiled at him. "Come in with me son." He ushered Gylippos through the open doorway.

Kallikradtidas halted at the top step just as the door squealed shut. He sat upon the steps and nervously began to swig the wine he had brought for Gylippos. An hour passed. The skin was half-empty. He unplugged the skin and began to tip it toward his open mouth when the door creaked open. "Well?"

Gylippos yanked the wine-skin from his friend and gulped down several mouthfuls. "I've lost the company!"

"What? They stripped you of your command?" He retrieved the wine and filled his mouth.

"Agis wanted to banish me. Polyakes and Pharax did their best to prevent it. Better to lose the company than my city." Gylippos kept his glance down as he began to walk

"Those fools forget that you are our city, just as Aristokles and Hipponoidas are. Just as Brasidas was. Men, not walls, make Sparta." Kallikratidas sighed. "But I suppose we must all study more than tactics and expand our skills beyond the gymnaseion and battlefield. Politics, too we must hone. It is not enough to be a good soldier, my friend."

Gylippos shrugged. "All I ever asked for is my shield, my spear, and clear understanding. You are right, my friend. Those simple things are no longer enough."

Chapter Three
Athens – 418 BC

Nikias waited for the soothsayer to reveal the portents for the day. He would not leave his town-house until he had the blessings of the gods and the calming interpretations of ever reliable Stilbides. The stony earth crunched under his sandaled feet as he paced the courtyard, brushing past the drooping branches of the mulberry bush that sprawled untrimmed near the fountain. Every so often he would peer into the shadows of the columned portico at the bronze statue of Zeus Herkaios and the spindly little man who worked upon the entrails of a splayed she-goat by the light of a flickering oil lamp.

Stilbides clamped his hands together, raising them skyward while nodding and chanting. Nikias needed nothing further. He swung the gate open and slipped out, checking the eastern sky for the first hint of daylight. He mulled the argument over in his head, how he would caution his countrymen from embarking upon another calamitous adventure. How to liberate their ambitions, without risking another war with the Spartans?

The Agora proper began to empty, men shuffling away and toward the Pynx Hill, ushered by slaves stalking the market stall with their paint soaked rope, ready to mark out any shirker with a crimson lash across their back. He looked up. The banner hung high and limp, signaling for certain that today there would be a calling of the Assembly. His legs, still stiff from sleep, ached as he ascended the polished marble stairs, finally cresting the hill and catching sight of his fellow Athenians crowding into the sacred precinct of the Pynx. Almost every man he squeezed by knew him, greeting him with a smile, a nod or a "good day". Some winced as if in pain when he edged past, men he also

knew—men who were comrades of Alkibiades.

Ahead and upon the stepped bema he could see the mantis portioning out the blood of the victims, a dozen or so sheep that had their throats slit, into bowls carried by a herd of boys. They dispersed with vessels in hand, and stood at even intervals around the perimeter of the Assembly. The herald, perched high above them stared out, checking to make certain that all who would come had made their way upon the hill. Finally satisfied he waved his kerykeion staff and the boys began to mark out a sanguine ring, enclosing them all.

Nikias would speak first today. He ascended with hesitating steps, the pain in his knees slowing him, but most saw not discomfit, but solemnity in his gait. He accepted the wreath and pushed it down upon his head while surveying the upturned faces of the crowd. He cleared his throat. The herald rapped his staff and the last murmurs of fading conversation ended.

"Another ten days has passed, and it is time to reconsider our treaty with Sparta," he spun the loose end of his himation cloak around his left forearm and continued. "You must be puzzled why now we call the entire Assembly here to reaffirm this pact." He now knew exactly where Alkibiades stood in the vast crowd of

Jon Edward Martin

six thousand Athenians, for all heads spun and all eyes became fixed upon his rival. "Treaties, as we all know, are not merely pacts among men, or agreements between cities, but are sacred oaths taken with the gods. We all know this except one of us, and this one alone will bring the wrath of the Olympians down upon us, men of Athens." Again heads turned to Alkibiades. "The Argives would not have attacked Sparta on their own, nor would the Mantineans. And do not place the blame on our general, Lamakhos, here for instigating this folly. The disaster at Mantinea was fully fashioned by Alkibiades, and it is only by the grace of

Zeus and the slowness of the Spartans that this treaty between us does not lie shattered like the army of adventure sent to invade Spartan territory." Nikias paused, the pain in his knees reminding him of his mortality, and his singular wish to become a private man, but so long as others like Alkibiades threatened the peace, he was compelled to step forward. Finally he ended his speech. "Or have you forgotten the ruin of war, of what it was like to run behind the walls of our city as the Spartan war beast slipped it reins each spring, devouring our crops."

Like a trireme cutting the swells, Alkibiades surged through the crowd and bounded up the steps with vigor and confidence. He stood next to Nikias, waiting for the wreath to be passed to him, waiting for the time to speak to be possessed by him. Just as the garland settled upon his head, he commenced. "So which oath do we break, my fellow Athenians? Which one did we, in truth not uphold?" He tilted his head down, squeezing his chin between his forefinger and thumb, imparting an aspect of careful deliberation as he paced the bema. "Argos and Mantinea are our allies and by treaty asked for our help. Could we ignore it? Did we attack Sparta? Did the Argives? Did the Mantineans? No! The Spartans attacked them. Our pact with both men and gods remains sacred and intact. Let no one trick you to believe otherwise."

Nikias' hands trembled with rage as he stood behind the bema, waiting for his turn to speak once more. Alkibiades turned away from the Assembly and grinned at Nikias, handing him the wreath. Nikias this time snatched it impatiently and settled it quickly atop his head.

"Alkibiades sounds like a philosopher now, making the weaker argument appear to be the stronger—making plain intentions seem unintended. Does anyone here think that by invading the lands of Tegea, our vaunted allies were not, in fact, attacking Sparta?

This so-called alliance was an innovation of Alkibiades, manufactured by him to rekindle the flames of war that the blood of many Athenians had extinguished. The gods, unlike men, always know our true purpose, and no twisting of words by a youngster can fool them." Nikias tore the wreath from his head and handed it to the herald, shuffling quickly down the steps of the bema, finally melting into the Assembly.

Alkibiades, not waiting for the wreath, shouted out, "A battle that cost us nothing nearly erased Sparta from the earth! Are those words plain enough, old man?"

Nikias did not acknowledge the outburst but kept moving deeper into the

Nemesis

crowd until he came to the far edge of the Pynx. He paused, the sparkling temple of Athena Parthenos filling his vision. Here he stopped and waited, to be certain that no aspersions, true or false, would be leveled upon him undefended. He listened to Alkibiades stir them up, easily moving thousands toward war, adventure, and ambition. But he kept it all less personal, not attacking Nikias but reminding them, no matter how tenuously, that the Argive alliance would counter the Spartan League. In Alkibiades' mind though, he knew it would not only counter it, but encourage Sparta and her allies to abandon peace: they could not accept so grave a threat roosting at their doorstep.

As the cheers rose and fell, Nikias clambered down the steps and onto the road that would bring him into the Agora proper. The smell of roasting meat mingled with the scent of draught animal dung as he moved along the road, past the boundary stones and amongst the cobbler stalls at the entrance to the Agora. He keep walking, finally stopping before the altar of the Twelve Heroes. He stared at the nails that once hung up the rolls of the army, the catalog of men called up by the Council and the ten strategoi, before peace had been restored. He was certain the rolls would be spiked up there soon. Alkibiades knew how to work the crowd.

"Nikias, greetings."

Nikias turned. He nodded with a smile. "Good day to you, Thessalos." He glanced quickly once more at the spot for his tribe's roll before grabbing Thessalos by the elbow, and began leading him toward the Strategeion. "I don't know how much longer we can keep him fettered in peace?"

"Alkibiades you mean?" Thessalos smiled. "Only the people that have nothing to lose want war with Sparta again. Look around you." He swept his arm as though he pulled back a curtain. "Merchants, landowners, fishermen—we all want peace. Peace is good for business. War only fills the poor people's fists with obols, not mine or yours."

"But peace is Alkibiades' poison. War is his antidote." Nikias winced as he felt a twinge of pain burrow through his back.

"Are you alright?" Thessalos' concern was genuine. He steadied Nikias with a hand upon his shoulder.

Nikias grinned. "That look of concern— it reminds me of your father, Kimon. A handsome man but he always carried a face full of worry with him."

"As you do now, I fear." Thessalos ushered them to an empty bench nestled beneath a broad plane tree at the foot of the hill behind the Tholos. They sat, first in silence, as the presidents of the council, the prytaneis, descended from the Pynx, wending their way along the road right up to the stairs of the Tholos. "They're looking for someplace cool and out of the sun too. It always seems a bit hotter when Alkibiades speaks."

"Sparta does not want war." Nikias began to rub his knees, kneading away the pain as he spoke. "But they do not wish to lose their allies in the Peloponessos. If we give the Peloponesians no cause to invoke the alliance, then peace endures."

Clouds of acrid smoke rolled over them, a sudden breeze carrying the exhaust from the smelters' furnaces and potters' kilns, all the way from the Kerameikos. Thessalos waved his hand, trying to clear the air. "They become intoxicated with each victory, the rabble that follow Alkibiades: the poor that can scrape up more coin rowing in the fleet, the young gentlemen who have never tasted the bitter broth of conflict in search of glory. They will spur our city toward war."

"And anyone that disagrees will be branded unpatriotic, as sure as if they pressed the blazing iron into our flesh as they would a horse's." Nikias leaned back, sighing. "They will say the wealthy do not wish to fund the fleet, not out of true concern for Athens but of distress for their purses. Yes they will mark us all unpatriotic, men putting our own interests before those of our country. And the mark will never wash away."

"Oh, poor Nikias, you sound like a pacifist. You, a general of the first rate. A general that has been victorious many times." Thessalos stared straight into his sullen eyes. "Please do not step down from the bema and hand your command over to Alkibiades, as you once did to Kleon. If you do that, even I will call you unpatriotic, for if you abdicate your command, you extinguish what sound judgment still dwells in there." He pointed to the Strategeion, the hall of generals.

"I am old now, and much too tired to contend with the likes of Alkibiades." He began rubbing his aching knees again. "But I have lived my life in accordance with the wishes of the gods. If they deem it so, then I will retain my command."

Thessalos grabbed the chiton of a young boy as he sped by them. "Here," he said as he dropped an obol into the lad's grimy hand. "Get us two cups of wine from the kapeleion there." He released the boy's chiton, but yelled after him. "Tell him no akratos, but some Khian!"

They sat there, in the shade of the plane tree, watching crowds of Athenians swirl amongst the stalls of vendors, and around the open carts laden with fresh olives, bales of fleece, and amphorai of wine. Nikias looked at it all, wondering how long this scene would last, how long Athens could remain sober and peaceful. His eyes began to fill and Thessalos noticed it.

"Is it your back? Has the pain returned?" Thessalos gripped Nikias' forearm intently.

"No, my friend. It is not my back, but another more familiar pain. For a moment I saw Athens as it was over ten years past. The Agora empty of food, but filled instead by corpses. The city crowded. The plague rampant. Athens at war. A vision of our future, perhaps?"

"Unfortunately, dear friend, their memories are short," said Thessalos with resignation.

"Is it so unpatriotic to reject such a vision?"

****

"There is a foreigner to see you, master."

Nikias rose from the divan excruciatingly slowly, rubbing the small of his back while wincing in pain.

Nemesis

"Your kidneys master? Are they shouting again?" Hiero had a quaint way of phrasing ailments of the body, as though certain organs, muscle and bone had voice, and could communicate directly.

"Tell him to go way. I cannot see anyone today." A bolt of pain doubled him over. "And call for the iatros."

Hiero dashed out of the andreion. In a few minutes he returned, almost out of breath. "Master, he will not leave until he speaks with you. He invokes your obligations as proxenos. He says he comes here at great risk to speak with you."

Nikias forced himself to stand erect, and summoned all the dignity he could, burying the pain. This man was seeking the proxenos of Syrakuse, and it was Nikias' duty to receive him. "His name?"

"He calls himself Athenagoras."

"He may enter." Nikias lowered himself back onto his couch, rearranging his pillows to support his back, but providing the appearance of relaxation. He lifted his kylix and held it up, waiting for his guest to enter. "Welcome Athenagoras," he announced cordially as the man stepped into the room. "Please sit. Have something to quench your thirst." Nikias flicked his fingers. Hiero filled a kylix and presented it to Athenagoras.

"I thank you for your hospitality, and I apologize for not arranging this visit beforehand." He sipped a bit of wine then continued. "I realize that I am not the ambassador of Syrakuse, and come now in no official capacity. I only come as a private citizen and a concerned friend to the Athenians."

Nikias grinned. If this man was indeed a friend to the Athenians as he says, then he is a traitor to his city. But he would listen. As proxenos to Syrakuse he was obliged to listen. "Hmm, a friend to the Athenians you say. Are you the only friend we have in Syrakuse, for you are quite alone?"

Athenagoras swallowed hard. He cleared his throat. He tried to speak but the words would not form, so he sipped more wine. His throat loosened. "My ship was on the way to Melos when a storm forced us to the Piraios. I come to you now, delivered by the gods, but I am not here, if you understand my meaning. None of my countrymen must know that I came here."

"If you are a friend, why are you so ashamed of this friendship?" Nikias knew the answer but asked the question just the same, to impart a bit of discomfort to the Syrakusan.

"Nikias, you know exactly why I must come here in secret; Syrakuse is a Dorian city, a colony of Korinth and an ally to your enemies. I know that you Athenians covet the wealth of Sikelia. Our island is rich in grain, grain that has been denied to you from the Black Sea since the loss of Amphipolis. Sikelia has horses in great abundance and lumber too. These things a great empire such as yours requires."

Nikias delayed his response, waiting for the ache in his back to subside. "And why would Syrakusans deliver such wealth to us?"

Athenagoras smiled. "Because Athens will deliver Syrakuse from the Gamoroi and give the city to its people. A democracy. On the Athenian model and a true friend to its benefactors the Athenians."

"So Athenagoras, you do not like the Gamoroi? Aristocrats offend you? Remember that my family too descends from Athens' aristocracy."

Athenagoras shook his head. "I mean no offense. You share power with the demos. The Gamoroi share little and begrudgingly. There are many Syrakusans that would come to Athens' assistance, if only your great city would come to theirs."

Nikias let him continue. He listened with feigned interest to these promises of bounty from Sikelia, but his mind returned to Amphipolis and the cities of the Khalkidike lost to the Spartans under Brasidas. He would prefer to recover these and reopen the grain shipments from Skythia. Still Sikelia and the west had promise. But Syrakuse was indeed far off. He listened long, but promised nothing, giving the Syrakusan a purse of silver as a token of Athens' friendship. It was a small investment, and he realized that it may never be recouped.

Nemesis

Chapter Four
Sparta – Late Autumn 418 BC

The Taygetos range plunged into the steely sky of autumn, shouldering the stiff winds and the boiling clouds that presaged the coming winter. Here, from his vantage upon the hill of the Menelaion, Gylippos stared across the tranquil valley, canvassing the sprawl of modest Spartan dwellings. Nearby a priest and attendant of the Menelaion plucked out tufts of weeds from the seams of massive limestone steps of the temple. All around lay strewn a multitude of votive offerings left by pilgrims in honor of Helen and Menelaos. He glanced northward, imagining the armies of Athens and her allies marching down the throat of the valley, but only for a moment. Even with the battle of Mantinea still fresh, it was a most difficult sight to imagine. *Thank the gods I will never see that day*, he thought. His current isolation reminded him of his mentor Brasidas, of *his* solo excursions and subsequent encounters with the goddess in these lonesome places. He prayed. He paused to search the holy precinct for any sign then prayed once more. None became manifest. He felt unworthy and abandoned.

With resignation he pulled his cloak tight to fend off the wind and the icy mist that buffeted him, preparing to leave his lonely outlook and descend once again into the world of his city.

Kanthos, his slave, hovered over a pathetically small fire he had kindled under a time-twisted olive tree, rubbing his hands and checking on his master in jerky, alternations.

A hand pressed upon Gylippos' shoulder. A voice commanded him to sit.

Without delay he complied, all the while staring at the far side of the valley, not turning,
neither commanded by fear to comply, nor by curiosity to disobey. He sat upon the cold stone step and simply listened.

"Years past, when you were but another beast in the herd of the Agoge, I told you to pray to the gods but to trust only yourself."

Now his heart began to drum in his chest. Brasidas had spoken these words to him, and only to him. He fought the urge to turn, to reach for the hand upon his shoulder and grab it, to clutch at what could only be a shade of his friend and Inspirer, but realized any such action would chase away this connection like waking from a dream. He drew a deep breath, then asked, "May I know who is speaking with me sir?"

The hand squeezed a bit tighter on his shoulder— a grip of reassurance and not control. "I am but a breath and a shadow. All men are nothing more."

Brasidas, many years passed, had uttered these words. A gust of wind buffeted him. No grip was felt. He turned around only to find Kanthos still bent over his fire, turning his cold hands above the flames, peering up at him. *There is no sense in asking him*, mulled Gylippos. *He saw only the fire, the dirt at his feet, and me.*

"Come, Kanthos," he called as he bounded up from his seat, no longer keeping his cloak tight about his shoulders only, letting its length billow and snap behind him like a massive crimson pennant. Kanthos snuffed out the fire with his calloused feet, stomping then scooping a mound of soil on the smoldering ashes, almost tripping as he hustled to catch up with his master.

The road twisted its way down the tall hill of the Menelaion, finally unraveling into the village of Therapne. The dwellings here were modest, even by Spartan standards, and strewn about the banks of the Eurotas, some carved part way into the steep slope of the Menalaion Hill. Kanthos trailed behind Gylippos, paying little attention to their path while whistling almost silently—exuberant happiness would only draw attention to him, and attention is a deadly attribute for any helot.

"What are so you happy about?" Gylippos heard his surreptitious whistles, and half-jokingly challenged him about it, knowing how it would unsettle Kanthos.

"Master Gylippos?" Kanthos barely lifted his eyes from the road, glancing—no wincing in his master's direction.

"Your ears are larger than any hare's. You know what I said." He imparted his sternest command voice, the one he normally reserved for orders in the phalanx or lectures to the paides in the Agoge.

"I'm sorry master Gylippos, but I cannot help but whistle when I know good things are happening—sacred things." He dipped his head low now, staring at the dirt just in front of his feet as he shuffled along. "As you know, I am a man who wants for little, and I take more joy in the good fortune of others."

"Get to the point, man. What good and sacred things are happening?" Kanthos talked much more than any helot. Not a surprise, since he was born neither in Laconia or Messenia, but was a war captive from the Khalkidike campaign. A gift from Brasidas. A man of many words and by his telling, much education, yet still a pious soul accepting his new life as the will of the gods and for him a novel and educating experience. For Gylippos it was refreshing most times to hear him speak, to elaborate and to play with words and language. Spartans used words as though they had to be purchased first with gold. Not so with Kanthos. His flowed like autumn rainwater.

"Master Gylippos, although it may not have been apparent, I overheard you speaking upon Menelaos' hill. Only crazy men speak out loud to themselves, and I know most certainly that you are not crazy, so a god must have been there with you. Why else would you be in conversation and quite alone?"

Gylippos' first reaction was to threaten the slave, but he thought better of it and realized that Kanthos was both candid and sincere. He calmed himself. Now he spoke. "Do you believe that daimons, shades, and gods can speak with us?"

"Most certainly, master. Why the Pythia of Delphi is the first example that comes to mind, but there are many, some very ordinary men, who have heard the words of gods. The one thing that I do know, master, and this is for certain: the gods

Nemesis

speak only to men singly, isolated, and never in groups."

Gylippos laughed a bit at this comment. "More likely is that the insane do not congregate in large numbers. Is that what you mean?"

"Kanthos shook his head violently. "No, no master, I did not mean to say, or to infer that because no one else seems to witness these encounters that they are not real. I speculate that the gods, when they do speak to us, speak in whispers, and only to the most pious of men."

"You are as nimble with words as I am with my spear. Just remember that both can be lethal, especially to a slave." Gylippos smiled. Kanthos swallowed hard.

As they followed the Eurotas northwards and toward the Babyx Bridge, the wind raked down the broad valley, rustling olive groves and scuffing up dust from the road. Ahead a goatherd shooed his flock along lazily. Through the reeds he caught site of the Phobaion, the temple to Fear, on the far bank of the river. His mind immediately stirred with thoughts of his days in the Agoge, the sacred rites, and the sacrifices of black puppies on the altar of the Phobaion, a simpler time when only gods and not men could harm his city.

Further up the valley, towards the north, clouds began to gather, boiling dark and

high in the iron sky. Soon Taygetos would be snow-capped. Nearer to the Babyx Bridge he spotted a herd of boys cutting reeds, and harvesting thistle-down for their beds. No shouting, let alone talking emanated from these patrols—only the rustling of reeds as they were hacked from the muddy banks. A procession of youth moved along the road now with arm-loads of makeshift bedding.

Few Spartiates stood amongst the youth. In days past and when not on campaign almost every herd was afforded the company of at least one Spartan warrior as tutor. Today, as Gylippos reviewed the troop of boys, he was reminded of how few of them there are. One entire division had marched out to Messenia, before the snow would close the passes. Even with Sparta technically at peace with Athens, the ephors sent this mora to guard the ripe coastline and enforce order on the estates in the west. More helots had become pressed into serving either as battlefield attendants, or manumitted into the ranks of the Neodameidois, or new citizens. The army thickened slightly, but not with true Spartiates.

The Eurotas churned beneath him as he crossed the Babyx. Behind him Kanthos bumbled along, head up and whistling when no one took notice, quickly slumping into silence whenever Gylippos turned around or any other Spartiate came into view. Two men strolled toward them, one of them limping, with a pack of Kastorian hunting dogs swirling around them. Further back several helots humped along, laden with wicker campaign packs and bundles of hunting spears.

"Praying to Menelaos again?" Lysandros said with a smirk as he came upon Gylippos. He stopped in the middle of the road along with his companion Aegisilaos.

Gylippos studied the pair for a moment in awkward silence. Lysandros began to move off. "Good day to you Lysandros," he said with a forced grin. Now he turned to

Jon Edward Martin

Aegisilaos. "And how fares your brother Agis?"

Aegisilaos' eyes sunk deep into his face. His lips tightened as though he bit down on something. "He fares well," he snapped in reply.

"I wish you a successful hunt," Gylippos said to Aegisilaos as he passed by, although he wished him nothing but malice. He mistrusted Aegisilaos because he was Agis' brother, a Eurypontid and by this an enemy to him, his father, and King Pleistoanax, But he could never be certain whom King Aegisilaos despised more—Pleistoanax or his very own brother. Aegisilaos' bitterness toward Agis could well be understood; he was stronger, smarter and more pious than Agis and by any measure of gods or men, infinitely more suited to rule.

"I'll send something along to your mess if it is," replied Aegisilaos.

The two crossed over the bridge, but headed north. The helots passed by Gylippos, their necks straining under the weight of the fully laden packs and armfuls of spears and javelins. He heard Kanthos whisper something to one of them, but decided to let the incident go unchallenged. Now they passed through Limnai, the village of Aegisilaos, by the Temple of Artemis Orthia, and straight towards the agora. The sight of the busy, chock full market-stalls encouraged him. Each autumn since the treaty of peace had been signed with the Athenians, the harvests improved, due in no small part to the helots being left to work the land and not tending to campaigns. Sparta indeed could produce enough grain for herself and her allies if the farms and estates were allowed to run routinely, uninterrupted by war, a distinct advantage over their adversary of Athens, a city that in the best of times imported vast quantities of grain to sustain herself. No, Sparta was now content with peace, a bit of breathing space to stiffen her economy and rebuild her battered army. Gylippos too began to accept the advantages of peace. He
knew Aegisilaos and Lysandros did not.

*****

Temo wrapped the loose end of the chiton around the kettle's bail, lifting it from the coals, waddling a bit under its weight as she made her way to the table where she plopped it down hard, losing her grip. Xenias smiled. She ladled out the broth, made thick and black from pig's blood and vinegar, into a bowl in front of her husband.

"They will kill you. Make no mistake about it," she blurted out.

"And who would that be?" he clamped the wooded spoon in his fist and began to fill his mouth, keeping his eyes upon Temo.

"Your masters, the Spartans."

"And why would they do this? They are short of men of the warrior class. That is why they freed us. To fight alongside them." He turned his attention to his spoon and the broth.

"You and the other Neodameidois will be always placed in peril, not the Spartiates. You will face the enemy's best, not them. Has the memory of Mantinea faded so quickly?"

Nemesis

He drew the spoon from his lips and dropped it into the bowl. "They are not all like Agis. I know. I stood next to Brasidas in battle. He asked nothing of his men that he would not endure himself. Men like him—Spartans—turned the tide of that battle because they disregarded peril. No, there are many that are not like Agis."

"My dear husband, you are fodder for their wars. And if by chance there was an end to it, an end to war, they would send the Krypteia to destroy you." She dropped her head into her hands and sighed. "And when the likes of Agis are done with you, they will turn on their very own. Think hard on Brasidas and his fate."

"I do not seem to think about him as often as you do!" Xenias threw the spoon into his bowl and stood up. The baby, sleeping until now erupted into a bout of crying.

Temo quickly snatched the infant from its cradle, all the while refusing to look at Xenias, staring up at the low rafters and cobwebs that she had missed when cleaning today. Yes, she did dwell upon the memory of Brasidas. How could she not. She married his discarded brother.

A soft rapping. Both Xenias and Temo snapped their eyes toward the sound. Temo wrapped her arms tighter around the baby, while Xenias walked calmly to the door and opened it. There stood a helot servant. "Mistress Argileonis sends this gift to her grandson."

Temo immediately set her glance upon Xenias, cautioning him with a look to say nothing. She knew he seethed with resentment. She also knew their son would benefit from Argileonis' attentions. "Please convey our heartfelt thanks to your mistress for her generosity." Temo reached with one hand to accept the small bundle, snuggling her baby with the other, and nodded as the slave turned quickly to depart.

Certain that the slave was out of earshot, Xenias stood then flung his stool across the room. The infant wailed. Xenias opened his mouth as if to speak, but checked himself before releasing a long sigh. He was through the doorway and into the cold night. His chest heaved as though he had been running, vapor swirling from his mouth in the frosty air. Above the stars broke through the patches of racing clouds. By now Temo had quieted her daughter, for only the wind tugging on the treetops broke the silence. He began to walk, but only to fend off the cold, no destination in mind—only thoughts of his mother tossing in his thoughts. She had abandoned him at birth, and for a brief moment after Brasidas' death, regarded him as her son again, only to abandon him again once when recovered from her grief. But she did remember her granddaughter, if only from afar and with gifts that could never be traced back to her. He wondered again, as he so often had a hundred times before, how different things would have been if he had a son, and his mother a grandson. Would she and Tellis have sponsored him? Would he enter the Agoge and leave it a Spartan warrior? As much as he wanted to cultivate his hatred of them both, in his heart he knew what they would do. Their son and his brother Brasidas was a noble man, an honest man, and so must be his parents. He hoped they were not the last.

****

"And why do you not push them back? Why do they have their friends as ephors and why do their families hold such sway over the Apella?"

Gylippos shook his head. "Arithmetics." He headed for the doorway, and escape from his wife's badgering.

"Numbers? Can they count better than you?" She was as fierce in debate as Gylippos was in battle.

Gylippos stopped in his tracks. "There are more of them. Seems you have not mastered *your* numbers yet. Perhaps we should engage a tutor for you?"

He charged out through courtyard and onto the narrow lane that would take him to the Amyklaian Way, pausing for a moment as he looked back at his house. *Strange,* he thought while staring at it. *When I am on campaign I cannot wait to return here. But a single night at home rids me of any such notion. I prefer battle over domestic life, and war to politics.*

"It's a cold one, isn't it?'

Gylippos looked up to find his friend Kallikratidas walking straight toward him. "It is winter."

"Where are you off to? The agelai are south of the city, past Amylklai, I think. At least the younger ones are." Often times the pair would train with the youth, assisting each bouagos with the instructions of combat. Kallikratidas stopped in his path, the wind whipping his long hair. He squinted against it as it lashed his face.

"I do not know where I am going, my friend. Worse than that, I do not know where Sparta is going." He tugged Kallikratidas by the arm. "Walk with me and I will tell you what I think, and I pray you can convince me that I am wrong."

Kallikratidas lost his smile. "Is your wife still arguing politics with you? That is the only time you become so melancholy."

They walked for several hours, past all the phiditia, smoke rising from almost every one as the cooks and bakers worked to prepare the evening meals for the army. Peace had brought all of them home—well, almost all of them. The contingent left to guard the coast of Messenia would not return until the spring melt, when the passes over the Taygetos range once again opened. Although at peace with Athens for several years, their one time enemy still maintained a garrison at Pylos and this had become a rallying point for runaway helots. A few helot desertions meant little, but this haven encouraged mass desertions, severely impacting the grain harvests. Only the presence of a Spartan mora could neutralize this base and ensure Sparta's food supply.

Gylippos halted before the Phobaion. "I do not fear that our enemy Athens will destroy us. What I do fear is our two illustrious royal houses and their constant feuding. Agis covets war but seems not to understand that victory is its aim. He had it in his grasp before Argos. With the most splendid army ever assembled he had the Argives surrounded. One signal from him to attack and our ancient rival in the Peloponessos would have been destroyed, our territory secured for generations. But instead Agis parlayed. Not only do the Argives despise us, but so too do our allies. We call upon them to fight alongside us and we have victory in our grasp then Agis

Nemesis

talks a bit and simply goes home. We all know if he had fought this battle, Mantinea would have proved unnecessary. Aristokles and Hipponoidas would still be with us. Thank the gods that *they* favored us that day." Gylippos' eyes filled up as he spoke. There was no false exaggeration of the earnestness of his opinion for in truth, well before the battle of Mantinea, the Spartan army had maneuvered to surround the Argives, assuring their destruction and Agis let them go. Kallikratidas nodded in affirmation while tugging his cloak tight to him. Gylippos continued. "And our king Pleistoanax still clings to ancient notions that Athens and Sparta can stand side by side as friends. He sees an Athens that no longer exists."

Kallikratidas, silent until now, offered his thoughts. "I am not as cynical as you are with regards to Athens. We will become allies once more as long as the Persian Empire smothers the horizon to the east." He stopped and pointed across the Eurotas. On the far bank a herd of paides lined up in rank and file, performing the Anapale, or battle pantomime. He smiled broadly as he watched them execute each move smoothly, with steady focus, and in silence. "Chances are that they will be fighting Persians and not Greeks. When you climb that hill," he said pointing to the Menelaion, "pray to Helen and Menelaos that what I say becomes true. Pray that like the ancients, we will be sailing to Asia delivering war to the barbarian."

"You, my friend, are much like Brasidas. You hold our traditions sacred. You hold honor sacred. But unlike Brasidas, you do not see the dishonor of evil men."

Gylippos wrapped his arm around the shoulder of Kallikratidas. "Exhibit honor as he did, but expect it not from others."

"You are in a sad state, dear Gylippos. You trust no one. You believe in nothing. Yours is a bitter existence."

"Ah, if you were married to my wife Andromakhe then you would know true bitterness." He laughed. Kallikratidas, after an uncomfortable pause, laughed with him. They walked for hours, but talked only for minutes. Their tour of the valley brought them past the Hellaneion to the Plane Tree Grounds, just as the night swallowed up the last bit of light to the west. The mountains beyond tore across the heavens, jagged and dark. A snake of torchlight slithered up one of the slopes.

"They are heading for the Deposits," said Gylippos. He immediately thought of the poor infant, condemned to be abandoned in a high mountain ravine, by this procession of elders. His own mind conjured up a vision of Xenias, brother to Brasidas, who also was discarded in that deadly place. *Sparta needs men*, he thought, *and they toss them away like broken pottery*. Kallikratidas could only shake his head as he too acknowledged the sight. The two men parted in silence, each almost expecting to hear the cries of the abandoned child waft down from the heights.

Jon Edward Martin

Chapter Five
Argos – Early Spring 417 BC

Endymion sat in the barn, mending together frayed pieces of grass rope that he would need for the plow. His fingers deftly flipped and twirled the tattered ends, creating long pieces out of many shorter ones, spitting onto his palms every so often to aid his grip. If it were not for the chilly air he would almost be comfortable. Argos was once again at peace with Sparta, although peace brought with it a certain compliance that was most easily delivered by the aristocrats now in power.

The door creaked open on rusty hinge pins. In the light of the portal stood his son Antiphemos, ax in hand. "Father, I gathered enough, I think."

Endymion rose slowly, letting the rope fall from his hands. "It will take much wood to make oh so little charcoal." He was lucky. His ancestral land hugged Mount Alesion and its thickly forested slopes, so charcoal burning proved to be an excellent supplement to his income from barley and grapes. The wind hit him hard and cold as he stepped free of the barn. He smiled. So did Antiphemos. Four wagon-loads of cut wood piled chest high lined the path to his house. Slaves had already begun carting it to the burners. Soon the air would be filled with the perfume of plane and oak, pine and wild olive.

"Son, I think you shall superintend the charcoal this year." He wrapped an arm around Antiphemos, squeezing his shoulder tight with his hand, giving his son a shake.

"Are the Spartans our friends now?" Antiphemos asked innocently.

Endymion thought for a moment before answering. "Well, at least for now they are not our enemy. That is somewhat of a blessing."

"So they are not our friends?"

Endymion chuckled. "Come on son. Let us see what mother has prepared for our dinner." He knew the mention of food would fill Antiphemos' mind and deliver him from discussions of politics. How could he explain to his son that friends and enemies are not so easily distinguished? What words could he conjure to explain that half his fellow citizens despised the other half and that any alliances with either Athens or Sparta were only tools for the advancement of their parties within Argos. Except that now the aristocrats ruled, and peace prevailed. A not inconvenient arrangement, as long as people remained calm. As long as people remained reasoned. Not being one, Endymion distrusted the aristocrats. But for today he would tolerate a little less freedom for a measure of peace and security.

"We have some fish tonight," announced his wife as they entered the kitchen, "to go with a loaf of wheat bread." She pulled the steaming loaf from the clay oven with a bent bronze rod twirling it as she stepped toward the table in the center of the room. With a deft flick she deposited it upon an orange-glazed platter, atop the neat row of palm-length grilled boarfish. She walked to Endymion, filled his wooden cup with wine then moved to her son's side and drained a portion into his, leaving

Nemesis

more than enough room for a hearty measure of water. Antiphemos almost snarled as she thinned his wine. "You two worked very hard today," she complimented while pulling a stool up to the table.

"I certainly did," confirmed Antiphemos. He snatched a fish from the platter and pushed it tail first into his mouth and began to chew.

"That will keep him quite for some time," said Endymion as he lifted his fish from the serving plate. He too worked upon the fish now, chewing around the bones, stripping every bit of meat from it without taking it out of his mouth until only a bare skeleton remained. He drained his wine.

His wife refilled the cup quickly. "Peace with the Spartans has allowed us to eat somewhat better," she said as she slid the pitcher atop the table. "And how long has it been since the fish stalls in agora have had anything to sell."

"I pray that this peace endures, but I would have preferred it to occur without a government installed by the Spartans."

From the courtyard his three hunting dogs exploded into a tirade of barking. He heard the wooden gate slam hard. The dogs growled and yipped.

"Get them back or I'll spear them!"

Antiphemos jumped from his stool and burst out of the kitchen, Endymion failing to grab hold of his son as he ran by. He bounded after him. In the courtyard five armed and armored men faced off against his dogs while Antiphemos struggled to hold them back. He could see in the eyes of these men that they would feel no compunction at driving a spear through his son, less so the dogs. "Stop! They will do you no harm." His wife flew out of the kitchen and along with Antiphemos, tugged the whirling dogs out of the courtyard and into the barn.

One of them stepped forward, planting his spear and raising his kranos helmet clear of his face. "Endymion, son of Antiphemos, of the village of Sepeia?"

Endymion nodded.

"You have been accused of treason by the council. You are to return with us to the city immediately."

Endymion glanced toward the barn where his son and wife began to emerge. He pushed his hand at them, motioning them to stop. By his look they understood this to be a command—not a request—so they halted in the doorway.

To each side of him moved a pair of hoplites while the leader stepped in front. They marched off in silence. Antiphemos and his mother rushed to the gate and peered out, watching Endymion and his escort fade slowly into the shadows of late evening. They could do nothing tonight, but tomorrow they would visit their neighbor Ekhinadas. He was once on the council. He would know what to do. At least that is what Antiphemos said to his mother, trying desperately to reassure her. They made their way slowly to the house, into the kitchen and pulled two stools together and sat. Antiphemos squeezed his mother's hand, saying over and over, "we will sort this out." His mother could only cry.

****

"I am no traitor." Endymion stalked the cell in the citadel, weaving in and out of the men sprawled on the floor, making his way to the thick oak door. He hammered it with his fist. "I am no traitor!"

"Doesn't matter." A voice bubbled up from the men who sat against the wall.

Endymion scanned the faces, but recognized none of them. Behind him, the bolt in the door rattled as a guard freed it. The door squealed open and four armed men strode through. They too scanned the faces of each man then heaved one up from the floor, shoving him quickly out of the cell. "Where are they taking him?" said Endymion as rushed to look out of the quickly closing door, but it slammed shut before he could steal a glance of the corridor beyond.

"Execution." A tall thin man, with a graying beard and gnarled fingers stood up. "They are murdering anyone who they think is a threat to the new government."

"You are Tisandros, the fisherman," declared Endymion as light from the high, narrow window struck his face. The man nodded. "I am no threat to this new government."

"Nor am I", Tisandros quickly added. "But they remember the battle of Mantinea, and recall with accuracy or not, the ones who raised complaints of how the generals conducted it." He paused looking around to see if any of their cell-mates listened too closely. "And the ones who so rightly noticed the lack of casualties amongst the aristocrats."

"I offered no complaints. I, in fact, said nothing. The generals did not lose that battle. We did! All of us!" Now the men in the cell began to grumble and shifted about, agitated by the truth that Endymion spouted. "The generals did not loot the Sparta baggage train. They did not break ranks and change from army to mob. We did."

"And were you there?" shouted out someone from the far corner of the cell. "Or did you hide behind your aristocrat friends as they entertained Agis and his Spartans?"

Endymion pushed his way to the corner of the cell and plucked up the man, shoving him hard into the cold stonework. "I fought there. I bled there. And I did not abandon the battle to stuff my purse full of booty."

Tisandros pulled Endymion off the man, "Settle down, my friend. Like it or not, we are now all enemies of the new government, a government of the few and of the rich. A government that has the backing of the Spartan army. Pray that we outlast the hysteria of the moment, and they let us all go back to our families and our homes."

"My life is changed forever, Tisandros. I was content to let others be concerned with the governing of our city, but look what has happened to me. Look what has happened to us all."

"We will have our chance," reassured Tisandros. "If they don't kill us all first."

Chapter Six
Sparta – Summer 417 BC

"Bastards!" Likhas pounded his fist into the table so hard that Gylippos' kothon flew into the air. A helot caught it before it smashed upon the floor. The feast of the Gymnopaidia had just begun, the middle of the three sacred festivals of the Spartan summer. The Argive conspirators had timed their move well.

"Are we certain that what this one Argive says is true?" challenged Kallikratidas. "Or is he anticipating something that he imagines might happen?"

"Oh, it is true, my friends. I am their proxenos and I know this man." Likhas squeezed the kothon in his ever-tightening fist.

Gylippos rapped his knuckles on the table. "And you would expect something else? Likhas, your *friends* in Argos, the very ones who assured you that they could control affairs and become a reliable ally, are murdering their fellow citizens. But I suppose that is one way to control them." The others in the phidition burst out in laughter. "When given a choice of death or revolution, it is quite easy to understand why Argos is in turmoil now. Would you go meekly to your death Likhas? Would you Kallkratidas?"

"So you would allow our friends in Argos to perish? Send no assistance to men who have helped us?" Likhas was beyond agitation. His kothon shattered in his hand. He hardly noticed, unconsciously licking the wine from his fingers.

Gylippos sighed. "By their actions they have proven themselves unfit to govern their own city. Send no troops. Let things take their natural course in Argos. A stable Argos, either democracy or oligarchy, is preferable to one in stasis. The Athenians woulduse this turmoil to insinuate themselves into Peloponnesian affairs. They will always use the excuse of coming to the aid of friends as a means of exerting their influence."

Likhas flung the remnants of his cup onto the floor. "You would really allow a wild democracy to take hold in Argos again, when we are so close to eliminating them as a rival? You and Pleistoanax talk much the same. He too, would prefer any form of government in Argos as long as it was immune to change."

"Would you try to put the rain back into the sky after it has fallen? Some things are never meant to be." Gylippos plucked a honey-cake from the platter. "Besides, if Agis leads us to Argos yet again, we will not fight. Some omen or another will turn him around, insulting our allies and emboldening our enemies. We might as well just stay here and enjoy the festival."

"But Agis says he would deal only with their oligarchs. That does not give him very room to maneuver. He may have no choice but to march on Argos," said Likhas.

"Why do we bother with them at all?" Kallikratidas shrugged his shoulders. "March on Athens, and obviate this Argive campaign. They have done us much harm even during this false peace. They hide behind the technicality of this treaty and poke and prod us. Pylos is still in their hands."

Jon Edward Martin

"Friends, you all know me well, and you know me to be no pacifist, but I think Sparta could do with a bit of stability itself. The Athenian Alkibiades is not the only man alive who would use war to enrich himself. I dare say there are more than a few here in Sparta who would advance their careers upon the battlefield, fighting not for our country but for themselves."

"Oh, well I knew you would have to find some way to insult Lysandros," said Kallikratidas laughing. "But I think he is busy attending to Aegisilaos. Besides, he is still
too young to command much more than a company."

A hebon, one of the young men just out of the Agoge, flew through the door, his chest heaving. "The festival has been suspended. The ephors have called up the first 20 age grades for battle." he nodded with deference then turned and ran off to the next phidition. Kallikratidas jumped up and chased after him. He would pose a question or two to the messenger. He was always gathering intelligence.

"Well gentlemen, at least the younger of you—assemble at the agora."

Gylippos rose slowly. "And who will be leading us? Likhas, since we are undoubtedly marching to Argos, you must be one of the polemarkhoi."

"I honestly do not know if they will allow me to go on this adventure, unless of course King Pleistoanax is in command."

Kallikratidas bounded up the stairs to the phidition, pushing the door wide open as he cleared the top step. "It is Agis."

They groaned a bit, but departed the mess-hall quickly. Kanthos was already waiting for him at the barracks, campaign pack filled, panoply laid out for inspection on Gylippos' sleeping pallet. His wife, more from duty than from love, had sent along a small packet of incense for his sacrifices and a wound kit of bronze needles, dried sinew, yarrow, and iskai moss. She knew he would not return to her before the march-out.

"Acceptable," he growled as he ran his fingers over the bronze facing of his shield. Kanthos had burnished it to perfection, its surface more reflective than any queen's mirror.

Kanthos clapped his hands together in delight. This was as much of a compliment as he could hope to receive from his master. He slipped the shield into its hide bag then carried it and a pair of spears to a waiting cart outside, hurried back into the barracks and quickly wrapped his master's kranos helmet, greaves and linothorax body armor in a large square of linen, tying it all up into a neat, almost symmetrical bundle. In moments he had this too, loaded upon the cart, had hitched up the mule and began to lead it to the agora to assemble with the others of the baggage train.

Gylippos slung his sword over his shoulder and checked to see that his skytale was securely fastened to his wrist. He stuck his pilos felt cap atop his head then headed off down the Aphetaid Road, toward the agora and his lokhos. As he walked the road was lined with people, mostly citizens and helots, but also many foreigners who had come to the Gymnopaidia as guests of influential Spartans, and

Nemesis

who would now, most extraordinarily, witness the assembly, organization and march-out of a Spartan army prepared for battle. This most uncommon spectacle to any foreigner.

As he walked by the acropolis, he saw many of the women gathered on its slopes, waving to husbands and sons as they moved by. There, amongst the women of his village stood his wife, performing her obligation for all to see. He tried to catch her eye, and did for a brief moment, but she stared away, her icy countenance a stark dismissal of his feeble attempt at a good-bye. Kanthos, ever-watchful, noticed this rebuff and thought to himself, *no wonder he prefers the barracks to home and war over peace.*

The army, a model of efficiency, assembled quickly—by mora, lokhos, pentekostys and finally enomotia. Once in final marching order with the king at the fore, a troop of cavalry sped off for the Babyx Bridge and would scout ahead until they reached their camp for the night. Word was passed down the triple column—they would march to Tegea and wait there for their allies and the Perioikoi. That would mean a hard march to get there by dark for they had less than half-a-day's light left to them.

****

"And are you happy that your predication has come to fruition?" Kallikratidas smirked at him as he spoke.

"Hardly a prediction. It is what he does." Gylippos pulled the baldric of his sword's scabbard, trying to adjust it for comfort as they marched.

"No my friend, it is what he does not do." Kallikratidas shook his head.

Exactly as Gylippos had stated before the march-out to Tegea, Agis had latched onto the first excuse to turn the army around. The oligarchy in Argos had fallen, its city walls now defended by the reformed democracy. They would not be helping allies, but invading a city. Agis had not the stomach for this improper and unseemly type of warfare that relied more on science and treachery than battlefield courage. Gylippos was disappointed only by the quickness of their return to Sparta.

The same familiar scenes greeted them as they crossed the Eurotas and into the village of Limnai. Sullen helots staring at them with hollow eyes, youth from the Agoge lined up singing the Embaterion, friends and relatives milling about the agora in anticipation. As always his wife was absent and as always Tellis alone greeted Gylippos.

"Have you heard any news from the allies? Has this retreat angered them?" asked Gylippos.

"Our allies are not the issue, but the Athenians." Tellis, hardly a man to betray his thought by countenance, appeared a bit disturbed.

"Have they attacked the coast?" Gylippos hoped this were true. He would force the issue with Likhas and command the Messenian garrison.

"They have invested Melos."

"But Melos is neutral. They serve neither us nor Athens," remarked Gylippos with a bit of astonishment laced in his voice.

"It seems a faction within Melos has called upon the Athenians to intervene. Athens needs little excuse to expand its empire," said Tellis. "One malcontent would provide all the grounds they require."

"But it is a Dorian city. Surely they would not risk open war again with us over an island that can do them no harm or provide no substantial benefit?" said Gylippos.

"There will be no war with us over Melos. Agis and the ephors would never risk it. By the Holy Twins, Agis will not fight on our very doorstep. The return of the army is proof of that". Tellis shook his head and continued, "But who knows? Maybe even Agis and the rest may show some courage in the face of the insult and provocation. Tellis paused a bit then continued, "Melos will receive no help from us. After all it is Agis we are talking about."

"Sir, I should go now. Andromakhe must be worried," he said laughing. Tellis did not smile at the remark, but could only shake his head.

Chapter Seven
Melos – Autumn 416 BC

Philokrates marched with his officers along the gravel beach toward the end of the siege works that punctuated the harbor entrance. The pyres had been erected, made from the timbers of Melian ships and houses, and were in size and number thought sufficient to burn the three-thousand or so corpses of the slain men. The female survivors and slaves of Melos carted the bodies to the base of the pyres then strained to clamber up the stacks of wood, dragging corpses and finally tossing them like kindling at the top. They wailed and beat their chests as they toiled, the Athenian hoplites that guarded them casting insults.

"Where are your Spartan saviors now?" yelled out one of them at a woman robed in black, two young girls helping her haul a body up the mountain of timber. She stopped, wiping the sweat from soiled face with her himation. Her daughters sobbed and sniffled. She wanted to respond, to retaliate with what words she could summon, but stayed silent, almost content in knowing that the gods would indeed punish them. She only wondered when and prayed that she would still be alive when the news reached her, wherever she might be, when these haughty Athenians climbed up pyres meant for them. One of the girls collapsed to her knees and began crying in fits. "Dianthe, get up," said her mother firmly, "or they will take you from me. Draw no notice from them."

The girl bounced to her feet and tugged on the arm of her father's corpse, and after almost a quarter hour they had placed him as gently as they could manage amongst the other dead. The woman slipped a coin into her dead husband's mouth, the toll for the Ferryman and insurance he would at the very least, depart this world and enter the land of shades.

Philokrates shouted out orders. "As soon as they are done, bring them all to the harbor. We'll auction them off there." He kept walking. The weather had been more than warm, bloating the flesh of the slain and luring the gulls, kites, and other carrion birds down to peck at the dead, the smell of rotting flesh saturating the air. Some of the younger Athenians vomited, overcome by nausea, but Philokrates, veteran of many battles, had become inured to the stench. He strode and surveyed, in no particular hurry, finally reaching the tower at the terminus of the harbor entrance. Here the wind shifted, a salty breeze filling his nostrils and carried away the fetid stench of death that hung upon the beach. Detachments of archers patrolled the high ground and the battlements, every-so-often unleashing a minor barrage at any of the Melians that attempted escape. To them it had become a game, with each successive fugitive initiating a contest amongst them, wagering to see who could delay the longest and therefore shoot the farthest in taking down a fleeing Melian women or child. They even started cheering each other as their arrows sprouted from the ever multiplying corpses.

"Send an officer up to the walls and order them to stop," bellowed Philokrates, "or we'll go home to Athens empty handed." He was visibly agitated at the gruesome contest, for in truth he found no honor in executing women and children, but more to the point, for every one slain meant less money in his purse—as commander he was entitled to just less than the tithe reserved for the god.

The officer hurried up the steep embankment, through the postern gate and atop the battlement. He carried out his order with extraordinary enthusiasm, berating the archers, cuffing one of them with the shaft of his spear, all as a show to his superior that he, too, himself possessed the qualities of command.

The woman looked up, squinting into the sun as it began to slip behind the high battlement wall. "Run now," she whispered, sending her two daughters into a sprint for harbor and the safety of the maze of quays. She, on the other hand, ran in the opposite direction, toward the beach and a clutch of abandoned fishing skiffs.

Philokrates yelled out again. "Get her!"

The woman was almost a hundred meters from the nearest hoplite as she shoved and heaved against the heavy hull of the boat, shouldering it finally into the meek swells. She pushed hard, then rolled into the belly of the skiff, the retreating tide pulled her slowly out to sea and away from the Athenians.

Philokrates stared up at the archers and his officer atop the battlement, shook his head in disgust then gave the order. A volley of iron-heads sizzled through the air, some ripping into the sea around the skiff while others thudded into the wooden hull. Another barrage. Fewer hit water. A third volley gruesomely filled the skiff.

*****

Night had come, lessening their anxiety but inflicting the pain of cold as they hunched beneath a quay in the harbor. The youngest of the girls, Elpida, began to sob again. "Shhh!" warned Dianthe, her finger before her lips, her eyes wide with fright. "They'll hear us," she whispered. She wrapped her arm around Elpida, letting her sister's face bury into her chest while stroking her sibling's golden hair as she looked out as the immense funeral pyres that illuminated the full expanse of the southern beach. The light from the flames reflecting eerily atop the water, reached deep under the quays as though the very waves carried it along. Dianthe continued to stare at the flames that consumed the body of her father, and prayed to Hermes to guide him to the Styx. Above her, the wooden boards that comprised the quays drummed with the footsteps of Athenian marines on patrol. Even on the beach, where the fires burned brightly, archers and infantry strolled about on guard. With all of them out there and above on the docks, they would never make the dash along the beach and to the stream beyond that would lead them up into the hills and their place of rendezvous.

Only two men now strode atop the gently swaying quay, moving directly toward them. Dianthe peered up through the gaps in the boardwalk. Loitering immediately above them, she made out the forms of two heavily armed hoplites, their armor made flashing, even in the gloom, by the nearby fires. Her heart pounded violently, and to her most loudly—Elpida's eyes screamed panic.

"Do you think Nikias will regret his opposition to the siege now?" asked the one hoplite, who ground the butt-spike of his spear nervously into the planking. He

Nemesis

slid his aspis shield from his shoulder, letting it slam hard into the quay. Elpida jumped. Dianthe hugged her even tighter. The shield rim rocked across the crevice of wood, so close that Dianthe could touch it. For a fleeting moment she almost succumbed to this urge.

"Never, my friend. Nikias wants us to sail to Thrake and forget these distractions," answered the second hoplite. He sucked up a mouthful of phlegm and spit it on the dock. "No matter. Alkibiades holds influence now. He wants no part in small battles. With him Melos counts for nothing. He is on the path to Karthage, by way of Syrakuse first, then Sikelia."

Now the hoplite re-hefted his shield. "Come on friend. Let us worry about our breakfast first and leave the grand strategies to Nikias and Alkibiades. They will keep each other in check, and if we are truly lucky, provoke only each other and not the Spartans."

As the night wore on she observed fewer and fewer patrols, but more laughter and shouting. The Athenians were drinking. *Good*, she thought. *Soon they will sleep*

Suddenly there was more shouting, but not from bands of revelers, but from voices of the clear-headed. Men jogged to the beach, gathering around a small boat that had drifted to shore. They hauled beyond the tide-line and near the base of the one of the raging pyres. Dianthe, from her hiding place beneath the quay could see them pull something—or someone from the boat. There was no movement and the men dropped whatever it was onto the gravel beach with no ceremony, and walked away muttering and chatting. Their shouts, for the time being, had been subdued.

Now she began to shiver, so she hugged her sister even tighter, but her feet had lost all feeling and her fingers refused to obey her mind. *I must get her out of the water,* she thought, swaying back and forth while continuing her embrace. *We must both get out or we will die.*

Almost another hour passed until she thought it safe enough to try to negotiate the beach to the stream beyond. Her sister was in convulsions by now, their violence increasing with each passing moment. "Come on. We must get dry." She waded through the waist deep water, toward the shore but keeping beneath the dock until it pinched them too tightly to the rock shore. Quietly they crawled onto dry land, for they could not walk yet, nor even stand—their legs cramped in pain from cold, muscles unable to flex. Dianthe began to rub her sister's legs, on at a time, to bring the blood back into them. Elpida whimpered as Dianthe kept to it, both doing everything possible to muffle their voices and smother cries. It was better than the water, but just barely. They needed fire. Their bodies were bereft of any warmth and the strength needed for activity to generate it. Dianthe began to crawl from the cover of the pier toward one of the smoldering pyres, dragging her moaning sister by the hand. The gravel rattled beneath them as they moved along, but it seemed that the guards had all succumbed either to sleep or the wine, and heard nothing. She pulled up next to the base of the fire, her sister next to her, and began to claw out stones from beneath the glowing embers. She wrapped these in her sister's chiton first and pressed them next to her belly, then quickly did the same. Like the healing touch of Apollo, the rocks poured life back into her. She pressed them even tighter to her body, clenching them, squeezing them, embracing them, trying to drawn out every bit of life restoring heat. After a time, they both had warmed up enough to continue to yank out more hot stones and placed then around their feet and legs, every so often handling them to warm up their hands also.

To the east the sky began to brighten, prompting Dianthe to forget her attempts at warming, forcing her now to formulate a plan for crossing the several hundred meters of beach under the walls and the eyes of the Athenian guards. Near the tide line, she could see a heap of what looked like discarded cloths, the contents of the drifting boat that the Athenians had beached earlier. Something compelled her to crawl toward it. She kept to her hands and knees though by now she had the strength to rise up and walk. As she drew closer she knew the object was no pile of laundry, but that of a body, the arms and legs clearly evident along with the span of the shoulders and the curve of the hips. She could not see the head, nor face, but was sure whom it was. She walked at first then began to run toward it, sliding to her knees as she came to the body.

She gently wiped the hair from her mother's face then twisted the arrows from her body, one by one. Her sister watched her. Her sister knew. But she stayed frozen as she was in the chilly water hours previous, unable to come any closer. Dianthe dragged her mother's body to the base of the smolder pyre, rolling it as far as she could upon the embers. Steam began to rise from her mother's corpse. She wanted to gather some wood, and thought about pulling what she could from the abandoned skiff, but it was too large and too heavy for her to haul up the beach, and the noise would certainly alert the guards. She crouched low and ambled back to her sister.

"We must leave now." She tugged on her sister's arm. Now Elpida's chest heaved with sobs. Dianthe pulled her arm violently, inducing such pain that her sister's sobs stopped. "Enough crying. She is dead. Honor her and Father by living." She pulled her up and they both began to cross the beach, passing the first two pyres without drawing any attention from the sleeping guards. Now she heard voices. From beyond the next pyre a group of Athenian soldiers sauntered their way. They were not drunk, nor recently roused and bleary-eyed. They moved with purpose and spoke with clarity. Philokrates took a sip from his kantharos mug before handing it back to his servant. "Do we have a tally from the auction yet?" His servant read off the preliminary figures. The numbers disappointed him. "Some of them ran off into the hills. We'll send patrols off today to round the remainder up and—." He stopped midsentence, the sight of a huge grain-lighter cutting through the swells on the way into the harbor arresting him. "Good," he said pointing to the large trading vessel. "We have buyers for our loot." He and his small entourage kept to their stroll along the beach, stopping at the base of the last pyre.

One of the infantrymen walked slowly over to it. "That is strange," he said as he poked the unburned body. "It didn't burn." He finally noticed the steam rising from

Nemesis

it. "By the gods, this one is wet!"

Philokrates and the rest rushed over to him. Another hoplite recognized the body. "That's the one that tried to escape in the fishing skiff last night. We pulled her out of it." He pointed to the skiff then spit into his chiton, an antidote for evil. "The dead woman crawled into the fire!"

Philokrates whacked the soldier with the shaft of his spear. "You fool! Someone dragged her up here. Rouse the harbor guards. Call the archers down from that wall and have them search the beach."

Huddled near the edge of the docks Dianthe and her sister had scant chance of crossing the beach now. "I won't go back into the water." Dianthe nodded silently in agreement. Berthed on the nearest quay, the grain-lighter that Philokrates had spotted was beginning to disembark its crew. The gang-plank was down, the vessel secured to the dock rings and the crewmen stood anxiously along the rail. The Athenian marines guarding the quay motioned them off. "Hope you boys have some money. The slave auction opens at dawn." They did all they could to steer the crew toward the agora and the slave auction, for they, of course, would receive their share of the profits. The ship emptied quickly. The marines drifted along the dock and away from the grain-lighter, inadvertently lured away by conversation with the departing crewmen.

Dianthe looked to her sister. They both knew, at that instant, what they would do. Silently, quickly, they scurried up the gang-plank and across the deck to the cargo hold of the grain-lighter, nestling in amongst the creaking amphorai filled with wheat.

Chapter Eight
Syrakuse – Autumn 416 BC

Hermokrates pulled back on the reins to slow his horse as it skidded down the hill-slope towards the harbor. The quays creaked under the swells. It was nearly midday, and the sun beat down on him like a molten hammer as he continued on with his inspection of the waterfront docks and warehouses. As the new Magistrate of Trade he could not neglect his duties even on such a scorching day as this.

"Ho!" a crewman on a freighter yelled out as he tossed a mooring rope onto the quay. A dock worker scurried to grab it and shoved it through a massive bronze ring, slung the end over his shoulder and began to tug the bow of the freighter closer to a berth. One and then another crewman hopped from the ship onto the dock then all along the length of vessel, this gang pulling it tight to the jetty using their calloused hands and thick-muscled arms. Once secure, the master of the vessel stepped to the balustrade, hands on hips, and looked up and down the length of the freighter, nodding his head as he inspected the moorings. Two other crewmen bounded down the gang-plank, their steps exaggerated by the steep incline and legs more accustomed to the sway of the sea than to solid earth. The ship master strode down confidently, all the while turning his head left and right as though everything he surveyed he owned.

"Where from?" shouted Hermokrates as he cantered his horse slowly over to the stranger. He rubbed his horse's neck affectionately while summoning his most stern and commanding face.

"From Melos, I am Tigranes, son of Kanduales."

Hermokrates almost slid from his horse to greet the man more cordially, but thought better of it. "You say you are from Melos?" He bent, extending his hand to the stranger in greeting.

The ship master shook his head most violently. "I have set sail from Melos, but my home is Kilikia."

"Then tell me: What are the doings at Melos? Last we heard it was under siege by the Athenians. How did you make it out?" quizzed Hermokrates.

"The siege, if one could call it that, still goes on. And so does the talk between the Melians and the Athenians. Both will come to their senses."

"What is your cargo?" Hermokrates asked as he dismounted.

"Some of this and a little of that. Mostly trinkets, nothing that would interest a man of your means."

"On the contrary. I may indeed find something to my liking." Hermokrates walked toward the gang-plank with the intention to board.

"Sir, I cannot allow anyone on board yet. I am obliged to meet with an important buyer first."

Hermokrates snagged a boy as he ran past, instructing him to fetch the harbor master as he pressed an obol into his palm. "You'll get another one of those when you return." The boy bowed then spun around and sprinted off. Now

Nemesis

Hermokrates turned his attention to the stranger. "Your vessel will be seized and its cargo inspected."

"What have I done? I had every intention to declare all of it or why else would I be talking to you?"

"It is a routine matter. If you have bills of freight and invoices for your cargo, you will have nothing to fear. But if you are but a pirate and a scavenger—?"

"A pirate!" Now the barbarian ship master flew into a rage. "I demand to see Athenagoras, the official in charge of commerce. We are good friends and he knows the value of reliable merchants such as me. He'll put you in your place."

"I think sir, that I shall put *you in yours*." I am Hermokrates, the new Magistrate of Trade for the Syrakusans."

The Kilikian's face drained. The quay rocked as the harbor master approached, flanked by two heavy infantrymen. Hermokrates nodded while pointing at the stranger. "He shall be our guest while we inspect his ship and cargo. Escort him to Long Stoa."The two hoplites squeezed around the Kilikian, gently nudging him forward to follow the harbor master. Hermokrates tugged on the reins of his horse, leading it as he walked slowly along the waterfront, surveying the vessels that had docked this day. The Great Harbor held scores of merchantmen closer to the causeway leading south of the city while the docks adjacent to Ortygia were lined with ship sheds for dry-docking war triremes. Farther off and along the beach near the marsh, fishermen began to return from with their morning catches, some scooped fish from the bellies of their boats while others dragged nets ashore, spreading them over wickerwork frames for drying. Children scurried in and about the fishing boats, anxious to assist fathers and brothers with the catch. The wind began to pick up now, bringing welcome relief from the midday heat—the Great Harbor stirred little, but beyond, the open sea commenced to churn with white-caps. Intensity of purpose increased amongst the fishermen as they quickly beached their vessels. A storm was brewing.

Hermokrates decided to return to the city, and to the bouleterion itself. Although the council was not due to meet until mid-afternoon today, he wished to be there before the chamber filled, to speak with his friends, but more importantly, measure his adversaries before the session commenced. Although today would consist of preliminaries only, he must gain what he could without confronting Athenagoras and the democrats. Life was very good in Syrakuse now. No war. Plentiful harvests. Any of his concerns regarding the Athenians would hardly be welcome as prudent cautions, but as fear mongering. He could not summon the specter of invasion unless it was imminent. But if he waited too long, there may be no time to avert the ruin war. Yes, times were good in Syrakuse. Few considered war and fewer were prepared for it.

Almost unconsciously, he retraced his way up the waterfront and to the commercial docks, passing the Kilikian freighter, as an Egyptian grain-lighter slipped into its berth nearby. Aboard, tall dark-skinned crewmen clad only in bull-hide loincloths tossed ropes and secured the vessel to the quay. "Sir, do you be the master of this harbor?" asked the only one of the men aboard dressed in robes and finery. His shaved head gleamed in the sun like a polished melon. He spoke in broken Greek, but proved understandable.

Hermokrates shook his head. "I, sir am not, but he will be returning shortly."

"Will it be possible for me to leave my ship?" He placed one foot upon the rail as he spoke, the wind rippling his bright robe, the sun flashing his bejeweled fingers as he waved them to add emphasis to his words. In the distance thunder rumbled, announcing a storm.

"Where from?" Hermokrates began to stare at the Egyptian. The man's eyes were lined with kohl as an remedy to the sun; his cheeks rubbed with ochre. Hermokrates laughed to himself.

"Naukratis, sir. Trading, I hope, in Egyptian wheat."

"But we are already content with our good Sikelian wheat. What else do you trade?" Hermokrates asked.

The Egyptian clamped his lips for a moment, before holding out his hand. "Much blue glass," he said, fingering the jewels upon his hand. "Oriental silk," he added, tugging on his robe.

"Sir, what we are in need of in Syrakuse is news. Can you accompany me to our council house?"

The Egyptian grinned from ear to ear while nodding furiously. "I will come, but I do not speak too very good."

Once upon the dock, Hermokrates introduced himself. The Egyptian dipped his head ever so quickly. "I am Djadao and at your service." Once the formalities had been dispensed with Hermokrates commenced his assault of questions. "Do you have any news from Melos? Our council meets soon and it would be of great interest."

The Egyptian suddenly lost his grin. "Taken by the Athenians. The men-folk for certain, they have slain."

"Killed them all?" Hermokrates could not believe him.

"All the men. I see the bodies myself when I be in their harbor. The women and young ones sold off right quick. The Athenians be hungry more for the loot than the houses or land. They wanted cold coin and fast." He wrung a clenched fist as though it was full of obols. Now he glanced to the Kikilian vessel. "They be at Melos before me and leave after me. Perhaps the pilot of that boat can tell you more? But if you still desire, I can relate these things to your council?" The man looked decidedly uncomfortable at the thought of speaking before so many foreigners.

Hermokrates paused before answering. To his dismay the Kilikian had told him much less. "Does the Kilikian know you to have been at Melos?"

Djadao's face wrinkled into a frown. "Why yes. We talk long time in the harbor."

Hermokrates could see the regret on the man's face. "You will not be required to say very much." Hermokrates waited for the gang-plank to be lowered. Djadao, his weight disguised by his billowing robe, bent the gang-plank as

Nemesis

disembarked, pulling up next to Hermokrates almost spent of breath. Hermokrates pointed up toward the city wall and Ortygia. "It will be a bit of a walk."

On board the grain-lighter, crewmen and slaves hustled about, fumbling with an immense litter that the Egyptian must so obviously use for ambling about; he did not move on his feet with comfort and every step proved the ultimate in exertion for him, but he waved furiously at his slaves preparing the litter, shouted something in Egyptian, then turned to Hermokrates. "They are always trying to get me to travel about in that unwieldy thing," he said, waving off the litter as though it were an infrequent nuisance.

Hermokrates, cognizant of his new companion's infirmities, slowed his pace considerably. He glanced back over his shoulder to the Egyptian vessel. The entire crew lined the balustrade, eyes wide with concern for their master as he ambled away from them. Some started to chuckle surreptitiously, covering smirks with their hands, or turning completely away to hide their mirth. He did not say much as he walked, knowing how uncomfortable the Egyptian was with his Greek and especially with this long walk. They passed men dragging full amphorai from ship to wagon and from dock to ship. Hermokrates though for a moment, *they most likely look at me as I look upon this Egyptian--a wealthy fop that could hardly feed himself without an army of servants.* Hermokrates grinned while inspecting his plump companion. *More likely he could feed all of them with one meal meant for him.* For most of the trek back to the city he interrogated Djadao in an affable manner, gaining what information he could about Athens and Sparta, for his guest had been to both the Piraios and Gytheion and he had exchanged goods with Athenian merchants directly, and with Korinthian traders, men from the city closest allied with Sparta. To his surprise, this Egyptian's father had been a guest-friend of the Athenian general Kimon many years in the past, having met during the civil war in Egypt, and he himself had attended a symposion at the home of Thessalos, son of Kimon. He had many interesting things to tell of Athens. Unlike the Kilikian, Djadao proved a wellspring of information.

It took them much longer than Hermokrates had at first guessed, finally reaching the bouleterion on Ortygia. The several hundred councilors were already seated. He scanned the faces, anxious to pick out his rival Athenagoras. Not so surprisingly, he spotted him and the Kilikian huddled together, and nodded politely—so very calmly—exhibiting not a bit of astonishment at seeing the foreigner released from the Long Stoa and in the company of his enemy. There they were, the Kilikian hunched over, Athenagoras whispering incessantly in his ear. Hermokrates stood just inside the doorway, motioning for the Egyptian to enter with him, and when he did, the chatter within ceased; all eyes turned upon them, adding to the foreigner's anxiety.

Sikanos, the president of the council, stepped to bema while the sacrificial goat was led to the center of the floor, to the small marble block that served as altar. A mantis anointed the goat with water, then without hesitation, slit its throat wide, pressing the animal ground-ward with a knee as it kicked and gasped away its last bit of life. Two boys entered and lifted the goat while the mantis slid a shallow bowl beneath the animal's draining wound, collecting the last of its blood. The boys lugged the carcass away; the mantis emptied the blood upon the puny altar. Sikanos plucked up the kyrkeion staff and began to address the council. "Fellow Syrakusans, we gather to debate what questions are to be put before tomorrow's Assembly." Here at Syrakuse as at Athens and other cities that practiced democracy, a limited number of elected or appointed men met as council, preparing laws, bills, and items to be voted on by the larger citizen body.

"Our first item, presented by Athenagoras, is the renewal of our pact of neutrality with Athens." This initiated a ripple of moans throughout the crowded, stepped seats. "Do we have anyone here to challenge this renewal or a speaker who wishes to confirm it?"

Hermokrates glanced at Athenagoras only to find his adversary already glaring at him. He smiled and winked at him, but made no attempt to stand and speak. Athenagoras looked up at the polished timber ceiling, as though he called upon the gods above to assist him. So far, it seemed, he would not need their help. Sikanos looked around the bouleterion, searching for anyone that would enter this debate. Most others looked either to Athenagoras or Hermokrates, deferring to these two, the right and privilege of oratory. Both men sat still. Both sat in silence. "Then we will put it to the assembly tomorrow, with the council's recommendation, that the treaty be renewed."

And so for an hour or more other bills of interest, and several law suits that required the participation of the entire citizen body, because of their magnitude, were brought forward, discussed and debated. Most survived to be added to the agenda of the assembly. The two most important bills, especially to Hermokrates, were now due to be discussed.

Sikanos plucked up a wax tablet from the small table adjacent to the bema. "And now to the matter of the Egesta." The council chamber, relatively tranquil until now, erupted into a chaotic explosion of shouts. Sikanos raised his hands, trying to quell the commotion. "We have reliable information, from our friends in Egesta that their city intends to petition Athens for military aid against our ally of Selinos, invoking the existing treaty of self-defense." Again Sikanos extended his hands. The shouting subsided.

Hermokrates, who until now had merely endured the motions and discussions before him, suddenly resurrected his focus and attention—he sat up board stiff as though he had been admonished by his tutor in youth, his gaze drilled straight at Sikanos as *he* spoke, his fists tightened, whitening his knuckles. He shot a hand into the air, Sikanos acknowledging him. "Fellow Syrakusans," Hermokrates began, "I pray and I hope that this news of Egesta's embassy does not seem trivial to you. I hope and surely I pray, that you all see with the same clarity I do, that Athens will rush to assist Egesta—at least that is what they will say. But they rush here to Sikelia, not to help a supposed ally, but to conquer us." He plunged back into his seat regretting this outburst. There was no need. He should have waited.

Now the council chamber erupted again with cries and hoots, insults hurled

Nemesis

at Hermokrates by some and others, his friends, tossing them back at his detractors in defense. In the midst of the tumult Athenagoras bolted up from his seat, extending a long thin arm above his head, while his head drooped, eyes locked upon the floor. The ruckus continued. Athenagoras waved his hand as he continued to stare down. Finally he yelled. "May I speak now?"

The turbulence of voices abated. Everyone, including Hermokrates, turned their eyes to Athenagoras. The portly Egyptian grabbed Hermokrates' elbow, squeezing it now as anxiety struck. "Is this how Greeks govern themselves?" he whispered.

Hermokrates smiled. "No sir, this is not government. This is the preliminary to it. A sort of ritual, if you like, that exposes both stories of fact and tales of fiction to light. We move forward with what we hope will be only the facts."

Athenagoras, not satisfied to speak from his seat, walked up to the bema. Sikanos nodded and stepped down, allowing him exclusive access to the platform. "Fellow Syrakusans, good Hermokrates here as somehow been able to crawl into the minds of the Athenian generals and discern future intentions." A few in the chamber laughed. "He has become an oracle, no doubt, but much better I think than most, for he does not couch his predictions in twisted verse, or ambiguous phrases, but foresees things with extreme clarity." Now even more laughed. Hermokrates rolled his eyes, waiting for his turn to speak. "Athens, I would remind you all, is somewhat preoccupied at the moment." In and amongst the councilors laughter erupted again, perfectly timed to enhance the flavor and intent of Athenagoras' speech. He had placed his friends well, and rehearsed them even better. "Their army must stay in Attika, in preparation for a Spartan invasion. Do you think they have the resources or the inclination to sail to our island? Hermokrates invents this crisis so he and the other Gamoroi can assume emergency powers. How else do tyrants in other places come to rule? People, when moved to panic, will choose security over liberty—but always with later regret. Do not fail to recognize where the threat to our city actually lies."

Hermokrates turned to the Egyptian and said, "Now you must speak." The Egyptian went pale. His eyelids fluttered. To all the world it looked like he would faint. "I-I cannot," he said, shaking his head. Hermokrates could not force the words from him, and besides, Athenagoras would fashion him into a fool if he could not speak willingly and with conviction.

Athenagoras, atop the bema, waited for a challenge, his eyes also searching out Hermokrates. Hermokrates only smiled back, unsettling him a bit. Athenagoras stepped down retaking his seat.

Sikanos stood up. "So I take it we will put forth before the assembly, the motion to send the one company of cavalry to Selinos, as promised, and no more?" Like a Spartan assembly, the vote was shouted, affirming his suggestion, so no voting tokens were handed out. He squinted now, reading the last of the motions to be discussed from the tablet. "Hermokrates has put forth the motion for an increase in funds to rebuild the ship-sheds."

Hermokrates stood up. Every man present, from the Gamoroi clans of the ancient Syrakusan landowners to the lowliest of potters, respected Hermokrates' intelligence, and his patriotism, so they listened to his words, and more often than not, took his advice. They knew he loved his city, and wanted it to prosper, but what they could never be sure of was whether he truly wished them all to enjoy in this prosperity. After all, as Athenagoras often reminded them, Hermokrates was an aristocrat, and by nature and upbringing compelled to rule—an attribute not always compatible with democracy. "I have just returned from my inspection of the docks, both military and commercial, and must tell you of the condition of them. The berths and quays for the merchantmen are in well enough repair, as the stream of goods from the waterfront to the agora attest. But the trireme sheds are ramshackles." He expected an immediate challenge from Athenagoras, especially since his adversary had just relinquished his term as Magistrate of Trade, and was indeed formerly responsible for the condition of the harbor—but none came. Today, it seemed, each man might at least come away with something. Both knew there would be many more contentious days to come, full of challenges. They would not exhaust each other so soon. The session ended, just as the light began to fade from the high square windows in the bouleterion, and the thunder growled with more frequency. Hermokrates ushered the Egyptian through the throng of councilors, leading him out into the agora and away from the milling crowds that inevitably formed after each session to discover what motions would be delivered at the full assembly. Just as the first drops of rain pelted them, they walked toward the Long Stoa, where Hermokrates and the other city magistrates maintained offices, although these merely consisted of polished tables and bins of scrolls, with enough space for each to review the business of his appointed magistracy upon, and for a clerk to record. At his table sat Dionysos, a brown haired and gangly boy of sixteen years, son of his neighbor and assigned to this job of trade clerk as a favor—at least initially. But now Hermokrates looked upon Dionysos as a favor to *him*. The lad worked incessantly, and was meticulous in his recording of each transaction, and every obol of tariff and tax brought in. He asked questions of everyone and about everything, remembering not only the obvious, but the seemingly trivial, a trait which proved invaluable to Hermokrates in his verbal bouts with Athenagoras. Wherever he could take Dionysos, he would. And the boy absorbed everything.

"Please sit," he said with extreme courtesy to Djadao. "Give your manifest to me." Hermokrates scanned the list slowly, humming as he did, for it was written in Attic Greek and he had to stop and reread certain words that differed from his Dorian dialect. He nodded. "My seal." He held out his hand. Djadao grinned. Dionysos placed the heavy seal in his palm. "Your cargo is below the limit. No tariff. You can unload what you like and take it to our agora, unless you already have purchase arranged?"

"No purchase arranged," Djadao answered. "To the agora I will go." He lowered his head while he spoke. "I am truly sorry I could not speak to your council."

"Friend, do not trouble yourself over the matter. It would have made little

Nemesis

difference." Hermokrates smiled politely. "Dionysos here will escort you back to your ship. I must see to other business in the agora." Hermokrates walked with them through the doorway and to the line of columns along the edge of the stoa. A slave began to light the cressets along the exterior wall, while the rain clattered off the tile roof above, the sound echoing off the hard marble floor. The last few still remaining inside began to exit as the night gathered, pulling up their himation cloaks overhead to fend off the storm. Hermokrates watched as Dionysos and the Egyptian disappeared into the soggy gloom beyond the temple to Apollo. He slowly took the steps down from the stoa, ignoring the splattering rain, his mind wandering and uneasy. He had no further business at the agora—just an excuse to relieve himself of Djadao, and unleash Dionysos upon him. The boy would drain the man of every bit of information.

"Are you feeling well?"

Hermokrates turned to find Sikanos approaching. It took a moment for the question to register. "Well enough, I suppose. Why? Do I look ill?"

"No, just wet. But you were most uncharacteristically reticent during the council session today." Sikanos tugged on his arm while peering from beneath the cowl formed by his cloak. "Come and dine with me tonight."

Hermokrates shook his head. "I am too worn out to attend one of your symposia, my friend."

"No symposion, just a modest dinner. Only my father Exeketos will join us. I too am tired, and must garner my energy for tomorrow. I think the assembly will be a lively one." He glanced skyward. "And moreover, my house is nearer and therefore you will be much the drier."

"The rain is a welcome distraction." Hermokrates stopped abruptly and turned to Sikanos. "My friend, I am furious. Oh, not with Athenagoras, but only with myself. I should never have blurted out the intentions of the Athenians."

Sikanos grinned warmly at him. Is it his words or how he speaks them which irritate you so?"

Now Hermokrates smiled in return. "Both!"

The pair started to walk out of the agora and toward the wall that ran along the seaward side of Ortygia. Hermokrates, conscious of it or not, was not bearing toward home but in the direction of Sikanos' town-house. Soon the rain slowed to a sprinkle. Without the clamor of a downpour to contend with they talked of routine matters of the governing of the city, and of the business before tomorrow's assembly, then Sikanos asked, "What was the Egyptian doing with you in the bouleterion?

"Oh, I thought he might have an interesting tale to tell, and could have helped us in getting the council to send more aid to Selinos. Once Athenagoras riled them I saw no use in this."

Sikanos walked on for a bit then asked, "What would this Egyptian tell us?"

Hermokrates stopped and put both hands upon the sopping battlement and stared out at the black of night, listening for a moment as the waves lapped up against the rocks below and the retreating storm grumbled at a distance. "He told me that

Melos had fallen to the Athenians."

"And you did not bring this news before the council?" Sikanos was stunned. Any news of Athenian aggression could only help our cause against the democrats.

"Oh, my friend, I had intentions of doing just that, but my Egyptian acquaintance had lost his tongue. Furthermore Athenagoras, I am sure, knew about Melos, and will have worked out a counter argument to his advantage. I can hear his shrieking voice again, pointing out to the council as he did today, that Athens, by the attack on Melos, is too preoccupied to bother with Sikelia and her allies here. No one will listen until they see the Athenian fleet first-hand, their dark sails on the horizon." He leaned out over the edge of the wall, as if it were daylight and he inspecting the harbors. "If they do come, we are hardly ready. And I fear that is exactly what Athenagoras wants."

"You must bring the Egyptian to the assembly tomorrow. He must be encouraged to speak," pleaded Sikanos. "If need be he must be forced to speak."

"You did not see him when the council broke into shouts, after Athenagoras riled them up and tossed insults at me. Fear was on his face."

"But to say nothing—that can only help Athenagoras." Sikanos grew more frustrated.

"Athenagoras would have challenged his every word, and forced new ones out of him, making him appear the fool. Like a bout of pankration, I will let Athenagoras throw the first punch, and I will counter. Besides, I stuck the Egyptian with Dionysos. That boy will drain every last bit of information out of him. Some of it, I hope, will benefit us."

He did not accept his friend's invitation to dine, although he was indeed hungry and oh so close to Sikanos' town-house, but instead walked back to the agora on his way to his house facing the Great Harbor. He arrived tired and wet, and most certainly hungry, and headed straight for the smaller dining hall reserved for his immediate family. His wife, quite unusually, was not there to greet him. He clapped his hands, but not a servant entered. Now, as tired as he was, he became furious, and stormed out of the hall through the main courtyard and into the women's quarters and the smaller courtyard within. In the middle of it he found his wife, daughter Kalli, and the young Dionysos attending to two little girls.

His wife, upon seeing him, rushed to greet him. "Dionysos brought them. Said they are a gift from a man named Djadao—an Egyptian friend of yours."

Hermokrates motioned for Dionysos to approach him. "Are these two slaves of the Egyptian?"

"Why, no sir. They are survivors from Melos. Djadao asks that you keep them, for he is not Greek and cannot understand them, and little girls make for poor sailors. He also said that they could speak to the fall of Melos better than he ever could."

*****

Shadows danced across the sooty walls and over the burnished bronze of the

Nemesis

pegged shields that stood mute sentinel over the great armory storeroom. Bundles of javelins bristled in huge stacks. Baskets of iron spearheads and bronze butt-spikes glittered in the orange glow of the oil lamps. Hermokrates slowly closed the huge oaken door. He was the last to enter. The rest were already here—nine of the fifteen generals, the men Hermokrates could trust. Men not beholden to Athenagoras and the radical democrats.

"Good Hermokrates, why did you not challenge him?" Pantheras hit him with the question before he had the chance to scan their faces, to see who attended this clandestine meeting. Others quickly added their voices to this single question.

Hermokrates sighed. "We would have a difficult time indeed trying to convince any of them."

Again Pantheras spoke. "But in your silence you condone the words of Athenagoras. The people look to you as a balm to his rancor. Your silence shouted assent.

You, by being there, listening to his talk of the benign intentions of the Athenians, and their preoccupation with the Spartan army that he insists, will bridle their ambitions and force them to attend to matters close to home. You have endorsed his every word with your reticence."

Sikanos moved to the center of the room, shouldering next to Hermokrates. "My friends, to confront Athenagoras now will gain us nothing, and only reveal our real intentions to him and his cronies."

Hermokrates broke in, "Listen to Sikanos. To press the issue now, when our argument would seem based more on opinion than on fact, will numb the people to the true danger. Ring the larum bell once and only once. Only then will it be well heard. Ring it again and again, and it becomes just so much clatter to be ignored."

"But we will have the opportunity to ring it at all, if we delay, waiting for the perfect moment that may never arrive?" Pantheras' words were laced with anxious concern. The eyes of the others in attendance confirmed the apprehension felt by all.

"You all know very well that Athenagoras will refashion our words to strengthen his. He plays the people like a kithara, strumming this string then that string, plucking out a tune that they are helpless but to follow. As he tells them, they lack wealth. We aristocrats do not. He has told them often enough that their lack of it is due to our greed, not to their lack of ambition. In his eyes, we are never patriots, but profiteers. And the poor fools believe him. If they only knew his power depends solely on them, and to no fine virtue or noble attribute that enables real power. The time will come when we will confront him and confront him we must. On this I am as sure as I know the sun will rise tomorrow. The Athenians will sail west. And when they do, no twisted words of that demagogue will be able to deny this."

Pantheras lowered himself onto an armorer's stool, hanging his head for a moment in thought, finally craning his neck to gaze up at Sikanos and Hermokrates. "Are you two so convinced that when the critical time comes, we can win this argument, and more importantly move the people to action?"

Three loud raps echoed off the oaken door, followed by two quick ones.

Hermokrates pulled hard on the thick bronze ring. The door groaned as he swung it open. From the blinding light of midday Dionysos peered in, surveying the faces of the men that stared out at him until he found Hermokrates. He turned around and bent low. "Come on, now. No one will hurt you." Silhouetted in the doorway were the figures of two small children, Dionysos' arms spread out with a hand on each one's back, gently ushering them into the dark armory. Hermokrates knelt low, eye to eye, to ease their fear and present a comfortably familiar face to them. "Do not be afraid, Dianthe," he assured, and repeated these words to Elpida as he smiled.

"What are these children doing here?" bellowed Pantheras. Elpida began to tremble. Dianthe wrapped an arm around her younger sister while launching a scowl at Pantheras.

Hermokrates rose up. "These two small girls may prove our most powerful of allies."

Pantheras snorted out a condescending laugh. "Are we now so desperate?"

"Come sit by me." He waved the sisters forward. They shuffled hesitatingly toward him. "Oh, pay no concern to him," said Hermokrates as he noticed both girls' eyes locked upon Pantheras. "An empty pot makes the most noise." Laughter spread throughout the gathering. Even Phion managed a forced chuckle. Dianthe carefully brushed the dust from atop a stool then offered it to Elpida. Her sister dropped into it hard. Dianthe stood behind her, hands atop her shoulders, gently rubbing away the anxiety with a surreptitious massage. "These two are Melians." Murmurs broke out. The men within moved closer to Hermokrates and the two sisters. Pantheras gasped audibly. "They have witnessed Athenian brutality first hand."

Pantheras, his eyes full of sympathy and his voice laden with concern asked, "But my friend Hermokrates, what can they tell us? Who would even listen to such youngsters?"

Dianthe bolted upright and cleared her throat. "I know what their general Alkibiades plans." He paused to compose herself. "What's more sir, I am sixteen years old and not a child."

Pantheras crouched down and with a patronizing smile looked her straight into her eyes. "Of course you are not. I apologize. But how could you know about Alkibiades?"

Dianthe, full of courage fired by her hate of the Athenians, recounted the death of her mother and father, her ordeal beneath the quay and the words she overheard from the Athenian soldiers' very mouths. There was no hesitation in the retelling, and the cold hard clarity in which she delivered it.

Pantheras sighed and stood up. "Alkibiades, their favored strategos, speaks so openly of his intentions that his own soldiers imbibe in this gossip. How is it that this strategy appears so familiar and obvious to the Athenians but so extraordinary to everyone else?"

"Commonplace or arcane—no matter," said Hermokrates shrugging. "One thing is certain: this little girl did not manufacture these words in her imagination.

Nemesis

The gods placed her there as our messenger, to deliver this warning to us. Can anyone doubt that these two children are protected by the Olympians? How else could they not only survive the destruction of their city and the extinction of their family, but then be delivered directly to us? These children are holy. They are sacred to the gods. And so must be their words."

Sikanos moved next to Hermokrates now. "I do not doubt this little one, nor do I read differently the meaning of her message, but what kind of witness would she or her sister prove under the scrutiny and interrogation of Athenagoras?"

"You are correct my friend. This poor child could never endure the wickedness of Athenagoras. And I suggest nothing that would require her to do so. I seek not to convince Athenagoras to rethink his opinion of the Athenians, so there is no purpose in subjecting this sorrowful pair to his harangue. What I must accomplish is to sway the others that have not been swayed. To convince—no, to educate and instruct, those men who have not succumbed to his wile, or have not yet been corrupted by his impossible promises. These are the men we must bring around to our way of thinking. The gods have conveyed the instrument to carry this task out." Hermokrates ushered the two sisters out into the daylight.

*****

Kalli licked her fingers then slicked back a few strands of hair from Elpida's forehead, tucking them under the garland of ivy and violets. "You look so beautiful." Elpida grinned, peering down at the silver gryphon-head clasps on her new sandals, swinging her heels out while touching toes and then clicking them back together nervously. "Dionysos will take you both for another walk."

Elpida glanced up. "And will we be telling our story again today?" She swung her arms back, grabbing hold of her wrists behind her back. She began to sway side to side.

Dionysos appeared at the gate now with Glaukia, chambermaid of Hermokrates' wife.

Dianthe pressed her hands down the length of her chiton, carefully smoothing out the smallest of wrinkles. "Mother had a peplos gown this color," she stated softly so only Elpida could hear. "Do you remember?"

Elpida nodded and sniffled, then reached out to clasp her sister's hand. Dionysos smiled at Kalli. "Are your new sisters ready?"

Kalli stepped back a bit, and nodded with satisfaction as she inspected them both. "I think they are adorable, don't you?"

Dionysos craned his neck, scanning the row of columns in the courtyard for anyone yet unseen. He leaned to Kalli. "It is you who is adorable," he whispered, blushing. Kalli pecked him on his cheek, satisfied that no one caught sight of them. Dianthe smiled and wagged her finger. Dionysos laughed. "Let us all be off. A pleasant stroll along the seawall today." He ushered Dianthe and Elpida out of the courtyard and onto the narrow, shadowed street, Glaukia slowly following them all.

The sisters walked along, almost skipping, Elpida's fingers wrapped tightly around her sister's hand. It had been almost a month since the Egyptian brought them

Jon Edward Martin

to Syrakuse, and by now they had achieved a sort of celebrity. Most people they passed knew the girls by name, and the ones that didn't whispered amongst themselves, "Those are the Melians." Finally, after walking for almost half an hour, they broke free of the cool shadows and crowded narrow streets into the expanse of the sunlit agora. Elpida, anxious to see the poultry vendor, let go of Dianthe and raced ahead, weaving in and amongst the throng of sellers' booths and curious shoppers, being quickly devoured by the crowd.

"Elpida! "Dianthe yelled out. Dionysos too called out. Only the neutral hum of hundreds of conversations echoed back at them. Now Dianthe panicked. She pushed

wildly through the mass of Syrakusans, scrambling toward the poultry crates, and began to dart in and out of the stacks of cages, setting the hens and roosters to a bluster of clucking and crowing. From the midst of the coops, amongst a storm of feathers, Dianthe caught sight of Elpida being led away from the agora by tall stranger. "Dionysos!" she screamed before sprinting after her sister. She ran as fast as she could, but it seemed as if she could make no headway, her path barred by a passing cart, or a wall of people crowding around a booth or stall. At first lost from sight then back again, Elpida, drifted inexorably away.

Suddenly a hand gripped her shoulder. "Did you see her?" Dionysos tugged Dianthe to face him. She pointed toward the corner of the temple of Apollo. Dionysos vaulted over an empty cart, instigating a chorus of insults from a fish-monger who stood nearby, but he barreled forward, catching sight of the girl before she turned the corner. He dare not call out, and alert her abductor, but dashed headlong toward them both as people scowled and cursed at him as he flew by. He saw where they were headed now, toward the high battlement that overlooked the rocky base of the sea-cliff. Only a couple of masons that worked on repairing the stonework of the battlement stood between Elpida and the end of the street and the cliff below. He would not reach her in time.

"Thief! Stop her! Thief," Dionysos yelled. The masons looked first at him, then at the girl, while still clutching their chisels. Elpida turned also and smiled at him. The stranger, startled now, looked at the two stone-workers ahead and Dionysos behind, letting Elpida's hand slip away. One of the mason's grabbed her by the chiton, shaking her so hard the garland snapped from her head. "I've got her for you," he cried out. The stranger spun around and began to jog directly at Dionysos while sliding a dagger from beneath his cloak. Dionysos, without hesitation, raced ahead. He had no plan, and certainly was no brawler. The man lumbered forward, raising his dagger hand high, preparing to strike down at the boy. Now only a few paces separated them as they headed toward collision, when Dionysos suddenly hit the ground in a tumble, rolling into the would-be abductor's knees, sending him hard to the paving stones. Slightly stunned, Dionysos sprang to his feet and sprinted to Elpida. She, by now, was screaming in terror, trying to free herself from the iron grip of the mason.

Nemesis

"She's all yours now lad," he announced with a measure of satisfaction.

Elpida flung herself into the arms of Dionysos, but he took no time to comfort her, but spun around to face his assailant. He sighed. The street yawned empty. From some distance he could hear Dianthe calling out her sister's name then his, in alternation. He looked up at the mason. "Thank you sir." The mason could only return a confused glance. Dionysos scooped Elpida up and began carrying her back toward the agora where Dianthe came into sight. Then Glaukia, followed by four heavily armed men, guards from the harbor tower, jogged into view.

Elpida squeezed Dionysos with a tight embrace and spoke softly directly into his ear. "Why did that man try to hurt you?"

He thought better of telling the truth. There was no need to frighten her even more. "Hurt me? Why it was one of Hermokrates' tests is all. He is always trying me out."

Dianthe pulled her sister away from Dionysos and into her arms. Glaukia passed by the two girls going directly to Dionysos. She looked him up and down, finding only a skinned left knee as any sign of an altercation. Now she glanced at Elpida and Dianthe. "These two are trouble indeed."

Dionysos shook his head. "Trouble yes, but not for me nor for your master Hermokrates. They are trouble only for his enemies."

Dianthe, satisfied that her sister was unharmed turned her attention to Dionysos. "You may think of us as mere children, but I know what is going on here, and I know why Hermokrates has been so kind too us."

Dionysos smiled, nodding as a polite indication for her to continue. He knew by now how headstrong this young Melian was, and decided not to contend with her but to indulge her, and experience, at the very least, a modicum of entertainment.

"He uses us as a tool against his enemies. Why else would he dress us up and have his servants parade us through the streets on the oft chance of meeting some important Syrakusan. We tell our tale of Melos, not for our sake but for his."

Dionysos limped over to Dianthe. "For a small girl you perceive much. But remember this: anything that benefits Hermokrates benefits us all, and in particular two foreign orphans." he reached out to grab Dianthe's hands, squeezing them firmly as he continued, "He never intended any harm to come to either you or Elpida." From the far end of the temple to Apollo he heard a voice rise above the din, calling his name. Hermokrates emerged from the stream of people flowing in and out of the agora. "Sir," said Dionysos respectfully and he tipped his head in a modest bow.

Hermokrates ran his eyes across them all in a quick survey before finally turning to the guards. "What has happened?"

The captain of the guards stepped forward. "Seems that some foreigner tried to run off with the girl." He pointed to Elpida with the tip of his spear before clanking it tall and straight to attention.

Hermokrates knelt before Elpida, concern welling in his eyes. "Are you hurt, child?" She shook her head. "Do you know this man? Have you seen him before?" Again she shook her head.

"Indeed he must be a foreigner," offered Dionysos. "I, for the life of me, have never laid eyes upon him before." Now he rubbed his bleeding knee. "But I think he left behind a token of his visit." Dionysos walked slowly toward the two masons, trying with all his might not to limp in front of Hermokrates. He bent over, snapping up a small dagger. "This belonged to him." He twirled the gleaming knife in his hand, studying its form and its jeweled hilt before testing the blade by carefully running his thumb across it.

"Let me see that." Hermokrates opened his hand to receive the dagger. "Certainly not crafted here in Syrakuse. In fact I doubt that it is from Sikelia at all."

Dionysos stepped closer to Hermokrates, but before he could speak Hermokrates added, "The girls must stay within the walls of my house. I have underestimated both their impact and the lengths to which Athenagoras would respond."

Dionysos exhaled slowly, releasing what seemed to him a heavy burden. He need not insist upon the very course of action his patron now embraced, requiring no uncomfortable confrontation.

Chapter Nine
Athens – Spring 415 BC

His knees ached, so stiff from cold, age, and ancient battle wounds. He hobbled a bit as he rose from his sleeping pallet, kicking aside the piles of fleece, firing more pain in his legs, before wrapping himself in his double thick himation cloak. His hands too, throbbed with pain, and he could neither grasp the cloak tightly nor open it fully. He hated the cold more than ever now. When he was young it was something to complain of it in a casual fashion, especially when soldiering, as all men do when gathered together preparing for difficult tasks, but now the early spring air gnawed at him with icy fangs, reminding him cruelly of his years. Shuffling out to the courtyard, he caught sight of Stilbides working over the limp carcass of a rooster, reading the signs. *I will not attend*, thought Nikias as he watched the mantis plunge bloody fingers into the belly-wound of the rooster, *unless the portents read benign*. Today, accompanied by this extreme discomfort, he almost wished the signs to portend evil, to provide to him his sought after divine justification to remain at home. No civic duty prodded him to ignore either his apprehension or infirmities, solely the fear of what would be said about him, what allegations would be tossed his way. Only the gods inspired more fear in him than the opinions of others. He prayed that all powerful Zeus would pardon him from the Assembly.

Stilbides raised his open arms skyward. Nikias' heart sank. The gods would grant no excuse for him today. From a dimly lit anteroom, Hiero jogged into the courtyard, a wax tablet and stylus in hand, anxious to greet his master. "Shall I go to the prytanies? I can tell him that you labored so long this night past, over the new chorus, the arrangements of the liturgies for the festival, and so on. I'll have them all apologizing to you, if only you let me." He grinned devilishly.

Nikias stuck out his hand from beneath his cloak, waving it meekly as he coughed. "No excuses today, no matter how beautifully constructed by you, dear Hiero. I will be on my way to the Assembly."

Hiero stared directly at Stilbides. Stilbides glared back at him. Now Hiero stomped across the courtyard to the mantis and bent low, whispering into his ear. "Can't you see he is not well? The coward that you are, you will not tweak the signs a bit and give our master a respite. A bit of doubt from you and he would have remained home today." Now he spun away from the soothsayer, walking briskly to Nikias. "The Egestians will be at the Assembly today. I spent last evening in Piraios, and met with rowers from the Eleutheria. They say the Egestians berthed their ship in late afternoon, and off-loaded sack upon sack of unminted silver."

Astonished at this news, Nikias fell back to a seat on a bench. His kidneys throbbed as he struck hard upon the marble. Hiero slid to a knee before Nikias, looking up into his master's eyes with concern. Nikias growled, "This cannot be. Egesta has no great surplus of wealth. It is a trick of Alkibiades, no doubt."

Hiero, gazing up into Nikias' face shook his head. "It is true. And although this new found trove of silver which the Egestians bring to sway the Assembly would benefit his scheming, Alkibiades, as far as I hear, had nothing to do with it. If there is scheming, it is exclusively by the Egestians. But I tell you, the silver in those sacks was as real as the gravel at my feet." He scooped up a handful from the courtyard and tumbled it in his hand, letting it shift slowly between his fingers.

Nikias had to hurry himself along. Dawn would break soon and he must not arrive late to the Assembly. No, he would suggest no weakness to his enemies, nor offend his friends by showing nothing less than ultimate respect for the laws of his city. Hiero jogged to his side, propping him by the elbow. He could feel Nikias shivering beneath the thick himation cloak. Hiero snatched up a torch then returned to Nikias' side, silently guiding him through the gate and into the street beyond. They came upon only a few others, and this immediately worried Nikias, for he was certain they were overdue. The narrow gutter slicing down the center of the street ran full with the icy water of early spring. The sight of it made his bones ache all the more. Soon they passed the boundary stones of the Agora, shuffling along quickly. Only metics lurked amongst the booths and stalls, not even the Skythian police, nor the slaves armed with ochre stained rope, ready to mark out any shirkers that headed away from their duty on the Pynx, could be seen. Atop the hill ahead, where they would gather, the pennant indicating an assembly rippled in the blustery early spring wind. Hurriedly, they ascended the bank of stairs that were flanked by twisted olive trees, to the bowl-shaped Pnyx.

Thank the gods, Nikias said, only to himself. Only a very few Athenians lingered on the Pynx: They were, by all accounts, more than early. Nikias walked unhurriedly to the bema, almost exaggerating his now relaxed gait, ascending the stony crest to finally stand before a fire that spit and crackled in a huge bronze tripod. At least for now he would be warm.

*****

Alkibiades flung the thick fleece blanket from him, exposing not only himself, but a young woman and a younger boy, both naked atop the sleeping pallet, to the cold dawn. He shuffled out of the tiny bedchamber, more a cell than a room, into the courtyard. He

too was naked, but the chilly air, at least for now did not concern him. It was the pounding in his head from excessive quantities of wine and his burning throat that occupied him. He looked up, hoping that the eastern sky would remain cloaked by night. Disappointed, he cursed Helios, as he found the belly of the clouds lit red by the rising sun. He swallowed hard, reminding himself of the bellowing choruses he had led the night before in his symposion. A slave hustled from the dark of the columns with a cloak, spreading it over Alkibiades' shoulders while apologizing profusely for rising so late, and not having everything prepared for his master's departure.

"Fret not, Thrakios. I do not think I could have awoken a moment sooner." Alkibiades, for a man in obvious discomfort, appeared in amazingly good spirits. He walked over to the fountain, tossed away his cloak and scooped up handfuls of frigid

Nemesis

water, splashing it over his head and face and across his body. "Lilac," he called out to Thrakios as the slave jogged ahead of him, into the andron. As he entered he saw a pair of slaves crouched over brooms, sweeping away the discarded scraps from last evening's meal. The room reeked of wine and vomit, but the cold ameliorated the stench of rotting food. He tugged and dragged an ivory-toothed comb through his long curly hair while Thrakios anointed him with splashes of lilac perfume.

Alkibiades plopped onto a couch. "My sandals," he commanded. The slave ran off, returning quickly with sandals, a heavy woolen chiton and a gold embroidered purple himation cloak. "Help me with this, will you." Alkibiades struggled to get the chiton over his head, finally pulling it down as Thrakios cinched a gold threaded belt around his waist. He sat, as still as his restless nature would allow, while his slave laced up each foot in the polished leather of his winter sandals.

"Alkibiades!" A voice boomed from the courtyard. Soon a man appeared in the doorway. "We must hurry. You don't want old Nikias scaring them off, do you?" Demostratos, a participant in the previous night's revelry, appeared hardly the worse for his attendance. He turned around, and said, "He's up and dressed," to others unseen in the courtyard. Now he looked to Alkibiades. "Hurry my friend. Theodoros is out there and Meletos. I think they are still a bit less than sober from last night." He coughed and shook his head while making a face as though he swallowed something bitter. "Indeed, I may still be drunk."

"Not so," countered Alkibiades. "You are not singing. That, as I have come to observe, is the measure of the wine. The more you sing the less watered the draft. This morning you are undoubtedly—and unfortunately sober. Last night, my friend, was a different story."

Presently Alkibiades and his entourage made their way on the Dromos to the Agora and the Pynx beyond. Now as he climbed the steps leading to the Assembly, men crowded around the entrance, some friends, others adversaries, but all anxious to see him, to hear him speak, to fire passions in them, both positive and negative. He was a man that could never be ignored.

Alkibiades, as soon as he had reached the groomed summit of the Pynx, looked about, politely ignoring the sea of faces that neither challenged nor supported him, searching out his opponent Nikias. High behind the bema, in front of the stoa and illuminated by a flaming tripod, he spotted him, slowly rubbing his hands over the fire. *He does not wish to be here*, thought Alkibiades. And he was right.

Within moments the Pynx was sealed off and the rituals performed. The Prytaneis walked up to the bema, wax tablet in hand, and read out the agenda for the day's business. The delegation from Egesta would address them first. But before they began a small party of slaves pulled two small wagons into view, their contents cloaked from the eyes of men by canvas shrouds. The head of the Egestian legation took the bema; but his eyes met Alkibiades'. He received a nod. The Egestian began, "Good Athenians, I bring you not unsubstantial gifts from my city." At these words the attending slaves furled back the shrouds of canvas, revealing heaps of uncoined silver, inciting a clamor. "Sixty talents in all," he shouted out, above the uproar.

Jon Edward Martin

Alkibiades, hardly awed by the treasure, looked instead to Nikias. His adversary bore the look of defeat. The Egestian, well-coached by Alkibiades, reminded them all of the treaty between their two cities, and pleaded for help against the aggression of the Selinuntines and their allies the Syrakusans. It did not matter what he said. The carts of silver spoke with more conviction and persuasion than any ambassador could. And besides, Alkibiades had invested in entertaining as many of the influential in Athens as possible, especially the younger men, men still untested by war, and through their inexperience, disposed to its adventure. Within an hour, the entire citizen body had voted to provide sixty Athenian ships for an expedition to Sikelia.

*****

Nikias climbed up the broad bank of marble steps, pausing but for an instant before stepping into the Propyleia. At the moment he stood in the world of everyday, but moved toward the threshold of the sacred and divine. Once through the columned passageway he would emerge upon the paved walk of the High City. Even from here he could see the gleaming statue of Athena, protectoress of the city, and the very goddess he invoked during this past morning's assembly. He walked forward into the forest of columns that dwarfed him. Finally he strode onto the sunlit Akropolis. No duty or ritual compelled him to visit today, only the desire to avoid the crowds of his fellow Athenians and the inevitable interrogations they would heap upon him concerning this morning's debate. Undoubtedly he thought the expedition a great folly, but to him even more absurd was the split command. He, along with Alkibiades and Lamakhos would share authority. He veered to his left, strolling toward the Erektheion, seeking the neat array of benches adjacent to the sacred olive tree of Athena. Before sitting, he leaned out over the battlement, straining to pick out his town-house amongst the muddle of tiled roofs and tangle of alley-ways beyond the Dromos.

"Trying to hide?"

Nikias spun around to catch sight of his interrogator and smiled. "I think after this morning's proceedings we should both find a hidden refuge, a sanctuary from Alkibiades and the mob."

Thessalos laughed. "My dear friend, I have never heard you speak so ill of our people. Alkibiades, on the other hand, is a different issue." He lowered himself to a seat on a long marble bench that butted against the wall of the Erektheion and the only one not veiled in its cool shadows. "Come and sit. We may yet have the opportunity to do something about this."

Nikias shook his head and sat down, stretching out his legs as he leaned back against the wall. "Only the gods could intervene with any hope of preventing it now."

"Do not be so certain. Today a pile of silver has intoxicated the mob. Tomorrow—who knows? They may awake with senses regained and think more prudently upon this adventure. But I doubt it." He sighed. "Then again they will listen to you. You must become the conscience of us all. Explain the risks. They will listen.

Nemesis
They must listen."

"Ah, if were only so. I fear that the few of us who have fought and suffered through real war will be far outnumbered by those youngsters who have only imagined it." Nikias stared now at the columns of the Propyleia, watching several men emerge, men he recognized as his brothers Eukrates and Diognetos, move briskly toward them. "Good greetings. What brings us all together?"

Eukrates smiled. "Concern for you, brother."

"For you, certainly, but for us all," added Diognetos. He sat next to Nikias, wrapping an arm around his brother's shoulder, shaking him affectionately. "Do not become so melancholy. It will be two months' time until the expedition will sail. By then, who knows, they may all have a change of heart."

Eukrates stood before Nikias. "Refuse the appointment. Your illness gives you good cause."

Nikias shook his head. "That mob, stirred on by Kleon's ghost, no doubt, would see my refusal as another instance of the wealthy avoiding their obligations."

"Brother, you have a point," said Eukrates as he gazed at the temple of Athena Parthenos. "But only sixty ships, hardly an invasion force. You will sail around the island, like Pythodoros and Eurymedon did nine years past, impress and awe a few barbarian cities, then return home. Nothing more."

"But the talk everywhere is of conquest. Alkibiades has every cobbler and potter, every shepherd and plow-pusher convinced that Sikelia is ours for the taking." Diognetos argued.

"Talk is one thing. Reality is another. Sixty ships. Sikelia is an island, I admit, but it is an extremely large island. Ships would hardly prove effective fighting on land, and as far I as remember, the Sikelians and even the Syrakusans live on land." Eukrates chuckled half-heartedly. "You, brother Nikias, shall have a pleasant summer sail and be home before the Thesmophoria."

The four men paused their conversation upon seeing Hiero step out from the dark Propyleia. He spotted them and hurried their way.

"Greetings Hiero," announced Thessalos. "How fortunate it is that we are all here together and not under the heady influence of either wine or the mob. Our mutual friend Nikias has a troublesome problem: How to deal with his appointment as strategos for the grand adventure to Sikelia?"

"Really now. Before I say what I would, let me hear your advice." Hiero leaned back nonchalantly against the Erektheion wall, stroking his beard with his right hand.

Eukrates spoke up. "I say nothing will come of this expedition. At least no war, and therefore no risk. It is all an exhibition, a parade of our fleet. That is the extent of it. What else could sixty ships hope to accomplish now that they could not achieve nine years ago?"

Hiero paced back and forth in silence, trying to accept Eukrates assessment as accurate. But still, he knew Nikias' health might not even tolerate a "parade of our fleet" as described. He also knew his friend would not reject an appointment by the demos. "Do not presume that sixty ships will restrain Alkibiades—or Lamakhos."

Nikias sprang to his feet. "I know you too well my friend. You hear and see everything that goes on in Athens. What moves you to say such a thing?"

Hiero looked around first then answered. "Alkibiades, as he departed the Assembly today, retired to the Strategeion with Lamakhos. I thought it very odd that they did not include the other appointed general, in their discussions, so I happened to wander into the anteroom of the Strategeion, drop a few coins into the more than obliging guard's hand, and promised to mind his post for him while he sampled some akratos wine from the nearby kapeleion of Antilokhos."

Thessalos, Eukrates, and Diognetos surrounded Hiero now, all anxious to hear what words and plans he gleaned from his surreptitious escapade. Eukrates pressed him first. "Well, what did our two conniving generals scheme in their meeting?"

"Alkibiades made it very plain. He intends to recruit not only our allies here in Hellas—Argives, Mantineans, Messenians, and such—he will also stir up the Sikels, Naxians, and Katanians, too. And of course there are the Egestians. Here is his army of conquest. He even talks of plans beyond the defeat of Syrakuse. For him Karthage is next. His ambition is boundless."

"What says Lamakhos to all of this?" asked Thessalos.

"Lamakhos?" chuckled Hiero, contemptibly. "That old mule just wants a fight. Any fight."

Nikias began to pace back and forth. "They all think the conquest of Sikilia such an easy thing. We will sail there, have others do the fighting, and be welcomed as liberators by the Sikelians? I think not. This is a mad scheme."

"But we cannot undo the vote of the Assembly," Diognetos said.

Nikias continued to stalk the area beside the Erektheion. "Five days hence, on the festival day of Adonis, the Assembly gathers again to finalize the preparations for the expedition. This will be my final chance to persuade them to rethink this misadventure."

Hiero moved next to Nikias and whispered, "I have an idea for a bit of theater that may help our cause, but it will require—"

Nikias cut him off. "How much, my friend?"

"Only a few drachmai. It should prove an excellent investment."

*****

The Pynx Hill swelled full of people, all anxious to hear of the preparations for the great expedition. Every so often, above the hum of conversation, the banging of drums and a distant lament would well up from the city below, reminding them all of the funeral rites of Adonis being performed by the women of Athens, a strange contrast to the grand optimism inspired by the enterprise at hand. Nikias accepted the speaker's wreath, placed it on his head, and ascended to the bema.

"Fellow Athenians, while it is true that we assemble here to discuss the preparations for the campaign in Sikelia, I wish to make few points and try to

Nemesis

convince you that we should not sail there at all." Grumbles rolled through the crowd. Nikias raised his hands to quiet things. He continued. "Let me say first, that personally, I would gain much honor by leading this ambitious undertaking. But as in the past—and you all know this well—I have never spoken against my convictions to gain honor, or any other advantage. I speak plain truth."

He looked out at the throng, his eyes settling on Alkibiades and his companion Demostratos, huddled in whispers. "Do not allow the ambitions of a youngster maneuver you into disaster, or rely on a fragile treaty of peace between us and Sparta, to make you think we are secure from war. It would take little provocation for the Spartans to attack us, and moreover, they have many allies who did not agree to the treaty and therefore are still at war with us. Even our own subjects disrupt the peace. Have you forgotten Melos? The Chalkidike?" Suddenly a piercing wail resonated from a nearby roof, part of the festival, but uncannily timed and appropriately unsettling. *Hiero at work again,* he muttered beneath his breath before continuing his speech. "Do not grasp at a new empire until you have secured the one you have." Again he paused to look out at the multitude of faces still unconvinced. Alkibiades, the Egestians and others had already manipulated the demos. *If reason cannot convince them*, he thought, *the vast expense of it might.*

Before he could continue his allotted time expired and he reluctantly handed the wreath to the herald as he descended the bema. Alkibiades brushed past him, took the speaker's platform and with confidence and restraint challenged every word, dispelling any remnant of doubt in the minds of the Athenians. Ambassadors from Sikelia, both Egestian and Leontine, pleaded with the Assembly for assistance, promising a quick and profitable campaign. Some followed, men known to be friends to Alkibiades, and others until now not associated with him, but all praising his foresight and patriotism, and attacking Nikias, although not directly, by casting doubt on anyone's loyalty to Athens who did not support the expedition.

Nikias, not totally discouraged, took to the bema one final time. "I see from the assent and approval, Athenians, that you all adhere to this plan unfaltering. So it is, and I will no longer try to dissuade you from it." He delayed briefly, mulling over his next words carefully. "If honoring the alliance with Egesta is truly our aim, then sixty triremes are woefully deficient. The Syrakusans alone would have no trouble engaging a sixty ship squadron. And we must consider their allies too. We require additional heavy-infantry, slingers, archers and other acontists. The increases to this invasion force, for this is what it is and let us speak to it plainly, must be substantial."

Demostratos, yelled, "Tell us now, just how many more ships, and infantry do you suggest?"

"Athenians, I think the numbers should be discussed at the Strategeion, in a calmer atmosphere, when and where rational assessment can be determined."

Again Demostratos shouted out, "No delays. Tell us all now, what is needed."

Nikias could not believe he was being challenged now. *By Cloud-Gathering Zeus*, he thought. If he wants numbers, *I will give them to him.* "A minimum of 100

Jon Edward Martin

warships. And this does not include the troop transports, supply freighters and ships for carpenters, masons, bakers and such. If we go to Sikelia, we must be prepared, like colonists, to establish our own city, and not depend on any of the Sikelians." He looked down his nose at the delegation of Egestians and ranted on. "And from our city alone we will need at the very least 5000 heavy-infantry. From our allies we will require that number and many more over. And by unit and organization, the standard compliments of archers, slingers and javelineers." He paused, waiting for shouts of protest to bubble up from the crowd. There were none. Unimaginably men throughout the Assembly shouted out, "Vote him the ships! Vote him the men!" These words echoed over and over. Nikias stood stunned into silence.

     Demostratos climbed up to the bema and shouted out. "What excellent advice. With such an armament we can only succeed."

Nemesis

Chapter Ten
Sparta – Spring 415 BC

The cicadas' chittering wafted from the groves that edged his house, while the sun, unrestrained by even a suggestion of clouds, set the air above the road to a shimmer. He did not speak, and neither did Andromakhe. They both trudged along, heading for the agora, followed by Kanthos and the household servants. Others merged onto to road offering greetings, which Gylippos returned most politely. One neighbor then another would walk along for a brief while, rendering pleasantries which Gylippos exchanged affably. He even managed a word or two for the servants he encountered, but his bitterness would not allow a single word to pass between his wife and him. Some people lingered at the entrance to the theatron, an impromptu meeting place, while he saw the figures of others atop the hill behind milling around the Bronze House of Athena. As they passed the kenotaphaion to Brasidas, the memorial to his Inspirer, he paused a bit, offering a quick prayer, and asked if he had offended him somehow, for he had not been visited by his shade for more than two years now. The reverse of things passed, for now in death Brasidas proved scarce during times of peace. Yet somehow Gylippos knew he would see him again.

Once they reached the agora, the women left their husbands and fathers behind, mounting the kanathra chariots that would take them to the Sanctuary of Apollo at Amyklai to begin the three-day festival of the Hyakinthia. These lined up behind the ceremonial cart that would carry the new robe fashioned for the statue of Apollo Amyklaios. Free of his wife, Gylippos felt as though his very soul had been unshackled.

Kanthos edged up to him, offering a drink from a wine-skin. "Sire?" He pried free the plug and held out the skin.

Gylippos waved it away. "I am not thirsty."

"It's not for thirst," replied Kanthos.

Gylippos laughed and snatched the wine-skin from his servant's hand. "Do I show it so openly?"

Kanthos wrinkled his brow. "I am only but an inferior, a base helot, and would not presume to evaluate a citizen."

Gylippos filled his mouth with wine, handed the skin back to Kanthos and swallowed. "You are no helot, at least not by birth, and by Zeus and Apollo, you judge me daily, measuring my every action and word. Why, I would dare say my very thoughts are subject to your review. You are a perceptive man. Entertain me and reveal what you see in me today."

Kanthos plugged the wine-skin and slung it over his shoulder. "I see a man who has angered the gods. Why else would they burden you with such a wife?" He flinched a bit while uttering that last string of words, holding up the wine-skin as a shield.

"Lower your guard. I shan't strike, at least not for speaking the truth." Gylippos increased his stride, trying to separate himself from the small band of

Jon Edward Martin

Spartan Peers and servants that began their trek toward the sacred Hyakinthian Way. He had built this wall between his wife and him, day by day, brick by brick and over the course of two years it had become immense and formidable. He would not now construct another between him and the only other soul that he could truly speak with. He purposely dragged their once quick pace to a crawl, letting others pass and his wife and her servant stretch far ahead. Satisfied that he and Kanthos were a comfortable, secure distance from others, he asked,

"In your village, what would be a solution to this problem." Kanthos surely felt his master's pain but he also feared his rage; Gylippos had returned home from a march mid-afternoon quite unexpectedly and found Andromakhe being raped by a helot—at least that is what she told Gylippos. He slew the man without compunction. Kanthos knew what Gylippos did not, but had only suspected. There was no rape. The tears were false and this was not the only helot, nor would he be the last one.

Kanthos stared down into the dusty track. "Sire, a divorce would be undertaken. But that can be an expensive thing with the dowry and all."

Gylippos knew full well the cost of trying to recover his life from Andromakhe. His father's exile and the debts he had left behind forced him to use most of Andromakhe's dowry plus all of his ancestral land in repayment. Now, precariously, his mess dues relied solely on the crops grown on his state kleros—in good years barely enough. If any of his helots deserted, or drought struck, he might risk his status as citizen. "I am certainly in the proper frame of mind for a day of mourning. For Hyakinthos certainly, but perhaps for me, also."

Divorce, at least for now, was no option. He had posted out to Messenia twice since Mantinea, providing a respite from this poisoned marriage, but without war he was committed to life within the confines of Sparta. Peace would kill him. Only the days spent training the youth provided him with purpose—a temporary remedy to his malaise.

"One day only, sire, for Hyakinthos. Then we all celebrate Apollo. Only a single day without bread or song. Today's small sacrifice makes tomorrow's celebration all the sweeter." Kanthos, having tried feebly to raise his master's spirits without success, knew to be silent now.

They walked for most of an hour along the Hyakinthian Way, its track narrowing and spiraling around the slopes of a meager hill as it carried them to its crest and the Sanctuary of Apollo Amyklaios. From here they could look all around the valley of the Eurotas, to the rock curtain of the Taygetos range and to the gleaming orange roof tops of the villages of Sparta to the north. Crowds of people swathed the hill crest and north facing slopes, grief for Hyakinthos fettering speech, producing an eerie silence broken only by chirping birds and windswept treetops.

Gylippos left Kanthos behind now and shouldered his way forward toward the throne-shaped tomb of Hyakinthos where the mantis had begun the enagismos sacrifice to the dead hero. A pair of attendants each hoisted up a likythos jar while the mantis sliced open the throat of a ram, pinning it to the ground as it kicked and

Nemesis

heaved away its last bit of life. Gylippos, for a fleeting moment, imagined himself as the mantis dispatching his troubles with the blade, but quickly whispered a litany of prayers, asking the hero forgiveness for his blasphemous thoughts. He stared, almost mesmerized, as the two attendants tipped their likythos jars, spilling wine into the sacral bowl that had collected blood from the ram. Once mixed, they solemnly lowered their jars to the ground and swung open a bronze door on the tomb's side through which the mantis emptied the bowl, as offering to the bones of Hyakinthos below. The priest and his attendants began to chant the dolorous hymn to the hero and in perfect synchronization pounded their chests, finally punctuating the dirge with a piercing wail.

Surrounding the hill and spreading toward the village of Amyklai he looked to the vast array of tents that had been erected for the evening's coarse meal as he moved along in perfect silence with the rest of the onlookers. Kanthos caught up with him, the other three servants of the household in tow, as he reluctantly sought out his wife amongst the women that had been temporarily sequestered prior to the ceremony. He spotted her just as she turned. Their eyes met, the smile on her face being swiftly erased as they exchanged frosty glances. He quickly looked away, and by chance caught sight of Xenias in conversation with Temo. Although he was only a freedman, Gylippos envied him, at least at this very moment.

"Still sleeping alone?" whispered Kallikratidas as he clamped a firm hand on Gylippos' shoulder. "At least find a helot to bed. You are in the prime of life."

Gylippos turned toward him wearing a grin. "You or any other Peer will never know if and when I lie with a helot. My friend, do not concern yourself over it. I do not."

Kallikratidas shook his head. "Strong talk, but I do not believe a word. You wear bitterness like an Olympic victor wears his crown."

"Now I am certain you are not as wise as others think. This is not bitterness, but hatred I wrap myself in. It keeps me warm, and is a constant and reliable companion."

"And seems to imbue you with a measure of belligerence beyond what is required of a warrior." Kallikratidas moved closer. "Divorce her. She speaks ill of you to anyone who will listen, even turning your own helots against you. She has bore you no sons." Kallikratidas stopped short of mentioning the most insidious of rumors, pausing awkwardly. After checking himself he went on. "The laws of Lykourgos make allowances for this. You cannot live each day, despising your wife's every breath."

"She turns my own helots against me? I would say they do not think much of any Spartan. And you forget that ancient apothegm of the Skiritai," reminded Gylippos.

"And what saying is that, my friend?" Kallikratidas stopped walking.

Gylippos halted also and whispered, "'Married men do indeed out live bachelors, but they are much more willing to die. What finer attribute is there for a warrior?"

Kallikratidas bellowed out a huge laugh, drawing looks of disdain from all around. Now he muttered a prayer of forgiveness to Hyakinthos. "By the way, did you hear of the brawl between Klearkhos and Lysandros?" Gylippos furled his brows, so Kallikratidas continued. "You know how Klearkhos is, so stubborn, so irritatingly single minded. And you will find favor with this—he hates the Persians more than you do. Lysandros, to his regret, brought up his scheme of opening relations with the Great King, to cultivate the Persians as allies against Athens, for he as Arkhidamos before him, believes that only money will win this war. And as you and I well know, no one has more of it than the Great King. Klearkhos bluntly reminded Lysandros and the others of his dining mess how the Great King acquired this wealth. Lysandros, not one to be lectured to by a rock headed enomotarkhos, lashed out with a deluge of sharp-tongued insults worthy of an Athenian playwright. Klearkhos responded the only way he knows. With a single blow he knocked Lysandros through the door of their phidition."

"That is a major breech of the code. What has happened to Klearkhos?" Gylippos was stunned by this news. Never had he heard of Spartiates fighting like this. Oh, as boys in the Agoge fisticuffs proved a common enough occurrence. In fact it was even encouraged. Not in manhood though. What puzzled him more was how anyone heard of such a fight, especially if it took place within the phidition itself. *Nothing that happens within goes out*, as the saying goes. "How did you come upon this bit of gossip?"

"It would never have been known except for the punch struck by Klearkhos. As I said, Lysandros shot through that door like a bullet from a sling. Many others saw him lying bloody in the dust as they exited their phiditia. A thunderous blow!"

"But what has happened to Klearkhos?" Gylippos worried for his new found friend.

"He is on guard tonight like a hebon at the Babyx, shield up till it breaks his arm." Now Kallikratidas lost his smile. "But I fear what Lysandros will do to him later. He can hold a grudge like no other, and with Agesilaos as an ally, he will exact his revenge."

Gylippos laughed. "It would not surprise me if Lysandros accused Klearkhos of medizing. It worked against Pausanias."

"I would think not. Lysandros will have his revenge, but he is clever enough not to have it reflect upon him." Kallikratidas started to walk away. "I must be off to the tent of my phyla and you off to yours. I will see you at the chorus tonight, won't I?"

Gylippos nodded while watching his friend disappear into eddies of people that swirled in the walkways amongst the tents. He ducked as he entered one of the tents of his phyla of Hylleis. Here piles of straw-stuffed blankets replaced dining couches, making for more efficient use of the confined space under the great canopy. He found his place near his wife and adjacent to Tellis and Argileonis.

Just as he sat someone yelled out his name. Quickly he scanned the row of

Nemesis

faces on the long array of make-shift cushions opposite, finding only full mouths over bowls of food. Again someone called out his name. Now he peered down the flank to his right. "Gongylos!" He spotted the smiling face of his friend from Korinthos. It had been over two years since they had marched together with Pleistoanax to invest Argos, but he could not forget the exuberant smile of this dashing Korinthian. Both men stood and embraced. "I am so very happy you have accepted my invitation."

"Dear Gylippos, I must make amends for not accepting it sooner, but last year, on the very day I was preparing to depart Korinthos for Sparta, my son was born."

Gylippos embraced the Korinthian again. "A son! May he become a boon to his city and family—and a source of strength to his father."

"I have no doubt he will. But I am remiss. How is Andromakhe?" He looked to Gylippos' wife, who acknowledged him perfunctorily.

Gylippos did not answer, but took his bowl and motioned for Gongylos to follow. The pair slipped out of the tent and into the warm air, taking advantage of the light of a protracted early summer evening. "Have you heard the rumors coming out of Argos?"

"The expedition?" Gongylos tipped the kothon to his lips and swigged a bit of wine. "Yes. Alkibiades the Athenian has exerted his influence over the Argives. They are provisioning their own contingent for the expedition. The Mantineans, too, are sending men."

"A good thing this is for Sparta. His adventures weaken our adversaries. Is it Sikelia?"

Gongylos nodded while gulping down the mouthful of wine. "The Athenians do not think Sparta will interfere."

"Sadly, my friend, they are correct." Gylippos led them away from the muddle of tents, up the slope toward the temple of Apollo, its painted columns glistening in the orange light of sunset. They were most certainly alone. "Agis wants no part of a war with Athens and clings to the spurious treaty. Pleistoanax, because of the maneuverings of the Eurypontids, holds no sway over the Gerousia, although I think at his age he does not have the stomach to contend with them anyway."

"And at Korinthos most believe that the Athenian fleet is sailing to intimidate, not conquer the Sikelians. But I know, as you do, that no city should depend on Athenian pacifism, especially with Alkibiades stirring them up." He tossed the dregs from his cup. "Things would be different if your father were here in Sparta. Things would certainly be different if Brasidas still lived."

*****

Xenias and Temo, finished with their meal, strolled out of the tent, so acutely aware of how unique this festival was here in Sparta. They walked past small groups of men, Spartiates mingling with foreigners, helots with their masters. It was an exhibit for all to see that for the span of three days, the very divisions that define Spartan society were shelved. High on the hill, torches flickered, illuminating the Amyklaion and the shrine to Hyakinthos. Above, stars pierced the deep sky. They followed one of the footpaths toward the temple, thanking Zephyros for the slight breeze that suppressed the ever-present swarms of mosquitoes. Nearing the hill crest Temo stopped, wrapping her arms around the neck of Xenias. He inhaled deeply, the perfume of her warm skin filling his nostrils and pulled her body tight to his. "I wish days such as this could last forever."

Temo looked up at him. "Days when they treat you like a man and me like a woman? Days when we need not give way to them on the road, or bow our heads to them as though in the presence of gods?"

Xenias slid his hands down the length of her, settling them on her hips. "Why do you refashion any pleasant moment to one of pain? Cannot you accept things as they are?"

Now Temo pushed him away. "Do cattle enjoy pleasant moments? Perhaps they do, because they hardly perceive the butcher. We have minds, and therefore cannot dodge the awareness of these things. Our butchers. Spartan butchers."

"Is your life so dreadful with me here in Lakedaimon?" Xenias gently propped her chin up in his hand. Temo said nothing in reply. "At least in Sparta everyone, even *they*, must obey. And it is for the benefit of all. Otherwise chaos would rule. In the forest animals are free. Men, no matter where they live, trade freedom for civilization. This liberty you crave is an illusion."

She knelt in the cool grass now, pulling on his hand to join her. When he finally sat next to her, she smiled at him and said, "So my husband is a philosopher now?"

"Hardly. All I am saying is everyone obeys: a child his parents, the soldier his officer—husband his wife," he added, laughing. "Why even the kings obey the Gerousia. In Athens they obey only the mob, and the mob is driven by greed. So which place is the better?"

Temo clasped both her hands over his. "I worry over you. The war will begin again. There is no disputing this. When it does, they will take you."

"Xenias, have you had your fill of coarse maza and bitter wine?" asked Gylippos as he marched up the slope toward the pair with Kallikratidas in tow. Xenias stood, dipping his head ever so slightly. Temo stood also, and quickly excused herself before hustling away. "I did not intend to frighten your wife. Please tell her I apologize for interrupting you." He winked.

"Whenever she sees Spartan officers approach, even you Lord Gylippos," Xenias answered, "she thinks there is a call-up."

"No fear of that, at least not now. You can reassure her that no war will separate you," Gylippos said with confidence.

"And your wife, too, must be happy in this," answered Xenias. Kallikratidas tried unsuccessfully to muffle a laugh, and turned away. Gylippos, stony eyed, said nothing. "Is there something you require of me?"

Gylippos cleared his throat. "Do you believe that the dead can converse with the living?" Xenias' tongue froze in his mouth. He expected a multitude of questions,

Nemesis

but not that one. "I speak of your brother. Has he ever appeared to you?"

Xenias grabbed the blue-glass charm that hung around his neck and squeezed it hard to fend off any evil. "By Hades, the Lord of Gloom, I swear he has not. No shade has ever afflicted me."

Gylippos shook his head in disappointment. "There is no evil in such things. I have seen him, and he delivers no curse—only solace." As he studied Xenias, his heart ached at Brasidas' absence, and verged on anger at the suggestion that there was any wickedness in his visions.

Xenias could see the troubled look upon his face, and attempted, as best he could, to remedy things. "Lord Gylippos, I mean no impiety by my remarks. Remember, by blood he was my brother, but I was raised not as a Spartan, and carry with me the uncomplicated superstitions of my rustic childhood."

"Xenias, how can you be more superstitious than a Spartan? That is impossible." Gylippos swallowed hard. "Moreover, you must be quite aware that the mere sight of you rekindles visions of Brasidas. You two are not dissimilar in either aspect or behavior."

Now Xenias, made uncomfortable by these remarks lowered his head and spoke. "Do not make such comparisons, sir. I do not deserve such."

Kallikratidas stepped toward Gylippos and wrapped an arm around his friend's shoulder. "Can't you see you're upsetting him? First you quiz him about the appearance of ghosts, and then you tell him he looks like one. He is a good soldier, and that is that. More than good enough for me."

"And for me." Gylippos allowed himself to be led away by Kallikratidas. They walked to a copse of olive, where others had gathered, using the gnarled trunks as back rests as they sat, while some lie back gazing up at the bright heavens. Gylippos interlaced his fingers behind his head and leaned back upon the cool grass.

Kallikratidas sat up, scanning the area for familiar faces. "They are up to it again." He shook his head as he sighed. "Lysandros and Sphodrias—you know their Persian scheme. Polyakes was at the Ephorion when they presented it once more."

"So they are convinced war will erupt?" Gylippos perfunctorily asked.

"They say it is only a matter of time, my friend."

Gylippos sat up. "And the thought of war disturbs you?"

Kallikratidas laughed. "Certainly not! We should, I believe, be more selective in choosing our allies. The Persians are hardly to be trusted. I agree with our unfortunate friend Klearkhos. We would, if we were truly clever and could see just a bit into the future, fashion a new treaty with Athens today, one that does not require that it be renewed every ten days but is a symmakhia. Then tomorrow, under the banner of this proper alliance, we should attack Persia."

Gylippos smiled in the dark. "This threat, no matter how real, is too distant for a city full of land-farers to grasp. Athens is closer—-a much more intimate enemy, I regret to say."

"Listen." Kallikratidas cocked his head to one side. "The women's chorus is beginning."

"You go my friend. I'll need a bit more wine before I can listen to Andromakhe's voice again." Suddenly a hand shot forth from behind the trunk of the tree, offering a brim-full cup of wine. Gylippos turned to find Kanthos smiling while holding out the libation.

"I wish I had so dependable a servant," said Kallikratidas. "You have never told me how you came by him."

"Surely you must know." Now Gylippos clearly observed by the look on Kallikratidas' face that he did not know, so he explained. "Polyakes, when he returned from Thrake with the Brasideio also brought back captives that served as attendants in the army of Brasidas. Kanthos, as you have already seen, exhibited exceptional service, and loyalty, and proved a benefit to the army. The man has been schooled in the arts of remedies of both the body, and by counsel, of the mind too. Polyakes said that Brasidas himself planned on assigning Kanthos to me as shield-bearer. So he honored this sentiment by turning the man over to me." He leaned forward so that only Kallikratidas could hear. "He is a true friend and companion as could be wished for, excepting yourself," he added, with a wink.

"Did he know this man could see into the mind of others?" asked Kallikratidas. "Is he Thrakian?"

Gylippos shook his head. "By Cloud-gathering Zeus he is not. Makedonian. Polyakes said they came upon his village on the retreat from Lynkestos. His village had been sacked. His master slain. Brasidas took him and the other survivors back to Amphipolis with him."

"A smart Makedonian and loyal too. An atypical combination. It seems Brasidas still watches over you."

*****

Gylippos snatched up the training spear from the pile of weapons and jogged over to the Wild Boars, the Agelai of boys formed up for drill. "The first strike must be executed in unison and without hesitation." He stalked the mock phalanx, ten boys in width and five deep. They stood rigid, their wiry, bronzed bodies hefting wicker training shields, each one wielding a blunted, counterfeit spear that had its tip wrapped in leather. "When the enemy appears, show no fear. Walk, do not run into battle. When the walls of shields collide, rejoice in their thunder."

Gylippos smiled. He heard the singing of the Embaterion March issuing from the tangle of reeds that separated the meadow from the road. In ranks of three, the Grey Wolves appeared at the far end of the practice field led by their bouagos. He marched to the distant edge and planted his spear, marking out the place of the first rank, first file. Smartly and in silence now, they spilled into formation. "Remember what I have said. When your shields collide with theirs, most will, by instinct, close their eyes. You must force yours open and strike. For this fleeting moment, you will have the advantage." He flung the end of his himation cloak around his left arm and trotted off to the middle of the field, holding his staff above his head. Both simulated phalanxes leaned their spears forward and brought shields up. Gylippos dropped his

Nemesis

staff and the two formations marched slowly toward each other. The beaten earth of the meadow churned up in clouds as they advanced. He watched, singling out the boys who strode with confidence, those that encouraged others around them with words. Only a very few exhibited dread of combat, but even these moved on, compelled forward by the deeper fear of shame. No matter the hours of repetitive drill, or the earnestness of instruction, the last few meters, contrary to all this practice and counsel, induce a running charge in most hoplites; here at the training field it proved no differently, except for the Wild Boars. They strode ahead at the same controlled pace while the opposing phalanx charged. Shields crashed together. Like a single mechanism the front rankers of the Wild Boars pumped their blunted weapons into the Grey Wolves, dropping half of their front rank in fits of pain.

"Drop spears!" Gylippos shouted out the command and both troops abandoned their weapons and commenced the othismos or shoving match. The mock attack with spears was limited in duration for even with blunted and padded tips, boys sustained broken noses fractured ribs and worse. The exercise was meant more to overcome the anxiety of the initial impact of a hoplite battle; real expertise would, in fact, be developed during hunting excursions where spear-work was no sham and the outcome dealt in death.

The Wild Boars, unimpeded by injuries, heaved into the quavering ranks of the Grey Wolves—groans of exertion, not pain, emanated from the churning cloud of dust, shields, arms and legs. The Grey Wolves began to crumble.

Gylippos summoned the bouagos of the Grey Wolves to his side. "Khirophos, call a halt to it." The young man sprinted toward the melee shouting the command to stop. From where Gylippos stood only shadowy outlines penetrated the dust, clarity gaining as moments passed. The boys of either Agelai hardly moved: most stood with shields tucked tightly to their shoulder caps as their chests heaved for air; some knelt on the ground spitting out blood; a pair of boys lay prostrate, apparently unconscious.

"Well, my friend," announced Kallikratidas as he emerged from the perimeter of tall reeds. "You took them from vanquished to victors in two short weeks."

"Get them to the river," yelled Gylippos. At his command the bouagos of the Wild Boars called his Agelai to form up for a march in columns of three, and led them onto a path that sliced through the reeds toward the Eurotas. The bouagos of the defeated Agelai, stooping over one of the injured boys, looked to Gylippos for orders. "Do those two require an iatros?" Gylippos asked as he walked toward him. The bouagos shook his head.

The injured boy sat up, a huge grin on his face. "I still have it!" He pushed his training shield into the air triumphantly. Indeed he did. Indeed, they all did. Not a single boy had relinquished his shield.

Kallikratidas caught up to Gylippos. "How did you accomplish it?" Gylippos did not answer. "By Artemis and the Holy Twins, how do you continue to do it? Your lessons are learned quickly. They are learned most painfully. But they are always learned."

"I am an adequate instructor, hardly as accomplished as Brasidas. I teach boys. He taught helots and in weeks transformed them into formidable warriors." Gylippos, hands on hips, surveyed the Grey Wolves, ensuring each had survived the contest with no serious injury. Finally satisfied, he dismissed them.

"Please my friend, you need not hide behind your false modesty. You do have a knack for this sort of thing. In fact, I have heard rumors that you will be nominated for paidonomos." Kallikratidas said, nodding.

"That sounds much like a rumor you would start." Gylippos leaned on his staff and gazed off at the Bronze House of Athena that glittered on the acropolis.

"Nothing like that," reassured Kallikratidas. "This rumor began at the Gymnopaidia, in the kings' tent."

Chapter 11
Argos – Summer 415 BC

Antiphemos listed to one side, shuffling into the courtyard with his father's shield on one arm. He struggled valiantly to keep it off the ground, but lost his grip. The rim scraped and banged along, but he hefted it again, tilting even more against its weight. Endymion hurried to his son and snatched up the shield and smiled. "In a year or two you'll handle it just fine. For now though, tend to my helmet and greaves."

Antiphemos scampering off, returning quickly with a kranos helmet cradled in his arms, its bobbing horsehair crest sweeping across his face as he walked. "Father," he said offering up the helmet. As soon as Endymion relieved him of it he ran off again.

Endymion knelt in front of his unfurled bedroll, taking a meticulous inventory of the essentials he would need for the expedition. This would not be a fast and fleeting march to a nearby battlefield, the only type he had known in his young life. His phylarkhos, whom they had nick-named Stump, had assembled the company a week previous explaining the extent and anticipated duration of their voyage. "Optimistically," Stump said, "you can presume to be away until autumn." Then he added, "But we have only three months' sailing time remaining in this summer so I would expect things to take us into next year's campaigning season." It felt to Endymion as though his body went hollow, heart and stomach shrinking into nothing at these words. He and his friends had talked about the price they would pay for the Athenians' help in restoring their democracy. They had all resigned themselves to battle, but none had expected to be abandoning home and family for so long, so very far away.

Smiling he lifted the small packet of medicines his wife had lovingly assembled for him. He carefully peeled back the linen to reveal a wad of moss, with a vial each of hellebore and fennel seeds, but finding an ampule he did not recognize, he pried the stopper free and sniffed, easily catching the scent of dried yarrow root.

"I will pray to Apollo and Asklepion every day that you will never have to open that packet." His wife stood over him now. She had entered the courtyard without making a sound, uncertain whether to speak to Endymion and risk another bout of tears, or to retreat into the women's quarters and return when she had composed herself. She drew a deep breath then sighed, watching her husband rewrap the medicines and pick up and inspect every item on the bedroll. He next checked the working edge of the curved whittling knife he would need for repairs to his spear shaft and for dressing game. He lifted the lid to the fire-pot, poking his finger in it to test the tinder. One item after another he examined everything.

While he tended to these small personal items, his son had packed away his panoply of helmet, greaves and linothorax body armor into a thick ox-hide haversack of the same type and ruggedness as the bag he used to transport his aspis shield. Once packed, Antiphemos tossed the haversack into a pannier on the mule, filling the other pannier with the bundled and tied bedroll. Endymion handed his wicker campaign pack to his son, the last of the items that he could handle, and once satisfied that it was wedged securely atop the pannier-harness he tied on three spear shafts, one with an iron warhead and butt-spike, the other two spares. Finally atop all of this he fastened his shield. He reviewed again everything, mentally counting and recounting his essentials in both possessions and duties to the gods. At first light he had already made sacrifice to Hermes, guardian of travelers, and a day previous left votives at the temples of Poseidon and Olympian Zeus. He had done what must be done and had packed what must be packed. Now he turned to his wife. She looked up at him, her arms stiff at her side as she tried to hold back the tears that despite her effort began to well up in her eyes. He wrapped his arms around her, squeezing her body against hers like no other time and she too could sense the intensity of this caress. She sobbed once then gathered herself, not wanting to upset their son who now wedged himself into their embrace.

"I must be off to the harbor now." He tugged on the reins of the mule, leading it out of the courtyard and onto the hard-packed road. His house, high on a hill, proved an excellent vantage for as he moved down the wide pathway he could see the glitter of sea-borne swells between the trunks of trees and through their gently tossing branches.

"Father, I will take care of the harvest for you," yelled out Antiphemos from the open gateway.

Endymion waved one last time to his son. His wife, standing behind Antiphemos and clasping his shoulders, lifted one arm as though to return his wave, but stopped, turning her head away for a moment. In was in this instant he realized that he most likely would never see them again. He knelt, scooping up a handful of earth, earth that had been in his family as far back as the combined memories of generations could recall. He squeezed it until it forced its way through his fingers, finally tossing away the rest.

In less than an hour he was amongst the other Argive hoplites waiting for his turn to board the troop transport, an old pentenconter with half the normal compliment of rowers, men excluded to make room for the infantry.

"This is a silly little voyage," said Tisandros.

"To Sikelia?" Endymion looked at the man oddly.

"I wish that was our destination. We must first sail to Piraios where the Athenians want the world to witness the vastness of our fleet, assembled in their harbor."

Endymion threw his hands up. "But Piraios is in the opposite direction from Sikelia."

"Don't you think I know that? Don't you think they know that?" he asked pointing to their commanders prowling the stern of the pentenconter. "Ours must be a heavy debt we owe to the Athenians and Alkibiades."

"The debt is theirs not ours," he said pointing to the same men on the deck of the transport. "Unfortunately we must pay it."

Nemesis

Endymion pulled back his wide-brimmed felt hat to look back at the city walls and the few people that, out of curiosity, had climbed to the battlements to watch their departure. This was hardly like the day they paraded out to Mantinea three years past. On that day every man of the hoplite class fell in the march, and families, neighbors and friends lined the road and tossed chaplets of flowers or handed them garlands as they passed by. Today it was different. Today only a few hundred mustered here, queued up to board transports that would ferry them initially to Athens port and then to the Ionian Sea and Sikelia. He could see amongst them none of the picked men, the ones trained and equipped full time, like Spartans, by the city. It occurred to him that these men were too valuable to throw away on an Athenian adventure. Neither could he spot any of the fervent democrats that overthrew the oligarchy. It was quite apparent that, discounting only the command staff, all the infantrymen selected were so very common, not distinctive in their politics or their wealth. "Men with little clout, even in their own city," he mumbled beneath his breath.

"What was that?" Tisandros asked.

"I said, were we better off imprisoned." Endymion received only a glare from Tisandros. Now he pulled on the mule's rein when his name was called, tromping up the brow-plank and onto the hastily crafted top deck of the troop carrier. The mule proved skittish and almost settled to a seat mid plank, but Endymion tugged hard while a pair of the crew pushed the animal from behind, finally getting them both on board.

Another crewman snatched the reins from Endymion and barked. "I'll take it now," leading the mule down into the hold. He tied it up next to the other baggage animals. Even now the stench of manure and sweat wafted up from below, amplified by the early summer heat.

Endymion moved forward to the mast, bracing himself there while looking back to the city. From here he could see the theatron, its bowl-shaped rows of seats carved high up into the hill. At the top row he saw a young boy. He thought he saw him wave. The last of the nautai, manhandling their oars and cushions, made their way aboard, and after running the gauntlet of curses and smacks, settled into their benches. The pilot shouted out his orders. The kaluestes hammered the stroke cadence, the bronze plate pealing out the very heart beat of their ship. Anxiously, the commanders shouldered their way through the crowded top-deck from the stern to the bow. The penteconter surged forward. The bronze rang out again. Another great heave almost sent Endymion tumbling. He scanned the sights of the harbor and the city beyond, his mind trying to capture in memory what a painter would in pigment, or a sculptor in stone—every detail of his native land.

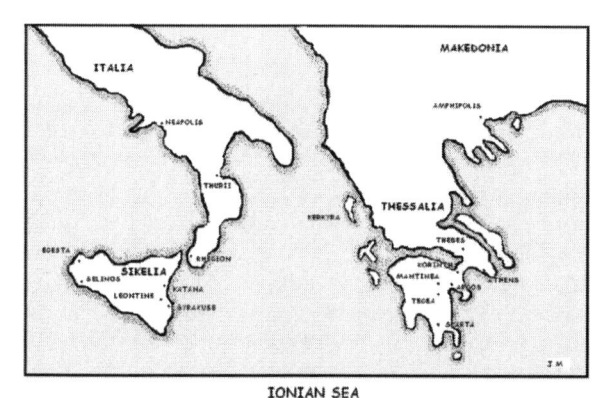

Chapter 12
Athens – 415 BC

Stilbides, almost out of breath, ran into the courtyard where he found Nikias dozing upon a wooden bench in the shade of the colonnade. By mid-day, the early summer sun had a somniferous effect on most Athenians, but with Nikias it was magnified, for the heat proved a soothing balm to his aching body. "Master Nikias." Stilbides gently nudged him. Nikias' eyelids fluttered open. "Master, an ominous thing has happened." Stilbides waited for Nikias to respond. He yawned, staring blurry-eyed at the soothsayer. Stilbides continued. "All the stone Hermes have been desecrated."

Nikias reluctantly swung his feet off the bench onto the ground and dipped his head low between his knees. "What are you saying?" he growled as he peered at the earth between his bare feet. Now he glanced up at Stilbides again.

Stilbides, a pious man, almost trembled as he gathered himself to explain. "Each and every stone plinth with the head of Hermes has been disfigured. The noses and phalluses have been hacked off." He clamped his hands on his head and wailed, "This portends doom for you and the expedition."

Nikias sat immobile, mulling over Stilbides' words until they coalesced into something intelligible. Immediately he calculated the impact of such an evil and sacrilegious act, and if any blame could be directed at him. He, too, was a more than pious man and without doubt he knew the gods would mete out punishment. He knew also that gods do not always discriminate when it comes to delivering their retribution. All Athenians, not just the perpetrators of this deed, would suffer. Now his mind whirred with thoughts of going to the council. They would need to delay, or hopefully cancel the expedition. The gate creaked open. Nikias and Stilbides found Hiero casually sauntering into the courtyard. *He must not know*, thought Nikias.

"Hiero, have you heard about—?"

Before Stilbides could finish his question Hiero began to answer. "About the

Nemesis

Hermes? Why yes. The Skythian police came upon them when they made their dawn rounds. Each and every one mutilated."

"You seem less than disturbed by this," said Stilbides.

Hiero strolled over to them, munching on a handful of olives. He chewed for a bit then replied, "This is exactly what we needed to convince them to abort the campaign. The timing could not have been better."

"You condone this sacrilege?" Stilbides grew visibly upset now.

Nikias said nothing. He listened to the soothsayer and Hiero argue over this unholy event. He, too, found this very disconcerting, but he also was quick to determine that this could be to his advantage—and to the benefit of Athens as a whole. He could put a halt to Alkibiades' folly immediately. The Assembly certainly did not listen to his advice—the advice of a man—but now they must heed the god. "And Hiero: What would be your counsel now?"

Hiero sat next to Nikias, looked at Stilbides then flicked his glance at the open gate. Nikias, without hesitation, perceived his request. "Stilbides, can you perform yet another sacrifice to Lord Zeus and to Hermes." Stilbides drew down his brows into a menacing frown as he stared at Hiero before departing. Hiero grabbed his matia charm that hung around his neck, invoking its protection, for if any man could direct a curse through a simple glance, it was Stilbides.

Now, as if rehearsed, Nikias' brothers Diognetos and Eukrates strode into the courtyard, brushing by both the door-keeper and the exiting Stilbides as though they were nothing more than ordinary household furnishings so common as to be invisible. Eukrates daubed away the sweat from his forehead with the trail of his himation cloak. "Good day to you, brother. Let me guess what the topic of conversation is."

Diognetos kissed Nikias on the head as he walked by on his way to the fountain. He sat on its edge, cupping handfuls of water onto his face. "This situation with the Hermes—."

"Is an evil thing," broke in Nikias.

Diognetos smiled at his brother. "It is an opportune thing too. The Assembly is now forced to postpone launching the fleet."

"And, everyone knows of your piety. Even the Assembly, as riled as it now is, would not force you to go against the will of the gods," Eukrates assured.

Hiero rose from the bench. "Gentlemen, may I suggest we retire to the andron and shun the mid-day heat. And certainly we would best be served if this conversation was continued away from prying eyes and ears." Hiero led them into the dark, cool andron where a servant stretched to light the triple spouted oil lamp that hung from the ceiling in the center of the room. The place reeked of stale wine and musty wool, the only antidote being the fragrant scent of the perfumed oil now flaming in the lamp. Nikias called in the attendant, and chastised him, ordering him, once they had all departed, to strip the andron of every cushion and fleece throw, launder them all and to scrub the floor yet again. The slave hurried away. Nikias apologized while offering each of them a couch before Hiero himself began to fill their wine cups, not wanting even Nikias' wine steward in their presence. Once everyone was comfortably reclined upon a couch, and the door secured, Hiero asked, so very politely, for the attention of all and continued with his plan. "I would expect that the defacing of the Hermes will more than upset the demos. Some say it was the act of some inebriated aristocrats. Others, and I have already heard this, are placing the blame on Korinthian agents sent to undermine the departure of the fleet. Personally, I believe this to be the most likely speculation. But I would like to put forth another possibility."

Diognetos sat up. "I myself delight in the notion of implicating the Korinthians. This would deflect blame from any Athenians, if you grasp my meaning?"

Nikias stared at his brother somewhat perplexed, trying to understand his last remark. Hiero, on the other hand, deduced it immediately and quickly interjected, "Alkibiades would prove the ideal suspect in this." Hiero finished off the last olive before speaking. "This morning, not too long after I learned of the sacrilege, I happened upon Thessalos in the Agora. He told me that the act was carried out by some drunken revelers. The very first person to come to mind was Alkibiades. Everyone knows he mocks the gods at his symposions, playing the part of sacred priests, ridiculing holy rites and such. For a small investment, I am certain, I can convince the proper men, men of influence, to expose the person responsible for this act of blasphemy."

"Those rumors concerning Alkibiades have been spinning through Athens for years," replied Nikias, shaking his head.

Diognetos, ignoring his brother's remark, bellowed out a laugh then said, "Why of course. He'll be arrested and put to trial. The fleet would either set sail without him, or be delayed awaiting the outcome of the trial. Hiero, you are a devious man."

Nikias, stunned to silence, sat on his divan as though he was a spectator at a play, watching the actors, listening intently to their every word—experiencing a wholly unreal and artificial world.

"If Alkibiades is implicated, and if he is arrested, the allied contingents—Argives, Mantineans and the rest, will withdraw from the expedition. The Assembly will not call-up more of our own hoplites to replenish this short fall. Without hoplites, Nikias my brother, you will enjoy a short cruise around Sikelia, flaunting Athenian naval power, returning home by summer's end. Without these hoplites, there can never be a land battle."

Eukrates nodded in agreement. "With Alkibiades out of the way, unable to beguile the demos with his ambitious promises, you, Nikias and the sane men of Athens may be able to deliver our city from these dangerous innovations. Hiero, I am glad you are a friend, not an adversary."

"As always Hiero, I am indebted to you for your good judgment and clear thinking," Nikias slowly rose from his couch. "Come with me and I will provide you with what funds you require for this *investment*." He stopped walking and abruptly

Nemesis

turned to Hiero. "But make no mistake about what I tell you now. There must be no connection between what you do next and me." Nikias led Hiero into a locked chamber adjacent to the andron. In moments Hiero exited with a small purse, which he quickly stuffed into his belt.

"He is a good man," said Eukrates as Nikias re-entered the andron. Diognetos repeated Eukrates' words in agreement.

"In that I have no doubt. He is loyal and perceptive." Nikias retook his seat on the dining couch, leaning back into its soft cushions, turning up his nose at the offensive odor. "But what if they do not arrest Alkibiades? If you can believe this, there are others that despise him more than I. What better way to find him guilty than to hold his trial after he has departed with the fleet?"

Both his brothers sipped their wine slowly mulling over the vintage and his words in a most deliberate fashion. After a long pause Diognetos spoke. "You, brother, are more devious than Hiero. Think on what you have said. If they let us sail and bring him to trial later, recalling only him, his supporters in the fleet and amongst the allies will be away in Sikelia. There will be precious few in Athens to vote in his behalf."

"Yes," added Eukrates. "It is a brilliant plan. If he stays, you will command the fleet. If he goes, eventually he will be recalled, and you will command. And in all of this no one could suspect you in undermining Alkibiades, for you will be far off in Sikelia."

*****

Put me to trial now!" demanded Alkibiades. Not one to ever exhibit uncontrolled emotion, he pounded a fist into his open left hand while pacing the floor of the Bouleterion, his face reddening. "If I am found guilty, carry out sentence. If you find me innocent then allow me join the fleet. Do either now without delay." He looked to the doorway and the shouts from men outside. One of the two hoplites guarding the bolted door rapped on it, barking out a command to quiet down.

This was quite an unusual session of the Council, the proceedings kept secret by closed doors. This very precaution beckoned the idle and interested to gather about the Bouleterion, all trying to catch any words. Athens, in its entirety, had been transformed by this one single act of sacrilege. A few considered it a random incident of vandalism—nothing more sinister, but most saw it as a prelude to the overthrow of democracy itself, planned by the aristocrats to cripple the government of Athens. It triggered a wave of paranoia and suspicion, the likes of which proud and confident Athens had not experienced before. This closed session of the council was not the only reaction to the Hermes. The *Committee* as it was dubbed, solicited witnesses vigorously, and many employed this opportunity to accuse personal rivals. Others manufactured testimony and evidence for reward. So wild was the panic to protect the state from enemies within and without, the ancient ban on torture was revoked to enable the *Committee* to extract information vital to the security of Athens. In a short few weeks the Athenians had undermined the very democracy they valued so highly.

Alkibiades continued. "You tell me we must convene on this matter behind closed doors, away from the people. What are we trying to hide? What do you fear from them?" He pointed toward the noise of the crowd outside. "You have trampled the very liberties you profess to defend."

Nikias enjoyed this. He watched as his rival squirmed and twisted, exerting every trick of oratory to recapture control of the situation. Not only did he revel in this, he took no direct part in challenging Alkibiades. No one could accuse him of politicking, or advancing concealed aims against his adversary. No, he simply crossed his arms in silence and delighted in his predicament. *Yes, the investment was well spent,* he thought.

Alkibiades, nearing the conclusion of his speech, gathered himself with a deep breath and genteelly clasped his hands together in front of him. "I urge the Council to bring me to trial tomorrow. The fleet sails in two days. I am certain of my innocence and so very certain that once all the facts are laid bare you will acquit me. Perchance my fellows do not believe my innocence. Then put me to death. Do it now. Do it before the armament departs." He paused, waiting for shouts of affirmation, the type and kind he most often heard in the full Assembly—an Assembly that admitted many of his friends who could initiate their vociferous approval. Here, today in the Bouleterion, no such endorsements became manifest. "If you suspect any of the charges of impiety against me are true, why, by the Holy Olympians, would you allow me to command? Would any of you sail away with such a charge hanging over *your* head? Would any of you find the deliberations and judgments of any trial carried out in your absence and allowing no defense just? "

Androkles stood up. "Now, now Alkibiades." He calmly strolled next to him, smiling. "The city has toiled these last few months over the preparations for this great expedition. The fleet is gathered in Piraios. Our allies have sent their troops and they are bivouacked on the waterfront. You and our other two generals have this endeavor well planned." He clamped his hand on Alkibiades' shoulder with false affection. "Lead our men. Sail with the fleet and prosecute the campaign. We are in no hurry to hold this trial. Your mind must be at ease and your thoughts focused on the fleet and its mission. When you lead our fleet back in victory we will bring up the matter of this trial, if at that time it is of interest to anyone at all."

The Prytaneis of the Council stood and restated Androkles' motion. The fleet would sail and Alkibiades would share the command with Lamakhos and Nikias. There would be no need for ballots today—most all the councilors affirmed Androkles' proposal. The pair of guards flung wide the twin doors of the Bouleterion, forcing back the crowd that had pressed against them. As the councilors exited they were barraged with questions. The single answer carried like a tall wave from the Bouleterion steps out across the Agora—"The fleet sets sail in two days!"

By chance, as the packed council house emptied, Nikias and Alkibiades found themselves shoulder to shoulder. They exited together, Nikias shuffling away from the stream of councilors that spilled down the steps, lingering near the last column that flanked the left side of the Bouleterion's porch. Alkibiades hung with

Nemesis

him. "You have a clever friend in Androkles," whispered Alkibiades, smiling to any who happened to pass by.

"He is no friend of mine. Not even an acquaintance," replied Nikias, bluntly.

"You no doubt realize the trial will take place once we sail." Alkibiades, for the very first time that Nikias could remember lost that aspect of confidence, the glimmer in his eyes that displayed serene control.

"Alkibiades, it is no secret that I do not like you. But it is also no secret that I have opposed this Sikelian scheme of yours. Did you not hear the proposal? We sail in two days." Nikias gazed off, his eyes fixed on passing clouds that scudded by above the tops of cypress and plane. Suddenly he returned to the conversation. "What do I gain from a delay in your trial? In fact, I had hoped that the trial did take place, and would expend more than a few days at the commencement of the sailing season. Any interruption of this disaster could only suit me." He answered firmly. He answered with conviction. Still, he would dare not exchange glances, for his eyes could not lie.

"Nikias, I know you to be a pious man, so I will relate to you the prediction I received from the oracle of Zeus-Ammon. This may set your mind at ease, and at least for the sake of Athens, allow us to cooperate in this endeavor." Alkibiades looked around to ensure no one overheard. "I understand that the mutilation of the Hermes seems like a curse upon us. I had no part in it. Secondly, this prediction from the god said, 'when the Athenians sail to Sikelia, they will capture all the Syrakusans.' This can only bode well for all of us."

*****

Nikias held out his golden kylix, ready to tip the sacral libation into the sea in honor of Poseidon and to seek his blessing. His hand quaked a bit as he waited for the priest to begin the prayer. Across the expanse of the harbor, trierarchs and captains stood poised on the sterns of their vessels awaiting the chant also. The whole of Athens crowded the waterfront—wives, sons, and daughters of the expedition's men anxious to say farewell, while foreigners simply enjoyed this resplendent spectacle. A hundred warships rocked in the mild swells, their sails furled, chaplets and garlands strung on every rope, balustrade and figurehead. The crews and commanders too, displayed crowns of blossoms, and further out, beyond the harbor fortifications, hundreds of support craft hung just off shore, sails bellying full on the morning breeze. He did not want to appear impious, but he wished the mantis to get on with his prayer so he could pour out the god's portion then relieve himself of his armor. The helmet baked his head in the hot summer sun and the weighty breastplate wrung the sweat out of him. Not even today's uncommonly persistent breeze offered relief, so once the priest commenced his benediction, Nikias quickly emptied his cup and handed it to Stilbides and without pause pried off his helmet. Hiero, always by his side, attempted to unburden him of its weight, but with his usual solemnity Nikias cradled it in his arm, wanting to exhibit to all his pious dignity, the precise quality that he always declared to possess and the one he attributed to his god-granted luck in all of his endeavors.

Jon Edward Martin

    Across the harbor, a battery of salphinxes blared out the signal to weigh anchors; this initiated a booming cheer from all the on lookers that had crammed the shoreline and quays, and from the workmen and young boys that straddled the peaks on the long and narrow trireme shed roofs. He looked out at the assembly of warships, each and every one of them well fitted, gold and silver shod figureheads gleaming in the hot sun, pennants swirling lazily, while the main histion sails distended, swallowing up the breeze. Presently crewmen scurried forward past Nikias and began hauling up the heavy anchor stones from either side of the prow while hammer strikes echoed over the deck, the beat marking time for the oarsmen as they heaved the trireme forward. Nikias threaded through the squad of marines that clogged the deck on his way to the stern. Here the pilot leaned hard into his rudders, carving the bow of the vessel hard to starboard and toward the open sea. His trireme, the *Amynta*, sliced ahead of all the others, the pilot using the island of Aigina as a target of navigation. To the port side and just trailing them, Nikias caught sight of Alkibiades' warship lurching forward in fits with every oar stroke, trying to gain the lead. Nikias signaled to the kaluestes who increased the stroke cadence. He peered down into the benches and saw the nautai pitching forward, then whipping rearwards in time with the hammer strikes, fully aware of the impromptu race, and displaying without any doubt their desire to win it. Aigina was still far off, more than an hour, and no ship of oarsmen could maintain such a pace for that length of time. They threw their backs into it for awhile, coasted along with the sails doing the work then took up the stroke again. The *Amynta* managed to out-pace Alkibiades' trireme. Suddenly a barrage of cheers echoed from the port side. Nikias turned to see Lamkhos' warship cutting the swells and pulling ahead of the entire fleet. The kaluestes looked to Nikias. Nikias threw out his hands as a sign of resignation. "Let them rest. This tiny victory is not worth the price." The kaluestes barked out the order to ship oars. Now the trireme filled up with the rattle of oar-looms banging and thole-pins grinding as the nautai withdrew their oars and let the sail propel them.

    "Why did you stop them?" asked Hiero as he watched not only Lamakhos' but also Alkibiades' vessel glide by them.

    "Look behind." Nikias pointed back toward Piraios.

    Hiero, his legs still quavering as he worked to grow accustomed to the tossing sea, turned slowly. The scene was one of utter ataxia, ships strung out in a jumble from here all the way back into the harbor. "I see."

    "Help me with this, will you," commanded Nikias, as he fumbled with the buckles on the side of his breastplate. Hiero unfastened both straps and swung open the twin halved breastplate on the hinges that fastened the right side of it just below Nikias' armpit.

    Hiero hustled down the ladder below decks with Nikias' armor, returning almost instantly with a flagon of wine. He looked to Nikias and Nikias returned a glance of misunderstanding. "Your kylix, sir," reminded Hiero.

    "I forgot I still had it." Without the strain induced by his armor, Nikias held

Nemesis

the cup quite steadily, even as the trireme pitched while cutting through the swells. Hiero filled it quickly. Nikias emptied it just as fast. Now he looked back, ignoring the chaos of the exuberant fleet, watching as the coastline of Attika faded in the summer haze. For a moment the thought that he would never see his home again crossed his mind, but the notion diminished as quickly as his view of the shore; his recollections of his duties to the gods and the funds expended on furnishing their temples and offerings at their feasts did plenty to bury this misgiving. He had invested much in his piety and expected a most beneficial return.

*****

For over a day now the great fleet moored off Korkyra, safe in the shadow of its crescent shaped harbor, finding a respite here at the final rendezvous where the balance of their allies would join them, and where they would fashion their plans and determinations before crossing the Ionian Sea to Italia. To Nikias, the scene had not much changed in the last week; the fleet stretched out vulnerably across a day's sailing—it took that long for the last troop transport to drop anchor. Still more disconcerting was the slackness of auxiliary craft, the ones carrying the masons, carpenters, cooks and such. These, as could be best estimated by the captain of the straggling troop transport, cruised leisurely a half-day behind and would most probably arrive just as the last of the main fleet would be departing.

Nikias had disembarked on the first day, along with most of the other Athenians, and took up quarters in the city of Korkyra, very near the acropolis that was built on a spit of land that flanked the north end of the harbor. From here he could look out from the rooftop to take account of the entire flotilla.

Enthusiasm still rode high amongst the fleet, even as they assembled for yet another inspection. To the men it seemed as the three generals held these reviews simply to wallow in the power they now wielded, but to Nikias especially, it meant honing every detail, maintaining discipline, and most certainly allowing any scouts from the Syrakusans or Selunitines to view with unmistakable clarity the force they would soon contend with. "Let rumors accomplish what the spear cannot." These words Nikias repeated often to both Lamakhos and Alkibiades. "Let the spears of our allies finish the job," the answer to this by Alkibiades.

As different as Alkibiades proved to be from Nikias, both did agree upon not rushing into battle. Lamakhos, on the other hand, espoused a less prudent approach. All three stood in full regalia upon the breakwater surveying the fleet as the last of the allied triremes slipped into place.

"Then we agree to send three scout ships ahead to determine which cities will allow us anchorage, food and water." Nikias, instead of his spear, leaned upon a walking stick, a persistent companion since their arrival, for his back and knees ached more than ever. This would suit him. He desired that word of the vast fleet to be foremost the concern of their adversaries. *Let their imagination expand the numbers— and the danger. Men fear the unknown.*

Alkibiades strutted across the paved breakwater, back and forth, the butt-spike of his spear clanking upon the stonework with every stride. He stopped in front of Nikias. "We should also send embassies to all the cities of Sikelia, excepting Syrakuse and Seline. And to the inland Sikels too. We must establish where they stand in all of this before we put any plan into effect."

Nikias leaned to Hiero. "What is the tally?"

Hiero, busy stabbing away at the wax tablet with his stylus looked up at his master. "134 triremes all told, plus four pentaconters from Rhodes. Thirty five supply freighters with the masons, bakers, cooks, and carpenters. I have not yet counted up the merchant traders that are still coming in."

Lamakhos sucked up a mouthful of phlegm then spit it out into the water. "We should sail to Syrakuse straightaway. Attack them before they can marshal their defenses. Shock them into surrender." His voice was low and hoarse, almost a growl.

Alkibiades moved next to Lamakhos. "Why risk any Athenian lives just yet? If we employ my designs, and collect first as many allies as possible, we can ensure certain victory."

Lamakhos glanced to Nikias. "What say you to this?"

"We should, after securing our anchorages and supplies, send ahead to Egesta and insist that they deliver unto us the remainder of the monies promised. Once we have the silver for our men, we can deal with the complaints of the Egestians and the Leontines with a well-paid and therefore agreeable fleet. We do not need any discontentment amongst our sailors, marines and infantry. Dear Lamakhos, I pray that we employ this fleet as a display only and resolve the disputes with Syrakuse to our satisfaction—and profit—through intimidation only."

"And what profit will there be for us? What will the Assembly think when we return from an expedition, this expedition with so large and fine an armament, empty-handed?" Alkibiades handed his spear to his shield bearer and now stood facing Nikias feet spread, hands on his hips, as though he prepared for a bout of wrestling. "A battle there must be, but not yet." He swung his arm out in an arc across the wide vista of the chock full harbor. "We have the instrument of victory before us. We must not sail back empty-handed."

Nikias brushed past him as he stepped to the edge of the breakwater, staring out at the fleet. "What victory is it that you propose? The Assembly voted for providing assistance to our ally Egesta. Is this not the aim of our expedition?"

Alkibiades laughed out loud. "Oh come now, Nikias. Even the men in the barber shops and perfume stalls know precisely why we are here. Why, I would suspect that even the Egestians know the true reason. Athens needs a secure grain source and Sikelia would provide it, once Syrakuse is subdued."

"Alkibiades, you are so like an impetuous child. As the saying goes, 'Be certain your pot is larger than your chicken.'" Nikias spoke to him as though he was a school boy, not a co-commander. Lamakhos rolled his eyes.

Alkibiades, all the while keeping calm answered, "Let us vote now on what course of action we should pursue. Once decided, we must, all three of us, swear to carry it out."

Nemesis

Lamakhos spoke next. "Since I am but a soldier, my plan is to fight. Fight now and let the gods deliver to us victory or defeat. But since I see neither of you wishes to employ this policy, I must side with Alkibiades. He differs only from me in a planned delay. Nikias, I am not certain that you have calculated battle into any of your schemes."

"Battle, for me, is a last option. I do not contemplate the like so casually, or with such eagerness. I did not advance to this age by being foolhardy." Nikias leaned hard upon his walking stick, a sudden twinge of pain crumpling him over. "Now that we have decided to follow your suggestions Alkibiades, I propose we divide the fleet into three flotillas. It will prove much more convenient to re-supply and locate sufficient anchorage if we spread across the coast. In a few days' time we should collect at Rhegion." He drew a long breath before continuing. "I must retire, gentlemen."

Nikias hobbled off the breakwater and began the climb up the ridge into the town above with Hiero at his side while his armor-bearer trailed, fully laden, behind them both. The road was barely wide enough for a farm cart, unpaved and scarred by wheel ruts—these he cursed every time his walking stick jammed fast into one, and again when a racing cart or horse sped by kicking up a choking cloud of dust. He was more than uncomfortable with his kidneys aching and his knees throbbing, so as a balm his mind filled with visions of Athens and the cool comfort of his own andron. *This is the best of it*, he thought as he trudged along. *Once on Sikelia no walking stick will banish the pain, or remedy what we have put in motion.* At the crest of the ridge, just where the roadway banked sharply to the right and along the city's wall he turned to look back at the precise rows of triremes, their pennants limp in the breezeless afternoon. Voices of men echoed from the decks, across the anchorage and up the ridge, for harbor's very shape resembled a massive amphitheater and projected even faint noise high to the crest. "Hiero, I have a very important task for you."

Hiero moved closer. "Master?"

"We are sending out three triremes ahead, to scout new anchorage and secure in advance of the fleet, our supplies. I am planning on sending out one additional vessel." Nikias winced as he straightened up. "You will sail directly to Syrakuse. I have a message you must deliver to a friend."

The pair finally entered their quarters where Nikias conducted Hiero into the storeroom, ostensibly to detail the packing of his belongings for the departure of the fleet, but in fact to present, in detail, the message he must convey and its recipient. "The man you will seek out is the very same man who visited my home last winter. His name is Athenagoras. Do you remember him?"

"Why certainly I remember him. He had the most annoying twang in his Doric speech." Hiero carried on, smothering Nikias in complaints about this visitor.

"Do not provide me with an inventory of his faults; only listen carefully to what I say, for I will give you no note—nothing written. This is for your own safety." Hiero, uncharacteristically silent, nodded. Nikias continued. "You will tell him that this armament—and spare no exaggeration in describing it—will without doubt be thrown against his city. Tell him also that if Syrakuse surrenders, I guarantee our terms will be fair to its citizens and more than profitable to Athenagoras and others like him who value democracy. You must impress upon him to render this vote soon, and come over to us quickly, before fickle war sets us all on a path neither of us can predict. Remind him also that Nikias is a true friend. Another Athenian commander may not be so inclined." Nikias ambled over to a small chest and fumbled with the clasp for a moment before prying back the lid. "And deliver to Athenagoras, this humble token, a reminder if you like, of the sincerity of my message." He held out a bulging leather purse. Hiero scooped it up without making comment. "It is, as you term such things as this—an investment."

    Hiero put to memory the entire message, word for word, in minutes and departed with the afternoon tide on a Kilikian freighter that was en route to Sikelia. Nikias, shrewd as ever, secured passage for Hiero on a vessel that traded with Syrakuse and would draw no undue attention. Although slower than his fleet of triremes, the freighter would sail directly across open sea, not needing nightly anchorage to rest and feed the oarsmen, for it could easily carry a week's worth of food and water, and its broad histion sail, unlike a crew of nautai, required no rest.

    Nikias, from the roof top of his quarters, beheld the teeming harbor below. He easily spotted the wide-bellied freighter bearing Kilikian markings on an incandescent orange sail, slipping by the moored warships of the fleet to the open sea beyond. Not long after, Lamakhos' flotilla, incited by the blare of salphinx trumpets, streamed out of the harbor, quickly reforming into squadrons before steering north. By then the Kilikian was lost in the haze, well on its way. Below him, in the narrow alleyways of the town, he could hear his own servants in argument. They cast insults at each other as they tussled with the bulky luggage of their master, some cursing the weight, others Nikias for requiring so much in what they dubbed, "personal comfort". *Fools*, he thought to himself as he listened to their vitriolic complaints. *Little comfort indeed! Armor, by its nature weighs more than clothing.* For a moment he wanted to shout out those words, to chastise them, but thought better of it. Now he heard footfalls in the stairwell and turned. "Ah, Stilbides. The sacrifice?"

    Stilbides smiled. "Both Hermes and Poseidon bless us. It is a good day to venture on the sea."

    "Excellent. Send for my adjutant."

    Before Stilbides descended half way down the stairwell, Euphemos emerged onto the roof top. "Your orders, Nikias?"

    "You are a good man Euphemos—loyal and efficient." Nikias moved toward the stairs. "Send word to the trierarchs and commanders to weigh anchor within the hour, while we still have the tide."

Chapter 13
Rhegion – Summer 415

Endymion and his companions from Argos swarmed from their troop transport to the beach outside of the city of Rhegion, slipping and sliding on the tide-polished rocks in their haste. A supposed friend and ally of Athens, the city had locked its gates, but did provide a market of sorts outside the walls near the temple to Artemis. Armed only with his hoplite xiphos, Endymion scrambled up the rocky beach toward the gleaming temple, following his friend Tisandros, who had replaced his sword with a small iron cauldron, which swung lazily from its bail with his every stride. The Athenians had kept good their promise on pay, and he had more than enough drachmai to replenish his victuals until they landed on Sikelia proper.

"It feels good to get solid land under me," remarked Tisandros, as they edged forward through the crowded market. "I can't see them but I can smell 'em."

"What are you after?" Endymion asked as he peered over and around the men in front of him, rising up on tip-toes to survey the food on display in the stalls.

"Chickens, man!" bellowed Tisandros. "I'll cook us up a feast." He shouldered his way ahead until he came upon the poultry pens, the stink of wet feathers and chicken scat filling his nostrils. "You find us some greens and maybe an onion or two."

Endymion pushed beyond the chicken vendors then turned back for a moment. "Meet at the temple," he yelled to Tisandros. Soon he was deep into the market and the press of men, mostly Athenians as their accent divulged. He came across an old man and woman with baskets full of mountain greens, onions and leeks.

"Good for the stomach," said the old woman as she shook a handful in before Endymion's face.

"Endymion held out an obol and his empty wicker battle pack. Immediately the old man scooped up the coin while the woman began to stuff handfuls of greens, onions and leeks into pack. He nodded. The old man bit hard on the coin and smiled back. "Where's the bread?"

"Nearer to the gate." The old man pointed with a crooked, wavering finger at the twin towered gate, not fifty meters further along the wall.

By the time Endymion had reached the bread vendors, all that remained were day old loaves, which cost him much less, but forced him to buy two instead of one, for his had to tear off large hunks that had molded over, yet two old loaves cost less than a single fresh one, so he felt he had bargained well. Soon he made his way to the temple of Artemis and climbed the stairs, searching for Tisandros.

"Over here, Endymion." Beneath a stunted cypress, Tisandros bent over his cauldron, his face glowing orange in the light of the cook fire.

"The most important ingredients," announced Endymion as he tossed the over-stuffed battle pack to his friend.

Tisandros, without looking up, thanked him and began tearing through the pack, pulling out handfuls of greens and leaks, which he dropped right into the pot.

"Help me with these," he said as he flipped an onion to Endymion, who peeled it quickly and sliced it into small wedges. "In there," said Tisandros. Hunger—compelling obedience—incited Endymion to plop them into the simmering stew promptly. Once the onions and greens had been added to the pot in quantities acceptable to Tisandros, he pointed to the twin piles of feathers nestled at the base of the tree. "Half for you, my friend. A few more meals such as this and we will both have pillows fit for a general." He motioned with a twitch of his head toward a knot of men walking toward them. "Should we ask the generals what kind of pillows they sleep on—yes?" Tisandros' questions invariably ended with 'yes' or 'no' depending on which reply he was fishing for.

"I have more suitable things to ask of them, if they venture on past." Endymion rose up, and brushed the dirt from his knees."

Nikias, with walking stick in hand, strolled deliberately through the temple precinct, offering brief greetings to each man as he passed by. Lamakhos and Alkibiades followed behind only slightly, deep in conversation and for the most part ignoring the soldiers and oarsmen eating their meals. "Enough food?" asked Nikias as he came upon Endymion and Tisandros.

"Why yes," replied Endymion. "But why do we eat out here beyond their walls? Are they not allies?"

Nikias held both ends of his walking stick, resting it across his thighs, as he spoke. "I think if we had landed with one vessel we would be eating inside. A few hundred is a bit more distressing—and intimidating."

Tisandros, still busy stirring the stew, looked up and asked, "Where to next, general?"

Nikias grinned reassuringly. "Do not worry, my Argive friend. I hear Katana is replete with poultry of all sorts. You will wear out that pot with all your feasting. Good day to you both." Nikias ambled away. Lamakhos and Alkibiades walked by also, but offered no greetings, other than perfunctory nods—the minimum display of recognition required.

"He seems a good old sort," said Tisandros as he spooned up a portion of the stew then blew on it before sampling. "Ready for soldiers, but not civilized men," he quipped, pointing to the flame-licked pot. "Can't say I think much of the other two, though."

"You speak of Alkibiades and Lamakhos?" Endymion sat down cross-legged holding out his bowl. Tisandros spooned it full. "Everyone in Argos talks of Alkibiades as our best friend at Athens. Still, I do not know about this."

"Indeed he is our finest advocate, or how else could we have hoped to be part of this great adventure without his friendship—no?" Tisandros stuffed a stew-laden spoon into his mouth and quickly traded it for a hunk of bread, keeping his cheeks bulging full.

"Can we trust any of these Athenians?" Endymion studied his bowl of stew while he stabbed at it with a flap of bread. "Are we to be treated any better than the

Nemesis

islanders?"

Tisandros chuckled beneath a most malevolent grin. "Trust is an illusion, my dear companion. The best we can hope for is that our aims and those of the Athenians are mutual and similar."

"But that may be the very issue. From what I can gather from the Athenian soldiers, the men leading us do not themselves have mutual and similar aims. How does this bode for us and the campaign?" Endymion kept poking his stew until the hunk of bread disintegrated. He tore off a fresh piece and had at it once more.

"Oh, I would think those three pursue the same end, just by different roads." Tisandros gulped a bit of wine then swiped his beard dry with the back of his hand. "They all want to return to Athens, victorious."

"I will pray to Hermes that they choose the shortest route."

*****

Nikias caused the fleet to dally at Rhegion for he wanted to supply Hiero with ample time for his mission, but also grew concerned that the limited markets provided here would not long satisfy the men, and he wished to suppress any indication of discord so early in the campaign. He timed their stay to coincide with the quantity of local resources, not departing before every last hunk of cheese, basket of fish, amphora of wine, and loaf of bread had been exhausted, for soldiers find contentment in full bellies—it is hard to complain when their mouths are busy chewing. Alkibiades had, like Nikias, sent his own spies ahead to gauge the mood of the various cities on Sikelia. Lamakhos, typically not thinking a day ahead and resigned to the plan of Alkibiades, paced the shore camp like a caged lion, snapping at men that exhibited any breach of discipline, no matter how insignificant. Nikias watched him as he riled the men and thought, *he should eat more.*

Four days after anchoring at Rhegion the three scout ships returned from their final port of call at Egesta, and brought with them information from their ally that proved more than unsettling. Hegasandros, commander of the scouting mission, hurried along the beach, a pair of aids in tow as he marched toward Nikias' tent, marked out by its swirling violet pennant. As his small entourage advanced across the tidal wash and gravel, men halted activity and stared, not a one calling out for information as was usual, but all frozen by the determined gait of the three men on their way to the commander's tent. Outside, a single slave worked on a tri-crested kranos helmet, polishing it with a wad of linen. The entrance itself was bracketed by two Athenian hoplites in full armor with their aspides resting against their thighs and their spears straight and tall, gripped in their right hands. Hegasandros flew through the tent opening, snapping back the flap as he entered.

"Greetings, Hegasandros." Nikias, bent over a small table peering at a map of the Sikelian coast, flanked by Alkibiades and Lamakhos. A slave held a small oil lamp over the table and shuffled awkwardly to remain adjacent to Nikias as he moved about, wanting to keep the halo of light convenient for his master. "Sit. There is wine." Nikias motioned at the three-legged table topped with cups and a wine-bowl which was flanked by a pair of couches. Hegasandros snatched up a cup and dunked it into the bowl then moved in beside Nikias.

Alkibiades, surprised that Nikias had not initiated any questions, spoke first. "Have the Egestians sent along the remainder of the payment?"

Hegasandros gulped his cup dry before answering. "They lied to us."

Alkibiades, his lisp agitated to extreme by his anger, challenged Hegasandros. "About what? Do they not have the silver, as promised?"

Hegasandros shook his head. "Thirty talents only. They duped our ambassadors. They do not have even a portion of what they promised."

Lamakhos flung his cup. "How do we pay the fleet?" He thought for a moment before adding, "Enact my plan. Sail straight for Syrakuse while we still have the fleet intact and the Syrakusans in disarray."

Nikias, oddly, seemed unaffected by this news. He stood apart from the other commanders and listened as they argued, ranted and restated what should be done now.

Nemesis

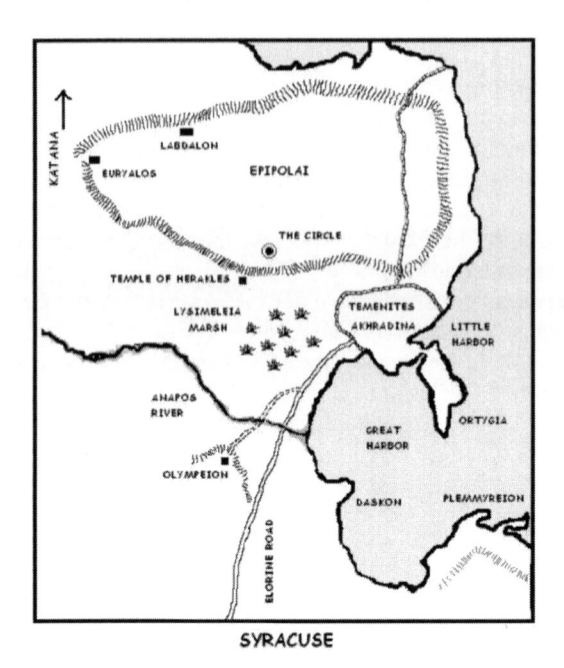

Chapter 14
Syrakuse –Summer 415

Athenagoras sat on the steps to the Council House, surrounded by his usual clique, discussing the rumors of the Athenian fleet's objective.

Diokles, the youngest of his companions, was not restrained by his lack of years. "Even if they intend to attack us, what can they hope to accomplish? Our walls are stout, our men numerous."

"My concern is not the Athenians, but our own Gamoroi." Athenagoras glanced over his right shoulder then his left before continuing. "They will undermine our democracy in the name of security." The sun beat down on them now as morning drifted toward noon; the agora started to empty with the rising heat. "Let us find a bit of shade." He slowly made his way down the bank of stairs followed by his associates, halting before an array of benches beneath a single plane tree near the Long Stoa. "We must whisper," he said while laughing, a cautioning finger pressed to his lips. "Hermokrates may be nearby."

They all laughed—briefly. Diokles stood up before the others who had sat upon the benches. "They control the cavalry, and do not forget about the *clubs*." He spoke of the conclaves, the secret societies of the aristocrats that worked outside the bounds of normal politics. These societies and associations were bound together beyond law, and were euphemistically dubbed *dining clubs*. Some were just that. Others grouped for more sinister purposes—at least that is what Diokles feared.

From the thinning crowd of the agora someone called out Athenagoras'

Jon Edward Martin

name. Soon a young boy burst into view, wearing only a loin-cloth and in full sprint. "Athenagoras!"

"Over here!" Athenagoras stood up and waved until the boy spotted him.

"A message for you," the boy announced as he pulled up, flashing a folded leaf of papyrus. He carried with him the stench of spoilt fish. His skin was bronzed by the sun, but it could not mask the filth that streaked his arms and legs—a blend of dried sea salt and tidal mud. He presented the message to Athenagoras, who recoiled for a moment as he caught site of his blistered hands and dirt-blackened finger nails.

"Here." He tossed the messenger a single coin. "From whom?"

The boy tested the obol with a bite then stuffed it into his cheek. "A man from a Kilikian ship." He began to turn away but stopped and added, "He spoke Greek."

Athenagoras peeled open the note. It did not take him long to read it, for he quickly crumpled it up in his fist. "I will see you all this evening. Invitations will be delivered this afternoon." He knew these men, his most trusted acquaintances, would not refuse to attend the symposion; they never did, and proved more than willing to drink his wine and eat his food if it meant listening to his tirades against the aristocrats. They were merchants, manufactory owners and such other brokers, each having little in common with the Gamoroi. He hurried through the agora and as he passed the temple to Apollo he tossed the crushed papyrus into a flaming tripod, soliciting a dark stare from the attendant. "Pah!" he muttered with a snarl and kept to his pace. As he followed the twisting harbor road down to the commercial wharf, he passed by the typical huddles of men chattering away, exchanging hearsay with rumor, but today and most uncommonly every conversation centered about the Athenian war fleet. Clearly he could no longer challenge Hermokrates directly in the assembly, for the past ridicule he had authored of such an invasion would be thrust into his face. No, he ought for now, with both patience and silence, allow Hermokrates this brief respite. He must, in all aspects, appear to support him. In future, there would be opportunities—there always are.

Activity here, at the height of the sailing season appeared somewhat diminished, this also the result of the sudden arrival of the Athenians in the waters around Sikelia. Officially, no state of war existed between Athens and Syrakuse, and if Syrakuse restored the land of the Leontines, the Athenians would have no legal reason to instigate hostilities. This, in truth, is exactly what Athenagoras wished for. If Syrakuse bent to the will of Athens, Hermokrates and the Gamoroi would be discredited. And of course someone within Syrakuse would be compelled to lead the city in its new relations with Athens. What better person than Athenagoras himself?

Once he spotted the furled orange sail and the balustrades swathed in bright ochre and saffron, he searched the deck for its captain. Instead, leaning upon the rail near the brow-plank he sighted someone unexpected but at the same time familiar to him.

"Athenagoras?" The man stammered out his name.

Nemesis

He stared for a somewhat uncomfortably long time; the face, at last, registered. He bounded up the brow-plank, not uttering a single word until he was close enough to whisper. "Nikias' slave?"

Hiero, about to roll his eyes caught himself. "I am in the employ of Nikias, son of Nikeratos, of Athens."

"May we go below?" Athenagoras did not wait for an answer but moved straightaway for the ladder that plunged into the hold. Hiero followed. Once in the belly of the ship they both lost sight momentarily in the confined darkness. They heard the squeal and scurry of rats, and the smell of the rowers' sweat and urine still hung in the air. The two men sat, each on an oarsman's bench, the sunlight splintered into shafts by the decking above. A swathe of light cut across Hiero's face while Athenagoras withdrew into the shadows, only his foot dappled by the sun.

"I bring a message from Nikias to you and to all the Syrakusans." Doubtlessly, Hiero recalled every word of Nikias' but he also had the cleverness and perception to refashion these to suit the occasion and the audience. "Nikias wants you to know that, if it were his exclusive decision, he would not make war upon the Syrakusans." Above, the deck creaked as one of the crewmen re-boarded. From where he sat Hiero could see the silhouettes of the man's scuffling feet, but not his face. It seemed he paused on deck searching, but soon disembarked, leaving the ship to Hiero and Athenagoras once more. "As I was saying, the decision whether to attack is not his alone. Restore Leontine. Any other action will result in war. Use your influence and this small gift from Nikias to persuade your council to heed this most prudent and lucrative advice." He held out the purse. A hand, disembodied by the shadows, snatched it up and withdrew out of sight. Hiero strained to detect Athenagoras' eyes, to gauge if his words were well met, but the gloom of the hold revealed nothing to him—only the rhythmic breathing of the Syrakusan. "Remember Melos. If it all comes down to a siege then even your benefactor Nikias will be in no position to help you."

Athenagoras rose from his seat. Still he said nothing but made his way to the ladder and the pool of sunlight that spilled around it. "Tell your master that in time, Syrakuse will appreciate Athens' friendship." He bounded up the ladder, pausing for a moment to poke his head out, scanning the wharf for idle, wandering eyes. Satisfied that he would remain anonymous, he left the freighter and began to hurry along the dock, trying to quickly distance himself from the Kilikian vessel. He peered back over his shoulder, curious to see if the Athenian messenger watched him, and met Hiero's eyes uncomfortably. He spun, quickening his pace but smacked into someone as he turned. "I beg your pardon," he said as he recovered himself."

"It is I who should apologize," replied Dionysos, as he stepped aside, allowing Athenagoras to pass.

Athenagoras, startled by Hermokrates' protégé, snarled at him. "What are you doing here?"

"Why I am here on business for Hermokrates, as I am every day." Dionysos summoned every bit of false humility he could, but he could hardly contain the satisfaction he felt at catching Athenagoras at something: he did not know what, but the man displayed the most obvious distress. He could not wait to tell Hermokrates. *But what will I tell him,* he thought. He scoured the docks and the vessels at anchor nearby, but nothing registered with him until his eyes came upon the Kilikian freighter. His mind filled with thoughts of the attack on Elpida and the knife—the Kilikian knife.

*****

"It could not have gone better," insisted Pantheras. "Even Athenagoras held his tongue. Hardly a peep from Diokles." He cantered his horse up to Hermokrates.

Hermokrates sighed, for his eyes and his thoughts were consumed by something distant. With a blink his trance broke and he stared at Pantheras. "We are hardly prepared for the Athenians." He prodded his horse forward with a gentle poke of his heels. "I, for one, would like to check the muster rolls at the Olympeion."

"As strategos, you can. Don't you realize what they have voted yesterday? Work will commence on the fortifications. The ship-sheds are to be rebuilt. Ambassadors will be dispatched across Sikelia. More importantly, we are sending out garrisons to keep watch on our less than trustworthy inland allies. All these things you have insisted on. Today, all these things are made to happen." Pantheras tugged on the reins of Hermokrates' horse, bringing the two men face to face. "The demagogues have lost."

Hermokrates clasped his friend's hand. "This is a temporary condition at best. Any setback and we will be out." Hermokrates pulled the reins from Pantheras' grip. "We must slow our pace. They are far behind." He squinted as he looked back down the road. The small column of wagons with their families appeared far off.

"They know where the Olympeion is. Indeed, how can they miss it?" Pantheras looked ahead to the temple hill and the small village that ringed its base. Pantheras blurted out, "And if they do indeed come against us, what can they do?" He drew a deep breath and checked the roadway with a glance. "Our walls are sturdy. Our cavalry will deny the countryside to them, and without access to our fields, how can they sustain themselves?"

"To the Olympeion!" Hermokrates drove his horse to a full sprint, splashing furiously through the marsh until they came to the bridge over the Eloros. He pulled up then slid from his mount and led it to the carved banks of the river for a drink.

"What was that race all about?" puffed Pantheras as he reined up almost breathless.

"To give us a bit of time to check the katalogos, before your wife and mine begin barking out orders." Hermokrates knelt on the bank and began to scoop water into his mouth. Finally he stood. "If they attack now, do you think we can stand up to them? The men in our assembly talk as though they all have fought numerous battles, and slain many a foe, but most have seen no more blood than in a street brawl. The Athenians are well seasoned in war, and merciless in victory. Ask Dianthe. Ask Elpida. I do not want my daughter watching the bodies of her family burn on pyres

Nemesis

outside of Syrakuse, as they cower from Athenian guards."

Pantheras, up until now, had graciously endured Hermokrates' gloomy talk. "By the gods above and below, what should we do? You speak as though this battle has already been fought. I too have a family. So do most of the men in that assembly that voted you strategos. We crave more inspiration than that!"

"Inspiration is a luxury only poets can afford. We need fighting men, not merely men that are willing to fight. Can you see the difference?" Hermokrates, tears welling in his eyes, clasped his friend's shoulder. "Courage alone is no defense." He vaulted onto his horse and trotted it up across the bridge and onto the narrow path that threaded through groves of perfectly manicured olive and mulberry trees. High above, the massive temple overwhelmed the countryside. It rose up, imposing, on an isolated hill, its gleaming, thick Doric columns buttressing the lustrous entablatures. Sculptures of the twelve Olympic gods seemed to push free of the azure painted marble of the pediment. It truly was the home of gods on earth. The wooden gate hung open as they rode through the entrance in the four meter high mud-brick wall that ran circuit around the entire base of the hill. Along the road within, cypress trees poked up straight and tall like an honor guard for the temple. "Hurry before they catch up." Hermokrates tethered his horse to a squat olive tree and hustled up the stairs. The tripods that flanked the door sputtered meek flames. A head bobbed into view within the pronaos. Hermokrates called out, "I've come from the board of generals." Cautiously the temple attendant shuffled into view clutching a well-worn broom. "Hermokrates?" he squeaked out while shading his eyes.

Pantheras bounded up the stairs and into the Olympeion behind his friend. Sight adjusted quickly and just as quickly Hermokrates found the crisscross of wooden receptacles that lined the wall just inside the doorway. "Where are the scrolls?"

The attendant appeared puzzled. "Taken not much before you arrived." He waved them out onto the temple porch. "See. They board the ship now to deliver them across to the city."

Hermokrates stepped out where the attendant began to swing his tattered broom this way and that, trying to appear diligent. "Sikanos wasted little time. He is more anxious than either of us." His sight wandered from the sacred trireme to the line of the wagons veering off the main road, a smoky trail of dust lingering in their wake. "I think they've picked out a spot."

Pantheras and Hermokrates left the temple and led their horses toward the jumble of wagons, where a few slaves worked to unhitch the teams while others began to arrange stools and food baskets for the afternoon picnic. "Melete, my dear," bellowed Pantheras as he approached his wife. She sat beneath a sparse-leaved olive tree, a slave wobbling over her with a linen parasol. His two boys had already wandered off with their hoop. He knelt beside Melete, resting his head on her lap. "No better pillow," he said smiling.

She cuffed him gently. "That is no way to behave," she scolded then added in a whisper, "at least not in outright view."

Pantheras, rubbing his head in mock pain, whispered in return, "I cannot wait for the night, and our bedroom." His wife blushed. He laughed.

Hermokrates approached his wife in a much reserved fashion. "I am so happy you decided to picnic with me today."

She smiled politely, twirling a small fan in her long slender fingers. "It is a beautiful day. And the girls needed to quit the city—and their prison."

Hermokrates winced at that last remark. He had ordered that his entire family remain behind the walls of his town-house since the incident with Elpida. Only now, on the eve of invasion did he finally relent and allow them this excursion into the countryside. He knew what was coming. So did the city. "Dearest, remember my offer to send you off to Korinth. There you may enjoy a bit more freedom, especially now."

Phaidra lowered herself onto the humble stool that her servant Glaukia had carefully placed at the foot of a shady plane tree; close to her friend Melete for conversation, but cordially distant enough for whispers to go unheard. "I will not abandon you, my husband."

"Do not think of it as abandonment, but a holiday. The Athenians will display little tolerance for a siege, and even less once the Peloponnesians come to Sikelia." Hermokrates looked around for his daughters, seeing only Kalli near a wagon, helping the servants unpack. She turned and waved exuberantly. He beamed.

Now she trotted his way swinging a basket, the gilded belt on her peplos gown gleaming in the sunlight. "Father, we have fresh baked bread, opson and figs." She emptied the basket upon an old cloak, arranging the contents fastidiously, every so often pushing back a loose strand of chestnut hair that brushed her cheek.

"Where is Dionysos?"

"Father, he does work for you, does he not?" Kalli replied smiling, as she kept looking down at her arrangement of food.

"He most certainly does, and I most certainly invited him." Hermokrates knelt upon a corner of the cloak, staring at his daughter, trying to get her to look at him and answer his question.

Kalli laughed. "He said he will join us after he attends to a most important task. I assumed it to be for you."

Hermokrates struggling to hide his anxiety, offered up a lie. "Yes, yes, I had forgotten about that." He shifted the conversation. "And where are Dianthe and Elpida?"

Finally Kalli tucked the defiant strand of hair into her chaplet of violets. "In the wagon, father."

Hermokrates found this a bit strange, so he meandered toward the wagon, pretending to check on his horse. As he grew closer he could hear sobbing. He peered in warily. Dianthe had Elpida wrapped in her arms, rocking while humming a lullaby as a balm to comfort her. "What is the matter?"

"Elpida overheard the guards, sir. She knows the Athenians are coming."

Nemesis

Dianthe began humming again.

Hermokrates stretched out his hand to stroke Elpida's head. "Now, now, who told you such a thing?"

The girl sniffled and looked up at him. Her eyes blazed red, her face streaked in tears. "The men working on the garden wall said the Athenians will attack us."

"Come on now and let us eat. You should not talk of such things while the gods have bestowed upon us such a splendid afternoon, and Glaukia has prepared an even more splendid meal." He reached in and lifted Elpida up and out of the wagon, holding her above his head. "Tell me, can you see the food from here?"

With a boyish vault Dianthe leapt from the wagon. She wanted to run, to where she did not know. She merely wanted to exercise this fleeting bit of liberty to its fullest, but painfully reflected on the schooling Hermokrates had generously provided her, with lessons on the behavior of ladies. She envied Elpida as she checked her own impulse to sprint, reining it in to a saunter.

Hermokrates, fully aware of her urge to charge off, scolded her gently with his eyes. She dipped her head, and slowly trudged toward the others. "Come and let us feast on some special delicacies. Glaukia has your favorite."

Elpida, hardly restricted by any hint of decorum sprinted off. Before she had approached to within a few feet Glaukia held out an epaikla honey cake. For the moment the little girl had forgotten the Athenians.

Dianthe turned and called to Hermokrates. "Look! In the Great Harbor."

Hermokrates squinted against the afternoon sun. His heart sank. There, in the flat water of the harbor, several Athenian warships, marked by their sails, swung in an arc toward the docks of Ortygia. "Everyone into the wagons. Into the wagons—now!" Hermokrates grabbed Dianthe's hand and called to her sister. Elpida, terror in her eyes, bolted toward them. Hermokrates tossed the girls into the bed of the wagon then shouted to his daughter Kalli. "Leave the food." Kalli scooped up what she could manage in an armful and hurried to the wagon. By now everyone, including Melete and Phaidra, had been loaded and the slaves led them toward the city. Hermokrates stood next to his horse waiting for Pantheras. "This appears to be no attack." He gazed at the Athenian squadron as it back-watered just off-shore. "Perhaps only heralds with our last warning to capitulate." The two vaulted upon their horses and set them to a gallop to catch up to their families on the Elorine Road, all the while eyeing the Athenians. For almost an hour the enemy warships lingered in the Great Harbor. As Hermokrates, Pantheras and the others hurriedly passed through the outer gates to the city, they lost sight of the harbor. The streets yawned empty, although mid-afternoon. Hermokrates ordered the servants to lead their families to their homes while he and Pantheras continued to the sea wall on Ortygia where they could glimpse the Athenians once more. Here the roof tops and battlements teemed with the people of Syrakuse. He cantered his skittish and snorting horse through the crowd, toward the main tower, dismounting at its base. Once inside he flew up the stairs, shoving aside the on-lookers that had crammed the roof, finally shouldering in next to Sikanos.

"Good that you are here." Sikanos pointed to the mouth of the Great Harbor and the sterns of the Athenian triremes as they departed. "Heralds. They offered any non-Syrakusans the opportunity to quit the city."

"That is all?" Hermokrates shrugged. "No terms. No list of grievances?"

"None, my friend. They mean to attack us—unless, of course, we surrender."

"What vessel is that?" Hermokrates stuck his finger out at a merchantman that had begun to unfurl its bright orange sail.

"A freighter, sir." Dionysos edged in next to Hermokrates.

"How are you so quick to answer?" challenged Sikanos.

Dionysos glanced at Sikanos with polite acknowledgment then spoke to his employer. "I walked by it last week, although Athenagoras may be able to enlighten you further. I saw him leave that ship. He was quite uncomfortable at the sight of me." Dionysos dipped his head. "I should have told you about this sooner."

Hermokrates held back a reply, working to summon up a slippery recollection, a memory, that still hidden, distressed him. "That is the very same Kilikian freighter that docked with the news of Melos," he blurted out with a bit of pride. "Little wonder that Athenagoras has acquaintances aboard."

Dionysos pulled out the dagger from his belt. "This also is Kilikian."

Sikanos eyes widened. "I think you carry these suppositions too far."

Hermokrates leaned to Sikanos' ear. "Are you saying he is not capable of murder?"

"Of you or me, he most certainly is, but I cannot believe he would harm a small child." Sikanos shook his head. "Not a child."

*****

Nikias and Alkibiades prowled the beach in anticipation, not quite together and in consultation, but near enough to each other to receive the news simultaneously while Lamakhos perched high on a boulder, his eyes on the horizon. The squadron would return soon. They yearned for word of its mission. Known only to Nikias, Hiero—gone for several weeks—was due back also. Nikias ran the two main points of the stated mission over in his head: restore the Leontines and help Egesta against the Seluntines. In reality, the attack on Syrakuse had been merely implied in the Assembly—only at a closed meeting at the Strategeion did the generals agree to this most ambitious aspect of the mission. If the Syrakusans proved wise and conceded the territory to the Leontines, he could apply token pressure against Seluntine; if successful he could take the fleet home, if not he could blame the Egestians for not delivering on the pledged silver and still bring the fleet home with little cost to Athens. But a siege of Syrakuse would prove a different matter, requiring more in provender, iron, horses, mercenaries and silver. So Alkibiades continued to work his schemes, enlisting more allies from amongst the inland Sikels, while exerting pressure on other cities to join against Syrakuse; his plan moved forward in fits—for every ally gained, another city stubbornly remained neutral. Nikias saw clearly where the strategy of Alkibiades was taking them—a year or more may be required before

Nemesis

they could enlist enough allies to coerce Syrakuse to submit. Still, if his rival showed progress, they all would be compelled to follow him.

In contrast, Lamakhos fumed at this lost opportunity of striking hard and striking fast. He desired battle. He craved resolution. At every evening meal he would say," We have already squandered the better part of the summer with elaborate diplomacies and protractions." He repeated it word for word, almost as a slogan.

Nikias, like a leaf buffeted by currents in a stream, navigated his strategy away from both, toward a flimsy but quick victory. Force the Seluntines to capitulate and he would have completed the major portion of the commission, still delivering on a promise to their Egestian allies, even if they had failed in payment for the fleet. Or settle the Syrakusan issue. Either would do. He did not require both. He mulled it all over as he walked the tidal shingle, hobbled by his aching knees, every so often glancing at Alkibiades.

Athenian warships crammed the Katanian harbor, while the local fishermen and merchants congested any open water between, trying to work their trades. For a moment a feeling of satisfaction overcame Nikias; he had limited the size of the squadron to ten triremes only and not the full complement that Lamakhos had urged. Ten would appear as a diplomatic mission, one-hundred an invasion. He was certain the Syrakusans required only a gentle nudge to render the Leontines their land. Any more than a nudge, say a push, or a shove and they would trade pliancy with stubbornness.

The first trireme ground ashore, followed by another, and another until all ten had beached. Brow-planks slammed into the shingle and the vessels emptied by the bunch, marines first followed by the nautai, all laughing and joking. Finally Euphemos made his way to Nikias. Alkibiades approached casually, seemingly in no hurry to hear the news, while Lamakhos leapt from his boulder and jogged to Euphemos.

"Well?" Nikias pulled his felt petasos hat from his bald, graying head.

"We sailed directly into their harbor, no warships, no booms, nothing to stop us." Exuberance mixed with contempt filled Euphemos' words.

"What did I tell you?" Lamakhos growled. "Attack now!"

Euphemos continued. "They piled in along their walls and gawked at us from their roof tops. By Athena, if the entire fleet had sailed we could have taken the city today."

Nikias face burned with rage. "You sailed into a harbor that had no walls. Their city is a different matter." He let a few moments pass to cool his temper. "What was their reply?"

"No reply." Euphemos rolled his eyes.

"None. Are you certain?" Nikias asked.

"We called out the ultimatum, waited for an hour then left."

"What ultimatum?" The question to be put to them concerned restoring Leontine, not for them to surrender." Lamakhos suddenly retreated from the conversation, ambling back toward the inland road. Nikias slapped his thigh with his hat.

"But I thought the change in orders came from you." Now Euphemos' face went pale. "It was you who altered the message, was it not?"

"What change?" Nikias pushed the hat down on his head.

"As we weighed the anchor stones this morning, a courier sprinted up the beach and tossed to me a scroll and blurted out, 'From Nikias.' Before I could unfurl it we had back-watered out into the harbor. It read: 'Ask for their surrender and nothing less.'"

"You fool, that courier may not have known it, but the note was most certainly a device of Lamakhos'. He proved cleverer than either Alkibiades or me. Now battle cannot be avoided."

"This should not worry you, Nikias. I am telling you, they are no match for us. We sailed around their Great Harbor like we were in the Piraios. These Syrakusans had only a few triremes dragged up into dilapidated ship-sheds. In fact, I know exactly how many men they can muster, and it barely matches our numbers."

"And how did you come by this bit of information?" Nikias thought of Hiero, and what word he would bring.

Euphemos waved to a pair of crewmen shouldering huge sacks. They glanced up from their crouches and slogged toward him. "Drop them." The men heaved the bags off their shoulders and onto the rocky beach. Euphemos plucked at the ties then stuck a hand in, pulling out a scroll.

Just then Alkibiades walked up to them. "What booty have you plundered from the Syrakusans?"

Euphemos answered quickly. "The name of every Syrakusan, tribe by tribe. Their complete muster roll. We captured their only ship afloat and it was running these from a temple to the city."

Nikias turned to Alkibiades. "Seems your soothsayer was correct. We did capture all the Syrakusans." Nikias snapped the scroll from Euphemos' hand. "Now if we could only fight our battle on parchment, we may be victorious." Nikias looked out at the mouth of the harbor to see a solitary freighter with Kilikian markings carve through the swells turning directly for the merchant quays. He made his excuses to Alkibiades and Euphemos and began his walk. Beyond the freighter he caught sight of a fast trireme tearing through the water, its oars glinting in unison, flying the violet pennant of the *Saliminia. What is the state trireme doing here? Why now?* He kept moving toward the docking freighter. The Kilikian's hull ground along the quay, planks squealing until shore-men grabbed the fore and aft ropes tossed from aboard and threaded them through the dock rings, finally heaving it tight to the quay. Hiero jumped from the freighter, not waiting for the brow-plank to be lowered, so very anxious to report to Nikias, and to be again in the company of his friend and master. He was a reluctant spy.

"Master, I have word from…"

Nikias cut him off. "Not here." He walked them off the quay and up a path to

Nemesis

a copse of trees. He wished for shade. He insisted on isolation. He eased himself down onto the soft patch of grass that circled one of the trees, his walking stick wobbling in his hand. "Now sit and tell me what you may."

Hiero sat and leaned back against the trunk of an olive tree. "Athenagoras sends his greetings, and his thanks."

Nikias smiled. "And what else does our Syrakusan friend have to say?"

"He assures you that there are many friends of the Athenians in Syrakuse. He also wanted me to convince you that he will do everything in his power to move the assembly toward accommodation with Athens." Hiero stretched his arms out and yawned, waiting for Nikias to speak.

"Can you convince me?" Nikias laughed. "Did he convince you?"

"Master Nikias, this man truly will work to assist us. What I cannot tell you is if he will be effective in this work. Enthusiasm is no substitute for skill."

Nikias laughed even louder. "Hiero, the philosopher." He collected himself, erasing any remnant of a smile. "What did you see? What did you hear? What is the state of their city?"

"Do not become cross with me when I say what I will say. Lamakhos is correct. If we had attacked quickly, we might have taken the city. But now, after a summer of preparations, this will testify more difficult." Hiero cleared his throat waiting for Nikias to say something; he did not. "There is a man called Hermokrates who, more than any one man, has been responsible for the renewed diligence of the Syrakusans. He has organized the building of forts, has extended the city walls, and dispatched embassies to the Sikels and others in an attempt to bring them into an alliance."

"You and Lamakhos are easily fooled. If we had attacked, and if we had been victorious, what would that have gained us? A few dead Syrakusans? We have no cavalry to exploit such a victory, nor do we possess the implements of siege. And do not forget the monies that such a siege would require. Lamakhos does not think a day ahead."

Hiero shrugged. "What should we do?"

"We should sail for home, but that will only bring disgrace upon us all. Circumstances and our fickle citizens force us to retrieve some scrap of victory, or I, along with our other generals, will be censured." Nikias face grew pale, either from the thoughts of a trial in Athens or from his persistent nephritis; both assaulted him constantly.

Hiero sat silent and confounded. A messenger barreled up the path shouting for Nikias. Hiero stood up then braced Nikias, helping him to his feet. Nikias raised his walking stick and waved it at the messenger.

"General, you must come to the command tent at once. Official couriers from the Assembly bring vital news and instruction."

"Ah, the *Saliminia*. I pray that they have reconsidered and are recalling the fleet. Who knows? Perhaps the Spartans have broken the peace?" He commenced the long walk toward the camp, keeping an eye on the high pennant marking the command tent. The messenger sped off, allowing no inquiries and providing not a hint of the specifics of the new orders. Still he hoped for the best. Throughout his life his devotion to the gods always testified to his piety and enabled his luck. He had come to expect their help. A spring returned to his step. Hiero, noticing this, smiled.

By the time the pair had reached the outer precincts of the camp, the crowd of men could easily be seen surrounding the commanders' tent. "Make way for the general," shouted Hiero as he knifed his arm ahead, parting the soldiers that had jammed their path. Guards on either side of the opening slapped spear against shield in salute. Nikias stepped in leaving Hiero behind. Inside he found Lamakhos and Alkibiades in conference with two others, men from the *Saliminia*; men Nikias knew.

"General Nikias," acknowledged one of the newcomers named Epikles. "The Athenians send their good wishes."

"And I humbly accept them. But I am certain you did not undertake so difficult a journey to deliver salutations. Our Assembly is hardly so gentile." Nikias removed his petasos hat and smoothed back what little hair that remained.

"We have come also to escort Alkibiades, son of Klinias of the deme Skambonides to Athens." Epikles stood back to reveal Alkibiades. The once proud general appeared wrapped in melancholy, uncharacteristically silent, and eyes downcast.

Suddenly Nikias' mind whirled with the implications. His enemy had been recalled just as he brother had predicted. Now only Lamakhos stood in his way from bringing the fleet home. Dark thoughts soon overwhelmed his short-lived elation. *How would the Assembly react?* "Are there no orders from the Assembly?" He directed his question at Epikles.

"I have no other message or any additional tasks other than to conduct Alkibiades and the men on this list to Athens for the inquiry." Epikles handed the scroll to Nikias.

Nikias pulled it open and quickly read the names. No surprises. Theodoros', Meletos' and Demostratos' names were marked prominently, with a few others, all associates of Alkibiades.

"One thing I will tell you, though, and it is nothing more than a bit of advice. Athens grows anxious of news from here, news of victory. You must give them something to rouse their spirits, for their mood is dark and bitter. May the gods help any commander who returns empty-handed." Epikles looked to Alkibiades. "We must leave on the tide. You will have time for your servants to pack up your belongings." He began to exit the tent but stopped just inside. "Oh, yes. The Assembly instructed me to clearly pronounce that you may sail in your own trireme. You are not under arrest."

Alkibiades began to follow Epikles but stopped before Nikias. "It seems your friends in Athens have been busy. Beware Nikias, or you may be next." He snapped the tent flap open and stepped out into the sun.

Nemesis

Chapter 15
Thurii – Late Summer

The modest Athenian flotilla cruised into the harbor at Thurii, a final stop in Italia before crossing the Ionian Sea for the mainland of Hellas. The *Saliminia* back-watered, allowing Alkibiades' trireme to dock first, ensuring he would make no dash for the open sea. Epikles, the commander of the *Saliminia*, had been charged with a most delicate task; he had to deliver Alkibiades for trial without placing him under arrest. No heavy-handedness and certainly no leg irons or armed guards. But he knew the man would try to ditch the escort before reaching Athens, and he could do little to restrain him overtly. Yet, all the while Alkibiades seemed resigned to his fate, even anxious to finally defend himself before the Assembly. Epikles felt somewhat assured seeing both ships docked, and their crews disembarked. He sent his contingent of marines to patrol the waterfront, all the while keeping both eyes on Alkibiades and his comrades.

"Epikles, am I permitted to speak with the locals?" asked Alkibiades.

"There is no need for sarcasm. You are a free man. You may speak with whom you like." Epikles, although schooled in the illusive talk of diplomats, had scant patience for dealing with Alkibiades. If it were up to him, he would have shackled him in the hold and sailed straightaway for home. This dainty approach unnerved him, but it was forced upon him by the Council in Athens, for they anticipated a coup if Alkibiades was arrested outright. More than this they feared his return at the head of the army.

Alkibiades and his friends bounded down the brow-plank and onto the dock in a most carefree manner, laughing, boisterous, and unnaturally cheerful. "We have quarters prepared for us. The marines will lead the way." Epikles and the officers of the *Saliminia* hung back, waiting for the others to make their way to the inn, not far from the waterfront. Alkibiades halted at the first stall he came to in the waterfront emporeion where a seller of oil lamps waved his goods before the faces of the Athenians as each one passed by. He spoke with a young boy, asking him questions and laughing; he could charm anyone. The boy sped off, but Alkibiades and his friends lingered at the lamp vendor, lifting one lamp then another, holding each to the light, tracing the etched figures with their fingers, bickering over price and finally returning each to its place amongst its brethren. Epikles, frustrated at this prolonged bout of shopping, waved the marines on. He felt sure he and his officers could contain Alkibiades, after all Thurri was a small town and the ships were secured. Where could he go?

After almost half an hour of inspecting lamps Alkibiades decided he had seen enough, so he ambled over to a perfume stall. Just as he began to uncork a small jar, the boy from the lamp vendor, exhausted at the end of his run, trudged from an alleyway. He exchanged whispers with Alkibiades, who slipped him a coin. The boy handed him a small single spouted lamp with the figure of Eros carved into it and returned to his stall while Alkibades lingered sniffing perfume, one vial at a time.

Epikles finally stepped up to him. "We should move on now to the inn before it grows much darker."

Alkibiades nodded. He began to walk away from the stall, a vial of perfume still in his hand. Epikles and his officers forced their way in front, determined to lead the way, and allow no more delays.

"Two obols for that one," the vendor barked out, waving his hand.

Alkibiades stopped short. "I forgot I still had this." He shook his head as though he was cross at his own absent-mindedness and turned around, heading back to the stall, holding out two coins. Just as he handed the payment, a wagon pulled by a pair of donkeys severed access to the main street that the squad of marines had taken. The wagon, piled high with fleece, blocked Epikles' view. He pushed it, rolling it forward enough for him to slip around it. Alkibiades was gone. So was the boy.

*****

Kleandridas sat upon his dining couch most comfortably, but Hipponoidas and Aristokles remained standing, arms crossed and in silence. "I am curious as to how you found my house?"

"You are not so anonymous, Kleandridas. It seems everyone in Thurii is familiar with the hero of the Tarentine War." Alkibiades artfully spun compliments into his speech, especially if he needed something. Today he did indeed need something. "So here we all are, men exiled from their motherlands. Men betrayed by their fellow citizens." He smiled as he scanned the faces of Aristokles and Hipponoidas, finally settling his eyes on Kleandridas once more.

"They will search for you. And if they bring enough money for bribes they may find you. Men here in Thurii are not rich. You may become a new source of revenue for them." Kleandridas snarled at the two Spartans. "Please, will you two sit." Finally Aristokles and Hipponoidas reluctantly took to their couches.

Alkibiades dropped a large purse upon the table in the center of the andron. "I think this will assuage any poverty of the curious."

"Keep your money Athenian. I was not exiled for accepting bribes. That is a calumny devised by my enemies in Sparta, as reviled a charge as impiety seems to be in your city."

Alkibiades felt a bit uneasy now. What could he offer, if the Spartan wanted no money? A servant entered with a bowl of water. Alkibiades dunked his hands then toweled them dry. The servant backed out of the room.

"Where will you go? No subject of Athens will take you in, and Persia is a long way off." Kleandridas sipped from his kylix, Aristokles and Hipponoidas following his lead. They barely touched the wine to their lips though, and did not hide their distaste for this Athenian. Kleandridas proved more subtle.

"I would think Argos," replied Alkibiades.

"Really? Will the Argives prove more a friend to you than to Athens?" Alkibiades did not answer. "Of course there is always Sparta."

Alkibiades knew that this option, a very dangerous one, was the only one

Nemesis

truly open to him. It would be more than difficult to gain Spartan trust. "How could I go about petitioning for a letter of transit? My family has long and ancient ties to Sparta through the family of Endios."

"Ah, Endios. I know of him. A good man and well thought of in Sparta. But he is not a king and only one of the kings could grant such a letter. They have power over all the roads and highways," Kleandridas stated. "Do you happen to know any Spartan kings?"

Alkibiades laughed. "I've but seen one and only briefly at Mantinea. We did not speak at all. He seemed a bit preoccupied."

Kleandridas laughed also. "Mantinea you say. And you do not recall my dining companions?" Kleandridas turned to the two Spartans. "My friends, you did not leave much of an impression on our guest."

Hipponoidas spoke up. "Our infantry could not advance as quickly as your Athenians retreated. Still, the Argives remember us—the ones who still live, anyway."

Kleandridas looked to Aristokles while addressing Alkibiades. "It just so happens that the brother of King Pleistoanax is seated beside you."

Alkibiades grinned. "The brother of a Spartan king in exile? And what service could an exiled Athenian provide to the king's brother in return for such a letter of transit?"

"There is nothing that we require," Aristokles replied.

"Let us not answer so quickly," said Kleandridas.

Alkibiades, more relaxed knowing he was in the company of exiles like himself, felt compelled to inquire. "Outside of Sparta looking in, men marvel at your Good Order. No civil strife. No violent transfer of power. Is this not truly the case? Why has she discarded so able a group of men?"

"Contrary to what we tell the greater world, there is always contention in Sparta. The two ancient houses of the kings were in years past from different villages, and in those distant times fought as outright enemies until Lykourgos, as wise as he was, divided rule between them—the Eurypontids and the Agiads. I hesitate to admit that this rivalry still exists. It cripples us. As you know, we Spartans are exceedingly deliberate, even when united. Any division in purpose exacerbates this circumspection. It most certainly benefits Athens."

Alkibiades nodded, squeezing his chin between his finger and thumb, imparting an aspect of rumination. "Tell me then: What could you have done to merit such a harsh sentence, Kleandridas? Indeed, what could your two companions have done to injure Sparta?"

Kleandridas chuckled under his breath. "Come now, you must know. It was by armistice with your city that I was accused of being bribed by Athenians. Arkhidamos, father of the present king Agis, used the peace Pleistoanax and I brokered between our cities as an excuse to levy the charge."

"A serious offense, crafting peace," said Alkibiades. "You must have a great affection for Athens?" His sarcasm, although pointed, stirred no offense—at least with Kleandridas.

"Quite the contrary, but I coldly appraised what could be gained or lost through another battle. We had, as you may recall, defeated your army and secured the Peloponnesos. We put you in check. What more could we hope to gain by continuing the war?"

"But why was Pleistoanax reinstated?" Alkibiades held out his empty kylix for a refilling. The wine steward obliged.

"Like it or not, the Ephors are required by law to read the stars every ninth year. The kings are judged not by men, but by Zeus. Heaven recalled him." Kleandridas sipped. "Unfortunately this ritual cannot be applied to non-royals like myself."

Alkibiades looked to Aristokles. "Pray, what fault could the Spartans have found with you after their victory at Mantinea?"

Aristokles hesitated then answered. "Insubordination." One word. No embellishment.

Kleandridas came to his defense. "He disobeyed the command of an idiot. Being the brother of Pleistoanax hardly helped the matter, though."

"Insubordination, you say." Alkibiades arched his brows. "Very un-Spartan-like."

"His insubordination was the cause of your defeat," replied Kleandridas. By now even he had succumbed to the wine. "But of course that blockhead Agis, resembling his more blockheaded father, could not admit his mistake. The Ephors were forced to side with him." Kleandridas sighed. "Which, I suppose is correct. On the battlefield the king is supreme. He must be obeyed." Now he shook his head. "Even if it means certain defeat."

Hipponoidas stood. "Kleandridas, I do not dispute what you say, but only question in what company you say it." He glared first at Alkibiades then Kleandridas.

"Agis' stupidity is no state secret," countered Kleandridas. "My dear friend Hipponoidas, you speak wisely. I will keep silent on this. But there is one thing I'll say for Agis: He certainly knew how to pick a wife. Without a doubt, the most beautiful woman in Sparta." Now he raised his kylix. "A drink to our queen."

Aristokles and Hipponoidas barely raised their cups. Alkibiades, on the other hand, reached for the ceiling with his. "I will always drink to a woman, and doubly so for one as beautiful as you say." He emptied his kylix with two breathless gulps.

Now to buffer the wine, Kleandridas called for the servants to bring in platters of bread, fish, figs and cheese. The conversation turned from the politics and graveness of survival to the triviality of weather and the games at Olympia. Wine continued to be drunk and serving trays replenished. A single flute-girl reposed in the far corner of room upon a low tripod stool, motionless, eyes shut, only the barely perceptible flutter of her fingers imparting any hint of life; a cascade of notes softly rebounded off the hard andron walls. Alkibiades, quite at ease with such gentile surroundings, engaged in talk as though Kleandridas was a life-long acquaintance.

Nemesis

Kleandridas, in return, did nothing to dispel this notion. But with Hipponoidas and especially Aristokles it was different. After almost an hour they had relaxed enough to unfold their arms, and nibble economically upon a bit of bread, their responses to questions and observations limited to not much more than a nod or frown.

Someone pounded upon the exterior gate. Even from deep within house and behind the closed door of the andron, shouts penetrated, mixed with more rapping until one of the servants burst into the room. "Master Kleandridas, there is a squad of Athenian marines at your door."

The flute-girl's melody continued to waft throughout the room, but everyone looked to Kleandridas. Alkibiades' smile had fled; he massaged his wine cup nervously. Aristokles and Hipponoidas, for the first time this evening, reached for their wine with smiles.

"Gentlemen, excuse me." Kleandridas, almost double Alkibiades in years, moved slowly to rise, using his Lakonian staff as a prop to gain his feet. By the time he had crossed the length of the andron, his back had finally straightened. Once in the courtyard he allowed a servant to assist him. As he walked, he could see the swirling torches of the Athenians just outside his gate, reflecting wildly off bobbing bronze helmets. His servants guarding the entrance parted, allowing him access to the intruders.

"What can I do for you gentlemen?" Kleandridas spun the end of his red Spartan cloak around his left arm.

A tall Athenian pushed aside the armored marines. He too wore a himation cloak, but one of fine embroidery, glistening in the torchlight. "Sir, my name is Epikles of the Athenian vessel *Saliminia*. We are searching for several escaped criminals."

"Criminals, you say?" Kleandridas stepped back, waving Epikles forward. "Please enter my courtyard—but leave your soldiers outside. Those weapons and that armor are all so unsettling." His servants grinned at these remarks.

Epikles turned to the captain of marines with a cautioning hand. He followed Kleandridas into the courtyard. "Thank you, sir."

Kleandridas shook his head. "Are these criminals Athenians?"

Epikles paused uncomfortably then answered, "Yes they are."

"You do know that I am Spartan?" Kleandridas smiled unseen in the dimly lit courtyard.

Epikles felt more than foolish. "I do now, sir."

"Would it seem likely that a Spartan would assist any Athenian? After all, we are mortal enemies, are we not?" He laughed. The Athenian did not. "If it were not so late, I would invite you to join me in a cup of wine." He rubbed his knee. "But I am old, and my legs pain me, imploring me to put them to bed."

Epikles began to walk to the gate. "*They* pain me also," he said, pointing to his chattering squad of marines, "and *they* too, wish to be in bed."

Before Epikles reached the gate, Kleandridas called to him. "Athenian, what can you tell me of these men?"

"Sir?"

"What have they done?"

Epikles shrugged. "They are accused of blasphemy."

Kleandridas grinned, tight-lipped. "This must be a very serious blasphemy if you have sailed all the way from Athens in pursuit of them?"

Epikles opened his mouth but checked his speech. "Sir, I beg your indulgence." He exited, merging with the squad of marines.

Kleandridas stood still, watching the torchlight dance on the adjacent houses and recede as the Athenians moved on. It took him awhile to cross the courtyard and re-enter the andron. Hipponoidas and Aristokles appeared as two bronzes, cast solid and unmoving upon their couches, while Alkibiades had lured the flute-girl to his couch and had exchanged her flute for a kylix of wine. Once she caught sight of Kleandridas she snatched up her flute and hustled back to the corner stool.

"Your countrymen must hold you in quite high esteem. They dispatch search parties at this time of night for you, led by a trierakhos of the Athenian navy." Kleandridas winced as he lowered himself onto his couch. "My knees do ache," he admitted, beneath his breath. "Alkibiades, do not fret over them. I will ensure that you go undiscovered." He sipped a bit of wine then sighed as he leaned back. "But there is one favor I would ask of you."

Chapter 16
Katana – Autumn 415 BC

 Endymion knew today felt different from the moment the gray dawn-light brought hazy detail to his world. Unlike other mornings, when chilled air of autumn enticed him to huddle in the embrace of his bed, the hum of activity had roused him. As always, it seemed to him that everyone knew what was going on but the infantrymen: rowers toiling in gangs under the supervision of shipwrights swabbed the long hulls of the triremes with pitch; men from the quartermaster company ushering teams of slaves humping foodstuffs onto every warship. By the time he had shaken Tisandros from his sleep and the two had scoffed down a breakfast of yesterday's bread and heated wine, rumors had tantalized them. Finally, after a summer of dallying, they would attack. Finally, they would sail against Syrakuse.

 The order came down from Stump by late morning that all were to draw three days rations, check their panoplies and bundle them up. Each man became fired with prospect of action. At sunset they would be on the ships, he said. He did not say to where. He need not. Every one of them knew it was Syrakuse. As the early morning air had reminded them, winter grew nearer, and none relished the prospects of enduring it in their make-shift city of tents outside Katana. No, Syrakuse—replete with hard roofs and soft beds—-had a certain allure, even if it meant they would have to fight for it.

 As the sun slipped behind the walls of the city, Endymion threaded a length of sinew through his worn sandal while fumbling with a scrap of ox-hide. His wife had spoiled him. His fingers worked blindly, as though they lacked any sensation, needle and patch, rarely intersecting. Tisandros, a fisherman by trade, and daily practiced in mending his nets, grabbed the work from Endymion. "You are lost without a woman." He pulled the sinew through his clamped lips, threaded the needle, and without a glance moved his hands over the sandal.

 Endymion pulled out a whetstone from his wicker battle pack. "I suppose I must return the favor?" He reached out and plucked up Tisandros' scabbard, sliding the sword free. He spit on the stone and began drawing it along the two foot long leaf-shaped blade.

 "I'm surprised there is any stone left." Tisandros tossed the sandal, repairs completed, to Endymion. "You spent hours grinding your sword. It must be razor sharp?"

 They both joked about their idiosyncrasies, the nervous habits all men exhibit when consumed by anticipation. Others in his platoon, like school boys, stood at the harbor's edge skipping stones; some, tension compounded by unexpended energy, had bouts of wrestling escalate into brawls; one man stalked the shoreline, spearing imaginary enemies day long. Night couldn't arrive soon enough.

 Now when Endymion looked up at the harbor, the scene had calmed. Men paused it seemed, to draw one final breath before departure. Over the sea to the east, the horizon steeped dark while stars flickered one after another into sight. The reflections of the triremes wobbled murky upon the swells. Torchlight sprouted up across the fleet. "Here they come." He pointed down the beach to the entourage of Athenian officers which had halted before a large boulder. This would be their speaking platform. Even before the salphinx sounded, the men instinctively collected around the boulder. It was near to Endymion. He would, for once, be close enough to these generals to actually hear them speak, and not rely on his own officers to convey their words.

Nikias, aided by Hiero, ascended to the peak of the boulder. "Men, gather round.'" He waved them forward. "Tonight we board our ships. Tomorrow we make our camp in the Great Harbor of Syrakuse." He had to wait for several minutes for the chatter to exhaust itself. "Some of you may be concerned. Some may say, 'how can we disembark, in the face of an enemy? They will attack us before our feet step upon dry land.' What if I tell you that we will sail into their Great Harbor unopposed then select our landing site, also unopposed? Would you still be so concerned?"

From the sea of grumbling and muddled shouts and single voice rang clear. "How is this possible?"

Nikias fought the urge to grin. "Because the Syrakusans will be here."

After the shock of his statement and the delirium it produced had subsided he explained to them how he had sent spies to Syrakuse, to lure their army here to Katana. "They think, since we have not attacked them, that we are afraid of offering battle. This contempt works in our favor. So we shall sail now, with night to cloak our fleet, into their harbor, erect our camp and force them to battle when and where we choose."

This speech, from the old man who most of the army had begun to ridicule as feeble and slow to act, transformed every one of them into fervent supporters. The entire expedition, revitalized, clambered aboard their transports.

Endymion hauled up his battle pack and bounced along the beach to transport, catching up to Tisandros. "It will all be over in a day."

Tisandros smiled. "Perhaps two."

The fast scout ships sliced out of the harbor first, followed by the *Amynta*. Nikias, with drama in his stance and helmet cradled in his arm, acted as an auxiliary figurehead to the warship. The sea spread inky, its voice reflective, echoing each oar stroke in a soft whisper, but the shore line, close and to starboard, loomed dangerously dark indeed. No moon. With all torches snuffed they would be difficult to eye from land and sea. By midnight they had passed the abandoned town of Hyblaia, marked out by a few towers that poked up in silhouette against the sky. The indistinct coastline soon transformed into the coarse profile of the cliffs of Akradina, slicing across the sky. Waves slapped the rocks. They cruised on, no flutes or hammers, only their years on the sea substituting for the row-master's cadence. Endymion lay back on the decking, pillowed by his shield, forming the stars into shapes of both men and gods. Now a gust slapped the trireme, rocking its hull and prodding the men topside with its chill. Endymion pulled his cloak tight to his neck

Nemesis

while Tisandros rubbed his crossed arms.

"Get up," whispered Tisandros.

Endymion, without a word, knelt, his eyes following Tisandros' outstretched arm. Ahead he saw the scout ships veer starboard then vessel after vessel peeled right, following the scouts. Endymion rose up as they passed by Syrakuse. No one, not even a lone sentry looked down upon them from the city's battlements. This great promenade of so impressive an armament advanced unnoticed. Ahead the Great Harbor opened immense and circular like a necklace of an Olympian goddess, Ortygia to the right one clasp and Plemmyreion to the left the other. Night continued to conceal them. Straight on he spotted a few vessels already beached and signalmen scurrying along the shore with marking torches. By dawn all hulls began drying on the beach.

Before the sun had risen much Endymion managed to gobble down a hunk of bread soaked in wine. Soon after he joined the gangs heaping stones on the promontory of Daskon, fortifying the one spot along the deep harbor shore vulnerable to attack. Others, mostly rowers and slaves, dragged sharpened pilings made of tree trunks to the water's edge and began planting them in the shallows. "The old Athenian has thought of everything," said Endymion as he heaved another rock upon the pile. Exertion combined with the mid-morning sun had warmed him. For a moment his thoughts brought him home. He imagined he piled border stones on his eastern wall. His chest expanded with a breath, the smell of turned earth filling his nostrils. Wood-smoke scudded by on a breeze. He could almost hear his son Antiphemos calling him.

"Endymion," Tisandros shook him by the shoulder. "I think they have arrived." Towards the sacred hill of the Olympeion, streams of dust stretched skyward from the road. "Cavalry."

Here and there from within the thick wall of dust dark figures of men on horseback emerged. They ventured no further than the outer precinct of the temple, made wary by the two companies of Athenian hoplites angled in formation just south of the river Anapos. "I wonder if they enjoyed Katana."

"Come on men, keep to your work. It'll be another day until the Syrakusan army arrives." The Athenian lokhagos prowled the expanding wall, offering encouragement and a hand, when needed, to heft larger boulders into place.

Nikias, too, roamed the growing fortification. He waded into the harbor directing the placement of palisade timbers. From there he took to his horse and rode out to the hoplites guarding the river. With the sun at its zenith, the men halted for a meal, but Nikias did not.

*****

Afternoon began to slip into evening and with it the day's gentle warmth of autumn gave way to darkness and its chilling winds. Nikias continued to patrol the encampment. Hiero chased after him. It proved futile. "Sir, you must take at least one meal today." Nikias acknowledged him with a nod and kept riding. He had toured the perimeter at least three times since noon, and weaved back and forth through the body of the camp more than once. Hiero, admitting that he was no military man, still could not understand the uneasiness in Nikias. The man worried about every detail. Masterfully, he had ensured they would land unthreatened, on the only ground defensible to cavalry. His ruse had even provided a day to improve and fortify their position. Only after the sun had set did he finally relent and follow Hiero back to his command tent.

"Master Nikias, we have tripe soup prepared, a cure most certain for your ailing kidneys." Nikias did not reply. Two servants helped him dismount. One handed him his walking stick, the other offered an arm as they ushered him into the tent. Once out of sight of any of the soldiers, he collapsed onto a couch, rubbing his face with both hands. "Has the pain returned?" Hiero trotted over to Nikias with a full cup. "The iatros has mixed up this posset for you."

Nikias winced as he inhaled a whiff of the elixir. First he tipped the cup against his lips. A sip. Now several. Finally he emptied the cup, wearing a puckered face. "Have the scouts returned?"

Hiero shrugged. "Lamakhos may know. He wanted me to send word once you had returned."

Nikias groaned. "By the gods, I have done what he asked. We are here before Syrakuse awaiting battle." He sank back into his couch crossing an arm over his forehead. A sigh. "Send for him."

Not long after, Lamakhos stepped into the tent. "General?"

Nikias slid his forearm free of his face to reveal a painful squint. "I beg your indulgence, Lamakhos, but the physician has slipped an anodyne into my wine and my head is heavy—."

"Rest. No need to rise. I have only a single question." Lamakhos hovered over him. From the corner Hiero observed, concerned. "Why have we not occupied the temple?"

"Why should we?" Nikias propped up his head with a pillow.

"It secures the high ground to our left. It may contain enough in gold and silver to feed our army through the winter. More importantly, it will deny such to the Syrakusans." Lamakhos sat on the edge of Nikias' couch. "I'll lead the Argives there myself. No need for you to trouble yourself over it."

Nikias shot up. "I will not risk all by desecrating the temple. Men, I fear not. The gods, on the other hand…"

"Be sensible. Do not leave the fate of our men to the fickle gods when we have it in our power to master it." Lamakhos bent to Nikias' ear. "No man is more pious than you. And do not think I am ungrateful for assenting to my plan, but I am no grand strategist—only a simple soldier. And as any soldier can see, you have relinquished good ground. I cannot stand by in silence while you squander opportunities—and lives. Athenians will perish because of that temple and its high ground now in Syrakusan hands."

"The temple is sacrosanct. This is the law of the gods, not of man. Besides,

Nemesis

its treasure will do the Syrakusans scant good if they cannot access it." Nikias melted into the deep cushioned divan, exhausted. "See to your men. This precious battle which you have so eagerly sought may manifest soon. That is what we must focus on. Not pilfering the treasury of Zeus."

Lamakhos stared at Nikias, watching his chest rise and fall laboriously. *The gods should take him,* he thought. *Take him and release us. Only then can victory fly to us unfettered.*

*****

Endymion, Tisandros and the rest of the Argives spent most of the day in loose formation south of the river, taking the place of the Athenians from the previous day. They watched the Syrakusan cavalry prance nervously in the groves near the temple hill, chasing down any foragers that wandered too far from the protection of the hoplites. Their phylarkhos Stump allowed them to kneel, with shields propped up by their planted spears, while guarding the camp. As the day slipped by, more Syrakusans filtered onto the opposite river bank, acontists at first—skirmishers armed with bow, javelin and sling—but by mid-afternoon hoplites, heavy with armor, lumbered into files.

"They're looking for us to move first," observed Tisandros.

"How so?" Endymion gulped down some water from his flask then handed it to his friend.

"They hug the river. Not even the light troopers cross it. He shaded his eyes. "Can you count their depth?"

"What?" Endymion asked.

"Their files: how deep are they?" Tisandros squinted against the sun, but the enemy formation melded to a blur.

"Sixteen men at the deepest."

"And they have just about filled the meadows from the river to the marsh." Tisandros tried to count the files, but he lost track not far into his calculation, forcing him to start over. After an hour, he quit trying.

"There he goes again," said Endymion as Nikias trotted by on his horse, his eyes remaining locked on the Syrakusans no matter which way his mount turned. "He wears me out. What is he looking for?"

"Who knows? Maybe he is having the same luck I am in my counting. Perhaps he has counted them all and refuses to accept the numbers. I would say there are more of them than of us." He turned to the sound of a galloping horse. "Here comes the other."

Lamakhos rode hard along the front rank of hoplites, slowing only when he had caught up to Nikias. Neither Endymion nor Tisandros could hear the words, but they witnessed, without doubt, a vigorous conversation. Nikias waved his hand across his chest while shaking his head. Lamakhos threw his arms up. "Tomorrow!" That single word bellowed from Nikias before Lamakhos kicked his horse into a sprint.

"With the gods' help it should all be over by tomorrow night. I am certain that Nikias has relented to an attack. What else would Lamakhos want from him?"

Tisandros rubbed the dirt from his knees as he rose. He looked up. Dark clouds rolled in from the sea, obliterating their shadows. The wind gained. Masts wobbled and ships pitched in the building swells. Gusts scuffed up the loose, dry earth. "I think we'll be wet before this one's over. It is that time of year," he added.

Night arrived early, relieving the Argives. They ate. They watched the enraged sky. Still no rain. The Argives, Athenians, Mantineans and the rest hunkered around their fires, flames squashed by the wind, each offering predications for the coming day. Many thought the inevitable storm would abort the battle. The less optimistic reckoned only a delay. The seasoned ones knew they would fight. Night proved long, sleep not so.

*****

Midday and they had been in formation since sun up. Endymion's' phyla anchored the extreme right of the phalanx, his file occupying the last spit of solid ground outside of the marsh. He peered left, down the undulating line of the formation, past his fellow countrymen and the Mantineans to the center where Nikias stood before the front rank surrounded by battle-priests. From the far wing he could see phalanx spit streams of men—slingers and bowmen—out into the empty expanse between the two armies. From the Syrakusan side also sprinted acontists. It was like a street brawl. No discipline. No cohesion. Men scrambled this way and that, launching missiles and ducking away before any could be returned their way. They might as well be tossing clods of dirt at each other.

A cheer welled up from the Athenians in the center; the sacrifice was good. All along the line men pulled down their helmets and hoisted shields. In the rear almost half the army had formed up into three sides of a square surrounding the slaves, attendants, cooks and other non-combatants, and the baggage train as a precaution against the Syrakusan cavalry. "Why couldn't we draw that duty," said Endymion, directing his friend's glace rearwards with the tip of his spear.

They'll be in the shit soon enough," replied Tisandros, "plugging holes, and pushing the faint-hearted onward." The salphinx blared. All the semaphoroi poked their flags high into the air then tilted them toward the Syrakusan line. Thunder rumbled far off in the mountains. The sky hung heavy above as rain began to spit down upon them. "Let's get on with it." He yanked his close-faced helmet down and strode ahead, trying to keep pace with the files on either side. Endymion followed, for the most part keeping his eyes on Tisandros' back, watching the shoulder flaps of his linothorax jog up and down with every step. Reluctantly he would steal a glance of the on-coming Syrakusans every so often until his belly knotted. Now the Dorian paian shook the air, roaring from the enemy lines. His Argives, not to be outdone, commenced the paian also; friend and enemy alike sang the hymn to Kastor. Whom would the god favor?

By coincidence the Argives had marched to a common cadence, each step magnifying the crunch and clatter of armor and leather, imparting rhythm and percussion to the advance. Endymion caught himself humming. Suddenly, sight,

Nemesis

sound and even taste became overwhelmed. Tisandros and all the other front rankers heaved into the Syrakusan line, releasing a roar of squealing bronze and grinding metal that overwhelmed the senses. Once the initial shock had rippled through them the uproar of battle rushed in to surround them. Overhead a forest of spears clattered and pinged, banging off helmets, shields, metal and flesh. Without thinking he drove his shield into Tisandros' back, the man behind him doing the same as the ranks compressed and the officers urged them on. "Push!" the one word command echoed a thousand times over across the formation. Men thrust their shoulders' deep into their shields and into anyone in front, friend or enemy. Some slipped. Others howled in agony, not from wounds but as muscles failed, or bones cracked under the multiplied heft of contending warriors.

Tisandros, his spear hand exhausted, dropped it to his side, using the shaft as a crutch to keep his feet. Endymion noticing this gap, plunged his spear into the enemy rank blindly, drew it back and lunged forward again. He had no target, only a mass of bobbing helmets and jumbled shields.

Now, eerily, the two formations, separated. Men re-hefted their shields, while attendants scurried forward to drag away the dead and wounded. The front lines stood less than a few of meters apart.

Tisandros, sucking air furiously, turned to Endymion. "This will take a while."

Endymion stared at the smile beneath the cheek pieces of his friend's helmet and watched the rivulets of blood twist down the bronze until it dripped free. *This is an immense duel, not a battle*, he thought as he tried to reconcile the quiet pause now with the chaos of moments past. The salphinx blared. Men yanked their shields up from the ground, but with less enthusiasm. Until now the rain had fallen unnoticed, but the clouds hung lower, discharging a sheeting torrent, turning a contused and bloody earth into a quagmire.

Tisandros looked at Endymion. "Don't let me fall," he pleaded before facing forward, brandishing his spear.

Again the salphinx shifted. Ranks tightened as each man edged into the shadow of the man's shield to his right. With two long strides the walls of shields collided again. Files compressed. Endymion could see the hoplite to his left shoving forward, feet spread wide, fighting for purchase on the slippery earth, all the while puffing out, "Push-push-push." Suddenly thunder crackled almost directly overhead. The sky opened. Rain gushed down upon them. The man in back rammed his shield into Endymion, almost toppling him. With two wild strides he regained his balance and heaved forward. From down the line he heard the command, "Push!" For a moment the Argives gathered themselves then rolled forward. The enemy seemed to slip, giving a bit of ground. "Push!" came the order once more, punctuated by a flash of lightening then a boom of thunder.

Endymion could feel it. His men began to secure momentum while the Syrakusans let it slip away. With every command or fortuitous peal of thunder the Argives gained ground while the Syrakusans lost some.

*****

"Sir, we are breaking in the center. And the left flank!" Dionysos, too young to fight, had been employed as a runner. He hung on the mane of Hermokrates' horse as he delivered his message.

"Tell Sikanos and the others to retreat. My cavalry will protect them." He drew his kopis sword free of its scabbard, whirling it over head. "Rearguard!" he yelled out. The three ilai of Syrakusan cavalry began to form into battle rhomboids, point forward, ready to charge into the flank of the Athenian phalanx if they pursued their retreating infantry with too much zeal. In the downpour all commands proved hardly audible; even the piercing wail of the salphinx became muted. He watched his blocks of infantry fracture and disintegrate under the Athenians' advance. His infantry seeped away from the phalanx, still maintaining discipline, but in the center, across from the more experienced Athenians, he could see men tossing away shields before breaking into full sprints.

"The center!" He kicked his horse sending it into a gallop toward the heart of the battlefield. Without hesitation his company followed, filtering around and through their panicked countrymen on foot. Athenian light troops cut down some of his Syrakusans as they fled, spears and javelins sprouting from his men's backs; even the enemy hoplites started to break ranks to enter the chase. Blinded by greed they ignored the closing squadrons of Syrakusan horse, intent to hack down enemy infantrymen before pausing to strip off their armor.

Hermokrates bore down on a solitary Athenian javelineer, who crouched over a fallen Syrakusan, twisting the shaft of his javelin until it unstuck. Now the Athenian rolled the corpse over with a kick and began to unfasten the muscled cuirass. Frustrated by buckles, he sliced the straps free, and unhinged the breast-plate. Hermokrates swung his kopis high then let it plummet down in an arc, cleaving the man's shoulder open. As he struck, the Athenian turned, his eyes wide and pleading, as if in supplication. He crumpled. Hermokrates hacked away until his own arm went limp from exertion. All around his cavalry had cut down the greedy; men isolated by their avarice. He reined up, wiping the rain water from his eyes. The meadow had turned to soup, the Athenians back-stepping into formation, presenting spears and shields to Hermokrates and his cavalry.

His cavalry reformed for battle, but he knew it was over. Ahead of him the Athenians seemed satisfied with winning the field if not the loot, and behind him the large portion of his infantry had stumbled back to the Elorine road and began the long slog back to the city. The storm had doused the rage of Ares, and the ambition of the enemy. He sat upon his horse, pelted by rain, watching the enemy melt into the brume.

"Master Hermokrates."

He looked down. Dionysos, soaked and slick with rain, stood beside him. "What are you doing here?" He did not wait for answer. "Get on." He pulled the boy onto the horse. "Hold tight," he commanded. Gently he urged his horse forward

Nemesis

through the mud, not wanting to lame the beast, but indeed desiring to get Dionysos to the city walls and both of them to a dry, warm house.

They rode along the Elorine Road, thunder roaring, rain drenching them. Hermokrates paused every so often to gaze out into the harbor, to sight the Athenian fleet, but only a few masts, here and there, were visible through the murk. The storm delivered a premature night. By the time they reached the city gates darkness had gripped Syrakuse along with the rampant news of defeat. "Off with you." Hermokrates kept his horse to station while Dionysos slid to his feet. "Get home to your mother and father."

His urged his horse forward, splashing through the flooded alleyways and across the puddle-pocked agora. Here men hunkered within the columns of the stoas, too spent to move on home. Thunder crackled, but farther off now. The rain slowed to a mist. Torchlight flickered in open windows. More and more wives, daughters and old men filtered into the agora seeking husbands, fathers, and sons. At the end of the market-place he spotted the generals huddling on the steps of the strategeion.

"It was the weather." Sikanos stood on the steps, helmet hooked by a finger and dangling from his limp arm. "We held our own, even in the center against the Athenians, but the thunder..." Other generals shouted out the same in affirmation.

Hermokrates boiled. "Only children are frightened by thunder and lightning."

Sikanos collapsed to a seat on the hard marble step, helmet ignored, rattling loose from his grip. "I could not keep them in line, not all of them anyway. They imagined Zeus himself had come down upon the side of the Athenians."

Heraklides nodded. "It wasn't many. But it was enough to start the others back-peddling, looking for a way out. The Athenians had us by the belt and never let go."

"Heralds?" Hermokrates walked the width of the steps leading to the Seat of Generals, surveying the faces of his fellow officers. None would meet his eyes.

"Riding out now," answered Sikanos.

"So we have no count on the dead? The wounded?" He knew it would be morning, at the earliest before they would reckon the harm inflicted upon them. Then he comforted himself with the thought that the counting proved difficult and the result of battle not so obvious. They had been hurt, yes, but they had not been vanquished. "Gentlemen, I suggest we dry off then see to our men. Gather your company commanders tonight and examine them. They should provide an accounting near enough to true. We must be prepared for the assembly tomorrow."

He led his horse away from the agora, too tired to remount, dragging his feet and kicking puddles like a schoolboy. He mulled over how he been duped. He had been out-maneuvered by the Athenians, and much too easily at that. The gods had punished his hubris and the rashness of all the Syrakusans. They were too ready to accept the words of the Katanian spy, because he told them exactly what they wished to hear. Now the Athenians patrolled the Great Harbor and controlled their most productive farmland. Solely the cavalry, his cavalry, delivered them from annihilation. Nevertheless, they stood shield to shield with the Athenians—finally offering up the field, but not from a scarcity of courage. They contended with Hellenes most familiar with war, and none more experienced, with one exception. Although in battle, where the Athenians proved competent technicians, the Spartans excelled as true artists. He wondered how the Athenians would fare against their Spartan cousins.

Even before he could unlatch the gate, his wife Phaidra, along with Kalli, Elpida and Dianthe had surrounded him, each full of tears. The ushered him into the andron—it was the closest room to the entrance and already had food and wine laid out for him; they expected him sooner. "Are you hurt?" his wife asked while trying to see past the mud and muck for any wounds. "We heard the others coming home, men up and down our street." She grabbed his arm. "Come and sit. You must eat." She immediately clapped for the servants to present him with some warm bread and wine. She knew no other way. No embrace. Certainly not a kiss. Food transmitted her love. He smiled at her. She wiped away the wet hair from his forehead and stared until he smiled but only briefly. His thoughts carried him back to the battlefield. Trance-like he gazed up, embraced by pillows and began tearing bread before stuffing the pieces into his mouth. He chewed. He swallowed. He chewed some more, even with an empty mouth, all the while fixing his eyes upward and at nothing.

Phaidra shooed the girls out of the andron and pulled a dry cloak over him. The chewing had ceased. The cloak rose and fell with each breath. Hermokrates slept.

In the courtyard the three girls hovered near the door as Phaidra departed the andron. "Let your father rest."

Kalli spoke first. "What has happened?"

Dianthe, not one to remain silent, quizzed Phaidra next. "Are the Athenians coming?" She wrapped an arm around Elpida to comfort her. "Have we been defeated?"

Phaidra shook her head while working to summon up a smile. "Do you think Father would be sleeping if the Athenians were coming?"

Elpida buried her face into Dianthe's peplos gown. Dianthe stroked her hair, murmuring, "Nothing to worry," over and over again, like the refrain from a lullaby.

Someone pounded upon the gate. Glaukia pried it open just enough to peek out then swung it open and in strode Dionysos. "I have a message for Master Hermokrates." He stood in the middle of the courtyard, hair slicked down by the rain, but wearing a dry cloak.

"Must he be disturbed?" Phaidra pleaded. "He is sleeping."

"He is not." There, braced in the doorway by his right hand planted on the frame, stood Hermokrates.

Dionysos took a few tentative steps toward him. "I have the count, sir." He handed him a marked wax tablet.

Hermokrates plucked it up and shuffled to one of the oil lamps that hung from the balcony. He squinted, forcing his sleepy eyes to focus. "Two-hundred and

Nemesis

fifty," he muttered. "Three times as many wounded."

*****

Nikias, with Hiero not far behind, strolled through the gaining mist of the battlefield, watching as men from his own taxis worked away on the olive tree. It was the tropaion, the turning point, the spot on which the battle itself had hinged and swung in their favor like a great door. Torches flickered around the trophy, guiding hammers as they nailed the discarded Syrakusan armor to the tree trunk. Bronze glistened, dampened with dew and blood. Dangling helmets ornamented the branches. Spears, driven deep into the turf stood guard around it all. The taxiarkhos, Kleonymos, approached. "Do we have a count?" Nikias asked.

"Fifty, sir." Kleonymos answered.

From the mist a small party of men robed in white linen emerged, led by Stilbides. "We are ready," reported the seer.

Nikias, remaining mounted, followed the entourage of priests into the dark and heavy air. Ahead torchlight, muted by the fog, marked out their destination. The barrow rose up from the trampled meadow, covered with the bodies of the slain Athenian and allied warriors. A procession of the army passed by, men solemnly tossing garlands, many chanting prayers. In a great semi-circle, torch-bearers ringed the base of the pyre while Nikias and Stilbides approached. Nikias took the golden cup from the priest and emptied it upon the earth, a libation to the dead. He chanted a prayer to Hermes then nodded. The attendants surrounded the immense heap of timber and commenced to poke it with their fire-brands, launching bursts of spark and flame through the stacks, silhouetting the linen-wrapped forms of men while igniting the wispy chaplets and garlands

Endymion and Tisandros ambled by the funeral barrow, finally moving off with the others that had passed by to view, trance-like, the consumption of the fallen. "He never leaves the dead behind," said Tisandros. "Be thankful he is our commander. There is none more pious."

Endymion, still gazing at the soaring flames, replied. "I'd rather have a commander who works to keeping us alive than one who tends to us when we are dead." A nearby Athenian glared at him,

*****

The last vestiges of the storm dripped from the tiles roofs and antefixes, feeding small puddles that speckled the cobbled alleyways and streets of the city. Hermokrates, along with Dionysos, made their way through the agora to the battlements overlooking the Great Harbor and the invaders. He wanted one final look at the Athenians before the assembly convened—a contemplation of his enemies without and within. He thought of his prepared speech to the assembly, how he selected, with precision, the words necessary to bolster the spirits and stiffen their resolve. In the aftermath of a defeat, this would prove difficult. He had more than expected to be greeted by Athenian heralds at the city gates by now, delivering final terms for surrender, making the upcoming session for both him and his fellow Gamoroi most difficult. *Athenagoras must be rubbing his hands*, he thought, *waiting*

Jon Edward Martin

to skewer me upon my own words. The stonework, still damp from rain proved slick. Hermokrates moved gingerly. Dionysos bounded to the top. Sunlight sliced the sky above the horizon, spilling golden upon the glistening battlements. The Great Harbor, kissed by a veil of fog was dead calm. The rattle of oars in their looms echoed over the water. He could see the Athenians, like ants, swarming over the promontory of Daskon. Cook fires dotted the strand around Daskon, but the thick mist that gripped the marsh obstructed his view deeper inland.

"They are boarding." Dionysos pointed a finger to the array of beached triremes. Men streamed up brow-planks. One then another slipped into the water, oars glinting and in unison.

Hermokrates leaned upon the stonework, extending his body as far over the wall as was prudent. He did not speak even though his mouth dropped open. A dozen or so warships backwatered in wide arcs away from shore until their bows faced toward the harbor mouth. They cruised out. More ships arced away. He kept no notice, but the battlement filled up with the curious. They all held vigil on the Athenians' curios departure. The Athenians, all of them, faded away with the morning fog.

*****

Stilbides sprinkled some incense onto the smoldering fire of the tripod releasing a puff of sparks and smoke. Nikias, as he had every single morning in his adult life, attended to the sacrifice, certain to give the gods their due. As the men well knew, he had a prayer for every occasion and today was no exception. "Mighty mover of earth and the unfruitful sea, the gods, Earth-Shaker, allotted to you a double distinction: To be both tamer of horses and preserver of ships. Hail, Poseidon, dark-haired upholder of the earth. Keep a compassionate heart, and help us who sail today." Finished with his invocation, he bowed his head, eyes closed, silently honoring the god.

Lamakhos, furious at their evacuation of the camp, waited nearby, no doubt aware that Nikias would not even speak with him until the sacred duties were complete and most probably now prolonged the ceremony to purposely annoy him. Hiero had already boarded the *Amynta,* ensuring that the servants stowed Nikias' impedimenta with care and was unavailable to fend off Lamakhos. "By the gods above and below, why do you insist on evacuation? You do realize that we were victorious yesterday?"

Nikias opened his eyes and turned slowly to face Lamakhos. "And what precisely have we won with this great victory?" His nephritis had battered him night long, leaving him exhausted. His legs had swollen and the pain in his back clawed at him. He would not wince, not in front of Lamakhos. He drew a long breath and started to walk toward the *Amynta.*

Lamakhos, with one stride, caught up with Nikias. "We could stroll right up to their walls. Their choicest farmland is in our hands. Move against them now and they *will* surrender."

Nemesis

Nikias shook his head. "I would caution against sauntering too near Syrakuse, or did you forget about their cavalry? And as for their farmland, it is well past harvest. And, of course, you *can* see their walls from here, can't you?"

"Curse you Nikias. Send a herald. They may indeed be expecting one."

Nikias kept on walking. "I know what their plans are, and surrender is not part of them—at least not yet. Their cavalry kept us from exploiting our victory. It will keep us from foraging if we stay here through the coming winter."

"And you would forfeit this ground?" I do not think they will allow us to sail into this harbor a second time." Nikias stopped at the foot of the brow-plank. "I hope they do indeed fortify the harbor. Let them concentrate their efforts here. That is what we must possess." He pointed with his staff to the high ground of Epipolai that loomed above the city.

Lamakhos could feel the passion draining from his own words. The old man, with patience, reserve, and cool logic, had worn him down. Three months ago they might have taken the city, or at least had the season with them to begin a siege. Three months ago his plan would have succeeded. He preferred to risk all at a stroke whereas Nikias employed his slow calculations—and although he did not admit so, his spies in the city. He did not relish spending the winter here in Sikelia. But what else could he expect from the old man. Nikias irritated him with his deliberate approach to war.

Hiero scrambled down the brow-plank to help Nikias; he initiated an overly boisterous conversation while surreptitiously bracing his master with a hand, ushering him away from Lamakhos. Nikias, once on board, remained at the stern with the pilot while Hiero, anxious to look ahead, worked his way through the squad of marines to the bow. Men onshore heaved into the hull of the trireme as the rowers dug their oars deep and pulled hard. The keel scraped free of the bottom and the warship pitched from side to side, gliding through the flat water of the Great Harbor. Nikias stared back at their cobbled fort on the point of Daskon, watching the last of the shore crew hop into their skiffs. Beyond the fort and deeper inland, the hill of the Olympeion rose up, the imposing temple dominating his view. He could see men of the Syrakusan garrison scrambling atop the precinct walls, all seemingly staring back at him. Once the last Athenian vessel had shoved off, squadrons of Syrakusan cavalry spilled onto the beach, horses whirling. Shouts echoed out loud but indiscernible from the beach and the battlements of Ortygia off to his left. All of Syrakuse viewed the procession of the Athenian fleet as it exited the Great Harbor, bearing north, keeping the city to its left, as their enemy sailed back to Katana, and with every oar-stroke they bellowed out insults, comfortable in this moment of their enemy's retreat. Nikias studied the shoals, individual bricks in the walls of Ortygia, and with especial care surveyed the trireme-sheds of the small harbor and the unmistakable profile of the arsenal abutting the dock as they cruised by. He knew that his fleet exceeded that of the Syrakusans in both quality and quantity and theirs would present no real threat to his expeditionary force. But he also knew that the fleet alone could deliver no victory. Without internal intrigues to assist his cause only his land army could furnish such a succes. Slowly he edged his way through the marines to join Hiero. The detail of Syrakuse faded behind him in the fog. So too did the shouting.

*****

Dianthe peeked through the planks of the gate. The wood had dried and shrunk under countless summers of heat, providing suitable crevices for peeping; she could watch passers-by without having to pry open the gate and reveal herself. Outside people scurried through the street. Their neighbor Philomena poked her head out of her second story window and yelled, "What is all this?"

A young boy skidded to a stop. "The Athenians have left." He sped off. Others shouted up to her as they too hurried by. Now men, who had mustered at the agora, waiting for the expected attack, began to lumber by in full panoplia, the butt-spikes of their spears scraping along the limestone pavement, too fatigued to be buoyed by the tidings of their enemy's retreat.

For the past few days since the Athenians first sailed into the Great Harbor Dianthe had been accompanied by her parents; this memory, so very strong, stirred thoughts of the final day of Melos, alternating with reflections of the last carefree moments of her life. These pangs of emotion, once enhanced, had now been mollified by this news. They were gone. At least for now, she could again consider better times. But she grew angry. The crowds outside the gate celebrated as though Syrakuse had expelled them for all time. She knew better. Dianthe was no general but she knew the Athenians would return again and again until either side would be destroyed. *Why laugh?* she thought. *Why cavort about with chaplets of victory?* Overwhelmed by rage she shouted out, "You fools! Can't you see they will return?" She felt a tug on her peplos.

"Will Dionysos teach the sword to us?" asked Elpida.

Dianthe smiled at her sister. Elpida neither grinned nor frowned, no joy nor tears adorning her grim face. Her question confirmed what they both perceived. "I will ask." In the past she would have convinced Elpida the folly of such a needless enterprise. Neither heart nor mind could compel her to do so now.

Suddenly the latch rattled and the gate swung open. "My two little spies." Hermokrates knelt with Dionysos looking over his shoulder. Elpida wrapped her arms around him. Dianthe dipped her head and stepped back. "What's all this? I've been gone only since morning." Still, the little girl hung around his neck. Gently, he pulled her arms away and rose. Phaidra stood wrapped in a cloak just outside the door to the women's quarters, partially obscured by the shadows of the courtyard columns. No words questioned him, but her eyes implored him to provide an answer. Hermokrates walked to his wife, extending a hand and led her to a bench near the fountain. "For now the assembly is rational. That is the good news." He could not summon up the courage to go on, so he awkwardly changed the subject. "Where is Kalli?" He nodded toward Dionysos with smile.

Phaidra tipped her head back to look up at the balcony. "Upstairs. She has been at the loom since you left. It soothes her mind."

Nemesis

"And why would she be upset? They have withdrawn, after all." He waved Elpida to him. "My dear, will you fetch Kalli for me?"

Elpida blushed. "You mean for Dionysos." She sped away up the stairs.

Hermokrates sat next to his wife. "Not only did the assembly listen to all of Sikanos' proposals, they have appointed me one of the three generals."

"And this is a good thing?" Phaidra squeezed her husband's hand.

"For Syrakuse it is. Fifteen generals proved our undoing during the battle. With three, our strategy will be more coherent. And just as important, there will be twelve less mouths to chitchat about it; twelve less ways for our plans to be divulged to the Athenians."

"Is it a good thing for you, husband?"

"What is good for Syrakuse is most certainly good for me." He sat silent for a while, watching his daughter Kalli beam as she spoke with Dionysos. He thought of them both, of their future, and the future of his city. He knew his skills, unfettered by the assembly or novice generals would be employed to the utmost to secure this future. Now he looked into Phaidra's eyes. "I am to sail in embassy Sparta." She said nothing. She sniffled as she fought back tears. Hermokrates, too, kept quiet. He could think of no embellishment, no words to soften the statement he had made.

"And Athenagoras remains here?" Phaidra blurted out. She knew the workings of politics at Syrakuse.

Her question surprised Hermokrates. "And this worries you?"

"I am surprised that this does not worry *you*. Your enemy remains here in Syrakuse while you are sent away on this errand. Have you not used this very device in the past to send away less than trustworthy men? An embassy indeed!" She pulled her hand out of his and rubbed her cheek. "And how long will this *embassy* last?"

Hermokrates reached for his wife's hand. "As long as required." He took more than an hour to convince Phaidra that he was the author of this mission and that Sikanos and Pantheras would tend to his business in his absence, and of course keep watch over her and the girls. It was only when he conceded to allow Dionysos to stay behind in Syrakuse did she finally acquiesce.

The next day he rose early, before the sun, and supervised the packing of his belongings. One chiton, his silver-clasped crimson sandals, a vial of oil, and a spare himation cloak were all the items he required. Phaidra had slipped some other more personal items within the folded chiton—a string of charms that she had assembled from blue-glass, amber, tiny votive figurines of Hermes and Poseidon and a linen packet containing a lock of her hair. His servant Hilarion finished securing the hide bundle before slinging it over his shoulder. The man proved reliable and dedicated, but no matter how Hermokrates and his family tried they could never get him to crack even the slightest smile, so Kalli dubbed him Hilarion, or Cheerful, and the name stuck. Hermokrates snapped up his petasos hat from the peg near the chamber door and followed Hilarion out into the still dark courtyard. Oil lamps flickered near the gate. Phaidra, Kalli, Elpida and Dianthe all were up and ready to say farewell. Even Glaukia had managed to pull herself out of bed before dawn. He was glad of the dark.

It masked his tears. He kissed his wife then Kalli and hugged little Elpida but when he got to Dianthe he knew that she would not offer or accept a silent parting kiss.

"Master Hermokrates—"

"Call me Father," interrupted Hermokrates.

Dianthe, eyes still downcast, hesitated a bit before looking at him. "Father, will the Spartans come?"

"That is a strange question, daughter. Why of course they will. Why do you ask such a thing?" Hermokrates meant no patronizing, but his voice was laced with it.

"We on Melos petitioned them too. They never came." She looked down again.

Hermokrates kissed her on the forehead, turned and walked through the gate. Glaukia pushed it closed slowly and fastened the latch.

Chapter 17
Katana – Winter 414 BC

Endymion squatted under the shelter of the tent, shoving bits of wine-soaked bread into his mouth while outside Tisandros toiled in the rain, scooping out a ditch with small jagged stone. He gouged and clawed at the soil, so desperate to carve out a channel that he hardly noticed the blood as it streaked from his hands, thinned by the rain. The storm pelted them without respite, miring the camp pathways and flooding every inch of dry earth beneath the army's tents and canopies. Inside, Endymion ate, cold and wet, listening to the thud and scrape of his friend at work as he attacked the ground with his make-shift shovel.

"That's it!" Tisandros flung the tent flap open and waddled in. He crossed arms and rubbed away the chill, water dripping from his bearded chin while he watched his friend finish off the bread. "The ditch is done." Even the ground inside the tent had turned to muck, so he squatted also, unwilling to sit.

"Here." Endymion whirled a blanket over his friend's shoulders. He poked the small fire with a stick then blew carefully on the coals. Flames licked the pot. "A bit of hot wine will help you." He studied the pot, waiting for steam to rise before sprinkling in some barley pearls. "That's the last of it," he said as he crumbled a thumb-sized hunk of goat cheese into the posset. He snapped up a wooden cup and dunked it in the pot. "Drink this."

Tisandros accepted the cup, wrapping both his hands around it, letting the wine warm his fingers and sting his cuts as he sipped. "Can he really hope to hold the games in this?"

"You speak of Nikias?"

Tisandros held out the empty cup. "Who else would convene such a farce? We've built the camp, the walls—even new roads. We won't drill anymore and he knows it. He conjures new distractions for us." Endymion filled his cup and handed it back. Tisandros gulped it dry. "As long as we are busy we'll have less time to grumble."

Endymion shook his head. "He's got every shovel man and stone-hauler working on the stadeion and the hippodromos. Why doesn't he have them build us a dry hut?" He smacked the mud with the palm of his hand.

Tisandros, still wrapped in his blanket, began to shiver. The pair, confined to the tent, rocked back and forth as their legs grew tired from crouching, while they sipped wine and exchanged complaints. After an hour or more, the incessant patter of rain finally ceased. Tisandros grinned. "Come on. Let's get out of this swamp and watch the games." He shuffled out of the tent, uncoiling from his crouch as he cleared away the flap and peered up at the bright patch of clouds that masked the sun. The rain had indeed paused, but the relentless wind continued to scour the meadows. He pulled the blanket tight beneath his chin with his fists and trudged off toward the stadeion.

Still inside the tent, Endymion continued to stoke the fire, rubbing his hands over the flames as he stared down at his mud-encrusted sandals. He clawed a bit of mud into his hand, rolling it over and over. He sniffed it. "Smells foreign," he said as he flung it back onto the ground. "This is not my earth I fight for." He rose slowly. His back throbbed and the damp chill gnawed at his stiff ankles. It did not take him long to abandon his fire to chase after Tisandros.

It seemed this abatement in the storm lured others from their hovels, all seeking diversion and relief from their discomfort, each seeking an opportunity to dry off. He easily spotted Tisandros, his wobbling gait hardly concealed by his dragging blanket. The droves of men slogging toward the stadeion appeared more like refugees than soldiers—there was no flash of bronze, no brightly colored war chitons, only lumbering forms dappled by mud and illuminated mutedly by lead-gray skies.

The stadeion had been scraped flat, with only a single low hill slope adjacent for seating, unlike Olympia or Nemea where graded slopes ringed the entire 200 meter courses. Even with this modest capacity the stadeion slope appeared almost empty; it held only a smattering of spectators, five-hundred at best, in Endymion's quick estimation. Thousands had preferred to ignore Nikias' attempt at morale building.

"Look! It's that Mantinean." Endymion pointed to an immense man in the blocks, poised to run the hoplitodromos.

"Yes, it's Aniketos. I'm certain of that. No one else in the army is so huge, or so swift." Tisandros spread his blanket on the wet and matted grass. "It's mostly dry," he said, offering a seat to his friend.

Only five competitors lined up in the blocks with the starter poised behind, clutching the lines that would drop the rods and release them. Now the sun began to peek out from behind the clouds, its light glinting off the shields and helmets of the runners as they crouched, ready to burst off the line in the race in armor. The starter tugged the lines taut, the rods dropped and they sprinted off, five of them chest to chest for the first 50 meters or so. At 100 meters only three contended, pulling far ahead of the trailing pair. At 150 meters Aniketos had opened a lead that only a stumble could relinquish.

"I am truly glad he fights with us and not against us," said Endymion.

Tisandros swiveled his head right and left. "Mostly islanders," he observed. Endymion shrugged. "I say the spectators are mostly islanders, and not many of them. Old Nikias can't even compel their attendance at his games, and they all serve Athens."

Endymion stroked the muddy ground with his fingers. "They miss their own dirt."

Chapter 18
Sparta – Winter 414 BC

Gylippos sat upon the gently banked hill that flanked the dromos watching the boys of the Wild Boars sprint in relays. They churned up the dust of the 200 meter track, their bouagos picking out a champion as each group tore across the finish line. "They're better, you know."

Gongylos the Korinthian turned. "Better than what?"

"Than us—I mean when we were their age. We make it harder for them, testing them against the false memories of our own accomplishments. For as I remember, my bouagos drilled us for an hour, but when I became one and headed an agelai, I would boast that we had actually drilled for two and forced it upon the new boys. We raise the expectations and they achieve, but our vanity and self-importance deny it. In fact, I would say the older a man gets the less he acknowledges the achievements of youth. It is human nature I suppose."

From the hill crest a man descended through the grove of twisting olive toward them. The sun hung low in the sky directly behind him, so neither Gylippos nor Gongylos could distinguish his identity until he bounced down the slope and into its shadow. "Hermokrates," shouted Gongylos as he rose. Gylippos flicked a glance over his shoulder at the approaching figure then stood. "My friend, it is so good to see you again." Gongylos embraced the stranger. He turned, and fumbling a bit with his words, added, "This is Gylippos, son of Kleandridas."

Hermokrates nodded and extended a hand. "I am honored, sir."

Now Gongylos motioned for them to sit. "I would guess that you are here in Sparta for the very same reason I am."

Hermokrates nodded. "To petition Sparta for help against Athens?"

"Specifically to petition on your behalf, and add the weight of Korinthos and the other allies to your argument. But do not worry. I have been working on my friend here all day. He has heard from me every detail of the Athenian plan for the conquest of Sikelia and how both Sparta and Korinthos must dispatch a force immediately."

"Sir, I do not come here to disrupt your leisure time with my badgering." Hermokrates turned his attention to the dromos. "Is your son running today?"

Gongylos winced and was about to speak when Gylippos said, "I do not have the honor of a son as of yet sir. I watch the races, for it is my duty: I observe the training of all our youth."

"So it is as people say. Spartans, when not at war, devote their energies to the development of the new generation. What a peculiar practice." Hermokrates scanned the slopes surrounding the dromos and noticed other red-clad Spartans clustered about in small groups, some chattering away as others pointed to this boy or that.

"Peculiar it may be, but is applied with earnest. Our youth revere their elders, but we in turn, cherish them," Gylippos said with a bit of pride. "And by that I mean every Spartan takes an interest in every boy in the Agoge. In Sparta we are all fathers and they are all our sons." He studied the Syrakusan for a moment then spoke. "Do you have a son?"

"The gods have blessed me with daughters only." Hermokrates leaned back upon his elbows into the cool grass and continued to watch the jagged lines of boys tear down the running course. From across the bowl-shaped dromos and voice boomed out. A single Spartiate stood up and yelled to the bouagos, "Send the winners from each group to the barracks and keep the others in races." The incentive proved masterful. The boys ran so much the faster now. Each winner pumped his hands high and trotted off to the south road toward the Agoge barracks. The losers reassembled, ran and produced a new winner. The groups shrank.

"And who is that man?" Hermokrates asked.

Gongylos replied quickly. "Aegisilaos?"

"You are correct, my friend. How did you know?" Gylippos smiled.

Gongylos pointed discreetly. "The limp—and his voice. The timbre of it is unmistakable."

They watched as Aegisilaos shuffled down the slope to the floor of the dromos, slightly dragging his left foot as he descended. He embraced the winners of the races and encouraged the losers to try all the harder next time. His voice rolled up the hillside, laden with enthusiasm. For a moment he stared directly up at the threesome then turned his attention once more to the herd of boys.

Hermokrates was truly impressed by this sight, a Spartiate and a noble one at that, devoting such time to a scruffy bunch of youth. It pained him too; he knew he could never watch his daughters in such sport, at least not at his home city. Here in Sparta though, he was well aware of the gymnastic training both girls and boys were entitled to receive—and endure. The competition appeared fierce, but not as violent as he was led to believe. Spartans did indeed celebrate victory, but in their own peculiar way they inspired the defeated.

"I have no son, yet I have a hundred," said Gylippos. He pointed to the racing packs of boys down below.

"I have no son, yet I am surrogate father to an exceptional youngster at Syrakuse." Hermokrates thought now of Dionysos and how he wished he could have taken him upon this voyage, to present him with pride to these new acquaintances, but prudence had dictated that he should leave Dionysos behind—his eyes and ears while absent from Syrakuse.

"Then we are both fortunate." Gylippos paused in his conversation, his eyes locked upon Aegisilaos. The man began walking across the floor of the dromos directly toward them. He halted at the base of the slope for a moment before heaving himself upwards. Gylippos, aware of his struggle to ascend with his injured leg, rose and walked to meet him.

"No, no," shouted Aegisilaos. "Remain where you are."

Gylippos slowed but kept moving toward him. They met mid-slope and out of earshot of Hermokrates and Gongylos.

Nemesis

"Entertaining the strangers, I see." Aegisilaos grinned at the pair and nodded. They smiled back.

"They were interested in how we train our youth." Gylippos returned only small talk.

Aegisilaos stared at the ground for a moment then looked up, not at anything in particular, but appeared to track the scudding clouds overhead. "I know you do not think much of me, Gylippos."

"Why do you say this?"

"Because I am Eurypontid and the brother of Agis."

Gylippos sighed. "To be honest with you, I really do not know you. But I do know other Eurypontids and what they have done to my friends—what they have done to me."

"By the gods! I did not choose my parents. I most certainly did not choose my brother, the fool that he is." Aegisilaos checked himself and lowered his voice. "Judge me for who I am and what I do."

"My judgment, in the scheme of things, means little."

"Damn you Gylippos! You make it very difficult. I came here to offer my support." Aegisilaos shook his head.

"Support?"

"Yes. The ephors are considering sending a Spartan officer to help the Syrakusans. Of course Likhas and Pleistoanax have nominated you." This bit of news stunned Gylippos. He said nothing. Aegisilaos continued. "And of course my brother will do what he can to prevent this. He has put forward Astyokhos."

"And why do you tell me this?"

"My thick-headed friend, you are the best one for this mission. I may be a Eurypontid, but I am Spartan first and foremost." Aegisilaos grabbed him by the shoulders and shook. "They look at this assignment as a diversion, and a distraction to the invasion of Attika, and this may work to your benefit. I will ensure your appointment by nudging along Astyokhos' assignment to the command of a mora. He will embrace this idea, for his ego could not neglect and ignore such a prestigious commission. He will lead a division of Spartan soldiers on a fool's errand while you will deliver an ally and inflict harm upon our enemy." Aegisilaos started to walk away, but stopped. "My brother fights your appointment only because it is you. Anyone else and he would not bother himself over it."

*****

"The Athenian traitor wishes to speak with you." Likhas hurried them both along as he spoke, past the wooded edge of the acropolis, toward the agora and the Ephorion.

Gylippos shook his head. "Why me?"

"Perhaps because you were trained by Brasidas" He stopped there, not mentioning his father Kleandridas—a good man exiled for the misdeeds of others.

Gylippos tightened his lips, exhaling audibly through his nose. The two Spartans strode past the boundary stones of the agora, finding themselves amongst the flimsy stalls and tilting booths of the Perioikoi vendors. Here and there Spartan woman strolled about, confidently inspecting pottery, or baskets of figs, or tugging on hares strung up by their lifeless hind legs. Cowering helot slaves shadowed them all, ready to lug away any purchase.

"Come on," barked Likhas as he bounded up the stairs to the Ephors dining hall. He pushed the door aside. The hinge pins grumbled against weighty oak. Unexpectedly, the gloom of the Ephorion doused the bright light of midday. Their eyes, though, adjusted quickly. The almost square room had walls painted in muted ochre and these were lined by seven dining couches, elevated slightly by an ankle-high platform. In the center of the room, framed by the couches, a jagged mosaic of Apollo and Hyakinthos stared up at them from the floor. The room went silent.

Gylippos quickly scanned the couches and the men reclined upon them. He recognized, one by one, each of the elected Ephors: Sphodrias, Lukarios, Endios, Leontidas and of course his escort, Likhas. Absent were both kings for neither Agis nor Pleistoanax reclined upon their couches; instead Endios occupied one in company with a Spartan he did not recognize. Tellis, not an ephor but the most influential member of the Gerousia, sat alone, adjacent to Endios' couch. He scanned the room again, trying to pick out the Athenian Alkibiades, but saw, excepting the Syrakusan Hermokrates, only men clad in scarlet chitons and sporting the long eight-locked hair of Spartiates. Suddenly his eyes fell upon Astyokhos. It seemed as though they had both been summoned as Aegisilaos had forewarned.

Sphodrias greeted them both. "Likhas, Gylippos, come sit and dine here with us tonight." All in all it sounded much like a polite request, but was in fact, a firm and pleasantly couched command.

Likhas sat upon one the vacant kings' divans while Gylippos edged onto the couch of Sphodrias, feet flat upon the floor and facing Leontidas and the unknown Spartan.

"Gentlemen, my manners are amiss today," announced Sphodrias as he glanced at his dining partner. "I must introduce our guest to you both." He motioned to Likhas then Gylippos. "This is Alkibiades, son of Kleinias, from Athens."

The man smiled at them both. Now he laughed. "By the look upon your face Gylippos, you are surprised. Did you expect a bejeweled fop in purple linen?" His Attic accent, immediately discernible, was tinged with a disarming lisp.

"I certainly did not expect to see an Athenian in such modest attire," answered Gylippos quickly. He lifted the heavy kothon tankard from the tri-legged table and began to sip the wine slowly, looking over the rim at this very Spartan Athenian.

"I am, what can be described as adaptable, my dear Gylippos. I hope that you prove to be as such." Alkibiades smiled as he looked directly at Tellis. "As your son Brasidas proved to be."

Tellis grinned for a quick moment, allowing an undetected bit of pride to swell before swiftly suppressing it. "Since, through the friendship of my son and the

Nemesis

sponsorship provided by me in your father's absence, I have become very much acquainted with you Gylippos, and understand better than most what service you can render to our country." He paused to sip from his kothon before continuing. "Sparta has a mission for you."

Gylippos looked directly at Astyokhos and said, "Attack the fort at Dekelea?"

Astyokhos grinned. "I am here to impress the ephors and our esteemed representative of the Gerousia of the importance of that mission and the care that must be applied when assigning the new polemarkhos."

Of the ephors, Likhas spoke first. "I would assume that you feel you are the more qualified candidate?"

Astyokhos attacked with his answer. "I certainly will carry out the orders of my king."

Gylippos, angered by this insinuation, opened his mouth to speak but Tellis challenged, "Do you infer that other candidates for this appointment would disobey?" Tellis waved at a servant to feed the brazier with charcoal, for both the winter chill and the discussion discomfited him.

Lukarios cleared his throat. "Gentlemen, I suggest we keep this discussion limited to abilities and not deficiencies."

Gylippos could not contain himself. "Then Astyokhos can offer only silence." He inflicted his rival with a murderous stare. "And do not impugn my actions at Mantinea. I fought, and I killed, and I bled upon that field while the only actions you witnessed were the asses of the Athenians as they ran away."

Lukarios gaveled his kothon on the table adjacent. "Astyokhos, Mantinea is in the past and punishments for any misdeeds have already been meted out. Gylippos, this is something you must accept. We are here to determine what is in our country's future."

Likhas shook his head. "Why do we go on with this? We all know well that Astyokhos will be appointed polemarkhos. It is simply a matter of numbers."

Tellis could not resist. "And we all know, my friends, that good decisions are based on knowledge, not on numbers."

"And that is why Astyokhos will become polemarkhos of the Ploas mora," said Leontidas, cousin to king Agis.

"We congratulate you," said Endios, perfunctorily. "You are dismissed."

Astyokhos dipped his head then plucked his sandals from the wall peg behind his couch. He fastened them quickly and strode to the door, but halted, looking at Gylippos, expecting his dismissal also.

"Well?" said Tellis. "You have been dismissed." Astyokhos stormed out. "Gylippos, he is your wife's cousin, is he not? I can only imagine what depth of hatred he would possess toward you if you were not related." The entire Ephoreion erupted in laughter.

Alkibiades, of all found this remark most humorous and once composed he cleared his throat then spoke, "Any Spartan officer can march into Attika. Not any

136

Spartan can deliver a city from an Athenian siege."

Gylippos' eyes widened as he too sipped a bit of wine now, mulling over what was about to be proposed and how to appear to be surprised when he heard it. "Skione? Akanthos?" He rattled off these and a number more of the cities in the Chalkidike, all the while watching the face of the Syrakusan Hermokrates; he gave away nothing.

"Your mentor Brasidas has instilled in you the vital importance this region holds for us Athenians," said Alkibiades. "But there is a greater city on the island of Sikelia, a city that Athens has staked her future on reducing."

"Syrakuse," Gylippos whispered into his cup.

Alkibiades' ears proved as sharp as his mind. "Yes, it is Syrakuse."

Sphodrias placed a firm hand on Gylippos' shoulders. "This task we commend you with will require much more skill than that of a soldier. Gone are the days when men stood against men in the open field of battle to end disputes. Now we must be diplomats also. Sparta is no school of diplomacy. But you, like Brasidas before you, possess such skills —skills so ably defined by Alkibiades here."

A pair of helots entered the Ephorion, one toting a cauldron of steaming broth and the other a platter with wooden bowls atop it. They halted before Tellis and Alkibiades first, one holding the cauldron while the other dipped a bowl into it, moving from one couch to the next until all the diners had received their portion.

Gylippos stared at the Athenian. He appeared most Spartan; long hair braided into eight locks; a blood-red chiton his only garment. He had heard of this man, this most audacious of a race of audacious men, the most Athenian of all Athenians, and wondered how he could so completely and flawlessly mimic the ways and manners of a Spartan. Alkibiades rose from his couch, sitting now upon Gylippos' couch. He leaned forward. "Your father sends his regards."

This was the last thing Gylippos expected. His father had written to him, but the last note he received was delivered by an acquaintance of Gongylos past four years ago. "How is my father?"

"I would say his better days have deserted him." Alkibiades sipped and smiled at the faces in the room. With the kothon hiding his lips he whispered, "Thank your father for this assignment. And thank me for delivering his wishes to your council and ephors."

Gylippos answered reluctantly, "Then we both owe you a debt, sir."

Alkibiades, his mouth still hidden, whispered, "Consider our debts even, if you introduce me to your king's wife. I'll say this for you Spartans: you don't hide your women like we Athenians do. And their beauty should not be hidden."

"Agis is a jealous man," cautioned Gylippos softly. Still, he thought what could be more fitting than to present this Athenian seducer to his enemy's wife. "You will need no introduction from me. She is often seen strolling the agora, as most Spartan women are. I am sure she already knows of you, sir." His dose of flattery was taken by Alkibiades without complaint. The Athenian rose and walked back to

Nemesis
his couch.

Jon Edward Martin

Chapter 19
Syrakuse – Spring 414 BC

Hermokrates pranced his horse along the front ranks of the Syrakusan formation, reviewing the newly strengthened divisions of hoplites assembled in the meadows near the Olympeion. In the past it would be hours before the fifteen strategoi would even decide who would ride first in the procession of inspection, but now, with the generals' numbers reduced to three—one for each Dorian tribe—the review commenced promptly. Alongside rode Heraklides and Sikanos. Each company's commander stood forward of his files, shield propped against a thigh and spear gripped mid-shaft and pointed toward the clouds. Hermokrates stopped at each one, asking how swiftly his men had assembled, and how quickly the new men were assimilated into the ranks. Each commander answered with the characteristic enthusiasm of inexperience. That is except for Diomilos, the Andrian. He had come to Syrakuse on the invitation of Hermokrates, and had a long career as a mercenary captain on the edge of the Persian Empire. Hermokrates had placed him in charge of a brigade of picked men, a quick strike force that would be first to engage the Athenians if and when they returned. It would not be long before they were tested.

"Your men?" Hermokrates wriggled his shoulders, trying to adjust the weighty cavalry breastplate that dug into his thighs.

"Ready, sir, every one of them." Diomilos said. Now he approached Hermokrates. "But I don't know about the rest of the army, sir." He flicked his glance down the front ranks. "They're shimmying and shaking like a bunch drunks waiting to piss."

Hermokrates scanned the ranks. The Andrian was right. Even the officers bobbed in and out of formation. Heads turned this way and that. Spears rattled and shields thudded upon the ground. Men argued.

A man on horseback tore down the road from Epipolai, waving an arm overhead while screaming Hermokrates' name. The three generals galloped off to intercept him and as they sped by each company the Syrakusan formation began to dissolve. "Hermokrates!" The scout reached out and grabbed the bit of Hermokrates' horse to keep them close. "The Athenians are coming from Euryalos. It's their entire army!"

Hermokrates face went grim. "Did you see them?"

"I fought with them. That is until I was ordered to warn you. They have overrun the fort and are swarming across Epipolai."

"Come!" Hemokrates retraced his way back to Diomilos, ordering him to follow the messenger back to Epipolai.

Diomilos said nothing. He raised his spear overhead and began to jog after the scout. His brigade funneled down to three columns and hustled behind him. Hermokrates called for the herald to reassemble the army, and soon afterward the salphinx blared out the command. The files, although wavering, shifted back into

Nemesis

place. The company commanders stepped forward, receiving the orders from the herald as he raced down the front rank. Now the block formations of the phalanx began to disintegrate and stream north along the Elorine Road toward Epipolai. Hermokrates raced ahead of the infantry with his cavalry, soon overtaking the columns of Diomilos. They passed by the marsh and followed the road that split away from the coast and the city toward the temple of Herakles that huddled at the base of the escarpment of Epipolai.

    Diomilos insisted that he and his picked brigade ascend first; for it was for tasks such as this that his unit was recruited, so they led the way up the steep and narrow road, through the rambling scrub and onto the heights. Once on Epipolai in the place called Fig-Tree he could see the vast army of the Athenians formed up beyond the groves and beginning their march toward the northern precincts of Syrakuse. He expected to find scattered groups of foragers and scouts. He swallowed hard and tried to summon spit but his mouth was dust dry. "Come up!" he yelled. "Come up quickly and into files." He marked out the front line of his formation by striding back and forth with spear out-stretched, shouting to each file officer to form his unit.

    The Athenians easily spotted Diomilos' men and without delay wheeled their phalanx directly toward them. For a moment they melted into the groves of olive and figs, broken forms of men shimmering between trunks and amongst foliage until finally the trees exhaled the massive enemy formation within half a stade of Diomilos' coalescing ranks. From across the diminishing space of 100 meters, a salphinx blared out. The Athenians broke into a trot.

    "Stay tight boys." Diomilos coolly slipped into his place in the center of his scanty phalanx. He calculated the length of the enemy's front rank, easily three times his own. They would be double flanked. Only Hermokrates and the cavalry could save them now. "Steady legs, boys. Steady legs."

    The Athenians thundered into them, spears clattering and shields thudding. They held, but only for moments. From both flanks the Athenian phalanx curled its grip around Diomilos' men, squeezing them tighter as it carved them up. The men in front struggled furiously, hoping that by some turn of luck they could advance through the Athenians and gain a respite. The men on either wing heaved their shields frantically this way and that, unable to defend against the whirling onslaught. If one faced right, he was struck on the left and rear, if turned to the left, spears skewered him right and front. Here, on the margins they fell in heaps.

    Finally Hermokrates and his cavalry burst onto the heights and began to form up into their diamonds. As soon as the first ilai jostled into line he pointed to the open ground between the battle and the city walls. "Wheel right!" His squadron of horse galloped right then spun left, hard into the flank of the Athenian hoplites. They were tough and disciplined. Not many fell out of the tight and trim ranks. His cavalry could do little more than slow down the enemy advance, for throughout the depth of escarpment he could see light troopers—archers, slingers and javelineers—hustling toward him and the flank.

    His squadron bounced and buffeted along the Athenian shield wall until forced into the fight he tried to avoid. Archers rained down arrows while slingers, well-spaced, whipped their bullets into his squadron, giving the javelineers courage enough to advance. They tossed their short battle javelins, aiming to wound and disable the horses. His men ran them down, and cut them up before more arrows and sling bullets forced them back. This parrying of forces went on for more than an hour.

All the while Diomilos' dying brigade held onto their small piece of Epipolai as the rest of the Syrakusan infantry ascended and formed up. Exhaustion from the double-paced march and steep climb left them with little stomach for battle, but it did provide a distraction, delivering the picked brigade from certain annihilation. They fought their way across Epipolai, trying to reach the walls of Syrakuse before the Athenians.

*****

Endymion and his company of Argives had turned the right wing of the Syrakusans and commenced to roll up their lines, but unlike the battle at Mantinea there was no prize, no loot, no alluring conduit to the enemy's camp, only the cliffs, and again so unlike at Mantinea, his men wheeled left and cut down the enemy from the rear. He was fourth in his file, so his job was nothing more than to push every now and then, and to nail any wounded on the ground with the butt-spike of his spear. It was dirty, exhausting work—nothing glorious. With each step they edged closer to Syrakuse, but as he moved on, the wounded at his feet thinned until the earth was bare. They halted at the edge of the grove peering at the walls of the city. From here he watched the last of the Syrakusan infantry scramble through the open gateway while their cavalry prowled not far off, suppressing any pursuit.

"One more tangle and that should do it," remarked Tisandros. He spiked his spear and dropped his shield to rest against his knee. "They have no stomach for it."

"A bit different than Mantinea, eh?" Endymion, for the first time since last summer, felt victory was close. He might be in Argos for the harvest.

"Vastly different. There are no Spartans here." Tisandros meant it as a joke, but it stuck deep in his gut, silencing him.

"I have to hand it to old Nikias. He had them fooled. Their entire army was on parade near the Great Harbor, traipsing about, expecting us to land there. By the gods, how did he know they would be out of the city and away from these heights? We have them trapped now and look down upon them."

"Those are sturdy walls and we have no engines to breach them." Tisandros rubbed the sweat from his brow. A salphinx trumpeted them to reassemble. "Time for dinner, I think." The pair turned around and faced the long stretch of the plateau. Battle dust hung thick. Within the haze dark figures moved about while sunlight glistened off bobbing bronze helmets and iron spear-tips. They trudged along slowly, melding into the stream of men ahead, hoping to find the camp already erected. By now wagons had been hauled up through the pass and food began to be doled out.

"No tents?" Tisandros asked the Stump as he passed by.

He laughed. "Tents—no. We're lucky to have food. Nikias has ordered all

Nemesis

the masons, carpenters and attendants to the spot where the Syrakusans came up. He plans on building a fort there tonight."

"We sleep outside?" Endymion dropped his shield and spear.

"Pick 'em up," barked Stump. "We set our own tents tonight. That is unless you would volunteer for rock piling at the fort?"

With a tinge of petulance, Endymion slowly retrieved his spear and shield. Tisandros smiled at him. "Why complain? Today we see Nikias move with swiftness and conviction. I don't mind working our own tents if it means we complete this siege all the quicker."

Endymion knew his friend was right. After months of inaction, this day raced by like a whirlwind delivering the prospects of victory. He said no more as they piled arms and shuffled along the wagons of provisions, snatching up their ration of bread, salt-fish and even saltier cheese. The wine steward proved generous. By the end of the first watch all had fallen into the haze of potent drink. The tents stood, not nearly as tall as they should, but they would certainly help keep the chill of the spring night off them. Through all three watches they heard the nocturnal hum of the engineers: the hack of axes, the scrape of shovels, and the strike of hammers on iron as the men toiled away on the fort. By morning, smoke hung thick in the air over the camp, seeping into every tent. Endymion expected the accustomed fragrance of bread to waft to his nostrils but it was the acrid stench of the smelter's furnace that assaulted him. He rose, rubbing sleep away from his eyes and left his tent and his sleeping mates to stroll along the edge of the escarpment where the brick manufactories and blacksmiths had set up. Beyond them a huge circular rampart topped by timber palisades had sprung up. As he approached he discerned the rectangular bases of stone towers at intervals along the fort's perimeter. It was more than large enough to hold the entire army. At what appeared to be the largest opening in the wall of the fort stood the two Athenian generals. He slowed his pace, determined to hear what these two spoke of.

Nikias leaned on his walking stick and said, "Give them a day to gather their dead."

"I'd give them less, but I won't argue with you over it," answered Lamakhos. "One more day will do them little good."

Now Endymion was but a few feet from them before they noticed him and paused their talking. "Good morning," he said with a smile as he passed by them. He kept walking, slow as he could manage without drawing undue notice, but they kept silent. He moved on until he came to the very edge of the cliffs facing the island of Ortygia. Mist filled the harbor and smudged the torchlight upon the city's battlements while dawn just began to cut across the horizon above the sea. Behind him the trees glowed in the orange light of the furnaces. The army began to rise.

*****

"Twice they have defeated our army." Athenagoras wasted no time in revealing the obvious to the Council. "We have an alternative to battle." Shouts exploded from the tiered benches of councilors. Athenagoras descended from the bema after an hour long speech. He had pointedly reminded them of past events here in Syrakuse and in other places more distant, and how protracted sieges had left the besieged with little to negotiate with. He insisted that to save their city they should sue for peace now.

Hermokrates' faction still held majority, but barely. He had little to offer them in contrast, but tried to encourage them that help would soon arrive from the Peloponnesians. He did not mention Sparta. The one thing his visit to that city had done was to reveal to him the less than united approach the Spartans had with regards to the war. They had promised him help. In his heart he could not count on it.

The entire session had been demoralizing. First the word of the Athenian herald and his truce for the recovery of their dead had begun the discussions. Soon the count had been delivered—three-hundred dead and double that wounded. The survivors had lost any battle-lust; courage proved a scanty commodity in Syrakuse now. And the people as a whole distrusted both the democrats and the Gamoroi. They thought of themselves as the prize of some game between the two, and would listen to anyone else—but up to now there were no alternatives.

Hermokrates filed out of the bouleterion with the other members of the Council into the crowd that had filled the agora. Hundreds had gathered. No one spoke. Blank eyes followed the leaders of the city as they shuffled down the broad staircase and melted into the press. As relatives and friends coalesced around each other, quiet bouts of inquiry erupted amongst them. Only the families of the battle dead were absent. They were on the heights carrying back the lifeless warriors who had fallen the day previous. Many had lugged jars of water, linen and alabaster flasks filled with oil for washing and anointing the bodies. They would have had more to say.

Phaidra was sitting in the outer courtyard when Hermokrates arrived. She did all to appear busy with Glaukia, planning the food purchases for the coming days. Hermokrates had scheduled two symposia, small affairs but requiring special care in planning, for above all other times these gatherings served as vital sessions of communication amongst the clubs. She fought off the anxiety, the need to rush to him, to quiz him on their fate and the fate of Syrakuse. With apparent poise she handed the wax tablet on which she had scribbled the wine list to Glaukia and smiled at Hermokrates. "How are you today, husband?" She fought to control the trembling in her voice.

He wiped his brow. "Hope is slipping away. Athenagoras gains influence with every defeat. Soon he'll convince them to negotiate terms."

"But what of your journey to Sparta? They did promise help, did they not?" Hermokrates sat next to her, hand pressed in hand, shaking his head. "They will come?" Her voice cracked a bit.

"Perhaps, but I fear it may be too late." He caught sight of a head bob in and out of view in the doorway to the women's quarters. "Dianthe, come out here." Dianthe stepped into view with Elpida standing behind. The two girls walked slowly

Nemesis

toward Hemokrates. "Why do you hide from me?"

Dianthe, quick to answer, said, "We were not hiding. We did not wish to disturb you, sir."

Hermokrates laughed. "You did not wish to disturb me," he repeated in a mocking tone. "Come and sit. You only bring joy to me." Dianthe and Elpida sat on the edge of the fountain facing Hermokrates and his wife. He smiled at them both and continued to stare at Dianthe." You have become a beautiful woman." He pondered the war and the uncertain fate of his city. "You deserve a proper husband."

Dianthe had thought often that the day would come when she must take a husband and hoped for any delay. The only eligible man she had contact with was Dionysos and he was betrothed to her new sister Kalli. She thought of him as a brother. She could only summon up a meek nod in response.

"I will talk with the father of Agatharkhos. He is a good man and his son is very bright. He's a cousin of Dionysos, you know." Hermokrates smiled gently at her as he squeezed his wife's hand. Phaidra tilted her head, which he took as a sign of agreement. Glaukia, knowing better, rolled her eyes. "Have you seen Agatharkhos?"

"No sir, I have not." She lied. She had glimpsed him on occasion when Dionysos took them on their tours of the city when they first arrived.

"Then we will introduce you to each other." Hermokrates rose up and smacked his thighs. "I'm glad that is settled. Now I must play the part of general again and ride to the gates. I will return before dark."

He kissed his wife on the head and left them all sitting and stunned in the courtyard while he fitted his armor and departed on horseback for the precinct of Apollo Temenites, the newly enclosed section of a suburb of Syrakuse. He was proud of this accomplishment, the enlargement of the walled section of his city. It would force the Athenians to double the extent of their siege walls. By riding through it, he truly understood the amount of ground they had secured. It was a small comfort. He arrived at the gate, and by rendezvous, rode out with Sikanos and Heraklides to the funeral pyre at the base of the cliffs. The army had assembled by tribal lokhos, the only time he had seen them exhibit true discipline of formation and crispness of file.

The timbers had been piled with care over three meters high and crisscrossed. Upon this, and with even greater fastidiousness, the bodies of the slain lay shrouded in linen. Chaplets and garland had been spread meticulously over all, giving the impression of a meadow blossoming over new fallen snow. Three hundred of their finest warriors had been lost, their best infantry commander, Diomilos, among them. Poked by blazing torches, the pyre crackled and flamed while smoke poured skyward. Moans and shrieks of the dead men's wives and mothers echoed back from the cliff wall. Suddenly the wind shifted, blowing in from the Athenian camp on Epipolai, forcing the pall over Syrakuse. Hermokrates looked up, beyond the roaring flames to spot hundreds of the enemy lining the heights and peering down at the fiery spectacle.

*****

The pattering of chisels upon stone echoed across Epipolai as masons hurriedly cut out base stones for the walls. Endymion, Tisandros and his company had toiled the day previous on the wall, lugging and fitting these heavy blocks, but today they wiled away their time on guard duty upon the road that slithered through the olive groves toward the northern gate of Syrakuse. Behind them ship-wrights worked on the beams and gate posts while other, less skilled ax men hacked points onto timber for the construction of the abattis. The smoke from charcoal burning furnaces wafted over the tree tops. The entire Athenian camp had been transformed to a manufactory of siege. A cheer went up from a cluster of men near the cliff edge.

Endymion glanced quickly at his friend, then handed him his shield before jogging off. A mob had surrounded a ditch, and had begun to slash at once-buried clay pipes, sending shards high into the air and releasing a torrent. "It's their water," said one of the men as Endymion shouldered his way to the ditch. They had stumbled across an exposed section of the pipes that delivered water to Syrakuse and pulverized ten meters or so. Turbid water swirled, filling the ditch.

"Dig it back." They all turned to find Lamakhos marching toward them. He waved and repeated the order. Men tore into the earth with picks and shovels, hacking away the hard packed soil to reveal more sections of pipe. "Dig it back to our wall." Lamakhos watched, grinning as the men scarred the ground and shattered the brown clay pipes.

Endymion, mesmerized by the liberated stream of water, watched as it gurgled and whirled, cutting the ditch wide, spilling over the cliff edge. He peered down at Syrakuse, at the guards along the city's battlements and upon its towers. They all looked up at the newly formed waterfall. In minutes he was back with his company, informing them all.

Tisandros called to him. "You forgot something." He rapped Endymion's shield with his spear.

Endymion pulled himself away from the crowd that had gathered around him and hefted the shield, falling back into line. He knew that, because of the destruction of the pipes, the Syrakusans might attack at any moment, so he quickly lost his appetite for chatter. One hour merged with another until midday sped past into late afternoon. They held their posts across the road, watching Lamakhos as he commanded the sappers as they cut off Syrakuse's water. He stood there all day, growling out orders, until they had destroyed more than two stades of the conduit, leaving a deep and muddy scar across Epipolai. So consumed by the work upon the pipes, Endymion and Tisandros had failed to notice how quickly the siege wall had grown, stretching on a northward axis from the Circle fort like a spoke on great wheel.

"We'll see them soon," assured Tisandros as he pointed toward the city. "They won't just sit in there, letting us cut them off."

He's right, thought Endymion. "Where is their cavalry? The Syrakusans may not want an infantry battle, but they have cavalry and more than enough to attack our men on the wall." Lamakhos had only a squad of archers protecting the demolition team at the pipes. Cavalry would have made short work of them. He gulped down

Nemesis

some water from his flask. Although still spring, the sun proved withering. He thought of the broken pipes and the thirsty Syrakusans. "How long?"

Tisandros looked up from his standing nap. "Them?" He flicked his head at the city. "Beginning of summer and they will have had enough." He pulled off his helmet and swabbed his forehead with his hand. "By Helios, I've had enough already," he said, grinning.

The shadows of the groves stretched out long across the plateau now. A cool wind swept up from the sea below. Soon the sun ducked behind the trees. "Dinner. I'm looking forward to it, my friend." Endymion saw Stump raise his spear overhead before marching off toward the Circle. They all fell in behind him in column, eyeing the handiwork of the sappers as they trudged along the ditch, following it right up to the stone and mud-brick foundation of their wall. Endymion swiped the still damp mud-brick as he passed by. The wall rambled away from him and into the gloom, marked here and there by newly fired torches and the glow of campfires. By the speed of the work he reckoned they would have this section of the wall completed within the month, but the lower section, the portion near the marsh and the Great Harbor would prove a bit more difficult.

*****

"Get up!" Tisandros appeared floating over him, fully clad in battle armor, shaking him in a panic. "They're here."

Endymion rubbed his eyes. His brows twisted as he looked up at his friend.

"The damned Syrakusans are spoiling for a fight today. They're on Epipolai and arrayed for battle." Tisandros grabbed Endymion by the arm, hoisting him to his feet. "Get your gear on. Nikias has called assembly."

Endymion crawled out of the tent and gazed up at the still dark sky. The seaward horizon had begun to lighten. What few clouds hung there glowed in crimson, announcing the dawn. "With the help of the gods we can finish it all today." He stood and brushed the dirt from his knees while searching for his greaves. Quickly he snapped these on, left leg then right, and fastened the ankle straps before struggling to don his linothorax body armor. He shrugged and twisted until it felt partly tolerable, snapped up helmet, aspis, and spear, then jogged off to rejoin his friend. His company had formed up on the right of the phalanx adjacent to the Athenian taxis commanded by Lamakhos. Reassurance swept over him seeing the crusty war veteran in command of his wing. He was a fighter, no doubt about it, with the destruction of the enemy his only thought. "With Lamakhos in charge, we will finish it all today."

Tisandros smiled in agreement. He looked left and right, his eyes peering down the straight, calm and motionless ranks of the army—veterans all. No novelty here, only routine. But across the vacant span of the battlefield, the Syrakusans could hardly keep still: helmet crests bobbed this way and that; spears rattled; shields clanged. They were barely tested in war and acquainted only with defeat. It showed in their fidgeting. Dust began to rise from the flanks of the Syrakusans. Cavalry poured in from the edges fronting the enemy phalanx.

Endymion began to laugh. "They're retreating." He pointed with his spear and shouted, "They're running back to Syrakuse."

"A curse upon their general." Tisandros slammed his shield into the ground. "No doubt we would have taken the fight today."

The Syrakusan cavalry galloped back and forth across the front line of their army, daring the Athenians to advance over the open ground. Yes they had received a small force of cavalry of their own a few weeks previous, but in no way could they match the Syrakusans—not yet anyway. From across the entire Athenian phalanx, insults flew hard and fast at the withdrawing Syrakusans. Endymion and Tisandros grew hoarse from their shouting. By midday they were once again piling stone and mud-brick along the wall.

*****

"What will we tell the Council?" Heraklides collapsed onto a stool. His empty cup struck the floor, sending echoes off the hard, dark walls.

"Tell them? Why every one of them was out there, shaking and shuffling, ready for anything but combat. What is there to say to a collection of shirkers? Delusion has induced them to think they can have both their freedom and their lives. At times such as these one is payment for the other." Hermokrates spent his anger in this single outburst before gathering himself. He breathed deeply then spoke. "We all know what would have happened if we had attacked the Athenians. We also know what will happen to our city if we allow them to complete their wall." Hermokrates paced the floor in the same manner he would stalk the front battle lines. "We must build a counter wall."

"On Epipolai?" Sikanos, by his tone disagreed.

"Through the marsh. The Athenians have concentrated all effort upon the heights. They have thought nothing of a move through there. It's closer to our walls—easier for our cavalry to protect it." Hermokrates paused, waiting for a determination from his two companions. Heraklides sat in silence. Finally Sikanos nodded. "It will mean stripping the crews from our triremes and all the men from the naval arsenal."

"We must cover almost a mile or more to cut off the line of their wall, but if we succeed, they cannot invest us." Sikanos grabbed Hermokrates by the shoulders. "I will present this to the Council. Hermokrates my friend, I think it best if you leave this argument to me, or Athenagoras may work his way into things otherwise."

Hermokrates agreed. Heraklides did not disagree. The three generals departed the Strategeion and walked briskly across the agora to the Council house, into the chamber chilled to silence by their entrance. Sikanos wasted no time in addressing them all. In short order he had convinced them of the plan. Early the following morning, while the sun still hung below the horizon, the Syrakusan cavalry led out the engineers, carpenters and masons to the edge of the Lysimelia marsh. Several squadrons of horses fanned out through the marsh, providing a screen for the laborers. At first they furiously shoveled a meter deep trench, piling the dirt and muck high to fashion a rampart. The ground proved soft. Heavy stone would sink in sections across this terrain, so as the shovel men toiled, carpenters dragged timber and

Nemesis

rough-hewn planks and commenced to throw up towers. Every so often they would look up from their labor to the cliffs above to catch sight of the Athenians gawking at them—but they remained upon their high ground for now, not wanting to test their luck against the prowling squadrons of Syrakusan cavalry fronting the marsh. At day's end contingents of darters and archers occupied the towers while a single ilai of cavalry patrolled the ditch and earthworks. Hermokrates rode out at sunset, bringing along Dionysos for an impromptu inspection.

"Damned mosquitoes," he said as he slapped one that had dug into his neck. "I should have come out here earlier."

Dionysos wanted to voice his agreement, but knew better. He swatted away the assault as best he could, all the while peering up at the Athenians on Epipolai, silhouetted by the descending sun. As uncomfortable as it proved for both him and Hermokrates, he knew the men posted out here for the night would suffer more. Mud splashed up as they trotted their horses along the ditch. Some of the archers had already begun slinging the muck over their exposed arms and legs as barrier against the swarms. The cavalry, though, would have no part in smearing dirt upon them, at least not now. Perhaps once their commander departed they would imitate the others. For now they rode by Hermokrates, exhibiting not so much as a wince or twitch as the mosquitoes feasted upon them.

Hermokrates, straining to eye the extent of the ditch and rampart through the gloom turned to Dionysos. "To your calculation, how much longer will it take our engineers to cross the road?"

Dionysos, to this point, had paid little attention to the distance they had ridden along the completed portion. The road, buried deep in shadows, could be seen only in his imagination. "Two weeks, maybe three.

Hermokrates smiled. "I did not see you today outside the Strategion." Hermokrates was certain Dionysos repeated what he had said during his estimation to Sikanos on their way to the bouleterion.

Dionysos—thankful that the gloom of dusk hid his blushing face—nodded. "Only there briefly, sir."

As they approached the very end of the day's work, they came upon a team of engineers. Some men, under torchlight, hacked tapering points onto logs, while others slid them into prepared holes on the rampart. The muddy ridge between the last pair of towers bristled with sharpened timbers.

"I think not much more than a week and we'll be at the road." He glanced up at Epipolai. "But cavalry will not do the job alone, if they decide to come down upon it."

Dionysos coughed out a single word. "Infantry?" He rubbed away the itch from his forearm.

"They won't like it, but it will take at least one tribe to guard the works."

Why does he care if they like it? It would be much easier to guard the engineers than to attack the Athenian wall, once complete, Dionysos thought. Prudently, he did not voice his thoughts, but added only a boyish question. "An entire tribe?"

    The pair made the return trip to the city in a much accelerated fashion, passing the towers without a glance, not stopping to converse with any of the engineers, cavalry, or archers on patrol. Hermokrates shouted out the watchword to the guards at the western gate. From outside he could hear the complaints as they drew back the bolt before shouldering open the huge, bronze clad gate. He rode to the house of Dionysos, escorting the boy, before turning around to retrace his path back towards his own town-house. Servants, vigilant as ever, greeted him at the gate and helped him dismount before leading away his horse to the mews.

    Dianthe peeked out through the crevice in her bedchamber door, watching Hermokrates as he lumbered, tired and yawning, across the courtyard to the andreion. Once she heard the door creak shut she turned away.

    Elpida, half asleep, rubbed her eyes. "Why are you still awake?"

    "No reason." Dianthe tip-toed back to their shared sleeping pallet and slipped beneath the single blanket.

    Elpida, now wide awake, bolted up. "You are still upset about your new husband, aren't you?" She giggled.

    Now Dianthe grabbed her sister by the shoulders. "Don't you say any more about it," she growled, her eyes ablaze.

    "Ow. You're hurting me," whined Elpida as she rubbed away the pain from her shoulder. "Don't be cross with me because he wants you to marry. Be cross with him."

    Dianthe knew she was right. She also knew Hermokrates thought only of her welfare. At his word she and her sister could have been slaves, but instead the man adopted them both, and accepted them into his family. It was the war, not her benefactor, which forced this circumstance upon her. She laid down to the sound of her sister's gentle breathing, thoughts of home flooding her mind: men hauling their boats ashore; boys and girls in chase around the quays; a family meal; her father; her mother. Suddenly her nostrils filled with the acrid scent of the funeral pyres on the beach. She buried her nose in the folds of her blanket and cried until sleep overcame her.

Chapter 20
Sparta – Spring 414 BC

Gylippos paced before the gray stonework of Brasidas' kenotaphaion waiting to meet with Likhas. The sun had just slipped behind Taygetos, plunging Sparta into blackness almost instantly. Finally, with most of his anxiety expended, he sat upon the step leading to the statue of his mentor. From around the corner a figure appeared, slow moving and with cloak pulled up, forming a hood, so at odds with the warm air of this late spring evening. The man hobbled a bit as he leaned upon a walking stick. "Beautiful night," he said as he approached. Gylippos expected the voice to match the man's apparent frailty, but it sounded incongruously robust.

I suppose it is," agreed Gylippos. He leaned back, his eyes catching the stars as they flickered on, one by one, in the heavens of the emergent night. He drew a deep breath. As the man stepped nearer he discerned the crimson of his himation cloak, marking him not as a helot, nor a Perioiki, but a Spartiate. "Do I know you, sir?"

The man let loose a chuckle then a cough. "Seems not." He halted a few steps from Gylippos and leaned upon a struggling plane tree, its trunk barely the thickness of a man's arm. "Hmmm. I needed to rest." He reached to his side, pressing an open hand upon his ribs. "Ancient battle wound."

"Old father, what are you doing out so late and alone?"

"I should ask you the same. I am indeed old and well past the age to be compelled to action—of any kind. But you? You are in your prime and neither with your mates nor your wife. Which of us is the more peculiar?" The old man tugged the cloak free of his head as he bent, fiddling with a strap on his sandal, face hidden in a shadow. Before he rose up, he slipped the cloak overhead once more.

Gylippos stared, his eyes trying to pierce the gloom, but only a fleck of light revealed the man's graying beard as he turned slightly to glance at the statue.

"Did you know him?" the man pointed up at the bronze likeness of Brasidas.

"Not as well as I wished." Gylippos hung his head. "Not as long as I wished."

"A friend?"

"More than that." Gylippos kept his eyes to the ground, shaking his head.

"A good friend is a valuable thing."

"He was that. And I could do with his advice now. I think Sparta is desperate for it."

"One man. So important?" The old man coughed.

Gylippos looked up at him. "Yes. One man can indeed be so important."

"Then I think your friend would tell you to become that man."

From the intersection of the Aphetaid Road voices rumbled. Gylippos stood, squinting in the darkness, trying to distinguish who approached. Clearly he heard the unmistakable laugh of his friend Kallikraditas. Next to him ambled Likhas, waving his hands flamboyantly in conversation. "What took you so long?" Gylippos turned to introduce the old man to his friends. The plane tree stood alone. "Did you see where he went?"

Likhas shrugged. "What?"

"The old man I was speaking with." Gylippos marched off to the corner of the kenotaphaion and began to circle it, looking for his departed acquaintance.

Kallikratidas called out, "Where are you going? We saw no one."

Gylippos returned from behind the monument. "He leaned upon that tree, not an arm's length from me."

"You must have dozed off. A dream—that is all you saw." Likhas tugged his arm. "I have good news for you. You are to depart for Sikelia tomorrow. The Korinthians have everything ready. Your triremes are docked at Asine."

"It is good news, but why did they not tell me sooner?" Gylippos shook his head.

"Options. If the order to depart is not given yet, the ephors still hold the option to reverse their decision," said Likhas. "If they could, they would walk you right to the end of the dock at Gytheion before telling you."

Kallikratidas embraced Gylippos. "May the gods grant favor upon you and your mission. You certainly are to be envied."

Gylippos shrugged "Why is that?"

"There will be no other Spartans to interfere with you. You will wield the power of a king, not just a general."

Likhas nodded. "He's right, you know. You plans, your commands, and your actions will determine the outcome. Grab hold of it. Let them see what you are capable of."

"Then good evening, gentlemen. I have much to attend to." Gylippos smiled as he exchanged final embraces with his two friends. He trotted down the road, past the tombs of Leonidas and Pausanias on his way to his house in the village of Pitane. He fought the urge to skip like a little boy as he hurried along, prospects of adventure, glory, but particularly absence from Sparta unleashing his spirit. He found the windows dark as he approached his house. With stealth he slipped through the door to the kitchen, deftly stepping over Kanthos, who had curled up next to the hearth. He roused him from sleep with a firm poke in the ribs. The man shot up to attention without even rubbing his eyes clear or expelling a yawn. "We are off to Sikelia," he whispered. Kanthos needed to hear nothing more. He lit a small oil lamp and shuffled off to the store room at the far end of the courtyard, set to the task of packing his master's panoplia.

Gylippos, meanwhile, crept into his bedroom. His wife slept soundly, or so it seemed, for she did not move as he quietly opened the lid to a chest and snatched his triboun war cloak and krepides boots, which he stuffed into an ox-hide sack. Every so often he would glance to his wife to be certain he hadn't disturbed her. Next he groped for the figurine of Ares and the blue-glass charm he always carried into battle and dropped these into his bag. He paused at the doorway, scanning the room and his thoughts for any forgotten item. Now he stared through the dark at his sleeping wife,

Nemesis

watching her chest rise and fall with each breath and for a fleeting moment thought to wake her, but he turned quickly and left the bedroom. She lie still, clutching the single blanket tight to her neck, eyes wide open as she watched him depart.

Kanthos stood alone outside the courtyard, holding the reins of their two horses and a baggage mule that had a pair of shields slung across it, one on either flank, plus a clutch of spears tied in a bundle bristling upon its back. His wicker battle pack hid beneath the shields. Gylippos stuffed his hide bag into the criss-cross of ropes and vaulted upon his horse. As they trotted out onto the road he peered up at the eastern sky, over Parnon, in hope of glimpsing the brightening sky of dawn; night still hung potent and dark over them. They rode slowly, past the dromos and the gymnaseion, keeping the dark form of the acropolis before them. In each and every public building he passed he found boys from the Agoge sleeping amongst the columns, all assigned as nocturnal guardians to the civic precincts. Within a quarter hour they came to the theatron and soon found themselves facing the Ephorion. Before Gylippos could dismount, the door creaked open and the five ephors filed out.

Lukarios stepped forward. "We had guessed that you would know before any of us could tell you." He frowned as he spoke, but smiled after uttering his last word. "A lokhos of Neodameidois will follow and meet you in Asine. The Korinthians and other allies have assembled a squadron of triremes and contingents of heavy and light infantry." Lukarios extended the skytale message stick to Gylippos. He accepted it with a nod. "You have no time to waste. The Athenians have begun their siege walls."

Gylippos twisted the skytale in his hands while he spoke. "What are my orders?"

Lukarios grinned. "Defeat the Athenians."

Any other person, from any other city would have accepted this statement as a jest, a prelude to more serious and detailed talk, but Gylippos knew his countrymen. No joke. No embellishments. No alternatives. He turned to depart. Before he could tug on the reins, the five had silently reentered the Ephoreion. His wish had been granted, to lead an army in the field, but this was certainly not how he had envisioned it: no herds of young boys cheering him from the slopes of the acropolis; no crowds of relatives of his troops lining the road; not even the surly glance of a helot toiling in the fields as he marched past. They would ride out alone, hidden by gloomy night. *Perhaps this is better*, he thought.

"Not even enough time for a farewell from friends?" Kallikratidas walked out of the shadows Persian Stoa. Two others stood nearby, cloaked by the darkness.

"My friend, so glad you could attend our parade." Gylippos jumped from his horse to embrace him. Likhas and Tellis stepped forward, and he embraced them also. He whispered into Tellis' ear. "I will do honor to you and your son."

Tellis winked away a tear. "I know you will. And so does he."

*****

The triremes rocked in the swells, their masts swaying, as gulls landed high upon them, scanning for a meal. Gylippos walked up to a Korinthian marine who stood guard upon the entrance to the quays. "I seek Gongylos."

Without a word he pointed toward a glistening trireme flying a violet and gold pennant. Gylippos bounded up the brow-plank. Gongylos turned as he heard footfalls upon the deck. "By Cloud-gathering Zeus, I am blessed that you are here." Gylippos shook his friend. "Are we ready?"

"We wait only for a single company of Arkadian mercenaries and your lokhos."

Gylippos looked out at the white-capped swells beyond the harbor. "The weather holding?"

"It will hold. I just hope the same can be said for the Syrakusans." Gongylos lost his smile. "Every merchant that docks here says the Athenians have just about shut them in." He looked into his friend's face, searching for a response. "What do we do?"

"What we are charged to do. We sail on until there is no doubt of the events. We sail on to Syrakuse." Gylippos drew a breath. "How long is the voyage?"

"Along the coasts—two weeks." Gongylos paused after his answer, knowing what question was to follow and formulated the answer. "A week if someone was to sail directly across the open sea."

"And do you know of anyone who is both brave and foolish enough to try it?" The smile returned to Gylippos.

"We both do." Gongylos grabbed his friend's arm. "But before I depart, at the very least allow me to dine with you—and introduce you to my commander, Pythen."

Chapter 21
Syrakuse – Summer 414 BC

Nikias and Lamakhos straddled the makeshift table in the command tent, studying the map of the island. "Attack by both land and sea," insisted Lamakhos. "They will not expect us to sail into the Great Harbor once again."

The plan rubbed Nikias the wrong way, for it was against his nature to risk so much at a stroke, but he possessed no counter argument and his nephritis had flared up to a point where he lost the capacity to dispute it. He nodded.

"Excellent!" Lamakhos pushed away from the table. "I will send the dispatch to Hegasandros to ready the fleet. Two mornings hence he will sail into their harbor and attack the Syrakusan wall from the south. I will advance from the north. "

Nikias winced, his throbbing kidneys crippling his thought. He swallowed hard against the pain and watched Lamakhos stride out of the tent. Outside men cheered, followed by the receding sound of hoof-beats across the plateau. Nikias called for his taxiarkhoi to be assembled. His team of division commanders had only a single day to develop their plan to attack the wall from the north and to pin down any Syrakusans that might challenge the landing in the harbor. Lamakhos, in the meantime, rode about the camp, inciting the men with the prospects of this bold action. He required no time for long deliberations and calculation; his plans had been prepared days previous, and he waited only for the opportunity to enact them. Orders streamed away from the command tent. Contingents of allied light infantry and acontists packed up and began their march back to Thapsos, to rejoin the fleet for the upcoming landing in the Great Harbor. A single company of peltasts, men armed for speed, had been retained by Lamakhos. His scheme was to refit them as hoplites, with heavy armor, shields and dory spears, a special group of picked fighters to exploit the Syrakusan casualness in protecting their wall.

The night passed with Nikias in long consultation with the taxiarkhoi and Lamakhos. By the middle of the second watch the details had been argued out, and the long session took its toll on Nikias. But he had a day and a night to recover before they launched the attack. Stilbides mixed him an anodyne, its effect so potent he slept through the entire day and partially into the next night. Severe bouts of vomiting awakened him.

*****

Endymion stood in rank of his company at the edge of the escarpment, peering down with the rest at the lengthening Syrakusan counter wall. The rearmed peltasts jogged by them, hustling down the road toward the temple of Herakles and the open, flat ground between the heights and the marsh. At midday the Syrakusan engineers had retreated to their tents, seeking shade and rest from the punishing heat of the sun. They hardly expected so ferocious an attack at so unreasonable a time.

The peltasts cut their way through the camp, slaying many napping masons and sappers still within the tents, until the enemy cavalry and a single lokhos of hoplites formed up to repel them. The Syrakusans tried to coalesce into formation but the Athenians slammed into them, cutting up their ranks, reeling them back toward the city walls. The cavalry, stunned and sleepy-eyed, struck and withdrew in cycles, trying to slow the Athenian advance, but it proved of little worth against the swarming peltasts. Finally the Syrakusans broke and flew headlong for the city with the Athenians on their heels. The slain dotted the fields and road from the camp right up to the gates. More than half had managed to shove their way back into the city, but their pursuers crashed through the gates and began forcing their way deeper into Syrakuse.

"They may not need our services today," quipped Tisandros. A few hundred wild men may do what our entire army could not."

The Argives pressed ahead toward the very edge of Epipolai, mesmerized by the spectacle below. The screams swept up the cliffs from the city. The alarm blasts of salphinxes cut through the roar of the tumult. Now men streamed out of Syrakuse and the gates ground shut.

"It took quite an effort to expel them." Endymion said as shrugged. "We will be next." And he was right. The semaphoroi raised up the flags for each tribe's taxis in synchronization with the trumpeting of a salphinx.

Tisandros peered down the ranks to the left, catching sight of the Athenian general Lamakhos. *Glad it's him again*, he thought. The army began to wedge itself into the narrow roadbed that descended to the fields below, delivering them into the Syrakusan camp and the outworks of their wall. But as they tromped down and with their view unhindered by hills or trees, they watched the Syrakusan army pour out of their city; not a mere lokhos of a few hundred men, but thousands jostled through the gates, spilling into block after block of phalanx formation. It seemed their midday nap was over.

Endymion's heart raced as he watched the ground between the Syrakusans and his Argives shrink. His wing would, by the oddity of the terrain and the disorganization of the Syrakusans, impact the enemy long before the others. His men started to raise the paean, the battle-hymn to Kastor. Eerily, the same chanting echoed back at them from the Dorian Syrakusans. The shouting rose in crescendo. Across the final few feet his vision filled with frantically wobbling helmet crests, bristling spears and glinting bronze. Their shield walls collided, war-cries turned to groans as men on both sides heaved all their weight into the othismos or shoving match. Endymion found himself almost cheek to cheek with a Syrakusan. Both men had their spear arms pinned low and in a tangle of shields. He could smell the man's sweat and the food he ate for breakfast. They shoved into each other, the bronze of their shields grinding and squealing. The Syrakusan spit a mouthful of blood through the eye slits of Endymion's helmet. He winked his vision clear, loosened the grip on his entangled spear and with a single swift draw had his sword free and into the belly of his opponent. The solid wall of shields began to dissolve; the Syrakusans to his left broke away, fighting their way back to the city walls, but the companies locked in combat directly in front had become detached and began to retreat across the marsh, heading

Nemesis

for the towers of their counter-wall.

Endymion, Tisandros and their company of Argives, urged on by their phylarkhos, Stump, broke out along with the lead element of Athenians in pursuit across the marsh. The soggy earth slowed both sides, forcing the Syrakusans to abandon their retreat and stand and fight. About twenty of the Argives, along with a dozen or so Athenians, Lamakhos amongst them, found themselves isolated in the marsh, about to engage Syrakusans more than double their number.

*****

Hiero blew into the tent. "Nikias! They are attacking the walls."

Nikias rolled off his sleeping pallet, doubling over in pain. He gripped his side, swaying as he fought to stand upright. "My armor."

Hiero stood frozen in disbelief—but only for a moment. He scrambled to pull the corselet off its rack and quickly fastened it around the unsteady body of his master. With helmet on, greaves fastened, and shield in hand Nikias leaned on Hiero as they emerged into daylight and the chaos of the Circle. Only a squad of archers had been left behind, exempt from the battle, to act as guards—the remainder consisted of workmen, cooks and bread-bakers, for no one had expected the Syrakusans to attack *their* fort. Nikias, racked by nephritis and barely able to speak, summoned every bit of strength and bolted upright to begin his march towards the main gate. As he strode by he summoned any and every man to follow; blacksmiths; carpenters, bakers, cooks, shipwrights, and cobblers crowded around him. He stopped, just inside the main gate, peering up at the archers that were frantically slinging arrows at the approaching Syrakusans.

"Cover us!" He yelled up to the captain of bowmen. He turned to the makeshift company of defenders that surrounded him. "Everyone! Torches! Fire all the timbers. Every scrap of wood we have gathered to build our walls is to be set ablaze."

They all scurried about, pulling the cold torches down from their sockets on the walls and towers, poking them into the smelters' furnaces to set flame to them. Others fashioned some out of the stacks of firewood cached about the blacksmiths' hearths and potters' kilns. Nikias grabbed a torch from Hiero and they moved through the open gate toward the stacks of siege timber.

"Pull it into the palisade!" Nikias directed a group of men to drag timber and planks to the spiked poles planted amongst the grove of trees as a deterrent to cavalry. The others soon realized his intent. They hauled and dragged the combustibles into the abattis, poking, packing tinder into the mix as quickly as they could. They needed no orders to ignite it.

*****

"We can't leave him!" Endymion shouted to the others in his company. He looked to them then back at Lamakhos and the tiny group of stranded Athenians as the Syrakusans reformed for an attack. "He can't run. Neither should we."

Endymion sloshed through the marsh, sweating rivers beneath his armor. He pulled up next to another Athenian hoplite who glanced his way, revealing a muddy face with a long slice of flesh hanging from beneath his left eye. Endymion nodded. The Athenian nodded back before facing toward the approaching enemy.

"Why are you always running?" Tisandros stomped in beside Endymion, splashing them both. Mosquitoes swarmed around their heads in clouds. "We'll even this up. Look."

Endymion turned around to see his fellow Argives splashing through the marsh toward them. Beyond them smoke billowed up from the heights; his heart sank. But before he could assess what conspired above, he re-faced the Syrakusans. Things *were* even. The Syrakusans, realizing the longer they waited, the more reinforcements would swell the ranks of the enemy, finally charged.

Unlike the immense clash of the two phalanxes earlier, men now jogged forward, arms hanging low from fatigue, moving toward death with both exhaustion and resignation. No formations, only small groups of four, or three, but mostly pairs, locked in combat, oblivious to their fellows. Endymion and Tisandros stood shoulder to shoulder, eyeing the three Syrakusans that strode toward them, no spears in hand, only battle swords, already swathed in black blood and swinging low from their blood-drenched arms.

But before the nearest could swing his sword overhead, Tisandros buried his own spear in the man's groin, doubling him in a howl. The other two, ignoring Endymion, slashed and thrust at Tisandros in succession, driving him backward. With two more flailing cuts they had hacked his neck wide open.

Endymion plunged his xiphos through one man's ribs. Blood spewed from his silent open mouth as he collapsed, but the blade stuck, pulling free of Endymion's grip. He searched the ground at his feet for Tisandros' lost spear or an abandoned Syrakusan sword, but finding neither scooped up a fist sized stone and slung it off the remaining Syrakusan's helmet, driving him to his knees.

Endymion, looking neither to his friend, nor the Athenians, hefted his shield before running back through the marsh toward the cliffs.

Chapter 22
Thurii – Summer 414 BC

    As soon as his trireme docked, Gylippos vaulted onto the quay and ran off seeking his father. A tired looking old man pushing a cart full of rank sardines told him of the house and the quickest way to reach it; this information only cost him a single obol. The man snatched it up, stuffed it into his cheek and without pause resumed mongering his day old fish. He had not seen his father since he was a rhobidas in the Agoge, but possessed such a clear vision of him he knew without doubt he would recognize him immediately. With each step forward he summoned this recollection and tried to account for the added years with his imagination. The alleyway— an unusually straight path uphill—led away from the lower town, the agora, and the waterfront manufactories. Here the white-washed dwellings gleamed in the hot summer sun, but as he neared the top of the hill, cool breezes refreshed him while the flawlessly blue sky overwhelmed his vision. He needed ask only one more person, a young woman sweeping dirt from the threshold of her home as he passed by. His father's town-house would be around the next corner. He rapped on the gate three times then waited. After a few minutes he pounded upon it. He could hear the echoes rebounding off the walls inside. Finally the gate cracked open only wide enough for an old man to peer out. "What do you want here?"

    Gylippos wrapped his hand around the frame of the gate as a precaution. "I seek Kleandridas."

    The ancient attendant growled, "What do you want with him?"

    "I am from Sparta. I am his son."

    Now the gate slowly creaked open, revealing the attendant standing within. The man possessed a single hand, his left one missing from just above the wrist. Mesmerized by the sight, Gylippos hardly realized the broad shoulders and thick neck of the old, but singularly powerfully built man. "Please follow me." The old man shuffled across the courtyard and into the darkened andreion. "Sit. I will bring you wine." He waved at a couch thick with pillows.

    Gylippos scanned the room, and preferring to recline on the single couch that had no multitude of cushions or other unnecessary adornments, lay back in it. The room seemed cool to him, not in temperature but in spirit—a room more often empty than full. At least that is how it felt to him. The servant, good in his words, carried back a large wine pitcher and a single kothon, managing them both with his right hand only. He filled the cup and presented it to Gylippos. Before he sipped, he asked, "Is my father at home today?"

    The old man did not answer straight away but opted to first pull a small stool from the corner. He planted it before Gylippos and himself upon it, tucking his handless arm into a fold in his chiton. "Master Gylippos, your father is dead."

    Gylippos, trying to place the cup on the adjacent table, dropped it, his hand frozen open. "That cannot be. I received a letter from him but two months previous. I spoke with men who met with him this past winter."

"The Athenian deserters, I suppose." The servant began to squeeze the fingers in his right hand into a fist, relax then squeeze again. "Sir your father died but ten days ago. Fever took him. It was swift and he went with little pain." He sat there in silence, looking down then up at Gylippos. Neither spoke.

Gylippos fell back into the couch and crossed his arms over his face. His mind recalled the last time he had seen his father; he stood upon the hill overlooking the dromos in conversation with Brasidas. Gylippos had just completed the single stade race. Victorious, he hurried up the slope to see them both, and neither said a word of the victory, as though they had expected it of him. Only after long moments of ignoring this feat did they both break out into laughter and boisterously congratulate him.

The man broke the interlude of silence. "Your father expected you would be coming. He arranged for you to claim your citizenship here in Thurii. This house and his kleros in the hills, orchards, and vineyards not far from here he bequeathed to you. You must present yourself to the magistrates."

Someone rapped at the courtyard gate. The servant rose slowly against his stiff knees and hobbled off. Meanwhile Gylippos sipped the wine unhurriedly, his mind flowing from thoughts of his father to this his new found property and citizenship in a city he had never before seen, amongst men he knew nothing about.

Kanthos stood at the threshold to the andreion. "Master, Pythen has *collected,* as he says, a number of merchant sailors who all admit to having news of Syrakuse. He asks you to return to the ships as quickly as you can."

Gylippos turned to the old man. "Are you a slave of my father's household?"

The man shook his head. "Sir, I was, and am still, employed by your father. I am the steward of his property." Gylippos said nothing. He stared at the man's severed arm. "Wondering why he would hire a cripple?"

Gylippos fumbled with his words. "I-I, well yes."

"We fought together against the Tarentines. I merely lost a hand while many a Tarentine lost their lives. I found it a fair trade. Your father, in his generosity, hired this one time carpenter." He shook his handless arm in the air. "Not much good at a trade missing this. But up here." He tapped his head with a finger. "It all still works."

Gylippos smiled. "Kanthos will stay here and gather all the details necessary for me to claim my citizenship. As my steward, I would expect you to assist him in every way." Now the old man smiled back. "What are you called, sir?"

"My name is Alexios."

"Alexios, guard my house and property as you would your own. The profits from the vineyards and orchards I leave to you." Gylippos stopped just outside the doorway. "Kanthos find out exactly what I must present to the magistrate and arrange what must be arranged. I wish to settle this before we depart." Gylippos mused that he would likely never return here, unless to recruit allies for his fight against the Athenians and reckoned his citizenship, fully claimed, would position him to do so. He jogged almost the entire distance back to the harbor, coming upon Pythen, a squad

Nemesis

of Korinthian marines and a band of recalcitrant seamen sprawled on the dock.

"Most of them say the deed is all but done. Syrakuse is surrounded and is now coming to terms with Nikias." Pythen stalked the quay, scanning the faces of the sailors as he passed by. "All except this one." He pointed to a sun-bronzed rower from an Etrurian grain-lighter. "Tell him."

The Etrurian unfolded from his seat and stood upright. The man was not tall, but his arms bulged and his shoulders appeared twice as wide as they should for so short a man. "My captain bought a Hykarrian slave from the Athenians just two days ago. The man says Nikias stopped short of completing the walls. The Syrakusans are still getting their supplies through the Euryalos pass."

Pythen shrugged. "Which of them do you believe?"

"I think they all speak the truth," replied Gylippos. "Nikias has most likely ceased building the siege wall if he thinks, in fact, the siege is over. His emissaries may indeed be in talks with the Syrakusans. We can only hope that Gongylos has made the crossing safely and has convinced the Syrakusans to hold out."

Gylippos motioned for the Etrurian to step closer." Tell me, my friend: Any other information that a Spartan might be in need of before landing in Sikelia?" He grabbed the man's arm, clamping down so hard on it that he could hear the Etrurian's teeth grind from the pain.

"The Athenians," he said, wincing, "they know you are coming."

*****

Pythen braced himself against the railing as he looked ahead, over the swells, to the commercial docks of Himera. "It will be a long march for you, my friend."

Gylippos nodded. "I'll feel much better with dry land beneath these feet—march, or no march." Yet for a Spartan, he moved about the rocking deck of the trireme like he had been born to it. "Yours will be the only vessel left with a crew, once we make port." He spoke of the other three triremes that would be stripped of rowers and marines and be rearmed as hoplites once on land. The troop carriers would disembark another thousand hoplites, bringing his total of heavy infantry to more than 1700. The talents of silver he also brought with him would be used to swell the ranks of light troopers and cavalry. "It may take us ten days to cover the distance from here to Syrakuse. I suggest you relax and enjoy the hospitality of Himera until then."

Pythen grinned. "Yes, yes, we all have to make sacrifices. By the way, have you ever seen the girls here? From what I've been told they're all three cuppers at least."

"That is much wine. Three cups and they should be more beautiful than Aphrodite."

The kaluestes barked out the order, "Check her down!" Without a moment's lag, the rowers plunged their oars into the water, digging the blades deep and shivering against their momentum, braking the vessel. Crewmen scrambled across the deck, tossing lines. Others on the quay snapped up the ropes and began threading them through huge bronze dock-rings. "Ship oars!" Over two-hundred oars rattled and thudded as they were pulled inboard. The trireme bumped and ground along the quay, finally stopping as the lines were drawn tight.

Gylippos waved to Kanthos. "Find Xenias. I want him and ten of his best to meet me at the agora. Full armor. All shiny and such. I would be certain we can impress upon the Himerians how much we require their help."

"I am sure you will do that, my friend," said Pythen. "With the help of the gods I shall see you in Syrakuse."

Chapter 23
Syrakuse – Summer 414 BC

Athenagoras could hardly suppress the smirk on his face as he tried to refashion it into a look of despair. He accepted the wreath and cleared his throat. "Fellow Syrakusans, we cannot continue to resist the will of the gods." He looked out at the multitude, the men who had been engaged in struggle with the invaders for months now and saw exhaustion. Man after man displayed both wounds of the flesh and spirit. They had fought hard and with courage, but the Athenians tightened the noose and it seemed inevitable. "You men, every one of you, have fought with distinction. At every turn you did, though powers beyond earth seemed to carry the Athenians to victory. Yes, we have slain one of their generals and were but moments from capturing their stores on Epipolai, but heaven itself intervened. In a short week their wall will be complete. If we wait for that week to end and they finish this wall, then we will have forfeited any strength in negotiations. Women crowd our temples as we meet, imploring the gods to not abandon us. Remember, Prayer, daughter of Zeus, follows behind her brothers, Folly and Anger. Do not continue to invoke her siblings."

Hermokrates could not wait for the wreath to be passed to him. "You speak of surrender, not negotiations," he shouted.

Athenagoras extended his arms, signaling the crowd to be silent. He waited. Finally the uproar instigated by Hermokrates subsided. Athenagoras turned toward Hermokrates and seemed to address him personally. "If we come to terms now, it may only cost us money, but if we try to hold out as Melos did then we are all doomed to slavery and death. The choice, I would submit to you, is an easy one. That is unless we should all prefer dying to protect the wealth of aristocrats such as yourself?"

The assembly, stirred up beyond all reason, would not listen to any counter argument. Hermokrates, lips pursed tightly, shook his head. Athenagoras insisted that they select ambassadors to ride to the Athenian camp now and open talks with Nikias. He reminded them that Nikias had been the proxenos to Syrakuse in Athens and he would deal fairly with them now. He shrewdly manufactured a landscape of terror before providing a pathway to hope.

"Our war funds dwindle away almost to nothing. Once depleted, how will we pay the mercenaries? Use this last bit of silver to soften the Athenians lust for spoils, before their wall cuts us off from any assistance."

The nominations for ambassadors commenced with no further challenges to Athenagoras. Names were put forward, votes taken, and the candidates called to the bema.

"Stop!" A man shoved his way through the crowded assembly toward Athenagoras and the array of newly appointed ambassadors. "I have news for you all." Gongylos, the Korinthian, bounded up the steps and snatched the wreath from Athenagoras' head, not waiting for permission to speak. Men, companions of Athenagoras, grabbed him and began to tug him off the bema.

"Let the man speak," yelled out Hermokrates.

Gongylos brushed away the hands of the two men who had tried to restrain him and stepped forward to the edge of the bema. "My name is Gongylos, from your mother city of Korinthos."

"Stop this now." Athenagoras waved his cronies to restrain the foreigner.

Again Hermokrates shouted out. "Do you fear this man's words, Athenagoras? Let him speak. The Athenians can wait a few moments before you kiss their asses." Laughter erupted from the crowd. Anonymous shouts from the assembly confirmed Hermokrates' request.

"I bring word of an army that is on its way to relieve your city. And it is led by a Spartan."

*****

Hermokrates fought to hold his horse steady amongst the press of men near the gate of Apollo Temenites. His cavalry would ride out first, to contact the Peloponnesian army that was crossing overland from Himera. Syrakusan heavy infantry would march out behind and hold the ground on the heights at Euryalos. The Athenians, since their victory at the siege walls, had moved most of their troops down from Epipolai into the massive encampment in the Great Harbor; only a few light troops and cavalry guarded the stacks of brick and timber carefully laid out for the final sections of their wall across the plateau. Hermokrates, in his wisdom, had kept open discussions of surrender, hoping to lull the Athenians into complacency, and by the barren look of the heights and the reports from the kataskopoi, his ruse had worked.

The double gates swung open revealing nothing but blackness beyond; it would be several hours until sunrise, so his squadrons of cavalry should be able to negotiate the distance across Epipolai unobserved. "No talking," Hermokrates barked out and his command rippled down the column in whispers as they exited the safety of the city walls.

Several hundred meters out, in the midst of a battered vineyard, an advance unit of acontists greeted him. The captain of archers assured him that no Athenian patrols had ventured anywhere near them. He pointed out the campfires of the enemy pickets; they flickered far off, almost ten stades by his reckoning. The cavalry advanced slowly, silently, until the gleaming fires became obscured by the gloomy terrain.

"Let's be off." Hermokrates whacked the ribs of his horse with his korthornos riding boots. Soon the entire compliment of horsemen galloped hard across Epipolai passing some of the Athenian siege-works left undefended for the night, but carefully avoiding the last enemy outpost at the fortress of Labdalon.

Now the sky hinted of dawn as the stars faded behind graying sky, and the bellies of the few clouds that hung near the horizon began to glow in hues of red and orange. Ahead Hermokrates could see the glint of bronze and men forming up into battle formation. Had the Athenians been forewarned? This could not be, for he had

Nemesis

Dionysos trail Athenagoras for almost every moment since the assembly rejected his motion for surrender. He could not prove it, but he felt certain what the Athenians knew of Syrakuse they had gathered from him. A single man in full panoplia jogged out towards the Syrakusan column. In the dim light of pre-dawn no color could be distinguished, but the man's shield bore the unmistakable lambda of a Spartan.

Hermokrates signaled for his column to halt; he proceeded forward, cautiously, eyeing this sole warrior as they converged upon each other.

"Hermokrates, son of Hermon?" the man asked.

"Y-yes."

"You do not seem so sure of your name, sir." The man slammed the butt-spike of his spear into the turf then lowered his shield to the ground, propping it up against his thigh. "We met, sir, in Sparta town. I am Gylippos, son of Kleandridas."

Hermokrates mouth hung open as he stared at Gylippos. Finally he summoned a few awkward words. 'It has been so long, I never thought that—."

"That I would come?" Gylippos spit. "Can't pass up a good fight. Now let's form up and greet the Athenians." He pointed to the rising dust beyond the tangled orchards that blocked their view toward the Athenian camp.

Hermokrates dispatched the order to evolve left into phalanx order and lock into the Peloponnesians who had already dressed their files, and although tired from their march stood facing the approaching enemy with a bit of insouciance, hardly anxious or concerned about the impending battle. Their demeanor settled the edginess of the Syrakusans. The dust cloud now began to filter up through the trees, expanding in breadth as the enemy advanced until at last the gleam of metal and the tromping of feet revealed the Athenians as they emerged onto the open meadows. They too exhibited confidence, displayed by the crispness of their march and their tight and trim files.

Gylippos stepped forward of his men and spiked his dory spear into the turf. He dropped his shield to rest against his knee while he lifted his pilos helmet to wipe the sweat from his forehead. Forward of them all by twenty or thirty meters, he stood quite solitary and exposed, but acted with no more concern than if he had just completed a morning drill near the Eurotas. The Syrakusans stared at him in awe. "Sosibos!" His herald came up running. "Go to the Athenians and ask them if their commander will meet me, out there." He pointed to a boulder near midway between the two armies.

Sosibos jogged out, his herald's staff held high for all to see, and headed directly for the most flamboyantly attired Athenians in their front ranks. After a few minutes he returned. "Their general, Nikias has obliged."

Gylippos sent for Hermokrates and they both strode out toward their approaching counterparts. "I seem to recognize Nikias, but do you know the other two?" Gylippos asked Hermokrates as they moved forward.

"I would have guessed Lamakhos to be one, but he is dead," answered Hermokrates.

The three Athenians and their herald stood astride the huge boulder that loomed above the other smaller stones that had been stacked to form a boundary fence, convenient for the local farmers and equally useful now to the two parties of adversaries—it neatly marked out a line not to be crossed.

Nikias, made obvious by his age and the ostentatious helmet and shield he displayed, wanted to speak but hesitated when he caught sight of the crimson exomis, and the lambda insignia on Gylippos' shield; he did not expect to encounter a Spartan on the heights of Epipolai. "I am Nikias, son of Nikeratos." He turned to his two companions. "Euthydemos and Menandros," he said as he pointed to each.

Hermokrates tipped his hand toward Gylippos, deferring to him. Gylippos offered no introductions. "Athenians, I come here to discuss terms of surrender." "Hermokrates went pale. Nikias, Euthydemos and Menandros began to grin. Gylippos continued. "If you stack your arms now, we will allow you to depart Sikelia unmolested." Nikias chin dropped. Euthydemos coughed nervously. Hermokrates, on the other hand, could do all he could to keep from laughing.

"I will make this offer only once. Save your army from the destruction that will surely befall it if you remain here."

Nikias spun away enraged and marched back to his phalanx with Euthydemos and Menandros trailing behind. Hermokrates shook his head. "I heard you Spartans had balls but that was something else. Can I tell the men?"

"About what?" Gylippos started to walk back to toward his front ranks.

"About your more than generous offer to spare the Athenians."

Gylippos nodded. "Of course. It was meant for them. But I would suspect that it may rile the Athenians a bit."

*****

The cavalry lingered on Epipolai as a rearguard for the army. Soon both the Peloponnesians and the Syrakusans had made their way back into the city, entering by the gate of Apollo Temenites. This one-time outskirt of Syrakuse hardly contained the amenities of the city proper, and not many of its citizens dwelled here, so the number greeting the returning army proved scanty, but the ones that did made up for their lack of numbers with their raucousness. The guards cheered from the battlements as Gylippos and his men marched in; little girls clung to their mothers and watched wide-eyed while boys ran along with the Peloponnesians as they marched in formation toward the statue of Apollo.

Hermokrates swept his hand out across the open ground surrounding the huge image of the god. "Your camp. Food will be brought up straightaway."

Gylippos passed the order for them to bivouac, built circular as all Spartan camps are, with Apollo acting as the hub. Both he and Xenias left the moiling troops behind, taking to the eastern sliver of Epipolai that had been enclosed by the Syrakusans this past winter. The towers here were of wood, not stone, but they provided a vantage across the plateau. "Look to the right, far off," said Gylippos. "The Athenian fort at Labdalon." The pair scanned the heights, locating the towers of the enemy fortress that poked above the trees. From here also they could see the

Nemesis

stacks of timbers, bricks and stones already laid out in a great line, ready for the Athenians to complete their siege wall. A scattered patrol of cavalry prowled around these supply dumps, but no permanent guards could be seen. "Seems we have not made much of an impression on them yet. This may prove a good thing."

"Is it their fort you have in mind?" Xenias saw the opportunity as clearly as Gylippos.

"We need something to stiffen the spines of the Syrakusans. You saw them today, prancing about in the face of the enemy. Too light on their feet, and I must be certain of the reliability of the men around me in battle. A victory, no matter how small, may boost their courage."

"Then you will not call a muster for the entire army?"

Gylippos rubbed his beard as he spoke. "A fast and light company. Picked men only."

"Then you'll want the first pentekontys of Neomdameidois?" Xenias knew his men could be counted on above all others.

"At first light. But I'll speak with the Syrakusan strategoi first. We must be polite to our hosts, and I do want to know exactly what the Athenians have at Labdalon."

"Am I dismissed?" Xenias turned to go.

Gylippos grabbed him by the arm. "Wait. Have our men move the encampment up here." Xenias nodded before plunging through the floor hatch to the ladder below. Now he heard others enter the tower as they began to ascend. A head popped up through the floor opening. "Commander Gylippos." The man waited for any sign of acknowledgement before climbing up into the tower. Gylippos nodded. The man heaved himself up the last few rungs and onto the tower deck. "My master, Hermokrates, has invited you to dine with him tonight." He handed Gylippos a folded piece of papyrus with the invitation inked onto it.

Gylippos glanced at it quickly. "Tell him I accept."

"Very good, sir. Shall I return at sunset to guide you to his home?"

Gylippos handed the papyrus back to the messenger. "Not necessary."

The man paused for a bit before climbing down the ladder, somewhat confused by the Spartan refusing his offer to escort him. He knew the Spartans could see in the dark; he did not think them god-like in this vision.

Gylippos leaned out over the portal of the tower, staring at the expanse of Epipolai, all the while wondering why Nikias had not completed his wall.

*****

Hermokrates had put on his best chiton; one fashioned of Egyptian linen and dyed in Phoenician purple. Beside him stood Phaidra and in a row behind her, Kalli, Dianthe and Elpida. His entire staff of household servants flanked the courtyard across from them as Hilarion solemnly opened the gate. There in the dim torchlight stood a tall man, crimson himation cloak draped over his shoulders and spun around his left arm, a conventional sight in dress, but his antediluvian, long eight-locked hair made the deepest impression on them all—especially Dianthe. This was her avenger, a hero sent by the gods to punish the Athenians and the image before her did nothing to detract from the one that she supposed. Hermokrates stepped forward to greet his guest and ushered Gylippos deeper into the courtyard where he introduced each member of his family.

Gylippos politely repeated each name as he received it, nodding slightly before moving on. He paused before Elpida and Dianthe, taken aback a bit by Elpida's reluctance to look at him. "May I see your face?" he asked, lowering himself to see eye to eye with the girl. Elpida looked at him sideways while clinging to her sister's peplos gown.

"Elpida, answer our guest," said Phaidra.

Gylippos whispered, "Elpida, I will not hurt you. Can I see both your eyes?"

Dianthe nudged her sister. Elpida turned to face the Spartan. "Am I so ugly you cannot bear to look at me?"

"Oh no sir," answered Dianthe quickly. "She does not think you ugly."

Hermokrates intervened. "These are my adopted daughters. From Melos and they do not have very fond memories of soldiers. For this I apologize. And to look at you sir—and there is no doubt—you are a soldier."

Gylippos could think of nothing to say while he looked into the eyes of Elpida. Hermokrates dismissed them all, freeing Gylippos from the little girl's trance and led him into the andreion. Two other men had already taken couches and Hermokrates introduced both Sikanos and Heraklides as they sat. Gylippos ate and drank, letting the Syrakusans provide the major portions of conversation.

After they had apprised him of what they perceived he should know, Heraklides addressed him. "Gylippos, I suspect we have overwhelmed you with all this detail about Syrakuse and our enemy upon Epipolai. I suggest you take a day or two to tour our city, its defenses, and inspect our troops."

"Splendid idea," added Sikanos. Hermokrates remained silent.

"Gentlemen, I have already inspected your defenses, and I must ask you not to be offended at my remarks, for I find them inadequate." Gylippos spoke with no emotion and exhibited little expression. It was as though he was a merchant tallying up his inventory at the end of a day at the agora.

"Inadequate?" Heraklides snorted as he spoke.

"I am a soldier, not a diplomat, so I shall not beat the bush with sticks but go straight for the game, spear in hand. I walked by your theatron and your agora, and the grounds of the palaistra. I saw not a single guard."

"We have placed our guards along the walls. Our enemies are out there, are they not?" Heraklides grew irritated at this stranger's insinuations.

"Yes, I saw every one of your guards. Very easy to count as they brandished their oil lamps. Ban these at once." Gylippos recovered his composure. "I blame no one." Pausing, he sipped from his cup. "I only wish to secure your city from enemies within and without."

Hermokrates nodded. "He is correct, my friends. One man with a bolt key

Nemesis

can relinquish what had taken an army to defend."

"Sirs, I will tell you what *must* be done at once. Then we shall have time to discuss what *may* be done." Gylippos paused for a moment as he organized his thoughts. Hermokrates, meanwhile, called for Hilarion to act as scribe. The slave dragged a rickety stool to a meekly lit corner of the andreion and sat, nestling a wax tablet upon his lap. "You will need more than that," remarked Gylippos as he watched Hilarion prepare. The servant looked to Hermokrates, who nodded. Quickly he departed and returned with several more tablets. "The first item which must be addressed is payment of the mercenaries. I would suggest that each head of household of the Gamoroi pledge wages for three men. Men of property, but of lesser means, should provide payment for at least one."

Heraklides opened his mouth, but Hermokrates cut him off, holding a finger before him. "Let our Spartan friend continue uninterrupted." Heraklides obliged, sinking back into the cushions of his divan.

"I will do my part in snatching some Athenian silver for you. Tomorrow we will attack their fort at Labdalon." The three generals stared wide-eyed at the Spartan. Gylippos smiled in return. "Do you think tomorrow too late?" He did not wait for a response but commenced a long and detailed lecture regarding the deportment of all battlement guards, how their precinct leaders should be assigned, and to the importance of the selecting only aristocrats for gate captains. Hilarion struggled to keep up with the copious instructions, furiously marking up one tablet, plopping it on the floor, and snapping up another. Gylippos paused in his disquisition, waiting until the slave had replenished his tablet and had stylus in hand. For the next hour he had described, with terse precision, exactly how the Syrakusans should defend their city. Once he had dictated these instructions, he asked for his kylix to be refilled.

While the Spartan drank, Heraklides snatched the opportunity to speak. "You have expounded in excruciating detail, what our responsibilities are, but what can we expect from you?"

"Leadership. I will be at the fore, beyond your walls and in the face of the enemy. That is my part of this bargain, good Syrakusans. I will not shy away from danger, and I will not ask from any man what I do not undertake myself in way of peril, but I do insist that you secure the city so that our army has a refuge to return to."

Hermokrates stood. "The hour is late, and we all have much to attend to gentlemen." The others stood also and reached for their sandals that hung behind their couches and fastened them quickly. Heraklides departed first, exhibiting barely a nod as he passed Gylippos. "He is a proud man," whispered Hermokrates to the Spartan. "But he is a loyal man also." He thanked Sikanos for attending, keeping silent until only he and Gylippos stood in the andreion. "Sir, you must remember that we are not soldiers in the Spartan army."

Gylippos smiled. "I am well aware of that, Hermokrates."

"Then why do you order us about like soldiers?"

"In more tranquil times, I would agree with you. I would, indeed, present my views as suggestions, not commands. But if I am not mistaken, there is an army up there on the Heights poised to annihilate your city. Be clear on this: only soldiers can protect Syrakuse and save your families." Gylippos paused. "I *suggest* that you assemble your men at dawn in the precinct of Apollo." He stepped out into the torch-lit courtyard, and turned just before opening the gate. "Thank you, sir, for a delicious meal. Tomorrow, after we have taken Labdalon, we will commence with reorganization and drilling."

Hermokrates shrugged as he watched the Spartan depart. Phaidra poked her head out of the women's quarters at the rear of the courtyard, making certain that all the guests had left before approaching him. "Husband, can this Spartan save us?"

"We are like a sick patient. The disease that afflicts us is Nikias and the Athenians. I pray we can survive the cure."

*****

"Once we move against the Athenian wall, you will attack Labdalon." Gylippos stabbed the turf with the butt-spike of his spear as he spoke. "Your company is to move as soon as we have stirred up the dust. I want to give those bastards something to look at as they wake up."

Xenias trotted off to his company of Neodamedois. They had stripped off their breastplates and greaves, retaining only kranos helmets and shields for armor. Mixed in with this pentekontys was a contingent of shield-bearers, slaves assigned not to attend to their masters, but to assist with gathering up whatever loot they might capture during the attack. Gylippos had been clear in his instructions; the fort and its contents must be taken. He needed silver for his own mercenaries.

Hermokrates, leading the first ilai of cavalry, cantered up to Gylippos. "We are ready."

Gylippos, surrounded by army heralds and commanders from each lokhos, handed his helmet and spear to Kanthos. "Gather close. Especially you Syrakusans." He stepped onto a small boulder, raising him above the others by not much more than a foot. "Remember, you men of Syrakuse, that you are Dorians like us Spartans, sober in thought and stern in courage, facing Ionians. By your race and lineage you are superior to these effete islanders and their Athenian masters. Never forget this." He stepped down, after giving the order to march. The heralds sprinted off, carrying his words. He moved to Kanthos to retrieve his spear.

"You cannot believe those words," he whispered to Gylippos.

"Men, particularly in groups, whether by family, nation, or tribe consider themselves favored by the gods and superior in nature to other men. It is to this sentiment that I speak and of course it is not true." Gylippos snatched the spear with a grin a hurried off to the head of the column.

No trumpets. No war-drums. Not even the unsettling echoes of Lakonian flutes. The Syrakusans and Peloponnesians poured through the gate and advanced across Epipolai in a great swinging arc, their left flank hanging near the walls, the right rolling along and protected by cavalry. Plumes of dust twisted skyward, glowing

Nemesis

golden in the early light of dawn. Across the meadows, from the depth of the Athenian encampment, trumpets blared out a frantic alarm. Gylippos halted the phalanx nearly three stades from the enemy occupied groves that bristled with spiked timbers.

Far off and hidden by the ridge spine of the plateau, Xenias and his company of picked men jogged along in silence, shields slung upon their backs and spears hanging low. He had already deployed a squad of javelineers well forward as scouts. As his column cut across an open field, they came up the perforated bodies of three Athenian day-watchers, with only a single shattered javelin evidence of the method of their dispatch. The squad had done their job. Now he ordered his men to form up in open order, sixteen shields across the front ranks and files eight deep, as they approached a grove that spanned the distance to the fort. They filtered through the trees, keeping to formation as best they could and emerged into a boulder-strewn clearing not fifty meters from Labdalon. The walls appeared just as Gylippos had described them to him earlier—low, patched with timber and unguarded. The scouts had already clambered over and ascended into the towers near the gate. Within moments bodies tumbled from the battlements, thudding morbidly into the hard, dry earth at the base of the walls.

Xenias led his men right up to the gate. "Fourth enomotai will remain here and keep watch for reinforcements." He spun around to face the gate, twisting his spear in his right hand, anxious for it to open. The bolt rattled. A timber thumped to the ground. Now the gate creaked and groaned as his scouts drew it open from within. His three remaining platoons streamed through the open gate, quickly reforming into a miniature phalanx twelve men across, shields braced hard against their shoulders and spears brandished high, expecting an onrush of defenders. Two then three Athenians stumbled out of a low-roofed mud-brick barracks only to be skewered by the spears of the Neodameidoi. With precision, his formation split into three parts, one moving right another left, each kicking in doors and flooding into buildings, one by one, while his center enomotai moved straight ahead for the arsenal. Just as they approached, the doors flew open and squad of infantry rushed at them, screaming wildly as they threw themselves against the Lakonians' shields. Five dropped upon impact, faces sunk into the dust. The survivors, convinced that they had performed their duty with their impetuous charge, tossed away their spears and shields, arms held out. Xenias' men waited for no command, no order to spare them, but cut them down as they pleaded and wailed. Like figures made of stone but somehow animated, they exhibited no malice and little enthusiasm for this work, only consummate economy in its execution—they delivered not a single spear thrust more than was required and walked over and away from the dead Athenians as if they were nothing more than storm-tossed tree limbs or fallen leaves.

It was more than he had hoped for. He strolled down the length of the arsenal, smiling as he passed stacks of javelins and caches of arrows. Several chests stood out conspicuously at the far terminus. He picked up a xiphos sword from a stack piled near some naval rigging and snapped off the seal from the largest chest before levering it open, revealing a shimmering hoard of silver coins and bars. One by one he cracked open each chest until he had all the silver exposed. He was no merchant and could only guess at the haul. *Perhaps thirty talents*, he though, as his eyes scanned the loot. By now the entourage of servants had entered the fort and had begun rounding up all available carts and wagons. Less disciplined troops would have slaughtered the draught animals in their battle-lust, but Xenias' men spared them all. It would be an easy trek back to Syrakuse—as long as Gylippos could cut-off any relief elements from reaching Labdalon.

As he exited the arsenal, he found his company slowly coalescing into a loose formation by platoon in the center of the compound. He shaded his eyes while scanning the towers; each scout acknowledged his glance with an exaggerated wave. "Anything?" he shouted up to one in the southern gate tower.

"Just dust and a lot of it, but far off," he yelled back.

"That's Gylippos. Keeping old Nikias busy so we can steal his money." Xenias whistled. His men turned to face him. "None alive?"

"None!" shouted the company, almost in a single, collective voice.

"Withdraw." Xenias pointed toward the gate with his spear. The three platoons marched out leading the train of carts and wagons laden with silver. Before they had all departed he ordered the last of the battle-servants to torch the fort. "Burn it all," he said as he made for the gate. He stopped in his tracks and shouted out, "Start with the arsenal."

Outside the fort he joined the fourth enomotai that had been deployed as security. He fell in with them, posting them as rear guard to the column as it moved back toward Syrakuse. Their procession of laden carts and shield-bearers proved extensive and stretched out longer than he would have liked, and if the Athenian cavalry attacked he most likely would be forced to abandon a good share of the booty. He sent a runner up the column to quicken the pace. Now a cloud rolled over them, smoke from the dying fort at Labdalon. He turned. Flames flickered above the walls while smoke billowed high. A gust of wind tugged and stretched it southward smothering them as they retreated, blotting out the sun.

*****

Nikias could not believe his good fortune. *This new Spartan commander— keen to show the Syrakusans his military prowess—lined up his army for battle less than a day after arriving. He had insulted my Athenians with a call for their surrender and now stands with a battered Syrakusan army, spoiling for combat. He has had no time to evaluate these men. No time to calculate his moves. He is rash and this encounter proves it.* He carried on with his thoughts as he peered across the battlefield and the fidgeting Syrakusans. It was sooner than he would have liked, but this battle could end it. He had hoped for more from Athenagoras' subterfuge and certainly expected more from a Spartan, but he would take it all the same.

An hour passed. Nikias would not maneuver away from the walls and into terrain that favored the Syrakusan cavalry so he held fast awaiting Gylippos to

Nemesis

advance. Another hour slipped by—still no attack.

"Look!" a front-ranker yelled out. More and more men shouted and pointed. Thick columns of smoke coiled skyward above the trees to the north.

Nikias felt his stomach twist. He knew, without a doubt, the smoke marked Labdalon. He held his men fast, issuing no commands to attack or to redeploy for a march to the fort. The Athenians stood rooted in their formation watching the dark, billowing smoke streak across the horizon. Men cried out. Others cursed. Nikias could only look away. Across the battlefield, the Syrakusan cavalry galloped forward, protecting their infantry phalanx as it commenced its withdrawal toward the city. Nikias thanked the gods that he had not relocated all of their stores and silver from the fleet's mooring at Thapsos, but more than that he thanked them that the enemy had moved first, removing him of his burden of decision and action.

Chapter 24
Syrakuse – Summer 414 BC

Athenagoras bolted to his feet. "You are very bold with the lives of others." The bouleterion hummed with dissent, stirred up by his words. Some shouted out in agreement. Not one defended Gylippos—not even Hermokrates. "Yes, you managed to capture one paltry fort and kill a handful of slaves, but what good did it do? They still occupy the Heights. And did you so quickly forget the defeat inflicted upon us by Nikias the very next day?" Athenagoras recounted briefly the first minor victory at Labdalon, but then expounded, in detail, the disastrous battle the very next day in which the Syrakusans sustained heavy casualties.

Gylippos stepped down from the bema and strode directly at Athenagoras, who raised his arm as if to deflect the blow that was certain to fall, and halted before him, not a foot away, before turning to face the banked seats of councilors. "This defeat you speak of was due to my haste, and not to the lack of skill or courage of you Syrakusans. Overcome with impatience, I ordered the attack too near the walls. This prevented our cavalry from coming into play."

Athenagoras backed up before speaking. "And why should we think you not hasty in this new decision?"

Gylippos answered, "Because I am certain where we will attack him, away from his walls and fortifications." He turned and spoke directly to Athenagoras. "And I will be in the fore, leading this attack. You, Athenagoras, can remain behind and guard the council house. The army will be on Epipolai, driving away the invaders."

The bouleterion shook with laughter as Athenagoras stomped out, followed by his dwindling entourage. Hermokrates edged close to Gylippos. "Let me spar with him. You don't need any more enemies."

Gylippos stared blankly at his friend. "Enemies?"

"Let us talk over some food, away from here," said Hermokrates as he scanned the faces near him; none seemed interested in them or their conversation, but he thought better of letting any words drift to unfriendly ears. They strolled to the far side of the agora, where the vendor stalls leaned one against another and black smoke wafted, masking the scorching afternoon sun.

"Ah master Hermokrates, you are hungry today?" A bony little man in a leather apron hovered over an array of baskets bloated with fish, waving away the swarms of flies. Hermokrates picked out two boar-fish. "Grill them for us," he said as he flipped the fish-monger an obol.

The man plucked up a pair of shimmering blue-scaled fish and headed behind his stall where a woman bent over a small brazier, poking away at the charcoal with a stick. She snatched the fish up while chattering, cursing the fire and the man then slapped the two boar-fish upon the grill. They sizzled and smoked, stinging her eyes. She cursed some more and rubbed her runny nose dry with the back of her hand. "By the time you get your wine they'll be cooked." He looked back at the woman and

Nemesis

the fish, shaking his head.

"Do you see why I won't have my wife talking with the customers?"

Hermokrates laughed. "Hmm? If I heard correctly, she was cursing you, not us."

Shortly they had purchased a small jug of wine, reclaimed their fish and found themselves sitting in the merciful shade of Long Stoa, away from the traffic, hawkers, and eye-stinging cook-fires. Gylippos unwrapped the grape leaves and began to pick at the steaming flakes of fish. "So I have been here less than a week and already I have enemies?"

"Men do not like their deficiencies pointed out, and you, my friend, do not hesitate to reveal any and every fault you perceive." Hermokrates sipped his wine slowly.

"Would you prefer I ignore these flaws—the very same ones that the Athenians will surely exploit?"

Hermokrates shook his head. "Of course not. All I ask is that you confine your discussions to the military and allow me to contend in politics. "

Gylippos threw his hands open and looked skyward. "By the Holy Twins, is not an assault by the army a military concern?"

"How we plan the assault is most definitely a military matter. *If* we assault is a political one, at least here at Syrakuse. Remember, my friend: we are not in Sparta."

"Believe me, I thank the gods we are not in Sparta," said Gylippos.

Hermokrates was taken aback by his answer. *All men loved their homes, their families, and their land. If not, why fight,* he thought. This Spartan, a man who truly had become his friend, proved unfathomable. "How is your fish?" he asked, studying Gylippos's face.

"What fish," he answered, grinning. He presented open palm with a single, barren grape leaf in it. "Delicious," said the Spartan as he observed a clerk from the strategeion hanging the katalogos upon the wall in the stoa, drawing a crowd just as quickly as the fish-monger's wares drew flies.

Hermokrates watched as the mob grew larger still. "The army will be assembled at dawn four days hence, in the precinct of Apollo Temenites."

"Then I have work ahead of me." Gylippos stood while draining his wine cup. "Thank you for the meal, and the advice."

"Where are you off to?" Hermokrates hurried after the Spartan.

Gylippos pointed to the cliffs of Epipolai. "Up there." He strode off, the crowd in the agora parting like swells before a trireme, as he moved north through the narrow alleyways and over the causeway toward the precinct of Akhradina. After not much more than an hour he came to his camp in Temenites where Kanthos stood waiting, holding the reins of Gylippos' horse, knowing exactly what his master had in mind. "Where is yours?"

Kanthos stammered a bit. "M-m-mine?"

"Your horse, man! You are riding with me." Gylippos swung his leg up and over the animal's back, clamping his knees tightly to its flanks. They rode swiftly, encountering the day-watchers as they returned from their posts for a meal and some sleep. He hoped the Athenian scouts did the same. By the end of the first watch they returned to the city, Kanthos to sleep while Gylippos pored over his map of the plateau, applying mental revisions to the hard set ink. Once his plan had formed, his eyes closed easily.

*****

By mid-morning a procession of rowers had formed up at the Little Harbor and began snaking its way through the alleyways toward the Temenites Gate. Gylippos had already ordered the cavalry onto the Heights and parties of light infantry, dispatched well before dawn, had secured the Athenians' stacks of brick and timber laid out for their siege wall. The nautai had traded their oars for shovels and axes.

Gylippos lingered outside the gate, in conference with the architect and his assistants. "You must push your men to finish it quickly," said Gylippos. "And it must cut across open ground—ground that will benefit our cavalry."

The architect lifted his petasos hat from his head and began swatting away a cloud of gnats that buzzed around them as he nodded. "The work parties have already been divided into three shifts. We will work through the day, the night, and the next day."

Gylippos vaulted onto his horse and tugged the reins to face the architect. "You must work quickly. And all this activity may provoke the Athenians' curiosity."

Now the leading edge of the column of oarsmen appeared from behind a corner, the clanking of their shovels, axes and picks echoing off the walls of Temenites. Several more allied triremes had docked the night before, adding to the teams of wall builders and to their prospects. As long as the Athenians, and especially Nikias, remained lethargic, and sent no patrols out across Epipolai, Gylippos felt certain they would complete the counter-wall. Nikias, though, concerned him. This wall was a lure, to pull the Athenians out into the open and most any commander would perceive the danger it presented. *The man is immune to the obvious*, he thought. He kicked his horse into a gallop and headed toward the open meadows where any battle would surely take place. Once amongst the clumps of heat-wilted grasses he traced with his eyes the location for the counter-wall then stared across the open fields toward the screen of orchards that hid the Athenian front lines and nodded.

*****

Endymion swayed back and forth from fatigue as he eyed the Syrakusan phalanx. For the last four days this was their enemy's routine—to march out from their city, rattle their spears against their polished shields, then withdraw in time for the midday meal behind a screen of cavalry. Just as Nikias had warned in his speech to the troops, this show of false courage was the last vestige of glue that held their army together. A few more displays such as this and even the dull-witted Syrakusans will realize what a sham they perpetrate by mocking both Athena and Ares with false

Nemesis

intentions of battle. His stomach growled at him. *Time for their cavalry to ride forward and cover their retreat*, he thought, as he searched the enemy formation for the dust of riders. His belly roared with hunger now, but no Syrakusan cavalry rode to the interval between the two armies. He saw pennants flash in the enemy formation. A salphinx bleated. The Syrakusans began their withdrawal.

Now every man in the front ranks began to chatter. He heard the voices, brimming first with disbelief then rage. "No cavalry screen," one man barked out. "Their turning their backs on us," another said. One voice cut like a sword through the air, clear, fast, and true. "Damn you Nikias: attack and take their wall!"

Endymion peered down the ranks to his left, toward the Athenian troops in the center. Nikias, surrounded by his herald and priests, hurriedly commenced the sphagia sacrifice. *There will be battle. We will attack!* The signal to advance blared out in three short bursts. No change in formation. They moved forward in open order, enabling them to close quickly with the retreating Syrakusans. Now, as always, his stomach acted as an oracle. Instead of growling, it twisted in him. *What if they are not withdrawing?* He spun as far to the right as he could without tripping up, trying to catch sight of their siege works. The walls slipped further away, and their protection with them. The backs of the jostling Syrakusans ahead reminded him of the vulnerability of men in retreat, and by their hurried, stumbling pace he knew panic might be only moments away. His stomach unwound as courage warmed his gut.

More signals trumpeted through the dusty, searing air, but he could not tell from where. Suddenly the Syrakusans stomped to a halt, and as the dust began to lift, he saw the tell-tale file and gap pattern of a Lakonian counter-march. The empty chasms began to fill up with flashing shields as each file spilled toward him, reversing, turning a withdrawal into an advance. Dust seeped skyward revealing the Syrakusan phalanx, a formation seething with bronze, shields overlapping, capped with a bristling forest of iron-tipped spears.

Endymion and all the other front rankers froze in their tracks. There was no order, no signal to halt and reform. They all had been in enough of these to understand exactly what to do, and what was to come next. They shuffled and shifted into close order formation and hunkered down for contact. Across the interval of fifty meters or so, he spotted a tall man with a transverse crest upon his helmet—a Spartan, no doubt, for his aspis shield bore the lambda ensign of Lakedaimon as did the all the shields of the men that flanked him. They seemed to glide forward, in no hurry, but still leading all others, their voices bellowing out the hymn to Kastor. They hit like an avalanche of muscle and iron.

*****

Kanthos knelt over Gylippos, swabbing away the grime as he scanned his master for any less obvious wounds. As he rubbed away the blood from his shoulder, Gylippos winced—not much, but enough for his servant to notice. Kanthos shook his head. "No sword cut. Not a bit of blood. You must take off your armor so I may see." Kanthos began to unfasten the ties on Gylippos' linothorax.

Gylippos, all the while biting his lip, spun away and sprang to his feet, trying to assure Kanthos by this very action that his injury was not serious. He squeezed his eyes shut and shook his head to clear away the pain. For the moment, he had buried it. "Find Xenias. Tell him to meet me at the town-house of Hermokrates." Before Kanthos could move to restrain him, Gylippos vaulted onto his horse and galloped away from the churned and scarred meadow toward the city. He glanced back, eyeing the stack of Athenian arms that formed the trophy of victory and the gathering of heralds that had just commenced to allow a truce for retrieval of the Athenian dead. With each bound in his horse's gait, his shoulder screamed in silent and inevitable pain. He had no doubt that it had been dislocated, and he also knew how clumsy Kanthos had been in the past when he had tried to snap it back into place for him. His shoulder would wait. First he must convince Hermokrates to urge the council to assault the Athenian Circle Fort, quickly, while Nikias regrouped his forces. The truce would be over at sunset. Offering no respite, at dawn they would be compelled to attack.

  By the time he had ridden through the gates and deep into Akhradina, the celebrations had already begun. Men still in their armor staggered through the alleyways, clutching wine cups and singing songs of victory. Women hung out windows tossing garlands and chaplets at the reveling warriors. "Ah, there it is," he said as he spotted the palaistra. He slid gingerly from his horse, handing the reins to a servant that hovered near the entrance. "The gymnasiakhos?" The boy pointed through the portal and into the sand covered arena. Two young boys grappled in the middle of the palaistra with a burly man wielding a staff circling them, poking one then another and bellowing out instructions. Gylippos lingered in the shadows of the columns, waiting for the bout to end. Before it could, the gymnasiarkhos caught sight of him. He plunged his staff into the sand between the two boys effectively ending the match.

  "Off with you," he commanded. He lumbered toward Gylippos, swinging his staff slightly with each step. When he got within a few feet he shook his head. "It's you left shoulder, isn't it?"

  "How did you know?" Gylippos tried to stand as straight as possible.

  "Oh, come now. You're as crooked as an olive tree." He waved Gylippos to follow him to a changing bench near a fountain where a boy, fresh from a scraping, was cleaning the scooped blade of his stenglis of oil and sand. "I can fix that shoulder, but I don't sew," he said, staring at the long gash that spanned Gylippos' forehead. The gymnasiarkhos waved a servant over. "On the bench," he commanded. "Face down." Gylippos reluctantly complied. The servant pinned his back down hard, wrapping an arm around his good shoulder. The gymnasiarkhos clamped down with both hands on his forearm and wrist. "I will count to three." Gylippos gritted his teeth and nodded. "One, two—." He yanked hard and quickly the shoulder joint separated for a brief moment before slipping back into place. "Not even a sigh," remarked the gymnasiarkhos with a bit of admiration.

  Gylippos tried to lift his arm to test the injury. It throbbed, but the joint

Nemesis

functioned, if only slightly. "By Apollo, you do know how to count, don't you? Where did three go?"

"Oh, I am sorry," he said grinning. "Three."

Gylippos stood and wriggled his shoulder until the pain insisted he stop. "Thank you. I'll have my servant come round with your payment."

"Not necessary." The gymnasiarkhos poked at Gylippos' crimson exomis with his staff. "You're the Spartan general everyone is talking about." He nodded as he looked him up and down. Now he tapped him on the forehead, just above his wound. "Better get that taken care of." He saluted Gylippos with his staff and began to make his way toward the center of the palaistra where a pair of servants worked to groom the sand. Within moments he attacked them with instructions, swinging his staff overhead.

Gylippos collected his horse and rode off, down the darkened streets and alleyways, for the sun had dipped below the roof tops, illuminating the few streaks of clouds that slipped by overhead. By the time he had reached the house of Hermokrates, night had steeped everything in gloom, only the intermittent flicker of an oil lamp visible through an open window displaying any light besides the emergence of the early evening stars. He rapped upon the hefty, wooden gate. It swung open almost instantly. There in the courtyard sat Hermokrates, still in battle armor and surrounded by his family.

"Come, come and sit down, my friend." Hermokrates stood up from the bench and clasped his hand upon Gylippos arm, ushering him to a seat. Phaidra stepped back a bit. The lamplight in the courtyard shined upon his forehead, revealing the glistening streaks of blood that Gylippos had ignored. He daubed it away from his eyes like sweat. "You are bleeding," said Hermokrates. He studied the wound for a moment before sending off Hilarion to fetch the iatros. Dianthe left them all, saying nothing, not even acknowledging the Spartan's arrival. In a moment she returned from the women's quarters with a wad of linen and a basket. She soaked the linen in the fountain then walked directly to Gylippos without a word. She did not ask permission but immediately commenced to daub the crusted blood and grime. Gylippos blinked away the trickles that ran into his eyes. He, too, sat in silence and stared at Dianthe as she stroked his forehead gently, gauging the length of the wound with her touch. Gylippos felt something more than mere flesh. Her very spirit lighted upon him. He could not keep his eyes from her. She leaned closer, straining in the dim courtyard to see the extent of his wound, her warm breath caressing the skin on his face. Glaukia approached them, an oil lamp in hand, which she wavered over his head until Dianthe snapped it away from her. Mesmerized, he stared at the flame reflected in her deep blue eyes, but his gaze proved no distraction to her: she cleaned the wound before pressing a wad of motos onto it; the last trace of blood withdrew into the poultice.

"Very good," said Hermokrates. "The bleeding has stopped."

Dianthe reached for Gylippos' hand and lifted it to the compress. "Keep pressure," she whispered to him as her hand lingered on his for a long moment. This

went unnoticed by no one. Hermokrates glanced to his wife Phaidra who returned a glare, while Elpida grinned from ear to ear.
Hermokrates reached for Gylippos arm. "Come. Let us retire to the andreion. You must be hungry, even if you do not admit it."
Gylippos did not argue. His stomach kicked at him and his shoulder ached, so much so, he had forgotten entirely about the foot long gash on his forehead. Food proved a soothing balm—wine more so. Not long after the two men had emptied their cups for the second time Xenias arrived as ordered, to provide Gylippos with an opportunity to leave the dinner.
"The orders for the morrow?" Xenias stood at the threshold of the andreion, reluctant to enter. "Or do you want to address the captains directly?"
Gylippos smiled. Xenias carried out his orders explicitly. He would deliver his commander from a cavalry assault or an awkward dinner engagement. "Prepare them for an attack on the Athenian fort at the Fig-Tree. I shall return by the second watch."
Xenias stared for a moment at Gylippos, doubting his ability to make even the short journey back to their camp tonight. "Very good," he said, wrinkling a brow. He spun around and departed.
Gylippos, uncharacteristically, drank more wine than usual, his throbbing shoulder compelling him to seek its mollifying effects, but he managed to impress upon Hermokrates how crucial an attack on the Circle Fort would be. The two also laid plans for the carpenters, masons and naval dock workers to hasten the new counter-wall across Epipolai. Gylippos meant to employ every means possible, as quickly as possible, to force Nikias off the Heights and to the lowlands near his fleet. Hermokrates could only agree with the logic of his argument.
Thoroughly impressed with the Spartan's stamina in the face of such quantities of wine, but still filled with concern for him, he summoned an iatros who secretly administered a potent soporific to Gylippos. The iatros, Hermokrates and even Gylippos understood that without sleep his shoulder could not begin to mend, but Hermokrates dared not risk trying to convince him of the need of any drug. Not long after Xenias departed the anodyne finally took effect; Hilarion and two other servants carried Gylippos to a spare room in the men's quarters, under the supervising eyes of Hermokrates. Finally, well after midnight, the entire household had retired.
*****
The heat woke him. A man like Gylippos was most usually up before dawn when the cool air, even in summer, was a familiar companion. Though he opened his eyes to darkness, he knew by the very scent and feel of the air it was late in the day. He fought to prop himself up, but collapsed back into a pillow, vision spinning, head pounding. He drew a deep breath and swallowed. He would try once more. Before he could, the door to his chamber creaked open allowing a shaft of blinding sunlight to pour in. A figure stood in the bright portal. He squinted. "What time of day is it?"
"Well past midday." The figure answered in a woman's voice. "I have some

Nemesis

bread for you." Now he knew it to be Dianthe. She dragged a squealing stool adjacent to the sleeping pallet and began to tear the bread into small pieces. One by one she slipped them into his mouth, watching him chew then swallow before adding another. Before he could ask she tipped a cup to his lips. He grabbed it with trembling hands and emptied it quickly.

"Why am I here?"

"Sir, your wounds are more serious than you realize." Dianthe pulled the empty cup from his hands and refilled it from a small orange pitcher.

He drank greedily. As the haze of drug-induced sleep began to lift, the pounding in his shoulder reminded him of the previous day's battle. Only when he tried to scratch his head did he remember that wound also. "Where is Hermokrates?"

Dianthe dipped a compress of linen into a water bowl then wrung it out before spreading it across his forehead. The damp cloth momentarily numbed the pain. "He is with the army."

Gylippos again tried to lift himself, but Dianthe gently pressed him back with a single hand. "The army has been gone since dawn. You must rest."

Gylippos sighed. "Can you send a message to my camp?"

Dianthe moved to the window and gently pushed open the shutters, the afternoon light revealing the youthful curves in her body despite her modest peplos gown. "Hilarion is at the Temenites gate waiting for their return."

"Kanthos?"

"Outside your door." Dianthe ducked her head out of the doorway. Kanthos entered soon after. Gylippos conveyed, without a single word, his displeasure at being away from the army to his servant. Kanthos could only wrinkle his face and shrug.

"Help me up," Gylippos commanded.

Kanthos, without hesitation, stepped forward to carry out his master's order until Dianthe intercepted him with a murderous stare. He stopped short of the sleeping pallet. "Remember the single condition you assented to," reminded Dianthe.

"And what condition is that?" challenged Gylippos.

Before Kanthos could answer, Dianthe spoke. "That no matter what you demanded of him, he could not help you up from your bed."

For a moment Gylippos could feel the anger rising in him until he realized that he still could not move on his own and that the restriction placed upon his servant was a sensible one. He also realized that until Hermokrates returned, this young woman controlled the household and anyone in it. Kanthos certainly exhibited no desire to challenge her and he did not possess the strength. "Is he allowed to speak with me?" Gylippos asked sarcastically.

"Certainly," answered Dianthe. She lifted the compress from his head, dipped it in the bowl once more and pressed it to his forehead.

"Is it the Circle?" Gylippos tugged at the compress to clear it away from his eyes.

"Yes." Kanthos replied, hovering near the foot of the bed.

"Ride to the gate. Have Xenias report here once he returns," ordered

Gylippos.

"Hilarion has already been dispatched to meet your captain," said Dianthe firmly. "Hermokrates ordered it so."

Gylippos, although grateful for the concern and care exhibited by the young woman, did not want to contend with her further, and wished also to speak uninterrupted with Kanthos. He manufactured a request. "My appetite seems to have suddenly returned. Is there something more substantial than bread to eat?"

Dianthe bounced up from the stool. "I am sure Glaukia has something prepared." She exited quickly.

"Sit there!" barked Gylippos. Kanthos shuffled to the stool and plopped into it. "How was the cavalry deployed? Did Xenias lead the assault?" He barraged his servant with these and other questions. The man could not answer. He had been loitering outside Gylippos' bed chamber night long and saw nothing of the army, and met with Xenias briefly before dawn when he came looking for Gylippos prior to the attack. Now he ripped into his servant for allowing this relinquishment of control.

The door swung open and in strode Dianthe with a serving tray. Steam rose from a black glazed bowl. Other smaller dishes overflowed with olives, sardines and goat cheese. Kanthos bolted up from the stool. Dianthe edged by him and sat, presenting the tray to Gylippos. "Black broth. Glaukia has tried her best to cook it up Spartan style."

She placed the tray on the floor lifting up the bowl, but before she could begin feeding him Gylippos snatched the spoon. "I'm not so helpless." He began to ladle the broth into his mouth, all the while presenting, as best he could, an aspect of delight and thanks. Kanthos did all he could not to laugh, for he could smell the zomos broth, it's pungent vinegar and blood combination wafted from the bowl—the taste undoubtedly horrible. With true Spartan courage he finished it all without exhibiting a bit of displeasure, but quickly stuffed a handful of olives followed by a healthy portion of cheese into his mouth to settle his stomach.

"You most certainly are in good appetite," observed Dianthe. "Would you like more broth?"

Before Gylippos said a word, Kanthos volunteered his service. "Stay here young lady and I will fetch it."

For a moment or two neither of them spoke, until Dianthe asked quite unexpectedly, "Is your wife beautiful?"

Gylippos paused a bit then answered, "That is an odd question."

Dianthe handed him another cup of wine. "Why is that so odd? Everyone talks of the beauty of Spartan women. Why Helen contended with Aphrodite in her looks. Is all of this fable or truth?"

Gylippos smiled. "Yes, Spartan women are beautiful indeed, but no more beautiful than you."

Dianthe looked away for a moment, trying to hide her embarrassment.

"I meant no offense, Dianthe. You lack nothing in flesh or spirit in

Nemesis

comparison to a Spartan woman." He could not believe what he had just uttered—not that he did not meant it, for he did, but that he expressed it—something he had never done before. He stared at her as she looked down at the floor. His stomach sank and his heart raced. It was almost as if he marched into battle. He felt something extraordinary, but would not allow himself another moment to enjoy it, but immediately fought to suppress his feelings with cool logic and memories of his wife. Thankfully, Kanthos returned. He handed him another full bowl of broth.

"I must see to my sister. Please excuse me." Dianthe, her eyes still down cast, left.

Kanthos took her place upon the stool. "Why was she crying?"

"Crying?" Gylippos pushed the bowl back into Kanthos' hands. "You eat it. And you better empty that bowl before she returns."

Gylippos watched his servant attack the bowl of broth, wincing after each mouthful, swallowing hard. He lay back wondering about what he had said and cursed himself for his honesty.

*****

Nikias trotted his horse well past the center of the battlefield, just beyond the breach in the abattis where the Syrakusans tried their assault upon the Circle Fort. Euphemos rode along with him as the surveyed the span of dead, the wrecked palisade and battered walls. They had repelled the attack, but barely. "Send for the captain of the Leontines. We will need his cavalry to provide a screen for our men tonight as they rebuild the wall."

Euthydemos nodded then asked, "What about the enemy counter-wall? We must attack—."

Nikias didn't allow him to finish. "Attack it again? Gylippos has fashioned those meadows into a slaughter pen. No attack. We must reinforce the walls near the fort, or risk losing it also."

Euthydemos, trying not to exhibit the exasperation that was welling in him responded in his high, staccato voice, "If they hold that counter-wall, our fort serves no useful purpose. If we cannot invest the city, our army serves no useful purpose."

Nikias knew he spoke the truth. Success would only come through a siege. The Syrakusans would not risk all in a single decisive battle. More to the point, neither would Nikias. Nikias also knew his men grew fatigued at this static fashion of warfare. They were soldiers, not brick-layers and masons, and performed these tasks most reluctantly. His spies within Syrakuse assured him that the city would capitulate soon; the Syrakusan command had scant monies to pay their mercenaries and held little hope in garnering reinforcements. Rumors of the new Spartan general being wounded added to the prospects of an imminent victory. He hoped and, with the help of Stilbides, prayed that the Syrakusans would break soon, before the autumn rains arrived.

Euthydemos began to laugh. Nikias, baffled by this display of joviality, reined up next to him. "What do you find so funny?" Nikias could only see the stacks of bodies and the battered, spilling bricks of their fortifications.

"This place," answered Euthydemos, still chuckling. "They call it Fig-Tree." Nikias looked around perfunctorily without speaking. "Can't you see?" Euthydemos twirled his horse in a circle." There's not a tree left standing." They both paused and scanned the dusty, churned earth that fanned out from their wall. No trees. Hardly a blade of grass or a leafless bush interrupted the landscape, their constructions and the Syrakusan attacks had reduced the once verdant orchard to a vast desiccated and barren expanse, its thirsty soil quenched only by the blood of combat.

Nikias absorbed the scene slowly for it reminded him now of his own life, and he recoiled at this thought, but could not deny it. Instead of patrolling the siege works, as he was wont to do each evening, he spun his horse around toward the main gate of the Circle, anxious to withdraw to his tent and consult with Stilbides. He required insight into the workings of the gods, for he had begun to lose faith in the industry of his army. By the time he had threaded his way through the narrow lanes of the fort to his command tent, the moon had exchanged places in the sky with the sun, its milky light distorting vision. He felt as though he rode in a dream. As soon as he entered the tent, Hiero ushered him to his couch and filled his shaking right hand with a cup of wine. The iatros hovered nearby, waiting to see if his services were needed. Nikias waved him away. "No pain tonight," he said. "Just fatigue. I need some sleep. And send for Stilbides."

The iatros looked to Hiero for permission to depart. He nodded. The physician pushed aside the flap and disappeared into the gloom. "How many more defeats can they withstand? How many can we?" Hiero asked as he presented a tray of figs to Nikias.

Nikias snapped one up and chewed away, savoring its sweetness and the comfort of his couch and its nest of cushions. "This war, my friend, is becoming a test of endurance. Our advantage is that Athens and its impatient, fickle assembly is far off, while the Syrakusans must contend with propinquity of theirs."

Hiero sat on a nearby couch, pondering Nikias' words. He had always thought that the Syrakusans having their council so near, and their citizens so quick and ready to assemble could only be to their enemy's benefit. Now he understood that decisions, although quicker made, may be wrong and hastily acted upon. And that is precisely what his master was hoping for. One rash and impulsive act by the Syrakusan council and the city would be theirs. But Hiero moved his thoughts beyond hoping to current reality and apprehended something quite different. This war hardly tips the balance and could go on indefinitely. Neither side is willing to commit fully. Victory or defeat is beyond reach. Hiero began to cry. He kept his tears hidden beneath his hands while he covered his face in them. He peered through his fingers at Nikias watching his chest rise and fall in sleep. Hiero tossed his shallow kylix on the ground and picked up a deep tankard, filling it with uncut wine. He gulped it down.

"Message for Nikias." A dust-covered rider stood in the opening of the tent waiting for permission to enter. Stilbides edged by the man and into the tent.

Hiero rose from his couch, wobbling under the influence of the wine. He

Nemesis

winked his eyes clear and stepped toward the courier. "As you can see our commander is sleeping. I will take the message."

The empty-handed courier cleared his throat. "The Syrakusans have reinforced their counter-wall toward Labdalon. It extends far beyond ours and cuts across its path."

Hiero nodded and the messenger spun on his heels, jogging out of sight. Although no tactician, he knew full well what this news meant: the Athenian army could not complete their wall on Epipolai. It was the cause of their attack earlier. He feared it would instigate more attacks still. He also knew he must awaken Nikias. He gently tugged on Nikias' shoulder staring at his closed eyes until they fluttered open. "A message has arrived." Still groggy Nikias could only manage a grunt. Hiero drew a deep breath. "The Syrakusans have cut off our wall."

Nikias pushed himself up on one elbow. "What did you say?"

"The Syrakusans have completed the counter-wall across Epipolai." Hiero extended a hand to help his master to his feet. "Should I gather the other strategoi?" Nikias nodded his consent.

Stilbides hovered before Nikias' couch. "You sent for me?"

"Come here, my friend." Nikias waved his seer closer. "You must make sacrifice to Athena. I seek the goddess' blessing for our next move." The soothsayer backed away a few steps before turning. He was out of the tent in a flash. Nikias felt a surge of relief. This most important task had been dispensed. Now he must engage in a more distasteful one—soon Euthydemos and Menandros would arrive. He hoped they would hear of the counter-wall from others on their way here. The inevitable sound of footsteps braced him for what would come next. Menandros entered first, followed by Euthydemos. "Gentlemen, rest," offered Nikias as he pointed to the empty bank of couches. Both moved to separate ones while keeping their eyes locked on Nikias. Menandros unfastened his sandals and tucked them under his couch, but Euthydemos, fresh from a mounted patrol, opted to keep his korthornos cavalry boots fastened and his feet upon the ground, using his divan as a chair only. Once they seemed settled and had a kylix each of wine, Nikias commenced. "We shall move our base to Plemmyreion."

Immediately Euthydemos challenged him. "And give up the high ground here?" Menandros shook his head in disbelief.

"The enemy has completed their counter-wall. To all purposes, Epipolai is lost."

Euthydemos, stunned by this news, paused while biting his lip, eyes darting side to side and up and down as his mind whirled. "Then we should attack their wall again."

"Yes." Menandros added in support. "Attack their wall. We should not so easily relinquish our advantage here on Epipolai."

Nikias sighed as a schoolmaster might before explaining an obvious lesson to a new and impatient student. "Did you so easily forget what happened this morning? We walked into their trap once. I will not allow us to make that same mistake again. Besides, the Heights will do us no good during this coming winter. We must secure a supply base closer to the sea and protect our ships in the harbor. If we control Plemmyreion, we control the harbor."

Euthydemos wrung his hands in disgust. Nikias, true to form, had made up his mind first then conjured up the rationale later. Both strategoi knew there would be no use in debating this decision. Both knew also that at some future date they would be compelled by every facet of strategy into recapturing Epipolai. The two abandoned their still full wine cups and Nikias. Their grumbling began once they exited the tent and continued on until each called for their company commanders. The officers gathered, received the new orders, and soon after trudged away, neither enthusiastic nor distressed by this new order.

By morning the Circle Fort boiled with activity as baggage-men and teamsters worked to load up wagons and carts with the freight of warfare. All the silver stores collected from their Sikelian allies moved first, followed by the entire contents of the arsenal. Most of the food stuffs also wended their way down the road from Epipolai, past the temple of Herakles and around the sweeping curve of the Great Harbor to the spit of land called Plemmyreion. The Syrakusan outpost at the Olympeion could only gaze out from atop the sacred precinct's walls in awe of the vast armament that paraded along the road. By dusk only a small garrison remained on the Heights.

*****

Endymion stood knee-deep in the chilling water of the Great Harbor staring across to Plemmyreion. Like ants, the Athenian engineers scurried over the barren spit of land, furious in their construction of the fortifications. The new walls and jagged towers grew quickly—Plemmyreion was a naked, empty peninsula, exposing every man and every task to view. *Long way for water*, mused Endymion. On the other hand, his new camp, just off the beach, enjoyed plentiful water; in fact more than he could desire for the marsh lie less than a few stades from his tent. The empty skies of summer now grew dark and swollen as autumn approached. The rains would soon be here, and he did not relish the thought of wallowing in mud through another Sikelian winter. He looked around at the men, some strolling along the beach, others, like him, wading in the water, taking advantage in the respite from re-erecting their camp for a quick bath. Since the death of Tisandros he had kept more to himself, not seeking companionship other than from an occasional porne. He thought often of how his dead friend would pine for the company of a real heitairai, a well-versed female companion, and not a cheap and quick whore that the infantrymen grew accustomed to hiring. But all the same it was the way he wished it—quick and cheap and meant to keep his mind off of Argos and his family.

"Argive!"

Endymion looked over his shoulder to the tide-line and the hulking form of Aniketos the Mantinean. The sight of the man still awed him: his neck seemed to pour from his ears and over his shoulders and his chest looked like a sculptor had chiseled

Nemesis

it from the hardest marble. His every physical attribute was an exaggeration. Endymion only smiled as the man lumbered by, watching him thrash through the water until he dived under, appearing ten or so meters out in the harbor. He wondered why he had never seen him at Zeus' games at Olympia. Who could contend with such a man in wrestling? In pankration?

As the sun slipped higher more of them went for a swim. The air indeed was chilly, but the water still held summer's warmth, but not enough for Endymion. He quickly dunked under then stood, scrubbing away the mud from his shins, every cut and insect bite reminding him of its presence with a sharp sting. As he washed he could still hear Aniketos as his arms cut powerfully through the water, and would look up for a brief confirmation now and then.

He heard Stump shouting the names of the men in his phyle, knowing his would be called out soon. Not waiting, he trudged up the up the beach, snatching up his chiton from a pile stashed near a log. "We have a job, boys," barked out the phylarkhos, "guarding wood-cutters."

"Why do they need guards?" Endymion rubbed his face dry with his chiton before sliding it overhead.

"Look." Stump pointed to the Olympeion. "Their cavalry there have been slicing up our foragers. Besides, this group is going further inland. It's not just firewood, but ship timber they're after."

"Ship timber?" Endymion snapped up his sandals and began making his way back to the camp, following his commander.

"They haven't been able to dry out the hulls." They both looked to the long bending row of triremes half in the water. Shipwrights and carpenters labored cutting what little timber lay on the shingle while the pungent odor of linen and pitch simmering in their cauldrons wafted over them. The phylarkhos jammed his spear into the sand. "I don't like it any more than you do. It's shit work. We'll be chased by their cavalry up into the hills and all the way back." He twisted his spear free and began jogging. "Let's go."

Within an hour Endymion's company had assembled in full panoplia, forming a rectangle with the wood-cutters bracketed in the middle. Before they even exited the stockade of their camp tower guards began shouting warnings to them. "Cavalry's forming out there!"

"How in Hades do they know?" a man croaked from behind him.

How do they know? he thought, as he looked around, searching for some dark silhouette in a tree, or high on a nearby ridge. The Syrakusans must have daywatchers stationed close by, but their vantage was not easily spotted. The gate swung open and reluctantly they marched out. His commander, along with a Leontine scout led them. A feeling of relief washed over him; they headed away from the open meadows and toward the path that snaked through the marsh. Rising above the orchards to his left, the dust cloud of cavalry marked their approach. If they picked up the pace, they should be in the swamp before any attack. The horsemen would not risk the soggy terrain. The teams of oxen though, even hauling empty wagons, ensured they moved slowly. Thankfully, his commander gave the signal for his detachment to race ahead to secure the road through the marsh. They rumbled forward, armor clanging, into the Lysimeleia, leaving their pursuers milling at the orchards' fringes. Once his squad had rumbled into the outskirts of the marsh, the Syrakusans reined up, far behind the wagons and their rearguard. He was certain they would be waiting for them on their return.

They shied away from the easy terrain near the Anapos, and hugged as best they could, the base of the cliffs of Epipolai, wary of any open tract that would expose them to cavalry, but the ground proved difficult even for men on foot and especially men humping seventy pounds of armor, so they slowed to a crawl. The oxen, although powerful, moved daintily over the rugged terrain; donkeys would have been better suited to it, and the light troops more appropriate chaperones. Gradually the low ridges grew to hills and ahead of them the hills began to stretch upward into mountains. Three hours into their march they halted.

The wood-cutters gathered around an old man who kept swatting away the mosquitoes with his petasos hat. He seemed to be directing them all. He kept pointing to the adjacent stand of trees while shaking his head. As one of the wood-cutters brushed by him, Endymion grabbed his thick-muscled arm. "What is going on?"

"He wants to go up into that mountain." He pointed with the head of his ax.

"Who is he? Endymion asked.

"Why he's the master shipwright. Says the pines down here won't do for planking or keels." The man swung his ax from his shoulder, dropping its head the turf while letting the handle rest against his leg. "Your commander's more stubborn than he is. Wants us to rest here for a while." Just as he finished he saw one after another of his company drop to a knee and jettison their shield and spear. Slaves collected around the mules, pulling baskets of bread and water skins from panniers. Endymion collapsed to the earth after planting his spear. The wood-cutter did the same. "Name's Pamphilos", he said, extending a hand to Endymion.

Endymion introduced himself then offered Pamphilos a drink from his flask. "It's a little stiffer than that water," he said mischievously.

"Let's have it here, then." He unplugged it and poured his mouth full, handing the flask back to Endymion as he eyes squeezed shut in delight. "Good wine."

"So tell me, friend: Why are we cutting ship timbers?"

"I'm no shipwright, nor am I trierakhos or pilot. I'm a simple oarsman, so I don't know what strategies and schemes our generals concoct or why we linger on a beach when docks and ship-sheds are only a day's sail away. But I will tell you this. Our ships are soaked and rotting."

"I'm no sailor so forgive me, but aren't ships made for the water?" Endymion gulped some wine and offered the flask to Pamphilos.

Flask still in hand, he waved it this way and that as he spoke, explaining in long breathless sentences on the maintenance of ships, the materials required, and the

Nemesis

discipline each trierarkhos must impose and why none of these requisites could be applied to their fleet. "And it all begins with the commander. Nikias allows this slackness. Why, I've heard that even some of the oarsmen have bought slaves to take their places at the rowing benches. Haven't seen it on my ship, but if this is so then our advantage of first-rate seamanship will be quickly forfeited."

"The Syrakusans will never attack us by sea. Why doesn't he pull the ships up to dry out?" Endymion asked. Now he caught sight of others in his company as they edged closer, apparently anxious to hear more of the state of the fleet from one of the rowers.

"Of course they won't. Most of their ships are hauled up in sheds in the little harbor. The remainder hid behind their forest of pointed timbers fronting the quays. They want no fight with us."

"Up! Everyone up—yes!" shouted the Stump as he strutted along looking down his nose at each man he passed. "We've got a hike ahead of us."

"Ambitious today, Stump?" called out Endymion.

"My ambition is to avoid ambition," replied his phylarkhos. "Get moving."

"Stump?" asked the wood-cutter. "He's the tallest one of your bunch."

Endymion grinned. "It's not his height we mock with that nickname."

The thickly wooded slopes proved cooler than the marsh and the meadows near the harbor, but only slightly. Endymion and his company spread out in a broad crescent with the wood-cutters behind them, each man scanning the fields and road for rising dust, the tell-tale sign of approaching cavalry. Endymion jammed his spear into the earth and dropped his shield, turning around to face the sound of the axes. Now he began to water the blanket of pine needles at his feet. It had been hours since he had relieved himself. Four wagons had already been stacked high with timber; slaves roped the logs to the wagon beds while the rowers kept up their assault on the newly fallen trees, hacking off the branches then felling more while the oxen munched on dry grass, their tails whipping away at clouds of gnats. He picked up his shield again and stared off toward the glistening harbor, where the sight of Athenian warships jamming the long, curving beach settled him. Occasionally he chatted with the man to his left or right, but after the death of Tisandros he balked at truly befriending another, so the conversations were cool and brief. He missed his friend. The sound of wagons rumbling toward him caught his attention.

"Time we're off!" shouted Stump as he marched by with exaggerated strides. "Want to be back before dark."

Endymion checked the long, stretching shadows and knew they would not. He hoped the Syrakusan cavalry would be withdrawing with the light and back at the Olympeion. The teams of oxen towed the over-laden wagons with little effort, but they pulled them slowly, too slowly for his liking. They would be fortunate to be back in camp by the second watch. They formed their rectangle once more, surrounding the rowers and the wagons and commenced the trek down-hill toward the marsh and the treacherous unbroken terrain beyond. Soon dusk enveloped them, its gloom stealing any chance they might see an approach of the enemy. The grinding wagons wheels and the snorting of the oxen erased any notion that he might hear them. Deaf and blind to the terrain ahead he and his company plodded along. Not a whisper of wind. Both the night and the mosquitoes thickened as they hit the edge of Lysimeleia. With two–thirds of their journey completed he now dreaded the remainder. He turned to look back at the lumbering oxen. *Whip them, damn it*, he thought as he sought relief from the swarms. In whispers the command to halt rippled down the column. Endymion dropped his shield and began scooping up the pungent mud and smeared it over every bit of exposed skin, even blackening his face with it. Soon all around him did the same. Once he had applied this soothing balm, anxiety again struck him. He wanted to move, and quickly. Ahead the open meadows spread wide, their last expanse of terrain before arrival at camp. Stump had them moving, to the relief of all but the oxen. The teamsters had been ordered to silence, relying only on their whips. Unfortunately, the beasts required more encouragement. The column lurched forward ever so slowly.

    With each step Endymion felt the change. No longer did his sandals sink into the sucking mud, but struck hard-packed, dry earth. The marsh slipped behind them, His heart raced as he knew they slogged into the midst of the open field. Shouts rang out from the column rear. Silhouettes of men on horseback tumbled into view, their arms swinging skyward, blades flashing in the moonlight. Men screamed. Without orders he and the men adjacent spun around and sprinted toward the wagons. Only fifty or so meters away, by the time they reached them the attackers had melted into the night. None of the hoplites had been injured, but nine of the rowers lay sprawled upon the road. Two oxen, still harnessed, swayed on wobbly legs, blood gushing from wounds on their backs. A third had collapsed, its neck carved open and gurgling with labored breaths. A pair of wagons had lost a wheel each. Two others seemed undamaged. It took more than an hour to transfer what timber they could and continue on. Endymion's estimate proved correct. Not long into the second watch they passed the line of pickets and entered the stockade.

Nemesis

Chapter 25
Syrakuse – Autumn 414 BC

"They hate you, you know," said Gongylos as he pointed to the banks of oarsmen. He was near enough to the pilot to be overheard—the man grinned as he leaned into the tiller, veering the trireme out into the whitecaps beyond the Small Harbor. The vessel began pitch as it climbed and dipped in the swells.

Gylippos, for the moment, ignored the comment. He motioned to Gongylos to order the kaluestes to double the pace. The flute skirled faster as the rowers escalated their cadence, inciting spray to shoot up over the ram, soaking the marines that stood near the bow. "Hate, you say?" Gylippos peered ahead at the four other Syrakusan warships that cruised in formation. "Attack speed," he barked. "Now we shall see how much they hate me."

Gongylos relayed the order and without hesitation, the piper accelerated his cadence and the rhythm of this mock battle. After a few minutes the order was given to withdraw oars. The drill was meant to simulate a ramming maneuver. The trireme coasted for a bit, the kubernetes holding it on course towards an anchored skiff that would serve as a target for the marines and toxotes. Their momentum proved more than sufficient to bring them to the skiff and well beyond, but Gylippos ordered another sprint, not so much to work the rowers—he wanted the vessel to pitch and roll as it would in battle to test the aim of the marines and archers. The skiff proved a small mark and the warriors on deck shuffled and skidded warily across the slick planking to brace themselves before launching javelins and arrows. Only a handful of their projectiles thumped into the open boat. The kubernetes shook his head in disgust, knowing they would repeat the run over and over, as they did every day for the past month. Two runs more and finally the greater share of missiles perforated the listing skiff than the waves. The marines had finally learned that not all of them could run to the balustrade at once—they tossed their javelins in relays, distributing weight more evenly across the rolling deck of the trireme, while the archers held the centerline and cast their arrows while sitting.

"Bring us home," said Gylippos. While Gongylos conveyed the order to the kubernetes he shouted out encouragements to the marines and toxotes. "Tomorrow, my friend, they will learn to hate you in my stead. I am off on a mission of diplomacy."

"Where to?" Gongylos walked from one side of the vessel to the other as though he were already on the quay. The marines, though, wobbled about as they moved away from the bow to their station amidships for docking. A single Athenian vessel, lingering well out to sea, caught his eye. "They watch us every day."

"Good. It will keep them occupied also," replied Gylippos. "The interior," he said finally answering his friend's question. "Since our minor but numerous victories over the Athenians, I would guess we have accumulated a few more friends than before. I will go to confirm these alliances."

"Let us suppose these allies are willing to send more troops," said Gongylos as he strolled about before the kubernetes, hands behind his back confidently exhibiting his sea-legs. "How will the Syrakusans pay them?"

"That is a secondary problem. I must focus on the primary. But I would think you Korinthians might donate a portion of silver to this cause. You have more of it than we Spartans."

"I am certain you will convince my countrymen of their obligations. You are visiting Korinthos, aren't you?"

"No, I remain on this island. A Syrakusan shall make the journey to Korinthos."

Now Gongylos leaned out over the balustrade, peering down at the hull of the ship as it buffeted along the quay. He turned to face Gylippos. "Dianthe will be upset at your departure." He smiled. "Unfortunate that you are already married."

Gylippos rolled his eyes. "She is barely a woman, and besides she is betrothed to a noble Syrakusan."

"Agatharkhos! He may be Syrakusan, but there is nothing noble about him. She fancies you." Gongylos embraced him. "She is beautiful, you know."

Gylippos shook his head in silence, trying as best he could not to let his friend uncover even the slightest bit of affection he might hold for Dianthe. Both men hung near the pilot, waiting for the marines to disembark followed by the nautai. Exhaustion was etched hard into the faces of the rowers as they ascended from their benches to the top deck. Most lumbered down the brow-plank without acknowledging either man, but every so often one would turn and snarl before departing. Gylippos' mind wandered. *It would be a good thing to be away*, he thought. *She shall wed mid-winter and I should be gone from Syrakuse until well after*. He felt a bit at ease knowing he would avoid this most painful event.

The pair stood on the quay surveying the squadron as it cruised back into the Small Harbor. Gongylos nodded in approval, watching the triremes coast then back-water smartly, the commands of each trierakhos carried out swiftly and with precision. Each day they improved in skill, but the Korinthian knew until they faced and defeated the Athenians at sea, their confidence was fragile, and their courage in doubt. "I think by the time you return, they will hate me as much as you."

"Do not sell yourself short, my friend," said Gylippos. "If you push them—as you must—they will utterly despise you in two months. Discipline is an unfamiliar quality here."

"I am certain Nikias conjures his own schemes now. What do you think he will be doing this winter?" Gongylos began to walk toward the arsenal.

Gylippos, distracted by the sight of a dock-man fumbling with a line, caught up to his friend. "He would be doing what I am doing—gathering reinforcements. Although I cannot believe Athens will send any more. Mercenaries, perhaps, or will she impress additional men from her subjects? Either way we shall be a drain on Athens' men or her silver."

"You speak as though Syrakuse is a mere diversion," said Gongylos as he

Nemesis

halted before the last trireme as it docked.

"Is it not so?" Gylippos laughed under his breath. "Syrakuse is a distraction. Come now. If either of our cities thought otherwise we would be in company with many more of our own countrymen defending this city. Would Sparta have dispatched a solitary officer? The real war will not be won here."

Gongylos shook his head. "Have you so quickly forgotten what Brasidas accomplished? He refashioned a *distraction*, as you call it, into a defeat for Athens that forced them to sue for peace." Gongylos swung his arms in a wide arc. "All of this, these ships and their crew: do they fight for a mere distraction?"

Gylippos sighed. "You must forgive me. A poor choice of words."

Gongylos grabbed onto his friend, forcing his to stop. "I would think those are the precise words that reflect how you see things. Damn, you Spartans are so single minded. Do you believe that only your only path to victory is in a Spartan phalanx?"

"It may not be," replied Gylippos as he clamped his hand over Gongylos', pressing it to his shoulder. "But it is all I have ever known."

*****

Nikias reclined on his sleeping pallet, while Hiero sat on an adjacent stool cradling a wax tablet, marking down his remarks. They had begun not long after sunrise, and now it was well past midday, for Nikias chose each and every word so very carefully, and he revised them singly then in sentences—again and again—trying the patience of Hiero. Finally the draft of the letter to the Athenian Assembly was complete.

"They will be furious," remarked Hiero. "But at least they will relieve you of your command."

"I fear that Assembly more than I do the Syrakusan army. Our enemy is much more predictable, even with this new Spartan commanding them." Nikias tried to get up, but the pain in his back held him in place. "Once you have transcribed it with ink and papyrus, bring it to me. I should want you to read it aloud, for that is how the Athenians will hear it."

"You would send me and not one of the officers?"

"Hiero, I have confidence that you will deliver my message and the letter in its true form and with conviction. I trust no one else." Nikias covered his eyes with a bent arm. "Now leave me to sleep for a bit, and finish your work."

Hiero left Nikias to rest and sat outside the tent, enjoying the afternoon sun as he scribbled away at the small table. His master had managed to reshape a simple thought into an elaborate document that relentlessly drove home his cautioning intentions, and Hiero, as he worked on it, doubted his capacity to deliver it orally to the Assembly. The words clustered together in awkward phrases, and stumbled along, heavy with qualifications. *This will infuriate them*, he thought, *to be lectured remotely by a failing general.* He tweaked what he could without revising too much and by the time he was done it was hardly mellifluous, but he considered it tolerable to the ear. Now he must hope Nikias either fails to recognize the changes, or better yet, accepts them as improvements.

Chapter 26
Athens – Winter 413 BC

Hiero finally felt at ease. The voyage had proved tortuous with the fickle winds of early winter tossing his vessel every moment since leaving the Great Harbor of Syrakuse. He strained to catch sight of any familiar face as the trireme ground along the quay; dock men pulled the lines tight setting the hull's planking to squealing. Once in full embrace of the wharf, a crewman slid the brow-plank over the side. It slammed hard, startling him.

"Hiero!"

He scanned the dock again, finally recognizing Thessalos. Hurriedly he made for the dock, coming face to face with Nikias' friend. "I have a letter of great urgency for the Assembly."

Thessalos put a finger to his pursed lips. "Many curious ears ply the waterfront. Let us get upon the road quickly."

*****

The clerk emerged from the shadows of the stoa behind the bema, carrying a papyrus roll in both hands, presenting it to the Assembly as though it was a precious and fragile gift. Hiero watched as the man peeled away the wax seal and curled back the edges of the scroll. For a long moment the clerk scanned the document before stepping forward then cleared his throat with a succession of coughs. Hiero listened and began repeating, word for word, the entire contents of his master's letter under his breath and in unison with the clerk.

"The report from our strategos, Nikias, son of Nikeratos," began the clerk. He paused then resumed. "'As has been our duty in the past, and continues now and into the future, we strive to keep the people of Athens well informed of our progress here in Sikelia. For a year and more, our army and navy have inflicted multiple defeats upon the Syrakusans, and we have secured from them much territory with the construction of various fortifications. But now a new army has arrived in their support and it is led by a Spartan. This body of reinforcements far outnumbers us in cavalry and light infantry, causing us to employ most of our infantry in futile attempts to guard the entire expanse of our siege works. Because of this we do not have the forces to attack Syrakuse—we have, in fact, become the besieged. The Syrakusans are now emboldened with the addition of these new troops and their Spartan commander has led them in a number of successful assaults upon our forts and siege works.

"'Our foragers are harried constantly, and even though our fleet and crew are superior, our ships lack maintenance, and we cannot harvest timber in sufficient quantities to refit and repair them. With each set back inflicted upon us, allies defect. Our grain supplies from the Italian mainland are threatened. Each morning, reports come in from every quarter of our camp that slaves have deserted. This situation grows more critical with each passing day.

"'These difficulties which I have enumerated, by themselves threaten the success of our expedition, but the diminishing control we have over our naturally recalcitrant trireme crews and marines—Athenians, like you who grow restless and are impatient for success, may undermine the entire operation.

"'To sum it up for you, Athenians, the armament you dispatched last year was more than a match for the Syrakusans and their allies, but a year in the field away from home has eroded its effectiveness, and now in light of the Peloponnesians sending additional reinforcements, we cannot hope to succeed. You must either recall the fleet, or dispatch reinforcements in the spring before more Peloponnesians arrive.

"'I also ask that you consider my past service to our city and to you, my fellow Athenians, and grant me relief from this command, as my health is rapidly deteriorating.'"

Hiero expected shouts of condemnation to be directed at Nikias for his blunt words. This he would endure if they only granted his master release from Sikelia. It would be an unpleasant and most difficult return, but at least he would receive proper treatment for his kidneys and could rest comfortably. Why would they harass a man who had in the past delivered so much for Athens and is now so ill? His stomach sank as he recalled the fate of Miltiades, hero of Marathon, left to die in prison from a wound for failing to pay a fine. No man, no matter how benevolent to Athens, would survive the ire of the Assembly; one failure is certain to undo a multitude of successes. But there were no outcries. No condemnations. To his surprise, men who he knew to be allies of Alkibiades defended Nikias, and proposed that reinforcements be dispatched at the beginning of spring. But they also insisted that Nikias remain in command, and voted to assign two other deputy commanders to assist him. *Poor Nikias*, thought Hiero. As always, h*e got what he asked for—almost.*

Chapter 27
Syrakuse – Winter 413 BC

Although only mid-afternoon, the winter's light began to fade, slowing her hand and frustrating her novice attempts at weaving. Dianthe's wedding, but two months passed, had dispatched her to a world more desperate and empty than the scorched fields of Melos. Her new husband, Agatharkhos, had provided her with two personal servants, but neither could weave much better than her, and since they were Sikels, they could not speak more than a few monosyllables that she could understand. She missed Elpida. She missed Kalli. The one person she most longed to see again might be gone from her life forever.

She passed the shuttle through the warp then pushed up on the shed stick, packing the weft and setting the loom weights to clinking like a set of wind chimes. Before she could begin another pass with the shuttle, voices spilled up to her window from the courtyard below. She dare not look directly out, but hugged the window frame and peeked at the gate as her husband, covered with dust from riding, lumbered through it. He tossed his cloak at one servant, disappearing into the andreion. There would be another symposion tonight, and she would only finally greet him deep into the night, after he was heavy with wine. These were the only nights he lay with her. With a little wine he was gentle. With more he could be brutish. She forgot about her weaving entirely and began to predict, with scenes of nights passed, what would transpire later. For a moment her eyes began to fill, but she fought back this urge to sob, to feel sorry for herself, by thinking of her parents, the fate of her countrymen and her hatred of Athens. Her only thought was to live long enough to see the pyres of the Athenians lighting up the Syrakusan sky.

Later, she took her meal as she always did, in a small room in the women's quarters alone. The ribald ditties sung by Agartharkhos and his wine-filled guests, plus the flute-playing of the female entertainers echoed through the courtyard, contrasting the dreariness and isolation of her evenings. When she had finished nibbling a meager portion, she ordered her servant to fetch a pitcher brimming of wine and to deliver it to her sleeping chamber; she would sip a little now, but save the larger share for Agartharkhos, hoping to nudge him from inebriation to unconsciousness.

"You may go now," she said to her pair of servants after they have filled the brazier with charcoal, a weak antidote to the icy night air. A chill shook her as she unclasped her sandals, so she kept her peplos gown on while slipping beneath the single blanket topped with scented fleece. With a soft breath she puffed out the modest flame of the lamp, plunging the room into total blackness, too dark to see the pitcher of wine or the cup, so she clenched the blanket under her chin, and tried to think of pleasanter times. Visions of her sister Elpida playing with the earthenware doll that Dionysos had given her induced a smile, but in her mind, as she watched her sister play in her adopted father's courtyard, the gate swung open and in strode Gylippos, with a flowing scarlet cloak, the very image of a divine hero. Elpida grinned and winked at her. In her dream she felt her cheeks blush.

"Good night," bellowed Agatharkhos, his voice shaking her from the margins of sleep. With the symposion over, he hovered in the courtyard below, ushering out his guests. By the sound of him, he had drunk more than usual; *it should prove an easy task to get him to sleep,* she thought. She groped for the pitcher. Her slender fingers clamped tightly around it and her arms quivered as she tipped it into the adjacent cup until the wine wet a finger that rested upon the rim.

Now the heavy slap of his feet echoed off the creaking stairs, growing louder, moving closer. The door swung open. Framed by the doorway Agatharkhos' diminutive, swaying silhouette hovered on the threshold. "By the gods, it is a frigid night," he said as he slammed the door shut. Dianthe sat up, cup in hand, trembling. He plopped onto the sleeping pallet and began fumbling with his sandals, kicking them against the wall after they had finally come free. He tugged his chiton over his head then turned to her, running his cold hands down her arms. Before she could offer him the wine, he collapsed into the fleece, naked and snoring. In three gulps she emptied the cup.

*****

"That is a beautiful gown, my dear," said Phaidra as she greeted Dianthe. Agatharkhos and Hermokrates had already fled to the andreion, leaving the entire courtyard to the women. "Forgive me," whined Phaidra as she grabbed Dianthe by the elbow, leading her to a sun-soaked bench. "In your condition you must rest." The two sat, Phaidra clasping Dianthe's right hand in both of hers. "Are the mornings—?"

Dianthe answered quickly. "Not a bit sick, not yet anyway."

"You are a strong girl. So is your sister." Phaidra turned to Elpida. Dianthe smiled and nodded. Elpida's expression of joy turned to dismay as she studied her sister's face. They communicated clearly without exchanging a single word.

"Where is Kalli?" Dianthe asked meekly.

"She is in the kitchen, instructing the cooks. She has planned a wonderful dinner for us all." Phaidra motioned for Glaukia to fetch her daughter. "She is so very excited at the prospects of being an aunt."

Kalli emerged from the smoky doorway of the kitchen, rubbing her hands in a cloth, a huge smile bursting across her face as her eyes fell upon Dianthe. She covered the courtyard quickly, and knelt beside Dianthe, wrapping her arms around her. "I haven't seen you since the wedding. Neither has your sister." Elpida, reserved until now, hugged both women, burying her head between them, sniffling.

"Now let her breathe a bit, will you," commanded Phaidra.

Kalli stood up and began inspecting Dianthe. "You are still as thin as ever," she said while gently pressing her hand upon Dianthe's belly. "Are you certain there is a baby in there?"

"There is no doubt, Kalli," replied Dianthe as she stroked Elpida's hair, pressing her sister's head to her breast. "And how is Dionysos?"

Kalli smiled. "He is well. He is training as an ephebe in the cavalry and has

Nemesis

been at the Olympeion for more than a week." Her smile melted away. "I miss him," she added.

"The Athenians?" asked Dianthe.

Her question seemed odd, causing Kalli to pause before answering. "Still in the Great Harbor and Plemmyreion."

The puzzled look on Kalli's face required Dianthe to explain. "Agatharkhos says women should not be burdened with the schemes of war or the state of the enemy. That is a concern only for men."

"And he is correct," said Phaidra. "Your husband is a good man, and thinks only of your welfare. There is no need, especially in your condition, to fret over such things."

With resignation Dianthe nodded. "Yes, Agatharkhos is a good man." She said nothing more. Neither did Kalli, nor Elpida.

Phaidra, uncomfortable with the pall of silence she had cast over them, stood up. "I will see to the cooks for now. Kalli, stay here and keep company with your sister."

Kalli followed her mother with her eyes, waiting until she disappeared into the kitchen then leaned to Dianthe, whispering. "He is fine," she said, shaking her head, "but you must forget about him and this infatuation. You are married now and soon to be a mother."

"Kalli, you are so very lucky to have Dionysos." Dianthe embraced her again.

Chapter 28
Sikelia - The Interior – Early Spring 413 BC

The smoke stung his eyes. Kanthos had been hovering over the pot of stew for almost an hour, slowly dropping in herbs, wedges of onion, and the cleaved portions of two hares that he had snared early that morning. Cold wind blew down the slopes of the mountains here in Sikelia, forcing him toward the fire. Gylippos strolled about the camp inured to it, his triboun cloak open and snapping behind him like a pennant on the mast of a trireme. After two months of scouring the highland villages and isolated valleys of Sikelia, Gylippos and his contingent had managed to obtain promises of men and horses, reinforcements that were desperately needed, although he knew not how the Syrakusans would pay for them. "Well?" he said as he stared the bubbling copper pot.

Kanthos quickly dipped his finger into the stew then licked it clean. He nodded. The cold had stolen dexterity; his fingers trembled as he snatched up a bowl, ladling it full before handing it up to his master. He filled a second bowl, but kept it clamped in his hands, allowing the warmth to seep into his fingers, alleviating, at least for the moment, the pain. Gusts shook the tree tops. Kanthos shuffled closer to the fire, squeezing his bowl, sipping from it slowly.

"The Kamarineans should arrive by nightfall," said Gylippos. "You'll be back in a warm bed in a day or two." He took his supper in hand and began to roam about the camp as he ate, passing through the mealtime huddles of his company of Neodameidois. They were hard men, not trained in the Agoge as he was, but hard none the less, toughened as they were first as slaves, then as fighters under the command of Brasidas, Polyakes and other Spartiates, consigned to battle far from home and against superior numbers. They had learned their craft of war quickly and had learned it well. When he first marched with them across Sikelia to the relief of Syrakuse, they all played their parts, he the commander and they the obedient soldiers, neither trusting the other, only discipline binding them together. After sharing battle in both victory and defeat, Gylippos felt a certain affection for these men. More importantly, they believed in him.

"Good evening, general." A soldier smiled and held his cup up as a salute. Others around nodded and saluted with their cups also.

"Warm enough, boys?" Gylippos asked as he knelt to share their fire, rubbing his hands over the flames. "Once the Kamarineans arrive, we'll be on our way."

"Do you think they'll still be there?" asked a soldier.

"The Athenians? I would be so very disappointed if they were not," answered Gylippos, inciting some muffled laughter. Heads began to turn toward the sound of hoof beats. "This may be them."

A solitary rider reined up in the center of the camp. "Where is Gylippos?" He scanned the men around him, easily picking out the Spartan. "Sir, messages from

Nemesis

Sparta."

    Gylippos took the small hide bag from the courier, instructing servants to feed him and tend to his horse while he made his way to his own tent. Kanthos stood outside, holding the skytale message stick that he would use to decode the dispatches. One by one, Gylippos pulled out the bundled and tied leather strips from the bag—six in all. "Bring me the messages after you have deciphered them," he instructed. Kanthos scurried into the tent cradling the bag, straps and skytale. Gylippos, meanwhile stared off in the direction of the western mountains, anticipating the arrival of his new allies. After almost half an hour, Kanthos emerged from the tent with a wax tablet in hand. Before he could offer it up, Gylippos commanded, "Read it to me."

    "'From the Spartans to Gylippos,, son of Kleandridas of the oba of Pitana.'" He hesitated a bit before proceeding. "'The Spartans have declared war upon the Athenians. Have dispatched 600 allied hoplites under the command of Ekritos, son of Polyakes, to Syrakuse.' That is the first part of the communication, sir," said Kanthos as he waited for a sign to continue. Gylippos rolled his eyes. Kanthos resumed. "'Korinthian agents report that the Athenians have dispatched a second fleet to Sikelia, to relieve Nikias. It is led by Demosthenes.'"

    Gylippos mind spun in interrogation. *Has their fleet sailed yet? How long for their crossing? Can we defeat Nikias before its arrival? Has Sparta invaded Attika?* His final thoughts dwelled on the Syrakusans. *Can Hermokrates hold the democrats in check once they hear this news?* "Where are they?" he blurted out, angrily.

    "Sir?" Kanthos squeaked, letting his arms fall to his side, still clutching the tablet and stylus.

    "The accursed Kamarineans. We must make for Syrakuse at first light. There can be no delay." Not waiting for assistance, Gylippos vaulted upon his horse and galloped out of the camp, heading into the shadowy mountains, his thoughts filling with the Athenian Demosthenes and how his arrival would afford an incomparable opportunity for revenge against so hated an enemy—the man who humiliated Sparta. The road had been scarred by the winter rains making the ride treacherous; he could imagine now why the Kamarineans were tardy. A figure stepped from the gloom, brandishing a spear overhead. Another lunged for the reins of his horse. Before Gylippos could draw his sword, a third tilted a spear at his chest.

    "Artemis!" growled the man with the spear.

    "Orthia," replied Gylippos. "At least you weren't dozing."

    "Sorry sir, I did not recognize you."

    "Then you did well. Never apologize for carrying out your duty." Gylippos rapped his heels into his mount. "I should be returning with some guests."

    He turned back for a moment and watched as the squad of pickets melted into the shadows. With darkness smothering his vision, hearing and smell became acute. Every rustling branch, each whiff of pine, sent his mind racing—evaluating—trying to glean evidence of the advancing Kamarineans. All sound, it seemed, was instigated by the wind, his sole companion on his ride so far. He thought now of the

Syrakusans and how, through patience, guile, and relentless drilling he had transformed them into formidable warriors. With another campaigning season he was certain he could defeat the Athenians. The report of this new and even larger fleet sent his spirits tumbling, so much so he called upon his mentor in prayer.

"Sir, I do not call upon you lightly. What must I do? How can I defeat our enemy if the gods seem fit to strengthen them beyond all measure?" He reined up his horse and listened. No answer. But then again he did not really expect one. The occasions proved rare when Brasidas' shade appeared to him, and never outside of the precincts of Sparta town. But what did come to mind is the war with the Medes at the Hot Gates. Leonidas killed thousands, but still more came on, a limitless supply of soldiers from the East. He did what he could, fought the ones in front of him, and did not concern himself with the multitudes queued up for battle. Unlike at Thermopylai, time, not geography, would fashion his choke point, his narrow pass that limited the amount of men the enemy could throw against him. He must attack Nikias quickly. He must find the Kamarineans now.

*****

Kanthos had required no orders. He commenced packing up his master's kit then searched out Xenias and found him snoozing, propped against a thick-trunked pine. Kanthos nudged him. "He has ridden out to meet the allies. I would think he wants the men ready to march at dawn."

Xenias sniffled before spitting his throat clear. "What is going on?"

"A message arrived this night. The Athenians are sending another fleet."

Xenias laughed. "I have found nothing upon this rocky island that would stoke such desires. What do you think compels the Athenians so?" Before Kanthos could reply, Xenias answered for him. "I'll tell you what incites them— they covet not so much a victory as they must obliterate any hint of defeat. Their empire depends on such."

Kanthos nodded and thought to himself, *and so it is with Sparta*. Now he recalled the more agreeable portion of the dispatch. "They are sending reinforcements and Ekritos is leading them."

"I knew his father. He was at Amphipolis with—," he hesitated then added, "—my brother."

"And so was I," added Kanthos.

Xenias dragged himself up and began to circulate amongst the men, passing along the order to be prepared to break camp at dawn. By now most had buried themselves under their cloaks and blankets, trying to fend off the icy winds. Most surprisingly they received the order with little complaint, for the prospects of a dry bed with a roof overhead roused their spirits. By the time he had returned to his tent, so had Gylippos, leading a battalion of Kamarinean hoplites and light infantry. The influx of Sikelian allies had been modest so far. The remaining city-states, villages, and hamlets hung back, not wishing to commit to either side until a certain victor became apparent.

Nemesis

Chapter 29
Syrakuse – Spring 413 BC

Gongylos had not waited for approval from the Council, but immediately put shipwrights and carpenters to work reinforcing the prows and catheads of each of the Syrakusan and allied triremes. His own countrymen had just demonstrated the effectiveness of these modifications; sea warfare had transformed from a battle of maneuver to one of brute force. The Athenian navy, at least at Naupaktos, proved unable to cope with an enemy determined to attack head-on. Their ships, constructed for speed and mobility, with lightly built catheads and long slender rams, crumpled under what they considered to be a most crude and blundering assault. As Gongylos watched the progress with great satisfaction he thought, *what better place to try out these innovations than the confines of the Great Harbor?*

"So you have become a shipwright?"

Gongylos spun round to find Gylippos smiling at him. He lunged to embrace his friend. "I never thought I would be so happy to see a lollygagger such as you. How was your holiday in the mountains?"

Gylippos stepped back and began smacking the dust from his chiton. "Restful," he said, grinning. "But more importantly, I have brought with me some friends."

"Cavalry, I hope? Any carpenters amongst your new friends?" Gongylos pointed to the flurry of work in the ship sheds and open berths. "We are applying a few modifications to our ships. Innovations that I trust the Athenians will not know how to contend with." His smile melted away. "Have you heard of the new Athenian armament?"

"Yes, by overland courier." Gylippos began to walk toward the nearest trireme, all the while inspecting the new, raw timbers being worked into the cathead. "You mean to attack them head on?'

Gongylos wrinkled his brow. "You do not seem overly concerned by this."

Without thinking he answered his friend's question, "Yes, head on."

"Dear Gongylos, we shall have some time before this new fleet of the Athenians arrives. Time enough to inflict much injury upon Nikias, if the gods allow it." He reached out from the dock and stroked the rough-hewn brace of oak that capped the out-rigger of the warship. "Have the Athenians obtained new lumber for their ships?"'

"Not over land. Hermokrates' cavalry makes certain of that. But word has it that the Etruskans have dispatched a squadron of triremes along with merchant ships of timber. And yes, we have already posted scouts to intercept them."

"Your premonition of a commander's orders makes you almost appear Spartan." Now he smacked the ship's brace with his palm. "We should test your innovations. The crews?"

"Much improved, but facing the Athenians is another matter. Their skill—."

Gylippos interrupted his friend. "Is it their skill or their courage that is lacking?"

Without hesitation Gongylos replied, "Both, I would say."

"Like their army, their fleet can only gain that final measure of courage and skill through combat. Training will only bring them to the threshold of victory—not across it." With Gongylos not far behind, he strolled the length of the trireme, ignored all the while by the teams of carpenters pounding away at dowels, laborers hauling fresh timber across its decking, and shipwrights barking out orders. "The refitting?"

Gongylos nodded. "A week. No more than that."

"Then I am off to visit with Hermokrates." Gylippos turned to his friend. "Dinner?"

Before Gylippos could depart, Gongylos grabbed him by the arm. "I know that look, my friend, and it unsettles me."

"And what look is that?"

"A look that tells me that you are not the least bit concerned that a new armament is being thrown against us. Could it be that the news that it is Demosthenes himself that leads it incites a bit of vengeance in you?" Gongylos finally freed his grip upon Gylippos' arm.

"This is the man that overwhelmed my fellow countrymen on Sphakteria, starving them first before swarming them with light troops, archers and javelin men many times their number. And he is honored for this? I will turn this island into his Sphakteria and swarm him with death."

For a long while Gongylos said nothing but stared blankly at his friend. He shook his head. "I will see you tonight." Distracted now by a wagon spilling its cargo of planking, he trotted away.

*****

Agatharkhos, while biting into an onion, picked up a corner of the cloak, inspecting Dianthe's work. He clicked his tongue in disappointment, letting the garment slip from his fingers. "I hope that is for you." She had been working on it for several weeks, and although her skill at weaving was indeed improving, it still did not meet with her husband's satisfaction; she could not now admit it was a gift for him. She nodded. He pulled up the other free corner then flicked it away. "Did they not have looms on Melos?"

"Yes, sir, they did," she answered meekly. She grew angry with herself for becoming so compliant, so docile. Only her respect for Hermokrates reined in her temper.

"Do not wait up for me tonight. After the council session, I will be attending a symposion at the house of Sikanos." He chewed viciously upon the last hunk of onion. "That Spartan fellow has returned and has asked to speak with us."

Her heart pounded so hard she was certain her husband could see it, even through her peplos gown and cloak. She would not let on and could not let on that this bit of information interested her. "Will Hermokrates be attending?"

"I suppose so," said Agatharkhos, his mouth bulging with onion.

Nemesis

"Please send along my regards to both him and Phaidra."

"Of course," answered her husband as he lumbered out of the room. His footsteps, as they faded going down the stairs, delivered relief; at night, on his return, they would instead bring dread.

No matter how she tried she could not work the wool, her fingers fumbling and discordant, as were her thoughts; anger at Agatharkhos' switched to flashes of joy upon hearing of Gylippos. This exchange of emotion threw her into a rage; she tore the half-finished cloak from the loom and ran to the window, tossing it into the courtyard below. One of her servants clamped a hand over her mouth, partially obscuring the look of terror on her face. The other ran out of the room and down the stairs, hoping to retrieve the cloak before their master caught sight of it. Dianthe buried her head in her hands, sobbing. Her unborn child kicked in protest at her outburst. "It would be easier if he were dead," she blurted out. She drew several deep breaths while pressing on her belly. "Go back to sleep," she whispered.

"Oh mistress, do not place such a curse upon your husband," said her servant as she hustled into the room, cloak in hand.

"It is not my husband who I curse." She grabbed the cloak and began daubing away the tears on her cheeks. *No, easier if I was dead*, she thought.

Jon Edward Martin

Chapter 30
Syrakuse – Spring 413 BC

Wary of spies, Gylippos had ordered the army to assemble every evening for the past week near the statue of Apollo Temenites and then march to the Akhradina Gate and beyond, parading noisily for all to see. By the third night, everyone in the city had become accustomed to the sight and paid little attention to this nocturnal drill. Tonight, though, he halted the column at the gate; Hemokrates soon joined him.

"Do you think they have seen enough of us?" Gylippos lifted his pilos helmet from his head. "Chilly night. Good. Their scouts will not venture far from their campfires."

"With the help of the gods, the Athenians should think this nothing more than routine. They would expect no less from a Spartan." Hermokrates grabbed his friend's arm. "We shall make certain they are quite preoccupied."

"You need only attack for an hour, two at most." He looked at Kanthos now. "We have made the proper sacrifices to Hermes. With his help we should arrive at the Olympeion by midnight, Plemmyreion by dawn."

"Be careful, my friend. You will be a long way from our walls," cautioned Hermokrates.

"I shall be much safer than you, for I will be on hard earth while you must be out there." He pointed toward the unseen waters of the Great Harbor. Silently he turned to face the black night beyond the open gate and led his force of Neodamodeis and mercenaries out, guided by a handful of Syrakusans—only five-hundred in all. The larger portion of the Syrakusans and their allies would man the fleet at first light. He felt quite at ease as they streamed onto the road with the walls of Syrakuse looming nearby, but as they marched southward skirting the marsh, the torchless battlements of the city faded into the gloom, heightening the sense of vulnerability expressed by Hermokrates. Every man had abandoned his bronze breastplate and greaves in the encampment, relieving each of forty pounds of armor, enabling speed and stealth while relinquishing the capabilities of defense; with no walls to retreat to, or armor to protect them, every one of them dreaded a chance encounter in the open with a massed phalanx or formation of cavalry. With this in mind, Gylippos had been anxious concerning the noise his company would generate, but the cacophony of frogs populating the margins of the swamp muffled their whispers and any incidental clang of metal. There also was a certain comfort in knowing that Xenias and a squad of infantry, along with two Syrakusans, reconnoitered far ahead. There should be no surprises on this night march.

Once they had passed the marsh the single track diverged into two roads; Gylippos led his men along the inland route toward the conspicuous hill of the Olympeion, easily visible, even at night, over the meadows and orchards that girded the Anapos River. From here they could clearly make out the Athenian siege wall, marked by torches above and the campfires of guards that blazed at intervals along its

Nemesis

base. Only now did he realize that they walked over a battlefield, the very place where the Athenians—at their initial landing— inflicted defeat upon the untried Syrakusans—the tree spiked with trophies of armor and weapons thrust skyward, solitary on the wide meadow as they marched by almost solemnly, glancing at this ominous reminder of the fate of the conquered. Any whispering had ceased.

Not far from the outer walls of the Olympeion Gylippos came upon an Athenian peltast emptied of his blood and lying twisted beside the road, his spear plunged into the turf acting as a marker. "Xenias' handiwork, no doubt," he whispered to Kanthos. His servant barely acknowledged him as he fiddled with his master's weighty shield; it spanned his back like a tortoise shell, forcing him to hunch. Kanthos peered ahead to the wall, anticipating the moment when he could rid himself of its bulk and relieve his spasms.

The guards barked out the watchword and without hesitation Gylippos responded with the countersign and his assault party began fanning out just inside the gate. Most knelt, keeping off the dank earth, but the more veteran lie down, their heads pillowed by shields, seemingly impervious to the damp and frosty ground, resting and regaining strength for the brawl to come. Servants, men, and boys already within the sacred precinct threaded their ways amongst the soldiers, offering skins of water and baskets of bread for refreshment. A boy approached Gylippos. "Water, sir?"

Gylippos waved him away. "Not now." He ambled about casually, but with every step inspected each man, measuring fatigue, for the longer stretch of their trek still lie ahead of them. Most all appeared no different to him than on any other drill, at any other time. A long winter's hiatus from combat seemed to have done them good.

"Sir, you should relax and take a bite yourself," insisted Kanthos. Of course he thought of Gylippos' welfare, but he also knew that if his master ate, he could rest, and an eighteen pound shield would remain off his bending back. Gylippos snapped up a slab of bread from Kanthos' shaking hand, choosing not to sit but instead continued to stroll about as he tore away small pieces and stuffed each slowly into his mouth. He strode up the hill toward the temple until his elevation afforded him a view of the Great Harbor and the city beyond. Campfires and torches blazed across the long crescent of the harbor shore and upon many of the beached Athenian triremes as well as the three forts at Plemmyreion. Even the sea played with light from the waning moon while an onshore breeze carried the salty redolence of Poseidon's realm with it. He could not help but admit what a beautiful night it was. Gylippos sighed.

"Quite a view." Xenias slipped from the darkness.

"And what do you see?" Gylippos tossed the dregs then pointed with his empty cup.

"Apart from the charming sight of so many Athenian campfires?" Xenias squinted as his sight fought against the darkness. "I see a deep and wide harbor full of enemy warships with a very narrow entrance."

"So do I. So does Nikias, for why else would he move his main fort to Plemmyreion at the mouth of the harbor. But he risks much by constructing it so far from his main encampment. He must have scant confidence that he can be re-supplied by land."

"He knows he can rely on his fleet to both provision him and defend the new fort." Xenias nodded, smiling. "I assume your scheme will somehow discourage him from this?"

"Let us rouse the men and discuss it with them." Gylippos tugged Xenias by the arm, leading him down the hill and to the sprawl of resting warriors.

"Up boys," he shouted then finished off his bread. The men rose slowly, groaning, chatter laced with minor complaints until they all stood. "Gather close. It is time I spoke to our plans and our actions." The grumbling ceased as they collapsed into a tightening circle around their commander. "Our mission I have deliberately kept secret until now because I value your lives and would not risk sacrificing a single one because of a spy," he turned and stared directly at the two Syrakusan scouts, "or a traitor. We shall attack the fort at Plemmyreion. But hear me clearly—we shall attack only on my order. Our fleet will launch at first light. We shall move against the fort only when they are fully engaged." He said nothing more but moved toward the gate, the crowd dissolving from in front of him as he strode ahead and by the time he had passed through the gate of the Olympeion a double column had formed behind him in silence. Again Xenias and his scouts hustled off, devoured quickly by the shadows ahead. Soon the entire column crossed the Elorine Road and moved at a jog toward the bumpy promontory of Plemmyreion, keeping low in gullies when they could not stay hidden behind the screening orchards and low scrub. Well before the sky began to lighten Gylippos had deployed his five hundred along the ridge, hidden from the guards at the Athenian forts. Meanwhile the Athenians, confident in their position and its distance from the city proved lax—not a single picket, guard, or road-watcher had been encountered since they left the Olympeion and none were upon the ridge. Not only could Gylippos and his men peer over the low walls of the main fort from this vantage but they also had an uninterrupted view of the Great Harbor and the spectacle to come.

Xenias bent low as he approached the crest of the ridge, finally slipping in between Gylippos and Kanthos. "We hid like this outside of Amphipolis, you know, watching the Athenians just as we watch them now."

Kanthos smiled but kept silent. Gylippos sighed and said, "Let us hope we can surprise them as you did." Now he motioned to the left wing of their contingent. "When the signal is given, you, Xenias, will attack the largest fort with your two companies. Move against it from the left. We will assault from the right. Ignore the other two lesser forts for now."

Xenias nodded and skulked away to the left flank. Kanthos edged a bit closer to Gylippos. "Why do neither of you mention his name?"

"Who?" Gylippos snapped back indignantly.

"Why Brasidas, of course. You both talk all around him, but never mention him, yet you both loved him. Why, I was his captive; even so I could not help but

Nemesis

develop an affection for so noble a man. Is his name a curse?"

"When it is appropriate, I speak of him. Why, on occasion I have spoken with him—only in spirit, of course," Gylippos added quickly. Now he stared straight at the Athenian fort as though he was deep in concentration over some detail of tactics or terrain.

"Yes, but neither Xenias nor you utter the name Brasidas when you are in each other's company."

"I did not realize that you were a sort of philosopher, Kanthos. If you were at some time in the past, you certainly are not now. And if you insist on practicing your art still, examine another."

*****

"Take a look at this!" Stump had torn back the flap to Endymion's tent and tossed his arms overhead wildly. He stood naked except for his crumpled felt hat. "The Syrakusans are rowing into the Great Harbor."

Endymion threw off his blanket and stumbled out into the gray light of dawn, rubbing the sleep from his eyes. He could hear the skirling of flutes echoing across the harbor and see clearly the gloomy silhouettes of enemy triremes cutting through the swells, passing so near he snatched up a stone and flung it; it fell short of the nearest warship by only a few meters. On the beach nearby, where only a small portion of his fleet had anchored, nautai and marines scrambled aboard their ships.

Stump began running toward the shore. "C'mon. Let's give 'em a heave!"

Every man sprinted away from the fort to the beach, all pouring around several triremes, sending clusters of scavenging gulls into the air, screeching. On board each a kubernetes or officer barked out orders to push, while at the same time the rowers dug and drew their oars. Moving slowly at first the hulking warships groaned as their keels plowed through the gravelly shingle until water slipped under their hulls, rolling them violently as they gained buoyancy.

Endymion stood chest deep in the sea watching as the two fleets converged. Half of the Athenian triremes launched directly toward the harbor mouth, intending to engage the Syrakusans that charged in from the Little Harbor, while the remainder formed up to receive an attack from the Syrakusan berths within the Great Harbor near the city.

"Our boys will get 'em," shouted Stump.

Endymion looked around and saw most of his company milling about in the water, watching and cheering as the battle raged. Across the harbor shouts of individual rowers and marines melded into a roar, the sound intermittently overwhelmed by an isolated explosion of cheers as one trireme tore into another. He could even see the distant figures of the Syrakusans on their walls as they too became entranced by this display of chaos. Suddenly Aniketos the Mantinean plunged into the water and began swimming toward the melee.

"By the Earth-Shaker, what is he doing?" yelled Stump.

Smoke from the burning ships drifted close over the surface, obscuring him for a moment. When it cleared they saw Aniketos swimming back toward them. Once in the shallows he pulled up a limp body from the water and tossed it over his shoulders and began plowing through the muted swells. When he reached the tide-line he dropped the man and turned around to face the battle. "Keep an eye out for more," he said. Sure enough other men, all from their fleet, swam frantically toward Plemmyreion, seeking refuge from the contest at the harbor mouth. By now the Athenian fleet had reformed and began to drive back the Syrakusans that had tried to force their way into the Great Harbor. Deeper in the harbor, the tumult of ships, wreckage, and smoke near the Syrakusan berths and quays revealed no clear victor or vanquished.

Suddenly two short blasts from a salphinx caused every one of them to turn around. Atop the low ridge behind them black figures rose out of the murk of dawn while pipes, of the very same type that Endymion had heard at Mantinea, shrilled out their marching cadence. His heart flew into his throat. "Spartans!" someone yelled out. Two separate and distinct walls of infantry advance down the ridge slope, trampling the few guards that stood their ground in futility. Even in the low light of dawn he could make out the dreaded lambda ensign on their shields and the glinting of sharpened iron on their spears. Others sprinted for the fort. Within moments the enemy formations slipped behind the walls of the largest fort, hidden from view.

"Get to the fort! Pick up your arms!" bellowed Stump. He raced up the beach toward the gate.

Endymion began to run until screams from the fort caused him to halt. Before Stump and others could reach the main gate, it flew open and what remained of the garrison poured out in a frantic sprint. Now an enemy column emerged from the shadows of the wall at a jog, spears lowered, and began to evolve into battle formation. Endymion spun around. "This way, Stump," he shouted. He spotted a pair of skiffs pulled up beyond the tide-line, small boats that had been used to ferry men from the main camp to Plemmyreion and also had been employed for unauthorized fishing excursions outside of the harbor. Six others had already gathered around the boats and began to heave them down the shingle and toward the water—Endymion and Stump added their muscle to the task. By this time the mouth of the harbor had been cleared of enemy triremes and an Athenian squadron, seeing the distress of the garrison and the flight of the refugees, rowed close inshore, picking up survivors. Endymion and his flotilla of skiffs rowed out to meet them.

*****

"I had hoped he would be here," said Gylippos, shaking his head in disappointment. Smoke drifted over and around him, burning his nostrils and blocking out the sun. He laughed to himself as he strolled the fort's interior, sighting platters of food and still full wine cups arranged as though a meal was about to be served; the surprise proved utter and complete.

"Who did you wish to be here?" asked Xenias.

"Nikias, of course. What a prize he would have been."

Xenias poked a shattered pot with his spear. "Ransom?"

Nemesis

"Ransom, yes: but information also. I think he would know the names of any Syrakusan collaborators." He wandered away from the array of tables toward stacks of trireme oars and warship tackle. "At least we seem to have captured all their spares. They will have a difficult time repairing the day's damage to their fleet." He looked up to the nearest tower and signaled to the day-watcher. "Any sign of our cavalry?" He shook his head. "They should have left the Olympeion by now." Gylippos and Hermokrates and ordered the horsemen and light-infantry at the Olympeion to sweep the land between the temple and Plemmyreion at day-break, hoping to run down any straggling Athenian foragers or refugees from the attack. Thinking them over burdened with this task he blurted out, "I cannot believe that many have slipped by us."

A messenger shouted for Gylippos, then skidded to a halt. "Food stores and plenty of them, sir, in the other two forts."

"We need the cavalry—any rider— unless someone has stumbled across a stray Athenian horse?" Gylippos looked around at his officers, each one returning only a blank stare. "We must send for wagons." He searched for his shield-bearer Kanthos and found him sitting on a stool munching on some abandoned figs and bread. "This is for you," he said as he slipped his aspis shield from his arm. Kanthos bolted up from the stool. "Relax and eat. I shall be at the shoreline." Kanthos accepted the shield with one hand while at the same time shoving a last handful of figs into his mouth. Gylippos, spear in hand, made his way clear of the fort and bounded down the steep incline toward the water's edge. "Clear them away!" He bellowed out, swinging his spear at the gulls that had descending to feast upon the Athenian dead. Servants rushed around waving their arms shouting, sending the rapacious birds airborne once more; they patrolled in slow, lazy circles, waiting for another opportunity.

Gylippos strode into the sea, scanning the waters. In the middle of the harbor he spotted a pair of enemy triremes pursuing a disabled vessel, most probably a Korinthian one as distinguished by its broad ram and beefy catheads. He kicked his way through shallow water looking for the detritus of battle, but found little if any debris either afloat or washed up. The Syrakusans had done their part, although he held the slim hope that they could have turned their distraction into a victory. The fleeing Korinthian trireme seemed headed straight for Plemmyreion with the pair of Athenian pursuers followed close behind by a third.

"Archers!" he shouted up at the tower on the fort. In moments two squads of Himerian bowmen sprinted toward him. "Form up." He spread his arms out on either side, standing knee deep in the harbor. A figure scrambled to the prow of the Korinthian vessel and waved at Gylippos. Gylippos, in turn, waved him toward his own position. "He'll bring them by us. Be ready."

Just as earlier in the morning, the men in and around the fort were drawn toward the harbor by the drama of combat, but now the Neodameidois moved down by enomotia and fully armed, ready to contend with any foe that might land upon the beach, or to assist any friend.

Gylippos shaded his eyes as he stared out at the figure on the prow.

"Gongylos?" he said, under his breath. As though taken over by the spirit of a god he strode behind the archers and bellowed out, "Only your arrows will save them."

The Korinthian tore through the swells, its glistening black hull buffeted by flotsam, the pilot fighting to keep his vessel true to course, for half the oars on the starboard side had been sheared off during battle, and the Athenians might overtake it before they would come into arrow range. Now at less than thirty meters off shore the kubernetes pressed both hands hard into the tiller causing the Korinthian to veer sharply left, turning so abruptly it avoided grounding, but it slowed and the Athenians pivoted also, fighting to stay in deeper water while sweeping around to cut off their prey. In their haste they had ignored the Himereans.

The captain of archers did not wait for Gylippos' command but ordered them to shoot once the lead Athenian trireme came into range. "Pour it into the stern," he yelled out. He wanted the kubernetes dead. Most of the arrows stuck dangling in the hide screens that shielded the pilot from missiles, but some flitted through. Not Gylippos, the archer captain, nor any one of the bowmen could see beyond the hide panels, but something had happened, for the trireme veered sharply toward the shore, its hull grinding into the bottom, the sudden halt of momentum flinging marines from its top deck into the harbor.

The remaining two Athenian triremes steered wide of the Korinthian, the shore, and their floundering companion, resigned to flight. In twin tight arcs they sheered away from Plemmyreion, marines and archers spilling from one railing to the other, all eyes locked upon their abandoned comrades and their floundering vessel. By now the Neodamodeis had swarmed up and into the grounded Athenian trireme, dispatching what remained of its contingent of marines and archers before descending into the lower deck of rowers; men pleaded while others cried out. The Neodamodeis slaughtered more than half—almost ninety—before Gylippos could put a halt to it.

Gylippos prowled the deck of the listing trireme, coming to the stern and the crumpled, perforated body of the kubernetes. The collision with the shore had flung his corpse against the balustrade and twisted his arms and legs into ghastly positions; blood soaked his saffron chiton. "Get them all ashore," he yelled into the dark, lower decks. Now the rowers stumbled up onto the deck, pushed and prodded by the Neodamedois. Most were naked. All were stunned and silent. "Strip the oars and tackle, then fire it."

Before departing the Athenian warship, Gylippos paused on the top deck and surveyed the disabled Korinthian trireme that had grounded not far away. He watched as rowers and marines began to evacuate the injured but saw no trace of his friend, Gongylos. As he hustled along the shoreline toward the Korinthian, litter-bearers scrambled by and in minutes returned in a much more deliberate procession, their wood and rope litters heavy with the wounded. He stared at each face as they passed. One litter, though, did not make its way to the fort, but lie in wet sand a few meters up the beach not far from the trireme's bow. Xenias stood over it. To Gylippos it seemed as if Gongylos reposed, napping, arms folded neatly and hair pushed clear of his face.

Nemesis

He stared, expecting to see his friend's arms rise and drop with each breath in his chest. There was no breath, not a bit of movement.

"He asked the surgeon to remove the arrow," said Xenias, his head bent low as he continued to watch over the body.

Gylippos knelt and pressed his hand upon his friend's crossed arms. "This was not meant to happen," he whispered. Gylippos had been careful in his calculations, or so he thought. Yes, they would trade a few Syrakusan lives for the Athenian forts at Plemmyreion, and that would be fine. After all, it was their city, their war. His arithmetic of battle did not include the life of his friend.

"I will fetch a wagon, sir," said Xenias.

Gylippos simply nodded. He stayed there, kneeling by the body of his friend through the morning, well past the time Xenias had returned with the wagon, all the while smoke drifted over him as the ruined Athenian trireme fed hungry flames. Kanthos sat upon the beach, close enough to respond if he were summoned but far enough not to hear the mumbled prayers and whispers that Gylippos engaged in for hours. No one dared disturb him, not until a messenger had made the run from the Olympeion in late afternoon.

*****

"Why do you insist on walking?" asked Hermokrates as they strolled across the causeway. "Agartharkhos' town-house is well past the agora."

Gylippos knew he must attend the symposion of the generals, but did not wish to hurry—this was a place he had hoped to never visit and the death of Gongylos left him bereft of appetite for both food and conversation and he certainly did not need his heart stirred by the sight of Dianthe. "Save the horses for battle," he answered quickly, with no elaboration.

"I am truly sorry about Gongylos. I know he was a friend. This is a terrible loss." Hermokrates leaned toward the Spartan expecting a response. None was given. The two men, followed by their servants Kanthos and Hilarion, strolled silently down the narrow alley-ways and across the expanse of the agora, finally arriving at the house of Agatharkhos as the last trace of light bled from the western sky. While still outside the gate they heard music, both flute and cymbals, waft over the walls, rebounding in echoes off the nearby houses. A slave, who had been undoubtedly peeking through the weathered planks of the gate, swung it open before either could knock. The entire courtyard glowed, bathed in the orange light of multiple hanging oil lamps. A small twirl of smoke hung above the altar to Zeus Herkaios, a remnant of an earlier sacrifice. The servant led them to the lone illuminated doorway. As Gylippos stepped toward the andreion, he glanced at the partially open door to the gynaikonitis, or women's quarters, noticing a glint of movement but no distinct form, so he turned his attention to the bright doorway, the music and the laughter within.

"Hail Gylippos, our Spartan benefactor!" Agatharkhos, already heavy with wine stood and thrust his kylix skyward in a mocking toast. The others, all five, held up their cups, but with less enthusiasm, quickly bringing them to their lips to empty them. Hermokrates grabbed the Spartan's arm and led him to the couch adjacent to

Sikanos while he occupied the couch nearest Agatharkhos.

"Why so glum, Spartan? Did you not enjoy your victory today? Why it only cost the lives of a few Syrakusans. A very economical transaction for you, Spartan" Agatharkhos' squadron took the brunt of the Athenians' attack. His own vessel barely limped out of the harbor while his brother perished aboard another, sunk by an Athenian ram. "What is a paltry two-hundred Syrakusans when measured against your valiant conquest of a stony, deserted beach?"

Hermokrates stood up. "That is the wine talking, Agatharkhos. Even you, as drunk as you as right now, know that in any battle men exchange lives for victory. It is the currency of war. The price, although high, cannot compare to the cost of defeat." Hermokrates, in a more solemn fashion, held up his kylix. "Let us first pour a libation to our comrades who did not return home with us today." In silence and with reverence they all, even Agatharkhos, lifted their cups while bowing their heads and tipped a portion of wine onto the floor. "To the fallen," they chanted in unison.

Gylippos, moved more by the memory of his friend than by the wine, stood up. "Agatharkhos, you accuse me of squandering Syrakusan lives with a diversion. I will present you and your fleet with an opportunity to avail yourself of one of *my* making. I will march out the army, with my Lakonians accepting the most perilous of positions, and attack the Athenian fortifications. I give to you a diversion. See if you can deliver even a portion of what I have today." No one spoke, not even Agatharkhos, as the flute-girl played on.

Outside the andreion Kanthos sat amongst the servants of the men who attended the symposion. They chattered away quietly, complaining of the harshness of their masters, their painful chores and the new discomforts brought on by the war. Krios, steward of Agatharkhos' household and a slave himself, exited the andreion with a platter of food cast off from the banquet inside. He handed it to one of the slaves and hovered before Kanthos. "You belong to the Spartan?"

Kanthos flicked a glance toward him, but did not answer. Hilarion hardly took notice as he snatched some figs from the platter and began to chew.

"Are you as mute and thick-skulled as your master? Can't you answer me with words?" Krios snatched away the platter before it could be passed onto Kanthos. The others, their mouths full, munched and smiled, as they watched and listened. Only Hilarion frowned, and shook his head; he knew Kanthos' temper and moved to the end of the bench, far away from both men. Krios grew angrier with the continuing silence. "Syrakuse has had its fill of your Spartan and you. You'll both be in the quarries with the Athenians when this is all over."

Kanthos slowly craned his neck, revealing his grinning face to Krios. "And who will do this?" He reached for Krios' chiton and pulled it up. "You'll need to grow a pair before you can do it. So will your master."

Krios' raw-boned face flushed red while his sunken eyes burned with anger; his knuckles whitened as he squeezed his fists. The other slaves grinned and nodded.

Kanthos glanced at the man's fists. "Is it women you beat with those, or

Nemesis

horses?"

The Krios lunged at him, and although twice his age, Kanthos managed, with the flick of a wrist, to spin the man beneath him, pinning his neck with his shin. He clamped his lips tight, staring straight at the slave as he pressed harder into his throat, watching his eyes roll back into his head as he let out a croak. Now the others, merely spectators until now, jumped on Kanthos and pulled him away. Hilarion sat still with his handful of figs, cracking a meek smile. The commotion demanded attention, for the symposion emptied out into the courtyard.

It was the home of Agatharkhos and his right to interrogate the slaves first. "How dare you fight here in my home!" He stared at the two servants that restrained Kanthos, stepping over the almost lifeless body of Krios, who still lay prostrate in the dirt. "Does this belong to you, Spartan?" Agatharkhos asked while pointing at Kanthos.

"Let us say he is on loan," replied Gylippos. "I apologize for his behavior." Gylippos nudged the slave that lay on his back with his foot. "Did you kill him?" Kanthos arched his eyebrows but said nothing. He kicked him again and again until a groan confirmed life. "If he is damaged, let me know and I shall recompense you, whoever the owner is."

Agatharkhos shook his head in disgust then booted Krios until he scrambled to his knees, moaning. "Get to the stables." He turned to Gylippos. "I would say our evening is at an end." He spun around and charged back into the andreion, a servant slowly closing the heavy oaken door, squeezing out the last shaft of light. One by one the generals departed along with their servants until only Hermokrates, Gylippos and their slaves stood in the courtyard.

"Come on, my friend." Hermokrates headed for the open gate, followed by Hilarion. Gylippos began to follow, but stopped in the middle of the courtyard; in the doorway to the women's quarters stood a veiled figure wearing a long cloak that hardly obscured her pregnant belly. He stared for a long moment until the door closed shut.

Chapter 31
Syrakuse – Summer 413 BC

Euthydemos and Menandros, each cradling a helmet in the crook of his arm, entered Nikias' tent and stood in silence. Nikias, for his part, reclined upon a couch, staring up, exhaling in loud, rhythmic puffs, waiting for the anodyne to deaden the pain in his back. Finally he turned toward the pair. "Are you here to tell me the Syrakusans are formed up again?"

The two looked at each other then Menandros spoke. "Nikias, they march out there upon the meadows, calling us out to battle. Our men hear the taunts. They grumble from inaction. With each passing day the grip of command is loosened. I beg you: let us lead the attack if your current health disables you."

"He wants us to attack," groaned Nikias through his pain.

"If you mean Ares, of course he does. But you need not invoke the god to reveal someone who desires combat. Pick any of our men. Each prays for you to lead us against the Syrakusans, if only to defend our honor. Your grand strategies and covert schemes mean nothing to them now. They crave action." Menandros, hardly an orator, spoke as though possessed.

Nikias propped himself up on an elbow. "It is the Spartan's schemes and strategies that you should concern yourself with and not mine, or the god's. *He* is desperate for battle. His only chance for victory is now, before Demosthenes arrives with the new fleet." He swung his feet off the couch and onto the floor. "Or is it Demosthenes' impending arrival that incites you to move? Do you balk at sharing victory with him?"

Euthydemos, silent until now, exploded with rage. "Inaction is not a strategy Nikias, but it is a policy and plan that you follow with unerring consistency. In any endeavor, you cannot succeed if you do not contend."

"My armor," he said as his face twisted in pain. He sucked in a deep breath then smiled. The drug had done its work. "Assemble the army." Menandros and Euthydemos paused at receiving this last order, surprised that Nikias finally relented. He glared at the pair. "Did you not hear?" Now they hustled out of the tent. Soon after, a salphinx blared out the call to battle.

Hiero emerged from the shadows deep within the tent. "Demosthenes should arrive within days. Why do you concede to this?"

"In a way they are correct. The facts present an undeniable case to intellect—wait for greater numbers to arrive. But men fight with their hearts and not their minds. Numbers are no substitute for courage."

Men criss-crossed the encampment in haste, all seeking their tents and panoplies, seemingly rejuvenated at the order for battle. On the other hand, the food vendors, wine merchants and others in the emporeion cursed the signal as the long queues of soldiers with money to spend evaporated away.

"Not but a mile off," yelled the day-watcher in the gate tower to Nikias as he

Nemesis

rode out, leading the army through the gate near the Elorine road, not far from Daskon. The column hummed with conversation while the ubiquitous clang and clatter of armor provided a familiar symphony, a symphony repeated so often that Nikias drew comfort from it. He smiled and tapped his heels to send his horse into a gallop. The sight of the Syrakusan phalanx caused him to rein up. Across the meadows, brown from the summer sun, the Syrakusans had assembled, their armor glinting brightly while their forms twisted in the waves of heat that rose from the interval. If the enemy crossed the road, he would launch the attack, for this would keep him still near his walls and his flank meshed with the vineyards to his left, protected from the swelling formation of enemy cavalry. Stilbides led the goat forward, and with flawless precision Nikas performed the sphagia sacrifice. He squinted in the harsh sunlight, trying to pick out Gylippos amongst the white-clad priests as he too, exercised his duty to the gods.

After having rubbed the blood away, Stilbides handed Nikias back his sword then held his red-stained fists overhead, thrusting them up, all the while hiding the fever-induced tremors that had begun to afflict him. The Athenians cheered. Nikias, as he slipped the sword back into his scabbard, glanced at the lifeless body of the sacrificial goat, its eyes staring back, black with death. Now he took the wine cup and sipped only a bit, before emptying the rest onto the blood-soaked earth. He could not help but gaze at their eyes. Awaiting the augury, the men looked to him, full of doubt and anticipation—full of life, and as with any battle, hours from now many will be staring back at him with eyes as black as these lifeless sacrifices. Above their heads and through the forest of wobbling spears he gazed at the workmen, sailors and camp followers that clung to battlements, only dark figures at this distance, but he knew also what must be in their eyes. He spun around to face the battlefield and the enemy beyond, expecting the same. He felt something cold, almost icy. The sound of flutes echoed from the Syrakusans and with a flash, the entire front rank presented their interlocked shields. The enemy phalanx undulated with movement. The advance had begun.

*****

Endymion hoisted his shield, pulling it tight to his shoulder as he watched the Syrakusans advance slowly but steadily, the interval between the armies diminishing to less than fifty meters now. In spurts arrows poured from behind the enemy ranks, pinging and rattling amongst his men. He tucked his chin beneath the shield rim and chanted a prayer to Athena, trying to muffle the accelerating beat of his heart. He looked to his right, to Stump and saw his commander standing upright, shield upon the ground and resting against his knee, taunting the barrage defiantly. To his left a front-ranker crumpled, wailing, an arrow pinning his foot to the earth. A battle servant rushed forward and dragged him through the files while another stepped forward to fill his spot.

Far off to his left he heard the rumble of metal upon metal, and the screams and cries of combat engaged. The enemy phalanx had advanced not in lines parallel to his, but at an angle, the combat igniting first at the far flank and inexorably rolling down the front toward him. Sweat streamed from beneath his helmet stinging his eyes and blurring sight. By the time he had winked them clear, enemy shields filled his vision. The collision skidded him backward almost a foot. He dug his left foot into the earth and pushed hard with his right, but it was like trying to move a mountain. The man in back shoved into him. He stumbled forward.

All of a sudden the fray subsided as the Syrakusans back-stepped. His first inclination was to pursue, to advance, and to pressure the enemy to retreat, but Stump restrained them all. "Hold fast!" he barked out. "It's a Spartan trick."

Endymion needed little urging to hold fast. Others, though, had become intoxicated by the thought of an enemy retreat and began to advance, breaking up their front line into a jagged swarm. Now a salphinx bleated out the order to halt. The fragmented contingents paused then tightened ranks while the bark of orders echoed down the line. Slowly these ambitious clusters of men slipped back to join the bulk of the phalanx. Ahead the Syrakusan army pivoted and presented their shield wall once more. Stump was right—it was no retreat. Nikias too, had seen through the ruse and had ordered the signal to regroup. What neither expected was the sight of billowing clouds of dust off to their left and the rumble of cavalry galloping towards them.

"They're coming up from the Olympeion," shouted Stump.

Endymion dropped his shield and glanced off toward the temple and its hill. Neither was visible through the rising haze. The Syrakusan horsemen had begun to advance and by the thunder of hooves proved not far off. If they had indeed advanced they would have been struck in the rear by this new contingent. For once Nikias' caution had saved them.

The order to withdraw rippled down the front rank, and in methodical evolutions, each lokhos in the phalanx oozed into columns and back into the camp. Endymion and his Argives held the right flank lingering upon the battlefield until all others had retired. "Our turn." Stump pivoted to the left, keeping an eye on the dissolving ranks of Syrakusans, and in particular on their cavalry. The company turned and began to tromp parallel to the battle line, moving toward its center. Ahead of them he spotted Nikias and his staff surrounding a lone body.

"What has happened here," asked Endymion as they passed by this odd gathering, trying to peer around or between the men. "It is the soothsayer."

As the rest of their company proceeded to the camp, Stump and Endymion stepped out of the column and hovered near Nikias, his retinue and the body of Stilbides . "Not a good thing," said Stump. "Not good at all." Litter-bearers jogged in opposition to the retired column of hoplites, their approach causing the ring of men to separate. They dropped the empty litter adjacent to Stilbides, waiting for the order from Nikias to remove his body, but Nikias seemed oblivious to them, his head bowed as he chanted some unintelligible prayer. His mutterings went on for more than a quarter hour. Nikias lifted his head, opening his eyes as though he had just awakened. "Carry him to my tent."

*****

Nemesis

    Dianthe insisted on an excursion to the agora, and only the absence of her husband afforded her even the chance of coercing her servants into allowing her to leave the town-house and make the short journey, riding in a small canopied litter. Once at the agora she ordered to be carried on toward the battlements that overlooked the Great Harbor near the shade of the fig tree that grew over the Spring of Arethousa. She waved off any assistance as she slid from the litter then draped her himation cloak over her swollen belly. With a servant on both sides, and her hands clamped in support, she ascended, step by step, the bank of stairs that led to an unoccupied section of the wall. The breeze lifted her veil while billowing out her capacious peplos gown and cloak. Only four steps and her breathing labored, but the sea air cooled her as she braced herself against the stonework. Suddenly a great shout rebounded off the stone crenellations. In the harbor below the fleet of Syrakusan warships fanned out from their berths near Ortygia while the remainder of their ships cut through the swells at the harbor mouth and charged in. Dianthe searched out Agatharkos' trireme but could not find it amongst the advancing formation of Syrakusan warships.
    A boy squeezed in besides her and began pointing toward the Athenian camp on the beach and to the plumes of dust rising beyond. "The Spartan is attacking them from the land," he shouted.
    She lost all thought of searching for her husband's ship, instead mesmerized by the clouds of dust that undoubtedly marked the battle hidden from view by the siege walls and orchards beyond. Frustrated at not being able to see the encounter she again turned her attention to the harbor and the fight. Individual ships sliced in and out of the massed jumble of combat, while shouts and screams spilled over the water and up to the spectators on the walls, but nothing clear could be discerned, although everything was visible. For almost two hours the fleets jousted in the Great Harbor with neither side gaining an advantage. Finally she found her husband's ship as it rowed away from the deep center of the harbor toward the quays and safety. She hardly felt any sense of relief. "What is happening now?" she asked as she tugged on the boy's chiton.
    He dipped his head in respect then answered, "It seems both fleets will pause a bit to rest and eat."
    Sure enough, as if through a previously agreed understanding, the Syrakusan warships withdrew to the docks near Orgtygia where food vendors from the agora had set up to provide food and drink, while the Athenian ships did likewise, retreating to their beach, a beach protected by a barrier of anchored merchants ships, where too, they might replenish themselves. To all it seemed the battle was over. The crowd along the battlements, too, began to drift away from the harbor with the spectacle at an end, but Dianthe delayed as she kept looking inland toward the assumed battlefield. The dust had, by now, been swept away by the onshore afternoon breeze, leaving no indication of the unseen combat. She gently ran an open palm over her belly, in a curve that replicated its shape while wincing a bit. He baby reminded her, with a kick, of her condition. She slowly slid her back along the rough stone wall until

she came to a seat at the base of it. She drew a deep breath. Her servant knelt beside her—one stroked her arm while the other gripped her hand. Neither spoke but only looked for a sign from Dianthe.

"I am fine," she said as she daubed away the sweat from her brow with her cloak. "It is still too early for him," she said smiling. She watched as the last of crowd abandoned the sea wall, most filtering through the alleyways toward the agora where food apparently awaited them also. The boy, her companion through most of the battle, lingered atop the battlement, dangling his legs over the stonework as he kept watch on the harbor. She glanced up at him. "Is your father with the fleet?"

He shook his head. "No ma'am. Killed a year ago by the Athenians. But my brother Phaidemos is."

"I pray the gods have delivered him from this battle today." She spoke the words to the boy but meant them for Gylippos.

The boy pulled his feet up and spun to his knees. "They're going out again!"

Dianthe, with the help of her servants, stood and leaned upon the battlement. From the close-by Syrakusan docks, the warships swept out in formation, streaks of churning white-water furrowing the dead-calm harbor in their advance toward the Athenian camp. Seemingly caught unawares, the Athenians could manage to launch only a few vessels at first, and by the time the larger portion of their fleet had rowed out from their barricades, the Syrakusans bore down upon them at battle speed, with their timber-thickened prows inviting them to clash. Without speed gained, the Athenians had no alternative but to accept battle head on—their vessels, built for maneuver and not collision, shattered under impact.

At first more young boys scrambled up to the battlements to watch, always the first spectators at any extraordinary event. They were soon followed by laborers and craftsmen from the nearby manufactories—sun-burnt carpenters, clay covered potters, and men black with soot from the smelters' ovens. In minutes the sea wall facing the Great Harbor seethed with onlookers. Dianthe, finally succumbing to the afternoon heat descended the stairs gingerly and aided by her servants, eased back onto her litter to be carried home. Cheers and shouts continued to boom from the walls as though the entire city viewed some sort of athletic games. As they approached the agora armored men—men from the land battle—began to filter through the market place. She tugged back the curtain on her litter just enough to peek out and ordered her bearers to halt near the strategeion. Hermokrates strolled by her, with his brother Proxenos and their shield-bearers close behind. Several more soldiers passed by until another she recognized—Sikanos—also appeared.

"Madame Dianthe, it will be dark soon," whispered her servant.

"I must rest for just a moment longer," she insisted. From across the span of the agora she spotted him, his crested helmet glinting orange with the light of sunset. A pack of young boys bubbled around him like hungry puppies yapping for a scrap of food. He appeared thin to her and his shield, always polished mirror-like, was now splattered with dirt and blood. He passed by so near she could smell the sweat on him

Nemesis

and almost hear him breathe, but he failed to notice her and he too climbed the stairs to the strategeion, disappearing through the dark portal. She scolded herself for not calling out his name, but then thought better of it. What would she say? Indeed what would he say, what words could he offer her other than some polite, dismissive phrase.

*****

"We have sunk seven of their front-line triremes," said Ariston, the Korinthian. He turned to Gylippos. "Your mealtime ruse worked to perfection."

The other strategoi shouted out mild acclimations of congratulations to Gylippos—except for Agartharkhos. He sat dark-browed and brooding upon his couch, unable to pronounce even the slightest approval of the scheme. The battle had been a draw—that is until the Athenians were lulled to complacency by the staged cessation. Gylippos had counted on Athenian hubris to execute this most modest of victories.

"The brave men of the fleet deserve commendation, not I. We honor them. We honor the dead that met their end in the Great Harbor today inflicting defeat upon an enemy unfamiliar with such setbacks." Gylippos could afford to be generous in victory; he must be generous, for words proved cheap currency when purchasing courage and he knew when the new Athenian fleet arrives they will need every measure of it.

Ariston swallowed hard. "Yes, we did best them today, but still lost three warships to their dolphins." He spoke of the three ships that had broken formation in an attempt to breach the string of merchant ships that protected the Athenian beach. They burst through convenient gaps only to suffer damage by heavy bronze weights fashioned to resemble dolphins that had been dropped from make-shift hoists at the Athenian barricade. Ariston had warned them before the battle of such machines. Now he scolded them. "Two ship and most of their crew lay at the bottom of the harbor. Only yours, Agatharkhos, managed to escape destruction."

Agatharkhos, shaken from his lethargy by this rebuke, could remain silent no longer. "I apologize for my zeal, and the zeal of my men, but if others had followed us, we would have indeed breached the ship-wall and destroyed their fleet once and for all."

Ariston restrained himself. Gylippos too. Hermokrates, even though Agatharkhos' friend, could not. "If they had followed you, we would have no fleet. The Athenians may appear to act rashly, but do not be so easily fooled. Everything they do, they do with extreme calculation. Do you forget who leads them? Nikias measures every action upon a scale, adding a weight to the balance of risk then accounting for it on the balance of success."

Agatharkhos offered no rebuttal, but tipped his kylix in salute then emptied it.

Gylippos stood. "Friends, what we have achieved today is no small thing. What you Syrakusans have achieved in the Great Harbor, you must not lose sight of. You have fought the Athenians in their element and prevailed. I would think the very scales that Hermokrates speaks of have been tipped in your favor. Remind your men of this. Until now, Syrakusans, you have entered battle trying to avoid defeat, to survive and withstand both the skill and reputation of the enemy. You have equaled their skill and by this action today damaged their reputation. Dismiss any thoughts of mere survival and replace them with notions of victory." His speech extinguished any further debate. How could it not? He told them what they wanted to hear and for once he could tell them the truth. Above the pleasant tunes of the flute-players and the verses of drinking songs that reverberated within the andreion, the unmistakable pounding of hoofs, penetrated the walls. Gylippos knew what impelled this courier to arrive with such haste. He prayed the Syrakusans could withstand his message.

Chapter 32
Syrakuse – Summer 413 BC

    Nikias, ailing evermore, still managed to drag himself with the aid of Hiero, down to the beach. Word had already reached him of the new fleet's arrival, delivered by one of his scout ships that patrolled the shores north of Syrakuse. He and his officers, all ablaze in polished armor, and helmet crests splayed by the wind, summoned what dignity they could as they awaited the landing. From the beach, behind the wall of merchant ships chained bow to stern that performed duty as a make-shift stockade, he could see nothing of the fleet. Only the cheers of the lookouts on the merchantmen gave any indication of its approach. His eyes drifted to his own, battered array of warships pulled up on the shingle and felt a bit embarrassed at their condition. Gone were the brightly painted balustrades and masts, the wind-bellied sails of dazzling saffron and gold. It was as if he viewed them through a gray veil. Now a single trireme slipped through the barricade, oars glistening, violet pennants whipping. With certainty it was the warship of Demosthenes. Men ran into the water to greet it, grabbing lines, forming in teams to pull it ashore. A squad of marines bounded down the prow-plank first, clearing the way for Demosthenes. He hesitated a bit at the balustrade, scanning the shoreline first before turning his eyes inland toward the encampment. Finally he descended to the shallows, meeting Nikias in water ankle deep.

    Nikias sucked up a deep breath and stood as tall as he could. "Greetings, Demosthenes," he said before fighting off an emerging cough.

    "By the gods, man, you look miserable," he growled. He took Nikias by the arm and began to lead him up the beach. "We must talk straightaway." As the pair moved inland more cheers exploded from the men on the beach. Both men turned. The new fleet had begun to flood by the barricades and into plain view.

    "Seventy-three in all," announced Demosthenes, answering Nikias' inquiry before it was posed. "Five-thousand heavy infantry. Double that in light troops and archers." He spit then winced. "I could smell your camp before we even entered the harbor."

    Nikias was at a loss of what to say. By now he and his entire army had become inured to the stench, the foul air of the marsh and the months of refuse both from men and animals that had covered the land between the Anapos and the marsh. Once off the beach the two wended along the broad main street of the camp that led to Nikias' command tent, passing knots of soldiers that here and there shouted out the name of Demosthenes. Nikias, Demosthenes and the other officers of the initial expeditionary force ducked into the tent, while the guard of marines bracketed its entrance.

    Nikias set his helmet down upon a small wobbly table near his couch and began to unfasten his breastplate, not waiting for Hiero to assist him. Free of its weight he sat, motioning for the others to join him.

    Demosthenes, however, remained standing. "I see the state of our army. Can you relate to me what the condition is of our adversary?"

Nikias answered. "They grow stronger each day. The Spartan Gylippos has garnered more allies from the Sikels and from the Hellenic towns nearby. They have cut our siege wall and now occupy the heights."

"Hmm," mumbled Demosthenes as he finally took his place upon a couch. "But what is the state of their army, of their men? Are they as disheartened as the army I see in this camp?"

Nikias fought back the trembling in his right arm as he reached for a kylix. "They have ample food—much more than us, and clean, abundant water too; but like our men they are wrought with a malady. They are sick of war."

"And you hope that this distress will bring them to terms?" Demosthenes kicked off his sandals and leaned back.

"There are many men within their walls that would make peace with us. They only need a reason to bolster their argument with their fellow citizens—a nudge is all it will require. I think your arrival with so vast an armament will provide this nudge and more."

"A nudge you say. You have been nudging the Syrakusans for nearly two years. By our very appearance today we have crushed their spirit. We must attack them and attack quickly."

Nikias cleared his throat. "You have not even disembarked your men, to say nothing of reconnoitering their walls, assessing the terrain or meeting to counsel with our officers."

"I do not need to walk upon Epipolai to know that is the key. And I am more than certain that if I offered the choice of delay or combat, which they would choose." He nodded to each of Nikias' officers. "I shall not allow procrastination to devolve this new armament into the wretched thing that sprawls across this plain."

"Has the Assembly given command to you?" Nikias asked him bluntly.

Demosthenes laughed. "We, sir, are co-commanders. "

Nikias smiled. "Then as your partner and peer in this endeavor, let me hear your plan."

Of a sudden the others started chattering and tipped their cups empty as if an unwelcome guest had just departed. For hours they discussed, in detail, the new plan of Demosthenes—a plan which he had weeks upon the sea to contemplate, formulate, and refine. He had accounted for every detail.

*****

A soft breeze swept up from the harbor, carrying with it the smoke from the enemy campfires that burned on the far shore. Gylippos ignored it and the Athenians for a moment, instead locking his gaze upon the far off mountains and the last sliver of sun that sunk behind them. Each and every day he would venture to this outlook upon the wall, surveying the Athenians, most times observing little change in their walled camp and barricaded shoreline then depart quickly to other tasks. Today he lingered. He smiled, thinking of Sparta then suddenly returned to the moment. "I

Nemesis

should say we have a day, two at most before he attacks."

Xenias spit. "His ships are indeed emptying quickly."

Both men had been here on the battlements day long, keeping watch on the newly arrived Athenian fleet, while others had come and gone, bored by the spectacle.

"What do you notice about these ships?"

Xenias frowned. "Besides their polished masts and gleaming figureheads?" He shook his head.

"Look to their decks," said Gylippos pointing. "They span full and are fitted for transport and not combat. He is pressing for a land battle."

Xenias scanned the Athenian camp, his eyes finally landing on the cliffs of Epipolai. "He covets the heights."

"I would, if I was him. He cannot hope to defeat us in the fields between the Olympeion and the marsh, but up there—there is where he can maneuver. That is where he must build his siege wall." Gylippos sighed. "He knows, as I do, that Epipolai is the key to victory. I would think we should not be so fortunate as to have two Athenian commanders relinquish then ignore so vital a piece of terrain."

Xenias measured the terrain with eyes. "We observe every move. How can he hope to assault the heights unseen?"

"At sunrise, perhaps? In a storm?" Gylippos turned away from the harbor and began to descend the long bank of stairs. "I should like to speak with Demosthenes. Come, we shall assemble the army and greet him. I could do no less for Demosthenes than I had done for Nikias."

Gylippos walked straightaway to Hermokrates' town-house, and convinced him to call a session of the generals. He wished to march out the army, not to induce battle, but to measure his new opponent. They would, as he assured Hermokrates, form up outside the walls late in the afternoon, with little day left for fighting, even if Demosthenes proved foolish enough to attack with the Syrakusan cavalry barracked at the Olympeion available to assail his flank.

*****

"The cadence must be slow," ordered Gylippos. "I want the Athenians to have the proper time to respond to our invitation." The gang of pipers dispersed to their divisions, while the lokhagoi continued to encircle him, awaiting their orders. Now he addressed them. "I would expect no battle today. But be alert nevertheless. March out slowly and smartly. This is an exercise in spectacle."

They grinned with understanding before jogging away. In minutes Gylippos gave the signal and the pipers commenced. In twelve columns they spilled left as they exited, so that on their return their shields would be presented to the enemy, and continued to advance along the base of their counter-wall until the last contingent marched free of the city. The signal to halt was piped, followed by the command to pivot right. Gylippos smiled. Across the meadow he could see the Athenians scrambling to form up, salphinxes blaring, dust drifting skyward in great clouds. He motioned to the herald. "Extend my greetings to Demosthenes and ask if he would meet me out there." He pointed with his spear to a broken portion of a stone wall that once marked the boundary of an orchard. The herald, staff held out before him, jogged off toward the Athenian center, but before he could reach their lines another man, most certainly a herald also, intercepted him. They spoke at length and this puzzled Gylippos, for his request was simple and straightforward and never felt quite easy when someone else was required to speak his words. After some time, the enemy herald returned to his ranks. Finally, after an extended delay, he trotted back to the empty land between the armies, nodded to Gylippos' herald, who in turn signaled that the parley was on. Gylippos hesitated a bit, wanting to see Demosthenes, and if he required an entourage as Nikias did; a solitary figure ambled away from the Athenian phalanx toward the battered stone-work.

Gylippos stared at him for awhile as he stood but a few feet away. The man wore a hard face, framed by a graying beard, with eyes unsmiling, dark, and intelligent. This was the face of the man who captured Sphakteria, the man who, in a single morning, defeated an island full of Spartans.

"You seem not much like the devil my countrymen think you are," said Gylippos. Demosthenes continued to stare at him in silence. "As you can see, we have both our armies assembled, each man armed and primed for combat. Why don't we settle this now? Your countryman Nikias has deemed it fit to make this war a life-long occupation."

Demosthenes cracked a grin and began to turn right and left. "We could resolve this now, but I think your cavalry would be hard pressed to stay at the Olympeion. Their attendance might spoil things."

"They are good boys, and might be cross with me if I did not invite them. " Now he mimicked Demosthenes, glancing this way and that. "I do see your concern. I have an alternative proposal."

"I am listening, Spartan."

Until now Gylippos' tone had been almost affable—now it turned steely. "I will give you and your army more than you gave my countrymen on the island. Lay down your arms and depart Sikelia now, and I guarantee your safety. This is the final time we shall speak with one another. There will be no other offers, no parleys, and no truces. Persist and you will have no soldiers left to ransom."

Unlike Nikias and his retinue of generals, Demosthenes did not scoff at this offer, nor did it anger him. He nodded once and turned away. Gylippos remained near the fractured wall, watching the Athenian phalanx swallow him up; now it began to shiver with activity then disperse, thousands of men scattering toward their walls and the beach. There would be no battle. The Syrakusan assembly would be thankful for that.

Gylippos made his way back toward his ranks in a most leisurely fashion, being met more than half-way by Ekritos and Xenias. "Sorry, but your men must wait to get bloody, Ekritos." He turned to look back over his shoulder. "But I do not think they will wait long."

"Was that Demosthenes out there?" asked Ekritos. "What did he say?"

Nemesis

"Yes, Demosthenes it was. How the gods favor us, my friend. They have presented us with an unparalleled opportunity." Gylippos waved the signal to disperse. "We have a chance to avenge ourselves upon the man who very nearly brought Sparta to its knees."

Ekritos, a young man, and barely tested in war, grew excited at the prospects of revenge against so formidable an opponent. Xenias, however, proved a bit more guarded. Until now and with Gylippos as his commander, he had fought coolly and with calculation against armies. He sensed for the first time that they would march not against many men, but just one, with logic replaced by obsession.

Gylippos ordered the officers of the Peloponnesians to assemble near the statute of Apollo Temenites, as soon as they had re-entered the city, asking nothing of the Syrakusan generals, for now. Over sixty of his unit leaders milled about waiting for him to speak, from junior officers leading platoons, to veterans in command of battalions. The few townsfolk that lingered in the sacred precinct also gravitated toward the Spartan as he stepped up onto the wide base of the statue of Apollo. "Are you Athenian spies?" he yelled to the pair of boys high in a plane tree; they shook their heads violently in the negative, mouths and eyes wide open. Gylippos smiled. The boys scurried away. His men drew closer, finally dropping shields against their legs while planting their spears. A single cough broke the silence.

"We have a different sort of adversary, a man very dissimilar from our long time opponent, Nikias." His men, pensive until now, laughed. "Demosthenes will not dally here long. He will attack, and soon, but I think we have this final night before he can settle in his new men and assess the others already in the camp."

Ekritos stepped forward. "The harbor or the heights?"

"Epipolai," Gylippos replied. "If I was in his place, I would attack our counter-wall and recapture the entire plateau." Not a man spoke. Not a man moved his gaze from the Spartan. "Tonight is our last night in comfortable beds within the city, so enjoy it. Tomorrow we bivouac on the heights in our forts. When he attacks, it will be most likely at dawn, advancing first under cover of night." He jumped down from his make-shift bema. "Then of course he could take the advice of Nikias, and we will be sleeping on cold ground for months to come, waiting."

Chapter 33
Syrakuse – Summer 413 BC

Day long the carpenters and masons had been gathering their axes, saws, chisels, baskets and other paraphernalia required to construct walls, towers and palisades. Shipwrights too, along with a company of sappers and pioneers joined them in preparation for the march up to Epipolai. Every man who could walk and bear arms had his named inked upon the katalogos. Demosthenes would hold nothing back on this bold assault upon the heights. His decisions proved quick and violent. Stump already prowled his section of the Argive encampment, checking on each of his men, joking as he moved about, as always mixing humor with precise and vital instructions.

"Every one of you draw your rations?" he yelled out as he turned in a circle.

Endymion lifted his battle-pack. "All five back-bending days worth," he replied.

"Good. You'll be hungry up there and thirsty. He'll want that wall finished in less than five days, you mark my words." He pointed to Demosthenes as he rode by upon a chestnut war-horse, purple boots clamped to the animal's sides and his chalmys cloak drawn stiff by the wind. His bearing was confident and his attire impeccable. His presence calmed them all. "Get some hot food in your bellies. It'll be awhile before you taste something warm again."

Endymion hunched over his bowl of leeks and barley, scooping out mouthfuls with a scrap of bread. He longed for a bit of meat, but even the salt-fish had been long since consumed and not all the new varieties of provender had been off-loaded from Demosthenes' supply vessels. The wind, that up until now had swept the mosquitoes away from their camp, petered out, so he moved close to a cook-fire, hoping the smoke would protect him. He inhaled savoring the cleansing scent of the fire, for it masked the stench of the camp, even if it was less than effective at keeping the swarms of flies and mosquitoes away. Finished with his meal he scoured out the bowl with a handful of sand and stuffed it into his battle pack. The army had become so depleted that a single slave on this night march would haul the kit of three hoplites; it was a Hykkarean assigned to him that hovered nearby, a man much closer to his home than Endymion was to his own and he reluctantly handed the slave his pack. He was unsettled by the fact that the Hykkarean could, if he wished, disappear into the night with their belongings and reappear in his own city within a few short days. The sun began to duck behind the curtain of mountains to the west, deepening the already bleak shadows of the cliffs they would be skirting. He stared up at this prized slab of land, imagining himself high up there and looking down once again upon a trapped and encircled city and thought how many times in the past two years he had foreseen victory, and now despised himself for allowing this tantalizing thought to occupy him. He fought to summon anger—and desperation. These are the things that must fill his mind as he marched and fought in the days ahead if he wished to see his home again.

Nemesis

He tied and re-tied his sandals, or what remained of them, making certain that they fit to his feet like a second skin; he wanted no flap of leather or loose strap to trip him up. He checked the blade of his sword once more, running his finger along its pitted edge, feeling only small portions where the sharpening stone had done its work. He tossed it aside and began to amble toward the physicians' tent, seeking out one of the wounded that would be exempt from the night's assault. The ones still conscious coolly stared at him as he moved amongst them, until he came upon the Mantinean Aniketos. "Wounded?"

Aniketos gazed up at him through clouded eyes. "Is that Endymion, the Argive?" He broke into a spasm of coughs.

Endymion knelt. "What ails you?" His gaze moved from the man's face to his scabbard and sword.

"It's the air. This swamp has sucked the life out of me." Aniketos chest collapsed as it emptied of breath. He inhaled and began coughing once more.

Endymion reached for the sword, drawing it free of the scabbard; it gleamed in the scant light of a flickering torch. "My friend, may I borrow this for the night?'

Aniketos, his huge body, once so powerful commenced to shiver in convulsions. "Take it in trade—for a blanket."

Endymion snatched up the sword and grasped his friend's hand, squeezing it with affection. "We have a deal." He jogged back to his tent, threading his way through the jumble of men as they worked their way to the assembly points, grabbed his blanket and returned to Aniketos. "Here is something to warm you up." He unfurled the blanket, spreading it over his friend, and noticed the shivering had ceased. He waved to one of the attendants. "You, fetch that torch." The man handed it to him and stood by shaking his head. Endymion drew the torch near to Aniketos' face and saw the light reflect off open, glassy eyes—eyes devoid of life. He tugged the blanket up until it covered his friend's face.

"Time to bang shields!" Stump bellowed as he waved to Endymion. The phylarkhos melded into the stream of men heading for the main road of the camp. Others pushed and jostled past Endymion, every one of them anxious to commence this great undertaking, this mission that should inaugurate the long sought end of the war. Endymion, though, shuffled past the litters of wounded and the dead, turning back only once to see a pair of blood soaked slaves haul up the body of Aniketos and toss it onto a wagon full of corpses stacked like sheaves of wheat or barley. Back at his tent he managed to buckle on his linothorax, and snatch up the remainder of his panoplia quickly, excepting his bronze greaves, and ran after his fellow Argives, catching up with them just outside the main gate.

"Forget something?" barked Stump as he wacked Endymion's bare shin.

"We are climbing tonight. Those will only slow me down." Endymion fell in behind Stump waiting for the lead elements of their triple column to advance. He grinned. *So quiet for so many*, he thought, as he watched men far ahead finally surge forward. Thousands of them marched in darkness—and in silence. Endymion stepped ahead, following the man in front, all the while amazed at the army's discipline and stealth. They would be upon the Syrakusan sentries before any could sound the alarm. In two short days Demosthenes had resurrected this army and instilled in them a cool resolution. Endymion was certain now of victory.

Their lengthy march brought them around the marsh and along the road that skirted the base of Epipolai as it twisted northwards towards the pass of Euryalos. The malodorous air of the camp faded away to be replaced by the scent of thyme and wild oregano that grew amongst the stunted pines at the base of the cliffs. Endymion looked up. *Long way to fall*, he thought. Suddenly the column halted, men shuffling into the ones in front who had already stopped, inciting bouts of angry whispers. Spears clattered. More rarely, bronze armor clanged. Heads turned as information rippled down the column. "It's started, boys," said Stump. "Shake off the sleep and get ready." He looked directly at Endymion. "It may get messy up there. Remember the watch-word—Athena-Proxima, and pray that the goddess is indeed near."

In fits the columns surged then halted then streamed forward again, until Endymion's company began to encounter an ever steepening grade. Their column generously formed at three abreast for most of the advance now squeezed down to two. Men slipped on the crumbling steep incline, tripping over rocks, fallen tree limbs, and each other. Sweat poured down Endymion's face beneath his helmet, stinging his eyes while his legs and lungs burned from exertion. Now he heard shouting, not of a single man, but of what seemed to him like hundreds, if not more, roaring like the surf on a storm-tossed beach. Mingling with this human cacophony, the unmistakable din of metal upon metal, pealed over the ridge and down upon them. As he lumbered to the crest of the ridge, he looked upon a most remarkable, almost trance-inducing scene. The moon, newly risen at his back, cast long gray shadows across the flat ridge top of his advancing army. The enemy fortress reflected this light reluctantly, appearing more shadow than substance, while the polished shields of the Syrakusans flashed like wind-scattered embers. It all appeared so much like a dream that he stumbled when the man in back of him had to shove him forward. "Keep moving," he barked at Endymion as he pushed him with his shield.

"Form up!" yelled Stump, holding out his spear, waist level and parallel to the earth. The Argives finally coalesced into a ragged file and rank formation. Once satisfied that his men were arrayed in something resembling a phalanx Stump thrust his spear forward and led them on. Ahead of them men streamed by, angling this way and that, the shadows formed by the full moon, multiplying their numbers and confusing direction and intention.

"Keep it tight and keep moving," barked Stump. Within minutes they had surged past the Syrakusan fortress at Euryalos, encountering only a rare few enemy dead at their feet as they advanced. Far ahead it appeared as if the very soil heaved and tossed, and took on the voices of men as the two armies swirled about the plateau, embraced in blind combat. All of a sudden he bellowed, "The paian boys. Let 'em hear it from you!" Now the Argives began to belt out the hymn to Kastor, this sacred chant stoking their courage and moving them forward. They struck a lone band of

Nemesis

Syrakusan light infantry, catching them confused by the paian that they most assuredly thought sung by their own Dorian kinsmen. They screamed. A few ran, but most all died and were trampled by the Argive advance.

Endymion began to breathe rhythmically, a breath in with his left foot and one out with his right as it struck the earth. They moved slowly, but inexorably toward their objective—the Syrakusan counter-wall. Alongside his formation and not far off he sighted a brigade of Athenians, marked by their leader Demosthenes, his triple crested helmet flashing in the moon light. Across the plateau, as far as his dimmed vision permitted, he saw clusters of men hastening toward Syrakuse.

"We have done it! They're on the run."

*****

"Reform!" Gylippos coolly walked before his battered unit of Neodamodeis, pointing to each surviving front-ranker or his replacement, marking out the front of each file. He had raced with his company to the fortress at Euryalos as soon as word reached him of the Athenian assault. Arriving there, he found his company outnumbered—*and* admitting as he cursed himself, out-maneuvered by Demosthenes. They had left the back door open and the cursed Athenian had shoved his way in. He reached for Kanthos, grabbing him by the chiton, pulling him nearer. "Find Ekritos. Have him lead the Thespiains to the first rally point." Yes, he had been surprised by this night attack, but beforehand hand had carefully denoted muster sites where his forces could reorganize and reform. This was the one small advantage that they still possessed; he had drilled and marched them repeatedly over the pock-marked terrain of Epipolai until they had intimate, painful memories of every rock, gully, and tree incised into their minds. He looked up at the moon, its muted light enticing the eyes, yet in truth revealing very little. "Men, look up there," he pointed with his spear to the great, scarred disc hanging in the black sky. "That is the direction where comes the enemy." He strained to see into the mass churning over and across Epipolai, trying to pick out any move toward the counter-wall. Suddenly a salphinx bleated out a signal from the Athenians and a jumbling mob streamed toward his right flank, heading for the wall and their last fort. He waved to the flute-player, who without delay, piped out the signal to advance as the order cascaded down the front rank to pivot right. They proceeded slowly, with an eerie calm and dispassion, in utter contrast to the boiling chaos ahead of them. Now, as they drew closer, he could easily calculate the size of the enemy phalanx, and his company did not compare favorably, but he must do what he could to slow them down, and buffet and bounce them off their path and away from the Syrakusan fortifications. Suddenly a second formation rolled toward them, also with the moon at their back, but reminiscent of a Spartan army, they sang the Dorian paian.

"Hear that!" The men around him cocked their heads.

"The paian?" shouted Xenias.

"The Argives, no doubt." Gylippos looked to the gap between the two advancing formations, the Athenians to the left and the smaller contingent of Argives to the right, reckoning the separation. He gave no new command; they continued to march toward the Athenians, whose ranks had loosened during their advance and oblivious to his company as it approached them. "The paian!"

Now his men belted out the battle hymn to Kastor. The Athenians, shocked for a moment as the singing commenced, slowed and began to thicken their ranks, pivoting their phalanx toward Gylippos. The two bodies of warriors collided almost blindly, shields squealing and thudding, men wailing as iron found flesh. They fought as much by feel and smell as by sight, for even the moon-light was quickly veiled by the rising dust of combat. Gylippos heaved his shield into the Athenian directly in front of him, but it felt to him as though four men shoved back. His men recoiled then slammed forward again, and again the Athenians responded with multiplied pressure upon his front wall of shields. Their legs wobbled. He could feel the formation beginning to break up.

"Withdraw!" his order quickly reached the piper who calmly sounded the brief flutter of notes that signaled retreat. They jogged away then at another signal spun around to re-face the enemy, but the Athenians too, were exhausted, and did not chase. Over the course of a hundred meters or so they retreated, spun around and retreated again several times before arriving at the rally point. Ekritos and his men moved out to cover the returning company.

"Orders?" Ekritos appeared from the gloom.

"Wait." Gylippos handed his shield to Kanthos before uncorking his flask. He sipped slowly.

Ekritos did not appreciate his serene demeanor. "Wait for what? They will be at the counter-wall if we do not attack."

"Look." Gylippos pointed to the Athenian phalanx that they had just engaged them, and moving quickly toward them was the Argive contingent, who had just taken up the paian again. The Athenians turned again as they had when Gylippos attacked, and just as his company had done the Argives began banging shields with them. "Now, let us join their party. Hold the files tight, close order, and keep the moon in front where we can see it."

*****

"Hit 'em hard, boys. The wall is close," shouted Stump. The tumbling mass of soldiers before them, who for a moment seemed as they headed toward the wall also, stopped and swung their shields to face the Argives. Men stumbled and pushed—and fell. Endymion could smell the sweat of his opponent but could not see his face until his spear found the man's groin, arching his back and tilting his helmetless head toward the sky. He yanked the spear free and lunged again at the dark form in front of him. Screams burst from the enemy ranks, but not ones of pain, but of anger—and the accent was decidedly Attic.

"Athena!" bellowed Stump. "Athena!" More and more of the Argives shouted out the watchword challenge.

"Proxima! Proxima!" the counter-sign cascaded from the enemy phalanx. Endymion pulled back his spear, but kept his shield high. Now the bellowing of the

Nemesis

watch-words drowned out the waning clash of battle. Endymion looked to the earth at his feet and the body of the Athenian he had just eviscerated, the blood still pooling beneath his crumpled body. An Athenian officer stepped between the two paused battle lines shaking his head. "Reform! We march to the wall." The two allied columns—Athenian and Argive—had struck at each other in the bewildering light and confusing terrain, but with order restored both contingents regrouped.

Endymion's file moved uneasily to mesh with the Athenians left flank so the combined phalanxes could move forward against the Syrakusan wall, but the passion of combat had all been extinguished by this disastrous encounter of ally against ally, numbing their minds, but still they kept on toward their objective. Endymion tripped, as did others of his company, as they stepped blindly upon the bodies of the fallen, their shields, and broken spears. Suddenly he vomited. The man to his left sneered at him. Endymion sucked his mouth clear then spit "Bad leeks."

Ahead, the wall cut across their vision, a black gash looming far off against a desolate sky, while their shadows shivered and swayed before them as they marched with the moon at their backs. The thunder of feet and the rustle of weapons poured out of the gloom to his left. Flashes of bronze danced about, undoubtedly from the helmets of advancing troops, but he could not distinguish friend from enemy. Suddenly a roar of metal detonated from the flank, followed by shouts of curses and divine invocations. More Athenians? Or did the Syrakusans attack? They struck from the flank, neither from ahead nor behind, so he could do nothing more than the rest of his men and only pivot and respond with death. By now his spear seemed to have tripled in weight and his shield pulled him down. For a moment he thanked himself for discarding his greaves, for this had kept his legs light and unencumbered, but now he felt hot liquid streaming down his shins and prayed it belonged not to him. He looked up at the sky in disbelief. *Day must come soon. We have been at this for hours.* Now the clamor of battle grew near. The ranks compressed. Reluctantly, he shouldered his shield, re-hefted his spear and waited in a crouch for the impact.

*****

Too bad, really. They have ceased killing each other. Gylippos could see clearly, even in the dark of night that the Argives and Athenians had combined and turned to move against him. He could hit again and withdraw, and hope that the momentary confusion that was inherent in night combat would allow him to extricate his men once more, but they were spent and he knew it. But he also knew if his men fought fatigue then the Athenians must be beyond exhaustion and wrought with indecision. He led his men directly toward the center of the enemy phalanx. Even the flute-player, who at the outset of battle had piped out a loud and robust tune, could hardly play for more than a minute or so without pausing for rest. For hours they had clashed with their enemy, in darkness and with uncertainty, but they still had not been overcome. The front rankers' shields crashed into the Athenians and the human machinery of slaughter was once again incited. Spears, propelled by tired arms, pumped into the enemy ranks, rebounding off bronze helmets and careening off shields, Gylippos and his company heaved forward, shoving the center of the

Athenians back, wading through their phalanx as though it had less substance than the sea until the mass of enemy reinforcements that kept pouring onto the plateau from Euryalos stopped them cold. He looked around, this way and that, and saw nothing but Athenians on all sides, except for a handful of his own men that had withdrawn into the shadows of their shields, fending off the flood of blows that fell upon them.

"Athena!" barked out Gylippos. One or two more of his men joined him in shouting out the Athenian challenge. Quickly he followed up with the reply, "Proxima!" This watch-word, meant to be secret and exercised discreetly, had been employed so often and so loudly by the Athenians that every man in his company knew it. The Athenians lowered their weapons. Now across the battlefield, the watchword and counter-sign burst from the melee—from both Athenians and the trapped Neodamodeis, quelling combat momentarily.

The Athenian phalanx momentarily broke its close order, allowing Gylippos and his trapped men to filter through it to their rear. Suddenly shouts and screams and the hollow thud of shield upon shield issued from the front lines of the Athenians. Ekritos and his Thespiains had struck, delivering the final blow that fractured their phalanx. Gylippos rallied his men into a circle, leading them obliquely toward his own lines and the Syrakusan fort. They sliced through the retreating Athenians, cutting down smaller pockets of them, and compelling others to toss away their armor and bolt.

Gylippos called for Sosibos, the herald. "Run to Ekritos and tell him we are advancing to the middle fort. He will hear the Embaterion march."

Sosibos sprinted off, dodging runaway Athenians as they stampeded toward the road at Euryalos and their only route of escape. Weaponless and without armor, the herald shoved fully armed soldiers out of his path, cursing them in Lakonian, squeezing through the thicker bands of fugitives until he saw the phalanx of Thespiains led by Ekritos methodically trampling down the slower, exhausted enemy heavy infantry.

*****

Endymion, by now overcome with exhaustion, could not hoist his shield up to his shoulder, and even if he could, he knew not which way to turn, whom to face and in what direction to move. The moon, which the Argives had hoped would illuminate the battlefield to their advantage, actually confused them, the shadows it created played tricks with their sense of direction, and recognition of both friend and enemy. Worse yet, the new men under Demosthenes, unfamiliar with the plateau, ran not to Euryalos and the road of retreat, but toward the cliffs.

Stump grabbed him. "Drop that shield."

Endymion stared at him for a long moment. His phylarkhos stood next to him with no armor, nor a spear, only his sword hanging low from a tired hand. He quickly flung off his helmet and let his shield slip off his arm, leaving him with no sword but only the shattered lower half of his dory spear. He nodded and trailed after Stump. They slunk low, shuffling south across Epipolai toward the old Circle Fort

Nemesis

and away from the chaos of retreat toward Euryalos. After a sprint of a hundred meters or so, they felt safe enough to pause and rest in a shallow gully.

"What has happened?" Endymion's chest heaved as he fought to regain both his breath and composure. He curled up into a ball, hugging his knees and rocking back and forth in the ditch.

Stump, with both hands, shook him until he looked up. "Our duty now is to return to camp alive. Keep your head clear and your eyes wide open."

Endymion did not answer. He began to sob, and with every ounce of effort tried to hold back his tears but could not. He had fought many times, and had held death close, but tonight it was different. Tonight his mind became overwhelmed with terror. He stood up.

"What are you doing?" Stump, still bending low, reached for him. Endymion stepped out of the gully and began walking toward the roar of battle and the cries of the dying. Stump tackled him and dragged him back into the shelter of the ditch. "This is not the time or the place for you to die, my friend."

Endymion cocked his head and stared into Stump's eyes. "You do not understand." He sniffled a bit, but his tears had stopped. "We are already dead."

*****

Nikias for hours now gazed up at the heights, listening to the rumble of battle that echoed from Epipolai like a storm caught in the mountains. It was long into the third watch, and by this time he had expected a courier from Demosthenes with news of the capture of the Syrakusan wall. Twice he had attempted to ride out of camp, but Hiero caught him, finally ordering the groom to stow the horse's bridle and caparison and lead the animal to the far end of the camp.

"At the very least sit. No matter what happens tonight, tomorrow will be a long day." Hiero snapped back the tent flap, but Nikias refused to move. He muttered prayers beneath his breath while pacing around the campfire until he finally shuffled away from his tent, heading along the main road toward the northern gate. Hiero caught up to him and slung a cloak over his shoulders, but said nothing. They walked by the sputtering campfires near the surgeons' tents and passed the wounded scattered about on litters, dull moaning rising up, mingled with echoes of coughing. Nikias pulled his cloak tight and stopped, scanning this human dump, this place where the injured and dying lie discarded.

Hiero looked at him. "What do you see?"

Nikias chanted something unintelligible as he rubbed the small pouch of charms that hung around his neck. "The Keres. Can't you see them hovering over our men, waiting to steal their souls."

Hiero felt the hair on his neck rise at these words. No, he saw nothing, and more importantly, wished to see nothing, so he stared straight down the road, daring not to let his eyes stray from side to side. As the pair walked, he realized that the only ones left in the camp were the wounded, dying and Nikias. The vendors, merchants and other opportunists that lived off the soldiers' pay had been quartered far away, near Daskon and the harbor shore; both he and Nikias proved to be the lone men moving about here. With the gate now in sight they heard voices, the guards, no doubt—men to speak with, to confirm that they were indeed still alive and not abandoned amongst the dying. He felt as though they had just departed a cemetery.

A guard in the tower hung over the railing and shouted, "Athena!"

"Proxima," replied Hiero.

From deep shadows along the wall two light-infantrymen appeared, their crescent shields held high, spears at the ready. One of them bobbed his head from side to side as he studied Nikias' face. "Sorry, strategos Nikias. We did not expect you, or anyone for that matter, approaching the gate from within."

"Glad to see you men are alert," said Nikias. Now he gazed up at the tower guard. "Any word yet?"

The man shook his head. "No, sir—and the noise up there has all but ended. Someone is victorious."

And someone is defeated, Nikias added in his thoughts. He cocked his ear, hoping to still hear the ruckus of battle, but he perceived only the chirping of crickets and the soft breeze stroking the trees. Nikias stumbled a bit sideways, Hiero catching him by the elbow and leading him to a stool near the wall.

"Please sit and rest a while." He eased his master onto the stool. "I will go up into the tower and watch for you."

Nikias puffed out a loud breath and nodded then leaned back against the wall, succumbing to sleep quickly. Meanwhile Hiero had scrambled up the ladder, joining the look-out. Both men peered out into the dark, trying to catch any movement on the road leading to their camp.

"Sick, is he?" mumbled the look-out, never turning toward Hiero. He spit.

"Yes. That is why he is not up there." Hiero flicked his glance up at Epipolai.

The look-out had not considered this beforehand. "Yes, this time was different. Demosthenes marched out anyone that could stand—even the cooks and bakers." He spit again, his eyes still gazing into the darkness. "He should be at the physicians' tents."

Hiero chuckled. "By the gods, I had to hide his horse tonight. He wanted to ride out there to see firsthand the outcome."

"And what do you think has happened?"

"I am no oracle, so I do not see the future. And I am certainly no general. I cannot speak to such things as strategies, schemes and maneuvers." Hiero walked to the railing facing the camp's interior, and found Nikias still sleeping upon his stool then turned around. "But I feel as though heaven itself is against us. That man down there is the most pious of Athenians. But more importantly he is the most lucky man I have ever known. Yet at every turn some disaster befalls us." Hiero rejoined the look-out, leaning upon the railing, staring again at nothing. "He has done everything possible to ensure the success of this mission, leaving no god forgotten or prayer unsaid."

Nemesis

The look-out laughed a bit. "May Zeus himself forgive me, but piety has never won a war, my friend. Our general should have been a priest." Now he clamped a hand on Hiero's shoulder. "But we have a general up there now. With Demosthenes we will fight or we will sail home, but at least we will do something."

For a moment Hiero felt anger rising, but he thought again on the man's words and although crudely delivered they rang true. Nikias was indeed a pious man, and a cautious one, traits that had kept them all from victory, but had at least kept them alive. In this night's work Demosthenes would risk all.

The look-out squinted and put a finger before his lips. "Something out there," he whispered. His eyes still could not penetrate the black shadows that consumed the road. "Athena!" he yelled.

"Proxima," a tired voice replied. Now a jumbled of black figures appeared from a turn in the road. "Forget the cursed watch-word. Even the Syrakusans know it!"

Hiero slid down the ladder and ran to the gate, helping the two guards peel it open enough to allow a man to slip through. He squeezed out and ran to the meet this first group of the returning. "What has happened?" Hiero inspected every one of them; none had weapons or armor and all were black with blood and grime. "Where are your shields?"

One of the men, a thick-chested brute with blood trickling from an eye, grabbed Hiero, twisting him to face Epipolai. "You little shit, it's up there. Go get it if you want it." He shoved Hiero away and staggered toward the gate. The others passed him by without offering a glance until the last in the party stopped. "We almost had it," he said. His eyes shone white on a dirt besmeared face. He alone amongst them had retained his sword. "This is what remains of my company." He followed after the six men that had already slipped through the gate. Although no soldier, Hiero understood what this lokhagos had just said; seven men out of one-hundred managed to survive the battle. *What could have gone so wrong?*

Others appeared from the shadows, stumbling along the road, some with spears and swords but only a few lugging their heavy hoplite shields. Hiero followed one band through the gate and there just inside stood Nikias, in silence, watching this procession of the forlorn scuffle past. "You should retire to your tent, sir, and wait there for Demosthenes." Nikias said nothing but moved along with the refugees toward the depths of the camp and his tent and retreated within, leaving Hiero outside; he looked east, and to the bellies of clouds that glowed like hot copper with the first light of day. *Well, it is finished,* he thought.

The flap whipped back and out stepped Nikias in full armor, cradling his triple-crested helmet in one arm. "My horse," he commanded.

The groom took one long stride then halted and looked at Hiero. He nodded and the groom sprinted off to the horse pens. Hiero sighed. "You would never have ridden out to meet them in victory, but you go now?"

"Once victorious, men, especially Athenians, require no leader. In defeat they yearn for one. The vanquished are like sheep, and will quickly lose their way without a shepherd."

*****

As dawn broke, it brought with it the flocks of gulls, kites, and other carrion birds. Slaves darted across the battlefield shooing them off the corpses, while others hauling carts roamed Epipolai for cast-off armor and weapons. Sunlight, stark, crisp and unforgiving, illuminated the scene revealing a swirl of death, and a pattern so unfamiliar, even to Gylippos that he felt compelled to inspect it all. He walked along the Syrakusan counter-wall, its mud-brick façade carrying him westward towards Euryalos. Near the third and last fort along its span, he stepped around a multitude of Athenian bodies intermingled with the brick, wood and stone they had torn from the fortification. *To have come this far,* he thought. Indeed, the enemy had captured this section of the wall and had begun to dismantle it; only a few meters more and they would have opened a gap that his men could have never closed. He walked further, heading south across the middle of the plateau, seeing in disbelief the heaps of armor and weapons abandoned by the enemy. The sun climbed higher, flashing golden off the vast deposits of hammered bronze and iron, of helmets, spears, swords, and shields that but a mere day earlier were wielded by multitudes of the enemy. With casual inspection he eyed the dead Athenians, hoping to come upon Demosthenes for with him dead, even the lethargic Nikias would have no recourse but to withdraw. And with him dead, Gylippos would have his trophy for Sparta and a victory for Syrakuse. And then a strange thought scurried through his mind; *Do I really want this to be done?*

As he strolled over the battlefield, here and there the moans of the dying wafted from piles of bodies. Slaves and servants of his Peloponnesian allies pulled these miserable survivors out of the tangled mass, offering them water, and a small bit of human comfort—the Syrakusans, on the other hand, dispatched them pitilessly on the spot. Now he came upon a ditch, not a very deep one, and barely the length of two men and in it a single man lie on his back, clutching a gash in his abdomen. "Water," he gasped.

Gylippos approached him while calling for Kanthos. "Bring a flask."

He knelt beside the man. His eyes stared at the Gylippos, pleading. "Water is on the way."

The man coughed his throat clear. "Spartan?"

Gylippos nodded as Kanthos handed him the flask. Gylippos looked to the man's seeping wound. "This will surely kill you." he said, as he pried the cork free.

The man smiled. "Last night, my friend told me I was already dead. He was right. Now I am merely thirsty." He grabbed the flask and tipped it, water gushed into his throat. "Thank you." His eyes widened and he groaned, the water making its way into his shredded belly. He shivered. Suddenly from above a spear-point plunged into the man's chest. Gylippos bolted up, grabbing the spear-shaft with one hand as he clubbed the blood-thirsty Syrakusan. "Animal!" He beat the man driving him to his knees, and kept pounding. Finally Kanthos along with several Syrakusans managed to

Nemesis

pull Gylippos free. The Syrakusan stood, wiping the blood from his lips with the back of his hand. "Did you forget, Spartan, what they have done to my city?" The man snapped up his spear and skulked away. He turned. "Kill your enemies. Or they will kill you."

Chapter 34
Syrakuse – Summer 413 BC

"You will have no argument from me. Go, and take the army with you," said Nikias. "But I will stay and play out the game here, for here is still a chance of success, whereas if we return to Athens with an army but without victory, our ruin is certain."

Demosthenes threw his hands up in the air. "Are you so convinced that the Assembly will take out its anger on you? But what has my curiosity piqued is—how can you cling to any hope of victory here? What do you apprehend of the goings on in Syrakuse?"

"First, think on our own Athenians, both here and at home. Oh, yes, if you ask the men—and I know you have asked many—they would wish to depart for Athens, and they would all agree to this quick fast. But once home, and their distress and peril a distant memory, they will accuse us of being bribed to withdraw from the siege, and recall with diminished accuracy the pain and discomfort of our present situation, and re-imagine a battle that should have been won, if not for the generals." Nikias eased himself onto his couch. "Is this not the way of our soldiers?" Demosthenes, reluctantly nodded in agreement. "And as far as the inner workings of our adversaries, I do know that they have already spent over 2000 talents. That was their total reserve, and they have nothing left to pay their mercenaries and oarsmen. They are but a hollow shell ready to crack."

"I think you forget about that Spartan. He is no hollow shell, and I think he would not allow the Syrakusans to crack." Demosthenes, still bleeding from a wound in his thigh, paced before Nikias, clamping the bridge of his nose between his fore finger and thumb. He limped, turned around then retraced his steps, this circuit he repeated in silence for more than five minutes. "At least move the camp," he finally blurted out. "Get us out of this swamp, to good ground where we can gather food and timber."

Nikias, his voice most often subdued, rose in pitch. "Leave and it will only embolden the enemy. I know. Two years ago I did as you now suggest and the Syrakusans grew more formidable, as we grew more despised by them."

"You would prefer to die here, rather than face the Assembly. It is as simple as that." Demosthenes flung his empty cup shattering it upon the tent's ridgepole. "If you persist in this jaunt toward suicide, than you should travel alone. I want no part in it, and I am certain there is not a man out there that wishes to join you in this pilgrimage of self-destruction."

Hiero, veiled by shadows, sat in the corner of the tent upon a stool listening. What Demosthenes suggested in anger seemed to him to be more than true. He had seen it in Nikias' eyes and it unsettled him. The man had surrendered to circumstance. Although ultimately motivated by fear, Nikias, in the past, would exhaust every option, and cultivate every deity to ensure success in his ventures. Now, in the face of

Nemesis

reason, he insists on remaining here, banking all on an elusive victory. He dredged up thoughts of Athenagoras, and what encouragements that man tossed Nikias' way for a swift and profitable resolution to this siege. *What if he believes him still? Does Nikias cleave to hopes attached to this man's promises? If so, he is doomed. And so are we all.*

The drumming hoofs, followed by shouting caused them all to stop in their tracks, listen and gaze towards the tent opening in anticipation. A messenger burst in. "More troops have joined the Syrakusans! We saw them marching across the plateau, directly into the northern gate."

Demosthenes moved to Nikias' couch and loomed over him. He said nothing, but could only stare. "We sail for home," Nikias said. "But no general order. We must not allow the Syrakusans to hear of our plans."

Demosthenes nodded. "We will have the men ready to move. They need not know to where—just yet."

Demosthenes stepped out into the unforgiving light of midday. His wound, though bleeding still, could not distract him from the relief he felt at the decision to evacuate the camp; he almost smiled. Hiero offered himself as a crutch to Nikias as he rose from his couch. The pair wobbled out of the tent.

"I shall dispatch the order for the men to prepare to move. They will think it another maneuver," said Demosthenes. He climbed onto his horse slowly and with care, but the pain from his wound doubled him over once mounted. His shield-bearer rushed to him, grabbing the reins. "Let me go." He snapped the reins away from the man. "I'll tend to it later." He urged the horse into a brisk canter, while his shield-bearer jogged after him.

"Fetch Menon, will you," ordered Nikias. Hiero could not argue with Nikias on this point, but he did not trust Menon. He really did not put much stock in the mutterings of any soothsayer, even old Stilbides, but at least when he was alive they had an "understanding,"-a way of coexisting because in the end they both loved Nikias and sought only to serve him. Menon seemed to Hiero of a different, more ambitious sort.

Just after sunset they had assembled near the make-shift altar of the camp: Nikias, Demosthenes, Euthydemos, Menandros and a small group of their attendants. "Look!" shouted out one of the grooms, as he pulled the reins of a skittish horse. Every one of them gazed up at the moon, tinged red, as it began to be swallowed by a black shadow. Some of them spit into their chitons to ward off evil while others frantically clutched for their amulets or charm bags.

"You have seen an eclipse before?" Demosthenes' impatience, exacerbated by his wound, caused him to erupt. "You are not old women, running from every shadow. This event is not unique or new to any of you."

"It is a sign from the gods," said Menon as he raised his hands up.

"Get on with the sacrifice, and let the god tell us if this be an omen of good or evil." Demosthenes yelled out the words not in discussion but as a command. Menon motioned for the boy to bring the goat forward to the altar. He lifted up the bowl and pulled the knife from it.

*****

With Stump dead, Endymion had become the new phylarkhos, a duty that he hardly wanted, but it kept his mind occupied, concerning himself with the welfare and readiness of the surviving Argives, and unable to dwell upon his own misfortune. He did, however, in this short stint, come to appreciate his old commander and how he had dealt so serenely with the constant vacillation of the generals. First command of the day was to pack up five days rations, and prepare to march, just as they had done before the night attack on Epipolai. He suspected that something more than the fickleness of his commanders was responsible for the countermanding of the order, after some of his men recounted the eclipse of the evening past; he had been asleep and did not witness it, but took it as truth from the more reliable amongst them.

"Pick that up," he said as he strolled by a lounging soldier that had dropped his unsheathed sword in the mud. "You'll surely need it." The man glared at Endymion. By the look on his face he wanted to speak but seemed too exhausted to bother. *Damn it, Stump. We need you more than ever.* He plucked the sword up, swiping the grime from its rusting blade with his palm. "This couldn't hack cheese." The man shrugged then leaned back upon his shield, using it as a pillow. All around him men lay about; weapons and armor tossed here and there like refuse, indifferent to both their duties and the necessities of life. He thought of their first miserable winter here in Sikelia, and how they had endured a similar malaise, but the mood hung heavier than the miasma of the nearby swamp. That first winter they were merely uncomfortable, irritated and annoyed. Now anguish had dulled their senses, and either life or death seemed equally acceptable. Endymion, too, wanted to withdraw to the realm of numbness, and would have if he had not the responsibility for his company.

"Curse the damned Athenians and their war. We are done fighting for them. Now we fight for ourselves and to see home again." He stalked the Argive precinct, pulling men to their feet, shaking others and if need be kicking some until he got them up and assembled for drill. They groaned. They cursed him. But they pulled themselves up from the mud, and began acting like soldiers once more. He ordered whatever servants that remained to gather wood and build fires, for cooking, warmth and more importantly, for their spirits. With drill complete, they all took their supper. Endymion, exhausted, collapsed beside a fire, too tired to eat.

"Here." He awoke to a man tugging on his arm as he hovered over him with a steaming bowl. It was the very same man he had scolded about his discarded sword. "You got us up. Now it's your turn." He handed him the bowl. Endymion nodded and pulled the bowl to his chest. He scooped the stew out with hunks of hard bread, eating so quickly he could hardly distinguish if the concoction was of animal, plant or a combination of both. "I have news from the Athenians." Endymion continued shoving bread and stew into his mouth, allowing the man to continue. "Their soothsayer has declared we must wait thrice nine days to propitiate the god and heed his warning not

Nemesis

to risk any new venture until the new moon." Endymion wanted to speak against this outrageous prediction, but knew, as Stump had known, that officers can have no opinions. That is a luxury afforded the regular soldier only. "Wine?"

The man handed him a cup and as he accepted it Endymion asked, "Is the god with us or the Syrakusans? It would seem his advice could only benefit them."

"I have no especial relationship with the gods. Neither do the Syrakusans."

Endymion grinned and thanked the man for his supper, but his thoughts dwelled on another twenty-seven days in this squalor, and wondered how many of his men might still be alive when providence finally allowed them to depart.

*****

Gylippos, once through the gate, climbed high into an adjacent tower to watch the procession of his triumphant infantry and also to tally up the prisoners from the Athenian foraging party that they had cut-off from the harbor.

"Congratulations, my Spartan friend." Hermokrates poked his head up through the trap door in the floor of the tower. Gylippos lent a hand, pulling him up then leading him to the portal.

"Seventy in all," he said pointing to the cavalcade of horses as his men herded them into the city.

"At least they will furnish pay for some of the mercenaries." Hermokrates turned to Gylippos. "You must allow at least a day's rest for the men."

"Good Hermokrates, our soldiers may be tired, but the Athenians are overspent, and I wish to allow them no respite, no chance for reconstitution of either spirits or supplies." He pointed to the bedraggled column of hoplites that trailed the band of captives. "Complain if they must, but their task of combat will prove much easier against a hungry and disheartened foe."

"Athenagoras is working the council, member by member, towards allowing the Athenians to flee. He points to our empty treasury, and the cost of prolonging this war. He is most expert at this art of inveigling."

Gylippos smiled. "And what would allow them to think that a fugitive Athenian army, resettled somewhere else in Sikelia, would not extend this war for years to come?" He buried his hands in his face, pushing back the rim of his helmet until it fell to the floor. "I apologize, friend, for I argue with the wrong man." He sighed. "I am remiss in my manners. How is your wife?"

"Phaidra and Kalli for that matter have been busy visiting Dianthe. Her baby is, as Phaidra calculates, very near birth. She weaves blankets, and has even ordered Hilarion to fashion a diminutive pair of sandals." Now he slapped his knees with both hands. "Enough domestic chat. Tell me what you would have us do."

Gylippos eagerly obliged, wanting to bury any thoughts of Dianthe and her baby quickly so he detailed a very simple plan that would require great and unrelenting stamina on the part of the Syrakusans. After three long years of war they had tipped the scales in their favor, and most were yearning to celebrate this good fortune, but Gylippos proposed no such frolic, but only tedious labors. "We must, every day, attack them somewhere, either their fortifications, their ships, or better yet, both. Take all the vessels we have captured and chain them stem-to-stern across the harbor mouth. Give them no hope of retreat."

Hermokrates lost any remnant of a smile. "I had always been told that you Spartans never pursue a defeated foe—that winning the battlefield was glory enough. What has spawned this ruthlessness?"

"Glory is a nostalgic commodity once shared amongst noble adversaries. This new world, with its new sort of war, can only accommodate ultimate and complete victory. We rest only when we have achieved this."

Hermokrates presented Gylippos and his plan to the council the very next day, and begrudgingly they accommodated him. Gylippos wasted no time in ushering Sikanos, Hermokrates and Agatharkhos to the strategeion once approval had been granted.

"Gentlemen. I thank you for your convincing appeal. The weight of your words carried the day for us." Gylippos continued to pace about the room while the others took to their couches, all pleased to be out of the hot summer sun but eager with thirst for a cup of wine. Gylippos shooed the wine-bearer away. "It is hot, and the men are tired, as are we all, but we must not relent."

Sikanos spoke. "I will see to the boom. The smiths, by now, have received the order for the chain. It will require more than a day to fashion it all—that is if we can gather enough iron."

"Take all the captured weapons and melt them down. You will, without doubt, have much more very soon." Gylippos ceased his circular stroll directly before Hermokrates. "When can the cavalry be ready?"

Hermokrates did not expect the question and hesitated before blurting out a question of his own. "What need is there of cavalry if we mean to provoke them at sea?"

"I wish to advance along the harbor from Plemmyreion toward Daskon with both infantry and horse. We ought to deny as much hospitable beach from them as possible. You sink an enemy ship and their rowers and marines swim to shore and are quickly thrown against us again. We must put an end to this."

Agatharkhos cleared his throat. "Spartan, should we not use this time to repair and refit our damaged vessels? Would it not be prudent to attack the Athenians with all the warships we can launch? In a week I can have every trireme fully fitted and manned."

Gylippos nodded as he stared at Agatharkhos. "You hunt, do you not, as all gentlemen do when afforded a respite from war?" He paused but not long enough to entertain any response. "You set out before dawn with your horses, beaters and hounds and stalk the wooded slopes of some nearby mountain, scouring the smallest of game trails for any trace of quarry. After many hours you find the tracks, and your hunting party now transforms. Your own pulse quickens, your senses of hearing and smell grow acute. The hounds swirl and bound, still held fast in their leashes. The beaters yell and before you a prize stag lopes by. Your javelin strikes and every man

Nemesis

is certain the wound is mortal. And do you now return home to rest, collect new javelins and hone your knives, or do you pursue this wounded prey relentlessly?" Now everyone except Agatharkhos chuckled at these words. Agatharkhos rose quickly and strode angrily to the door and departed without another word.

*****

Before sunrise Gylippos rode back to Ortygia, leaving his camp, his breakfast, and Kanthos behind. He passed a few men pushing carts partly full of olives, mulberries and grain toward the agora. With each passing day the Syrakusans had reclaimed more of their farmland and orchards, and with each day the carts heading for market grew fuller. Once across the causeway he headed east toward the Little Harbor, catching sight of the round, dark merchant ships swaying gently in the snug confines, allowed to berth in the naval harbor while the fleet patrolled beyond. Like the land, the sea had only recently begun to render provender and goods in any real quantity. The sight encouraged him, if only for a moment, for his thoughts moved quickly to the Syrakusans and the complacency that these things might contrive. They had endured years of war, and desperation had, indeed, hardened them for battle, but he could not rid himself of the notion that these men, like all others outside of Sparta were inherently weak and would trade glory for pleasure. As he rode along, the echoes of hammers cascaded along the battlements, luring him toward the glowing furnaces of the smiths. The pinging of iron upon iron grew louder. He turned down a narrow alleyway guided by the orange light that rippled across the whitewashed and densely packed houses. There, in a tiny spot of ground that connected the shops of the smiths and metal-workers, he saw burly men plunging glowing loops of iron into the raging coals while others worked the bellows, inciting fountains of sparks and embers to spurt from the furnaces. Searing, orange-red and shimmering the newly formed links of chain, once extracted from the flames, were pounded, quenched and reburied deep into the coals. Not a one lifted up from his toil, nor did the men now standing even acknowledge him, but they kept to their tasks, like loyal servants of the fiery god, Hephaistos. Nine wagons creaked and groaned under the weight of chain, but it would require many more.

Above the sky brightened. On the tallest of the buildings in the agora antefixes caught the first light of dawn. He rode on, finally halting near the fountain of Arethusa. From here he could peer down at the nearby quays of the Great Harbor and see firsthand, the work of Sikanos and his shipwrights. Old, worn out hulks of grain-lighters and some of the captured Athenian warships, thudded against the docks, while workers swarmed over them, constructing full top decks and fighting platforms for the infantry and archers. Here was his wall of ships—his boom that would choke shut the Great Harbor.

"Will it be completed in time?" Hermokrates cantered his horse next to Gylippos.

"Good morning, friend." Gylippos nodded. "The work goes well."

"Athenagoras has been spreading talk of an accommodation with the Athenians, and many are listening." Hermokrates leaned forward, shaking his head while tugging the reins tightly.

"Only a blind runner would veer away from the finish line when it is so near."

Hermokrates laughed. "In my mind's eye I can see Athenagoras stumbling away from so apparent a victory."

"I pray he is as clumsy as you believe he is. No matter. The fleet will be in battle soon enough, providing the boom is complete."

Hermokrates looked up at the cloudless sky. "It would be a beautiful day, I think." He sighed. "If you have your way, my friend, it may be the last day for them—and many of us."

"I pray a single day is enough, for once the enemy sights the boom crossing from here to Plemmyreion, they will attack. Even old Nikias will be forced to act, and this may prove to be the toughest fight of all."

*****

Demosthenes limped into Nikias' tent, employing his spear as a crutch, almost poking it through the canopy as he entered. Nikias did not bother to look up; he bent over a small table, stylus in hand, stabbing figures onto a wax tablet. "Is the leg mending?"

Demosthenes eased himself onto a couch. "It will not mend here." He waved his hand before his face as though he chased away smoke. The air moved, but the ubiquitous stench hung heavy as ever. "We cannot delay any longer, even if it means angering the gods." He rolled his eyes. "Are you certain that soothsayer is not Lakonian?" His attention was drawn to the sound of trickling water. Near the entrance a large basin, cracked at its base, leaked away it contents. "Our army is much like that bowl," he said pointing to it.

Nikias finally abandoned his figures. He glanced at Demosthenes. "You speak of a bowl?" His eyes found it. "Clumsiness!" He waved at a servant to remove the basin. "Now tell me about your observations of pottery and armies."

"Our spirit, good Nikias, is much like that water. With each passing moment it trickles away. And like our dwindling supply of water, we have no excess reserve of spirit—no surplus courage or tenacity that we can summon to reconstitute our army. The only certain remedy is escape."

"Do not be so certain that only *our* spirit fades. I have word from within Syrakuse that their council still debates coming to terms with us. They tire of that Spartan and bemoan their empty coffers. Unlike you, my friend, from where they sit they see no fractured pot trickling away our perseverance, but only the same Athenians who subdued Potidaia and Melos. Would you relinquish victory at the very moment of possessing it?"

Demosthenes held his head in his hands. "You entertain fantasies. In fact, I am more than surprised by their recent benign and most gracious actions. In this slight pause in their attacks, they may not be considering negotiations, but instead be contemplating our destruction. It would, I surmise, require some tedious planning to

Nemesis

annihilate us fully." He wanted to laugh, for he spoke half in jest, but thought again and was sobered by the possibility.

Menandros, with two officers in tow, burst into the tent. "They are attacking along the harbor coast."

Demosthenes swung his feet upon the floor, wincing as he rose. "From where?"

Menandros turned around urging one of the officers to reply. "Plemmyreion. Smoke is rising from stockade at Daskon."

"Strange technique of negotiation, is it not?" Demosthenes ambled past Nikias to stand before Menandros. "Reinforce the shore wall. We cannot allow them to squeeze us much more." Now he turned to Nikias. "This is only a preliminary. He means to command as much of the shoreline as possible before he strikes with his fleet. This Spartan considers no terms, but is single-minded in our destruction."

"And what do you propose?" Nikias slammed the wax tablet hard upon the table.

"Attack with our fleet before they attack us. Only the sea can preserve us."

*****

Endymion grabbed his helmet, spear and shield then sprinted along the beach with the other Argives heading toward the twisting coils of smoke that marked out the fort at Daskon. Without thinking his first inclination was to seek out Stump, but he quickly realized that the men would be looking to him for orders, so he burst ahead of them all, getting to the wall near the mouth of the Anapos River first. "Form up. File leaders front!" His depleted company spanned only ten shields across, with some files eight deep, but most falling in at six or less. More than half of his company had been lost—the larger portion during the night attack on Epipolai.

Guards in the tower screamed out. "Hurry! Run!" Other encouragements, laced with vulgarity also issued from the towers and battlements. The gate, barely open, spit men through one by one, until finally an Athenian officer order it shut. Five men heaved their shoulders into it, slamming it so hard the surrounding mud-brick shivered, releasing a yellow mist of dust pierced by shafts of sunlight.

Endymion jogged over to the Athenian. "What has happened?" He gazed up, beyond the walls to the smoke-filled sky.

"They have taken the fort at Daskon." The Athenian scrambled up a creaking ladder to the battlement. Endymion bounded up after him. From here he could see the promontory of Daskon and the small, curving bay formed in its shadow, the very place where their fleet landed two years previously. A stream of corpses fanned out from the fort toward their wall; Squadrons of Syrakusan cavalry sliced the interval in brief charges, cutting down the very last survivors. His sight drifted away from the fort, out to the Great Harbor, for he discerned far off movement, even in the fading light of late afternoon. Black silhouettes skimmed over the water just at the harbor mouth, ships for certain for he could make out their slender, naked masts poking up into the flawless sky. The procession of vessels grew from what at first seemed to be only two or three to dozens as they attempted to span the harbor opening.

"By blue-balled Poseidon, they're sealing us in." The Athenian continued to stare out at the line of ships. Then he added with a bit of disdain, "They cannot hold us."

Endymion stared at the empty harbor. He contemplated the inevitable, knowing that soon it would be crammed with warships, both theirs and the enemy's and he would be out there on one enmeshed in battle. "I do not think their intention is to hold us, friend. I believe they wish to destroy us."

The Athenian did not reply. His face went pale. He pushed away from the battlement and descended the ladder quickly where he became absorbed by the milling crowd near the gate.

Chapter 35
Syrakuse – Summer 413 BC

Dianthe, as she did every day, cracked the door to her bedroom and peered down into the courtyard to watch Agatharkhos depart, and as with every sunrise his presence was revealed by abusive commands hurled at the servants. "Polish it again!" he shouted. She watched him fling the helmet at his shield-bearer. He prepared for no speech in the assembly or sacred procession. This day he girded for war. In a few moments the shield-bearer returned with a gleaming helmet. Agatharkhos snatched it from his hands and marched out of the courtyard. Dianthe had not noticed but her hand-maid squeezed next her, trying to peek out.

"Prepare my clothes. We are going to the fountain." Dianthe pushed the door shut softly then shuffled to a chair while pressing both her palms into the small of her back. The hand-maid did not respond to her command. Her face flushed red. "Did you not hear? I wish to visit the fountain."

Slowly she moved as if to comply, hovering over the bronze clad chest, somewhat reluctant to pry open the lid. "The baby may come at any day. You should rest." The servant poked a hand deep into the chest, but removed nothing.

"I will go to the fountain, with or without your help."

Now from the streets a great commotion erupted, hundreds of voices mingled with the multiplied slap of sandaled feet upon the hard-packed earth. She flung open the shuttered window that faced the street and saw it crammed, boys and women all moving along hurriedly toward the agora.

"You boy!" she shouted at a youngster that shimmied along the wall beneath her window as he was buffeted by the crowd. He glanced up. "What is going on?"

"A battle in the harbor," the boy shouted.

A woman pushed the boy from behind and looked up at Dianthe. "No battle yet, but the Athenians are in their ships."

Dianthe pulled the shutters tight. "Please goddess, delay at least by a day this labor." She clamped her hands over her rounded belly. "Oh." She drew a deep breath.

Her hand-maid rushed to her side. "You should not invoke Elithyia so." She spoke of the goddess of child birth. "I will fetch the mid-wife. Come, let me help." She lifted Dianthe from the chair by the elbow and guided her to the bed. With every step Dianthe winced in pain. The sun had barely climbed above the horizon, and her portion of the house stood in the shade still, but her flesh burned hot. Perspiration beaded across her face and began to soak through her peplos gown. "Send word to Phaidra—and to my sister."

The hand-maid bolted out of the room and down the stairs, inciting an uproar in the courtyard below. Dianthe heard the servants cackling away, the gate slamming and the pounding of feet as more than one bounded up the stairs. The door swept open revealing the entire servant staff of women. From outside the pungent scent of pine resin wafted into the room, overwhelming her sense of smell. She tilted her head to peer out; the cook, bucket in hand, worked at swabbing the door frame with pitch as an antidote to any evil spirit.

Slowly the servants edged into the room, one shouting instructions to another, while a third, the laundry-woman, waved them both away. "Cool water and a cloth. That is what she needs until the omphalotomos arrives. Now leave her." She pressed Dianthe's hand in hers and smiled at her. "We have sent for the midwife. You will do fine my dear. You are strong and you are young." She began chanting a circular verse intended for Elithyia, but to Dianthe it sounded more like a lullaby, the sound pleasant and the rhythm soothing. Dianthe shut her eyes. Suddenly her eyes opened wide as she squeezed the laundry-woman's hand, wringing her knuckles white. The chant continued, interrupted only by a momentary, consoling smile. The pain subsided. Dianthe collapsed deeper into the pillows.

*****

Nikias climbed into the skiff then instructed the rowers to take him out to first squadron of triremes arrayed closest to the stockade entrance. They rowed him between the two lead vessels whereupon he called out to the trierakhoi and the crews. All crowded the rails, leaning out to catch sight of their strategos—even the nautai, buried deep within the hulls bent to their oar ports to look out at him.

"Men of Athens," he began. "Today we have provided you with every advantage. Your decks are crammed with archers, javelineers and marines. In our last encounter with the Syrakusans they benefitted from some innovations which we have countered." He glanced to the grapnel hooks that dangled near the prows. "We possess more in both quantity and quality of the things most necessary for victory. You, Athenians, are the best seamen in the world, and you sail in the finest warships. Our vessels are more numerous and our skill superior. But even with such advantage, I must remind you that not only our lives but the existence of our city is in the balance, for if we lose this battle, our enemies will descend upon Athens like carrion crows. You fight for your sons, your daughters, your wives and your country. But today one thought must compel you all—break through the barricade at the harbor mouth. Only then will we be able to see home again.

"To the next ship," commanded Nikias.

Hiero shrugged. "We have almost one-hundred ready to launch. You cannot hope to speak to each and every crew." Nikias lowered himself to a seat as he snarled at the oarsmen. The skiff heaved forward, thudding along the hull of the nearest trireme. No one cheered. The crews of both triremes stared in silence as the small boat slipped away.

"I shall. I must be certain that all that can be done is done, and that all that can be said is said." He sat, arms crossed and eyes straight ahead but focused on nothing in particular as though he posed for a sculptor, becoming as rigid and lifeless as any statue of marble or bronze. Hiero stared at Nikias. He knew of no man who could endure such pain and reveal none of it, no man who could work himself all hours in his calculations of battle and logistics while continuing to function. It all made no sense to him. Here was a man, when good fortune smiled, took no

Nemesis

advantage, acting without vigor or determination, but now, when all is against him, and doom is most inevitable, he is potent and acts with vitality. This thought, instead of prompting tears, incited anger. Their small boat wandered from ship to ship until both the morning and Nikias were used up.

*****

Gylippos stood atop the battlements overlooking the merchant harbor now bursting with Syrakusan and Korinthian warships. From here he could easily spot the preparations of the enemy triremes as they jockeyed along the shore, protected nonetheless by their stockade. From here also he could see the jammed decks glistening with bronze and iron, set to motion by the muscle of thousands of warriors jostling about. He leaned over the stone-work looking for the Korinthian admiral. "Pythen, they are priming for attack. Good luck. We will hold the shore for you."

Gylippos trotted down the wide bank of steps, making for the gate where his men had assembled. His Lakonian troops, reinforced by newly acquired Sikel allies, stood in formation by lokhos. All eyes followed him as he climbed the tower ladder, gaining the height necessary to address them all.

"Men, it seems as if the enemy has not tired of you." A few isolated laughs broke the silence then soon faded. "Today we win back more land from the invader." He looked out at the men, and saw faces full of trust. He saw Xenias and in him Brasidas—this extinguished the last trace of anxiety. He wanted to say much, but knew only little was needed. "Men, there is no secret technique, no special art in warfare other than this: Look to your right and look to your left, directly into the eyes of the men that stand next to you in battle and remember that it is for them that you stand and fight and do not retreat."

Quickly he scrambled down the ladder and moved to the head of the column. They passed through the gates, following the road that traced the shoreline until it intersected the stone and earth causeway spanning the harbor side of the marsh. It surprised him that no Athenian infantry blocked his way, for this was the natural choke-point, a location where he could bring only a handful of shields to bear in a forward assault. His column compressed into three abreast while the Sikel light troops scurried along the flanks, splashing through the marsh. Some even waded in the shallows of the harbor. The Athenian wall loomed ahead. He watched as the sentries bobbed their heads and waved frantically to others unseen within the encampment. Now salphinxes trumpeted their alarm across the harbor, their notes of terror skimming the water, enticing his men to pause and stare at the spectacle. They turned to see the Athenian naval stockades exhale squadrons of triremes—three spearheads of warships sliced toward the barrier at the harbor and the single opening available for the Syrakusans vessels to use as an entrance. They seemed to move slowly, their motion frozen by distance. The Syrakusan response appeared equally deliberate as their warships oozed from the docks at Ortygia toward the harbor center.

Ahead of Gylippos an empty patch of ground stretched away from the Athenian wall, an ideal place to form up if they could reach it before the enemy, but the gate flung open and out poured companies of heavy infantry, squeezing quickly into phalanx formation and swallowing up every last bit solid earth on the far side of the causeway. Gylippos halted their advance less than fifty meters from the gathering enemy and called for his company commanders.

"We hold here." He pointed out at the converging warships in the harbor. "This strand belongs to us— a haven for our ships and a sanctuary to our rowers. Protect them, if they land. Deny any refuge to the Athenians."

His Lakonian officers nodded, expressionless, but the Sikel xenagos grinned wickedly. "Let no Athenian reach this shore alive," he said before trotting away to his men. Gylippos increased his front, but hardly equaling that of the Athenians arrayed before their wall, but enough to discourage any advance by them. For now both contingents stared across the empty fifty meters, content to hold their ground and furtively view the impending clash in the Great Harbor.

*****

With each surge his vessel crashed through the building swells, showering him in spray. He was no marine or sailor, possessing no balance and steadiness that the true marines exhibited, for his legs quaked against every pitch and roll of the ship, reminding him of this deficiency. Endymion squinted through the dousing. *We shall make it*, he thought as the chained barricade at the harbor entrance grew closer. His vessel was one of the first squadron assigned to breach the string of ships anchored from Ortygia to Plemmyreion. He had been ordered to exchange his battle sword for an ax, as had all the infantry on this trireme. They would cut their way through then break for the sea. At the speed they approached he could see no need for any axes; their velocity along with their ram should do the job most easily. The distance to the barricade diminished, but their speed did not. Upon the decks of the Syrakusan ships, figures scrambled to evacuate the perceived point of impact. Now arrows showered down upon them.

"Ship oars!" The kaleustes bellowed the command and the rowers complied quickly.

For a fleeting moment only, he heard grinding before the air shook with a thunder clap that enveloped them. His feet flew from beneath him upon impact, but he quickly rolled upright then skidded and slipped toward the bow along with the spilling mass of archers, javelineers and marines. The vessel shuddered and again he tumbled. Now he shook his vision clear while regaining his feet, and shuffled ever forward, herded along by the men around him. Screams exploded from both the bow and the cat-heads, where his Argives fought to board the impaled Syrakusan ship. The enemy swarmed from the extremes of their vessel toward the collision point, while their archers flung arrows recklessly. He shoved his way ahead, buffeting men with his shield, his ax in hand. His balance proved elusive, imperiled by the slick deck and the awkward weapon he was forced to wield. A few vaulted over the balustrade and onto the deck of the enemy ship but were swiftly cut down. "Archers!" he shouted out the command, the voice and action so unusual for him that it seemed to come from another. The bowmen pushed forward to the railing. "Clear a path for us." They

Nemesis

hurled volley after volley point blank at the portion of enemy deck directly before them dispatching foe-men in heaps. "Over, boys," he yelled before hurdling the balustrade. The deck came up fast and hit him hard rolling him awkwardly onto his shield. Something cracked in his wrist. Pain surged up his arm. Quickly he gathered himself and tucked his shoulder deep into his shield while brandishing his ax overhead, poised to strike. More of his Argives poured around him, locking shields.

"To the stern!" They heaved forward carving up enemy marines with their heavy axes, but they too, fell to death launched from afar. An arrow flitted by Endymion's head striking the man adjacent in the ear socket of his helmet, snapping his head to the side as though he had been clubbed. Another buried deep into his shield but missed his arm and shoulder. "Forward!" In spurts they advanced across the deck toward their prize—the thick links of chain that trussed the barricade. It took almost an hour to clear the deck of the enemy warship and only six of his Argives survived to draw their axes against the chain. Endymion, at first, tried to swing his ax one-handed while still holding his shield; an effective and prudent technique against targets of flesh, but his ax blade caromed off the hard iron, leaving only glinting streaks of metal as proof of impact. He dropped his shield then wrapped two hands around the haft, rising high on his toes as he swung the ax overhead. He lunged violently, the blade glancing off as the haft twisted in his hands. His mangled left wrist exploded with pain. "Come on," he screamed. Two of his Argives stood over him, screening him with their shields as the last remnants of his boarding party joined him, slamming their axes into the chain like a team of blacksmiths pounding out a plowshare. His ax blade shattered. Endymion scanned the deck then lunged for a discarded spear shaft, plunging it through the battered link. He twisted it, fighting to lever apart the joint. The shaft splintered. He grabbed another. Finally the link separated. Frantically, they split the chain apart, and tossed the loose end over the side and into the foaming harbor water. A cheer went up from his men. Endymion signaled to the pilot, and the command was given to deploy oars and reverse. Just as Endymion and his men set foot again on their trireme, the deck pitched violently as a deep, grinding moan bellowed from deep within the hull. Endymion lost his shield as he slammed hard against the balustrade. Spray shot up into a fountain higher than the mast. Now another roar obliterated all other noise; splintered planks showered down up them. As the cloud of spray and debris subsided he looked first to starboard and saw an enemy trireme back-rowing away from his vessel, its ram squealing as it withdrew from the gash in his ship's hull. Volleys of arrows arced from the Syrakusan, some perforating his men while the rest sprouted from the deck like a field of white flowers. To port another enemy trireme had plunged deep into the hull but could not so easily withdraw. His ship groaned and listed suddenly, sending him skidding to the opposite rail. From here he could see miniature squadrons of rowboats and skiffs circling his vessel, loaded with javelineers and archers. They darted under the oars and hurled death in amongst the rowers, their wails echoing up from below.

He pulled himself to his knees, trying to see beyond the plight of his own ship. Fires had erupted sporadically across the boom, but no Athenian ship had punched through the barricade. Even though his squad of marines had hazarded to cut a breach in the boom, his very own trireme, disabled and sinking, proved an effective plug. He looked back into the harbor but his vision could hardly penetrate the rolling curtains of black smoke that scudded over the water.

"Come on! That's our way home!" He yelled to his men as he moved toward the stuck Syrakusan trireme in a low crouch, searching for a discarded shield and spear. The spear he came upon quickly—it pinned one of his own marines to the deck. He twisted it free and moved forward pausing near the railing adjacent to the enemy's ship. "Tell them to pick up what they can," he commanded as he watched rowers emerge from below deck. About twenty or so oarsmen filled in behind him with an assortment of weapons, some with knives, others with swords or axes while many wielded only splintered boards. His men followed without hesitation. "By Zeus and Athena!" He vaulted onto the deck of the Syrakusan warship, plunging his spear into lightly armored archers that rushed at him. His spear, good only for a handful of thrusts shattered as it stuck fast in the ribs of a collapsing foe, so he snatched up an abandoned bow and swung it like a whip, keeping his adversaries at a distance until he spied a dead Syrakusan marine with his still sheathed sword slung around his bloodied torso. He freed the blade with a twang and commenced to hack his way toward the stern and the enemy pilot. He could hear the Syrakusan row-master barking his cadence furiously and hear also the oar blades as they thrashed the water, but the two vessels remained locked in this murderous grapple. The deck shifted slightly beneath his feet. Wood crackled. All of a sudden the ship pitched severely as the ram slid free, propelling the bow up and out of the water momentarily. With a death moan, his damaged and abandoned ship rolled onto its side before slipping beneath the foaming water, leaving him and his small boarding party stranded on the enemy warship. The last of the Syrakusan marines locked shields, spanning the deck and blocking his way toward the pilot and the steering rudders; although his men outnumbered them, their weapons consisted of pieces of debris and discarded, broken swords and spears, not one of them still possessing a shield. They could not advance. His contingent of impressed oarsmen discerned this most quickly; they leapt into the water. Now the Syrakusan marines shuffled forward emboldened by this desertion.

"Over with you," Endymion shouted as he tossed away his sword before diving into the harbor. No sooner had he crashed through the surface and bobbed up to grab a breath than small craft began to collect toward him. He could see the Syrakusans holding javelins overhead, cocked and ready to hurl at him and any other of his men that broke the surface. His lungs burned and every muscle in his body was wracked with fatigue, and for a moment he thought to cease any struggle and let them skewer him—death would release him from this pain. The thought fled quickly. He dived beneath the swirling water and mats of floating detritus and swam toward a motionless ship hull, hoping to use its bulky form as cover. A spear plunged into the water, cutting through the flesh of his shoulder cap. Another penetrated the surface,

Nemesis

barely missing his flailing legs. The sound of dying ships, of crackling timbers and prodigious collisions coursed through the water, shuddering his very bones as he swam. Finally, as his breath failed him, he broke through to gulp the air, braced against the hull of a trireme. He felt his way along the black planking, bobbing beneath the surface with each breathe to remain unseen until he reached the ram, and a splintered timber that afforded him a grip. He scanned the ship's hull: an entire bank of oars dangled into the water, creaking in their thole-pins with each passing swell. He could not tell if it was an enemy ship or an Athenian, but for certain it had become a casualty. He pressed his ear to the derelict hull and heard nothing within.

All around scraps of timber floated by. Now a body drifted close, arms and legs hanging limp, its head swaying in rhythm with the swells, several gashes in its back staining the water red. Not far off two ships cruised toward each other with oars flashing. One veered sharply, grinding its way along the hull of its adversary, snapping oars, and rolling along it until its keel surged into view. He hung on, now a spectator, witnessing relentless combat and unable to apprehend the victor, praying for light-stealing night to arrive.

*****

"Hold your ground," shouted Gylippos as he heaved forward, thrusting his shield into the chest of a stumbling Athenian before driving its rim sharply upward, cracking his opponent's jaw. They fought with fury, but so did the Athenian heavy infantry, for Gylippos and his men could advance no further than the end of the causeway, leaving a good portion of the shore still in enemy hands, enabling the recovery of their injured.

He recoiled and slammed forward, turning sideways as he buried his shoulder deep within his shield, leaning hard and steep. They had been at this now for many hours, collisions of shield walls and massed contests of shoving, only occasionally lacing these assaults with flashes of spears and swords, each side pausing momentarily for recuperation before beginning the cycle again. Gylippos looked at the earth near his feet and to the very same stone he had strode over and retreated past numerous times this day. Again shields disengaged.

"Look!" Gylippos flicked a glance toward the harbor and the raging, smoke-laced battle, where a bevy of men thrashed through the water toward the shore—the very shore they contended over now.

Their front-rankers snapped their shields forward as the rear ranks compressed in behind them. Flute-players commenced skirling the advance and once more the two phalanxes crashed together. Gylippos eyed the stone as it slipped by and behind him—he spied new earth. They pressed forward, gaining only a few meters, but he knew from battles past that such a precious few meters may trigger a collapse of a phalanx if exhaustion is near. His men knew it too. They redoubled their effort, driving forward hard, pummeling the Athenian front ranks with a torrent of overhand spear thrusts, the multitudinous pinging of iron upon bronze overwhelming all other sound. The Athenians gave ground but did not break, while the refugees from the naval battle seemed to care not which side held dry ground but crawled and staggered to collapse upon the beach where the Athenians retrieved theirs while quickly dispatching any luckless Syrakusans. Gylippos' Sikel warriors reciprocated with enthusiasm when they came upon an Athenian but offered no succor to any wounded Syrakusans. Xenias, seeing this dispatched three of his rear-rankers to their aid and to ensure the Sikels made no error in discriminating friend from foe.

Eventually darkness crept over the battlefield and the melee in the Great Harbor. Ship-wrecked oarsmen continued to swim for land, but now many paused just off shore, trying to distinguish which army held the ground before plodding out of the water. Debris, scattered and sparse in the early afternoon, now washed up in clinging mats, conglomerations of timber, sail cloth and twisted, bloated corpses. To the west the sun sank below the mountains, casting deep shadows and ushering the cessation of combat for at least another day. Gylippos held his men in place until the beach could be cleared of survivors before ordering a measured, deliberate withdrawal toward the city. The Athenians, desperate to retrieve something from this long day, exploded into cheers. Gylippos stood at the shore as his men passed by in column, watching the bizarre spectacle in front of the Athenian wall.

Xenias, limping and bloodied, stepped beside him. "What goes on?"

Gylippos shook his head and answered with a smile. "They are erecting a trophy. They despair so for a victory, they concoct one."

"But who won this day? I see only wreckage and smoke drifting in the harbor and a myriad of dead upon the shore."

"It is a meager feast that Nike has set before us. But we all have seats at her banquet." Gylippos pointed to the band of Athenians that had just finished nailing armor to a tree as an emblem of victory, "For we are alive. Today, that share is enough." He turned to the Great Harbor, sighting the still intact boom that secured the entrance. "But I would think we have managed to steal a greater portion than them."

*****

Endymion clung to the shattered hull, fighting to keep his eyes open. If he drifted into slumber, the water would surely swallow him up. The sun had long set, but the sky still held traces of daylight and now the flotilla of Syrakusan skiffs and row-boats prowled the harbor looking for survivors, circling and zigzagging when they spotted anything afloat, probing with their spears, letting nothing alive or dead escape their attention. He saw not one Athenian vessel cruise near him since his own vessel sank. Far off and deep into the harbor he detected torches flickering and dancing along the shore of the Athenian encampment, a puny ribbon of light in comparison to the vast, dark coastline that encircled him. *A long swim,* he thought as he gauged the distance. A scream echoed over the water followed by laughter. About fifty meters away he saw a small boat with three dark figures in it pumping spears into the water. The day, for certain, had proved long and hot, but the cool water of the harbor had quickly sucked away any warmth from his body and sent him into shivers. His teeth began chattering, and he was sure the Syrakusans would hear them, so he clamped his jaw tight, trying to silence them.

Nemesis

After several hours and with the departure of the Syrakusan boats, he latched onto a shattered oar blade and began to swim deliberately and in silence toward the glimmering torches on the far shore. Mist began to seep up from the water, smudging the light and affording him a sense of concealment. The harbor was dead calm. He hoped the mist would not completely obscure his destination. Every so often he dropped his head upon the oar blade, but only for a moment before fighting off the urge to sleep. He kept to it, his submersed legs fluttering, propelling him forward. A body bumped against him. He pushed it aside with no more though than if he was brushing aside a drifting timber.

It took awhile but he found himself in the deepest part of the harbor, near its center and far from any shore, friendly or not. Now he heard oars thudding in the hollow belly of a boat. Men spoke. The voices grew louder. He saw two frosted spheres of light, oil lamps no doubt, suspended in the fog. *They cannot see me.* He tried to reassure himself. But the small boat sliced through the flat water of the harbor directly at him. He waited until they were almost upon him, filled his lungs with an enormous breath then slipped off the oar blade sinking quickly. Even underwater he could hear the boat as it struck his abandoned float. He palmed the keel as it passed overhead, his hand drifting free as he counted away. At ten, he bobbed up through the surface and gulped air. The fog had swallowed up any trace of the boat, but his oar blade was gone and so were his bearings. He could see nothing but the milky blanket that enveloped him. He muttered a prayer to Poseidon and to Boreas for a whisper of a breeze, something to sweep away this sight-stealing veil, but the fog hung thick and persistent so he swam on anyway.

Luckily, he encountered no more bands of Syrakusans. He was surrounded by water and without sight or sound so dreams seeped into his mind. He could hear his son Antiphemos call his name, and smell the charcoal-burners as they chugged their smoke, perfuming the air in the field near his house. His wife called him also—for dinner, so he dropped his ax near the wood pile and caught up with his son. They ran to the kitchen door, doused themselves with water then entered. He sat quickly at the table, reaching for a slab of flat-bread which he tore in two, handing a piece to Antiphemos. They both munched away, grinning, as his wife ladled out portions of stew, filling three bowls. He wanted to speak to them but he could form no words, and they too could only smile at him in silence. The room grew dark. His eyes grew heavy.

*****

Dianthe drifted in and out of sleep, the anodyne dispensed by the iatros had lessened her pain, but kept her from holding her new-born daughter. Through bleary eyes she glanced to the nurse and the bundle of cloth that she cradled in her arms, infrequent quavering wails the only indication of the infant within. Shouting echoed in the courtyard below. Her hand-maid's eyes grew wide. "The master is home," she said as she ran to the doorway. She cracked it open, just enough to peek out. Phaidra followed along and looked out also while Elpida and Kalli remained on either side of Dianthe's bed.

Dianthe coughed. "Is it Agatharkhos?" She coughed again inducing more pain.

Phaidra nodded, still peering out of the doorway. She watched as Agatharkhos looked up, seemingly at her, but he checked for the sprig of wild olive, a token announcing the birth of a son, but saw instead a tuft of wool hanging from the door post. Phaidra could see his eyes falling upon the wool, and see also his rage. He flung his war-helmet across the courtyard, and with amplified strides disappeared into the andreion. The midwife scurried about the room picking up several cloths that had been tossed upon the floor then nervously began rearranging the water pitcher and bowl that sat upon a small table near Dianthe, barely moving either, her fingers dancing from vessel to vessel.

"Is he coming?" Dianthe, hands quivering, pushed the hair from her face.

Phaidra turned and shook her head. "He went straight to the andreion." Noticing the dismay on Dianthe's face she quickly added, "He must be tired. I am certain he wishes to see you and his new daughter once he has rested a bit."

Tears began to force their way out, but she willed them to stop. She would not cry anymore—certainly not because of him. In fact she thought little of him all day long while he fought the Athenians. Her concerns lie with Hermokrates, Sikanos, Pantheras and the other Syrakusans who had shown her and her sister nothing but kindness. But when her pain was at its worst, as she brought her daughter into the world, she could think only of Gylippos. Now she cursed the gods for filling her mind as such. Elpida squeezed Dianthe's hand.

"We shall be off," said Phaidra. She turned to Kalli. "Someone must greet Father." Phaidra stepped near the bed. She crouched over Dianthe, smiling, and stroked her cheek gently. "Sleep, child. The morning will change things, I am certain." She stared into Dianthe's eyes then stepped back, and as though she had awoken from a trance began chattering instructions to the hand-maid, the omphalotomos, and then to her daughters. "We shall see your sister tomorrow," she assured Elpida before ushering her and Kalli out of the doorway and down the stairs.

Dianthe watched them depart and when the hand-maid closed the door she drew a deep breath and closed her eyes, allowing the dark healer—Night—to do his work.

*****

His ribs felt as though hot iron pierced them. Another explosion of pain burst from his side. "Get up!" Endymion winked open his eyes. Three men stood over him, all brandishing spears, but no other weapons or armor, only the random flickering of their torches revealing any feature of their faces. "Get up Syrakusan." A foot caved in his ribs, folding him into a ball.

He spit out a mouthful of blood and a single word—"Argive!" His response stopped a kick just short of his face.

One of the men dropped his spear and knelt to his side. "Well, let's go boys. Help him up."

Nemesis

Endymion staggered to his feet. He looked down, finding himself naked, except for the charm that dangled from his neck. Even his sandals had been lost. He could see he had washed ashore near the mouth of the Asopos River and the terminus of the wall that enclosed his encampment. Here wreckage congested the shoreline while Athenian patrols stalked the beach, partially obscured by the heavy fog that seeped in from the harbor. "The battle?"

"Not so good," said the man bracing him up with a shoulder. "We lost almost twenty war-ships. Again that many are damaged."

"Many survivors?" Endymion snapped up a flask offered to him by another and began gulping from it.

"Some, but I would think the harbor has taken most. Or the Syrakusans. They hold the larger portion of the shoreline."

Endymion handed the empty flask back to the Athenian, nodding a thank you and lowered himself onto the gravel of the beach where he sat staring out at the blank fog, clutching his shattered wrist.

Jon Edward Martin

Chapter 36
Syrakuse – Summer 413 BC

The sight-robbing fog had finally withdrawn into the bosom of the sea, but night lingered on—an anodyne to war, an interruption of battle. Gylippos, in anticipation of a day full of crucial activity had slept only briefly, and now well before dawn, made his way through the empty streets of Syrakuse to the town-house of Hermokrates. He tried to talk himself out of the anger that he felt as he walked the bleak alleys, seeing no watchmen, no guards on the battlements, no evidence of the vital precautions so necessary in war. *They are not Spartans*. His rational mind tried to tame his emotions, but he was tired and the kernel of his nature overwhelmed him. By the time he reached the house of his friend, he was fit to break in the gate. He pounded the bronze-clad oaken door, but did not yell. Finally it creaked open. Hilarion, lamp in hand, gazed at him bleary-eyed.

"I must see your master," demanded Gylippos. He pushed the man aside and stepped into the courtyard. "Wake him now."

"But it is late and he recuperates from the battle." Hilarion stood by the gate, unmoving.

"It is an urgent matter. He will sleep much sounder with no more battles to fight."

Hilarion finally complied reluctantly. He left one angry man in the courtyard only to awaken another. After a brief lambasting, he lit the way for Hermokrates, the lamp flickering wildly in his quivering hand, spilled oil tracing his path.

Hermokrates approached Gylippos stiff-legged and partially bent over, dealing with the remnants of a day-long battle at sea. "I am, perhaps, your last friend in this city. You do much to over task even this unique and rare bond."

"Forgive me, *friend*, but I must press you to assemble the entire army." Gylippos cut straight to the point. "It is vital that we secure the roads, the river crossings and the defiles near Epipolai." He stared now at Hermokrates, waiting for his response.

"Impossible." Hermokrates shook his head while dropping onto a nearby bench. Now he clamped his head in his hands, refusing to look up.

"This is not impossible. You need simply issue the order." Gylippos spoke with an irritating economy of words.

Hermokrates craned his neck and looked up at the Spartan still clutching his head as though it would flee from his body if he released it. "Oh, the order is not, but its execution most certainly is. The men who were not entirely exhausted or wounded during this last battle are sleeping off their wine. I know, because I was one of them until you awakened me." He turned to Hilarion. "Fetch us a bit more wine. There is little necessity to endure sobriety now."

Gylippos, his eyes imploring the heavens above, sighed. "The Athenians should have struck again at the boom. Since they did not they must be planning to

Nemesis

march overland to Katana."

Hilarion returned holding a pair of deep cups. Hermokrates grabbed one, sipped a bit then asked, "How do you know this? Is this Spartan augury?"

"Augury—no! Any competent commander would have ordered another attempt on the boom, most especially after your fleet withdrew." Gylippos waved off the cup offered to him by Hilarion.

"Oh come now. Do you really think that old Nikias would move so swiftly?" Hermokrates brought his cup to his lips, but did not drink, pausing for Gylippos' answer.

"No, but Demosthenes shall and with purpose, allowing us no chance to recover. If he did not move by sea then he most certainly will move by land. Their assault on the boom was one of desperation. Did you not witness close hand how they overloaded their vessels with infantry and acontists. That was no technique of elegance and ingenuity, but one of brute force—so very un-Athenian."

"And if you convince me, what good will this do? I cannot rally our men to battle again. They know the Athenians are beaten. Allow them at least a day to savor this victory." He gulped the wine now. "They have earned it. After all they have been at the point of spear for two long years."

"I have been at the point of a spear my entire life." He paused regaining himself. "Think on what you have said, my friend. Do you believe that they are beaten? Do you not realize that if they escape to Katana, or some other refuge here in Sikelia, that they will return again with an even larger force? As long as Athenians tread on this island your city will be at risk."

Hermokrates placed his empty cup upon the bench next to him and slowly rose to his feet. "Our army will not march this morning, but I think I might fashion a device to confine the Athenians to their camp for at least another day. He called to Hilarion, speaking briefly with his slave and the mission assigned. Even this fleeting moment away from discussions with Gylippos lightened Hermokrates' spirits. He insisted that Gylippos raise his kylix to join him in a toast. "Today Dianthe gave to me a new granddaughter."

Gylippos smiled politely and raised his kylix. He could see in his friend's eyes rejoicing, but he felt only bitterness, and was ashamed for it. "And are both mother and daughter as happy as you appear to be, Hermokrates?"

"That I cannot say. Phaidra, although she stayed with Dianthe all day long, spoke little of it. Perhaps tomorrow she will prove more amenable to conversation." He laughed, staring up at the fading stars. "It is tomorrow already."

*****

Dionysos rode alone toward the Athenian wall near the marsh, keeping watch for any enemy pickets or foragers. Up until now, he had seen no combat, assigned as were all the epheboi to guard duty, but he relished his new mission, and could hardly keep the grin off his face as he approached a dozing sentry near the wall. The man had fallen asleep upright, knees locked as his back rested against the trunk of an olive tree.

"Friend," Dionysos announced softly. The man grabbed for his spear and thrust it blindly. Dionysos yanked on the reins back peddling his horse to stay clear of the whipping blade. "Ho, friend. See," he said waving his hands overhead. "I come with no weapons."

The sentry shook the sleep from his eyes. "Whaddya want?" he growled then planted the spear by its butt-spike to lean upon it.

"I bring word from friends within Syrakuse. Friends of Nikias. Friends of Athens." Dionysos cantered his horse closer. "Athenagoras sends warnings. Do not attempt to retreat by land today. That Spartan has dispatched troops to all the river crossings and inland roads. They are poised to fall upon you if you move. In a day or two they will tire of this and withdraw to the city. Then move as you please."

"This is some trick, is it not?" The sentry held his spear at the ready, its tip pointed directly at Dionysos.

"I am only a messenger. You may accept this message for what it is. Or you can ignore it. But you look like no general to me." Again Dionysos backed his mount away from the sentry, fighting against a grin that threatened to appear. "My advice is to tell your generals of what I say, and let them decide." He rapped his horse with his heels and yanked hard on the reins galloping back toward the city.

*****

Gylippos rode up to Epipolai along the road that skirted the temple of Herakles, the very same temple that the Syrakusans now toiled upon, adorning it with lavish decoration. Garlands had been strung around the gates and atop the precinct walls, while tripods sparked and sputtered full of extravagant portions of incense sending aromatic clouds skyward. Beyond it he ascended the plateau as morning slipped away toward noon, and could see the Athenians still clinging to their encampment near the harbor shore. He scanned the pathways and roads for any sign of movement but apparently not even token parties of enemy kataskopoi had been dispatched to reconnoiter.

Xenias, followed by a company of Brasideioi, jogged toward him. "You sent for us?"

Gylippos un-corked his flask and held it out, as if to offer a drink to the Athenians. "Their supplies of water must be exhausted. The streams near their camp are merely a trickle now and they are still far from the Asinaros River." He looked up, shading his eyes. "Helios has proved unrelenting. No rain for weeks." He drank deeply. A distant rumble caused him to turn. Far off on the northern horizon the clear sky retreated from an advancing storm. Iron-black clouds boiled while Zeus slashed the heavens with fiery bolts. Thunder shook the ground. In time the clouds rolled overhead, muting day into dusk. Rain spit upon them, so lightly that Gylippos watched it dot the parched earth at his feet, the random pattern quickly vanishing as the thirsty dust absorbed every drop. Gusts buffeted them. He looked up. "With all piety due to you, Father Zeus, I implore you to cease. Give not a drop of water to them."

Nemesis

Xenias smiled, shaking his head. "I have never heard a prayer intended to stop rain. Even more odd, I have never heard *you* pray to any god."

"My prayers are few for I ask little of the gods, for I require little." He grabbed the hilt of his sword. "They have already provided in all the necessities." The wind snapped at his cloak while scouring dust from the desiccated plateau. Men averted their faces. The horses bucked and spun. Abruptly the wind died out. No rain fell. Above the clouds thinned and stretched until shafts of sunlight bored through them. Gylippos smiled before dipping his head reverently, muttering. He waved for one of the shield bearers and tossed a pouch of coins at him. "To the city with you. Fetch for me a bull and lead it to the temple down there." He turned to Xenias. "A prayer such as that is not for the frugal." He motioned for Xenias to come closer. "Take your company to the ravine beyond Euryalos, near the Akraian Heights. Masons and sappers will accompany you. You are to act as a wall until one can be built. That is the most direct route to Katana. That is the route Nikias will take, and he will depart soon enough, I suspect." He shook his head. "Those Athenians." His eyes grew darker than the retreating storm. "We must break their army here. We must break it now." Xenias said nothing but his silence spoke for him as he stared at Gylippos. "Why you and not Ekritos?" He leaned over and clamped his hand upon Xenias' shoulder. "I trust you. He may be the son of Polyakes, but there is something about him…" He kicked his heels hard into the flanks of his horse, tugging the reins. "Ha!" He galloped away, churning up a smoky trail and fading hoof beats.

"Boys, let's get there right quick," shouted Xenias. "I wish to nap a bit before our guests arrive." The men at the fore of the column and within earshot laughed at his remark and began to jog after Xenias. Within an hour they had easily traversed Epipolai and descended by way of Euryalos heading northwest to the defile known as the Akraian Heights. As they approached the importance of the place grew obvious. The terrain from all around funneled toward a cleft in a stony ridge, offering no alternative to escape the plain. Buried deep in shadows it appeared even more formidable in the fading light of dusk. Xenias nodded approvingly. One of his men bumped him as he passed by. "Cozy, isn't it?"

*****

Endymion left the assembly of commanders, trudging up the muck near the harbor's edge toward the Argive camp. He had tried to ignore the hundreds of bodies strewn along the shore, bloated in death, enticing the flies, gulls and dogs to feast upon them with their stench. Most of the men had seen worse. All grew so accustomed to it that they strolled amongst the corpses, stepping over and around them like they were so many fallen tree limbs or nuisance stones for they lie there in silence unattended and ubiquitous. Once into the camp proper, he came first to the hospital precinct and surgeons' tents where a hasty splint and bandage had been slapped around his wrist earlier that morning. It was a foul and miserable place and he wished never to endure it again, but that now proved unavoidable. Many days past, the tents had become overburdened, so men with less serious wounds lay out in the open, rolling on the bare earth in fits of pain, some moaning, others sobbing.

Scroungers threaded their way amongst the sick, confiscating what food or water lie about, running off with armfuls of provisions toward the marshalling areas near the gates.

A man reached out and grabbed Endymion by the ankle. "Brother Argive, you won't leave us here?" The man had one eye covered in a bloody bandage and a leg shattered from the knee to foot all purpled and twisted. Endymion stared at it for a moment, mesmerized by its gruesome contortions. He reached down and gently pried the man's fingers from his leg, locking eyes for a long uncomfortable moment. He saw hollow desperation in this man's face and welling tears in his eyes—eyes that implored him to stay, to aid and not abandon him.

"Do you not remember me?" the man wheezed as he spoke. Endymion tried to read his face, to jostle some memory but could recall nothing. "I am Pamphilos, the wood-cutter."

Endymion, struggling to summon even the simplest word, gazed upon him dumbstruck. This hardly looked like the burly ax-man dispatched with his platoon to gather ship-wood. Injuries aside, he appeared to be wasting away, with little muscle left clinging to his bones. Endymion could only turn away. He quickened his pace to exit this most forsaken of districts and to escape his own inability to deal with this renewed acquaintance. Others around him struggled to their feet and began to follow, some stumbling while most collapsed, either stricken with fever or bled dry from festering wounds. They sobbed. So too did the healthy that hustled by as quickly as their feet would carry them. Ahead, men moved toward the main gate, burdened with provisions and weapons. Most all the battle servants had either been slain on the beaches or had, by now, deserted, leaving the infantry to haul out every type of necessity, both of war and sustenance. He wondered, looking at it all, how would they fight? How could they fight saddled with more than each man's weight in baggage? Still he felt somewhat comforted by the sheer number of them. It seemed to him thousands jostled about near the assembly grounds with still more draining from the camp pathways.

The Athenian general Demosthenes, leading his horse by the reins, crossed in front of Endymion. Both men paused not sure who would proceed first. Endymion stepped back. Demosthenes nodded. Before moving on Endymion asked simply, "How many?"

Demosthenes, chin high and a sparkle in his eyes answered, "Twenty-thousand to fight. Another twenty-thousand to protect." He rubbed the horse's snout affectionately, grinning and turned back to Endymion. "We'll do alright. Keep alert and keep alive, my friend."

Endymion, upon reaching his tent, looked around for what remained of his company. *Not many.* The living scrounged through the possessions of the dead, taking any serviceable weapon or article of clothing and on occasion a stash of food, stuffing smaller items into their belted chitons and jamming the rest into their tattered battle packs. To him they appeared as peddlers, or worst, destitute thieves, filthy, ragged

Nemesis

and over-burdened with paraphernalia. To a man they proved anxious to depart, to vacate this scene of destruction and humiliation, and to move beyond the cries of their discarded comrades. He snapped up his bedroll and stuck a curved knife deep into its folds, slipped the cord of a water skin over his shoulder and picked up only his shield and spear. He would take a sword if he found one, for he lost his in the camp and his kranos helmet lie at the bottom of the harbor. For a moment he considered donning his linothorax but laughed at the idea. If he caught spear in the chest, better to die quickly. Besides, he would conserve what strength he had remaining to fight and not to hump freight from here to Katana. He could not understand why so many were still ruled by possessions and not sense. He ambled by a flattened tent, his eye catching the shape of a helmet. He groped for an opening in the swirled and flattened canvas, finally retrieving an open-faced Attic helm, stripped of its crest. *Light enough.* He dropped it on his head and moved along.

Past midnight, deep into the third watch and with daybreak not far off he received the order for his Argives to move to the agema of the column. A platoon of Athenian bowmen lingered at the fore along with a smattering of cavalry. Most often he dreaded leading the formation, but now, nearly exhausted, he relished the thought of being in the fore, to be first into Katana and salvation, or first to be delivered from this horrid nightmare by a spear of the enemy.

*****

Exhausted and aching Nikias shuffled toward his horse. The breeze swept on-shore fanning the acrid smoke of burning triremes that his men had thoughtlessly set alight. Thinking to deprive the Syrakusans of any trophies of battle, they unwittingly confirmed their intentions to march overland. Anger welled up in him but subsided, smothered by futility. With resignation he looked to the source of the smoke and sighed. "The gods have abandoned us," he whispered. Hiero rushed to his side, offering a hand as he struggled to swing his leg over the horse's back. For a moment he blacked out as a bolt of pain shot through him. He slouched, hugging the horse by the neck, fingers clamped tightly to its mane, recovering consciousness. "Demosthenes?"

Hiero nodded. "He confirmed he would command the rearguard." Hiero thought, *He has no choice. He and his men hardly are acquainted with the terrain. Better Nikias lead.*

Tents began collapsing across the encampment. Many, like the warships, fed the self-inflicted flames of denial—only the surgeons' lean-tos and canopies near the marsh stood erect. He stared for a long while at these tents, finally realizing that he, like his men, must move on. He rode slowly along the main road of the camp, overtaking a column of hoplites laden with battle packs and dragging their spears. Few looked up as he passed. Most glanced down at the dry earth with despair. Many hacked out coughs. Some vomited. What pack animals had survived queued up near the gate, their panniers crammed with sacks of water and the scant remnants of grain that had not been lost aboard the triremes.

He halted just outside the camp, compelled by either piety or habit to perform the sacrifice, but quickly remembered Stilbides was dead, and had little faith that Medon possessed any relationship with the gods. He rode on. Less than a stade along the road he came to the head of the main column, comprised of the veteran Argives and some Athenian archers. The cavalry had already moved ahead. Slowly he made his way to the fore, seeking out the commander. "Sir," he began so very formally, "I regret that I do not know your name, for if I am not mistaken, we have never met."

The commander pushed back his helmet, craning his neck to look at Nikias. "I am Endymion, phylarkhos of the last company of Argives."

"Endymion, we will march for Katana, and your men will lead us."

Endymion could only stare, bereft of speech, at Nikias, until finally he blurted out. "The gods punish us, do they not? We have been prideful and full of hubris. Is this not what we deserve?"

Nikias shook his head. "Endymion, look to my life as an answer to your questions. Have I not the reputation of being moist pious? Have I not always honored the gods and consulted with them before any venture? Is any man more reverent?"

Endymion felt almost embarrassed at his questioning. "No, none are more pious that you, Nikias."

"And still these misfortunes have befallen me, just as they have befallen you, and the rest of our army. We have done nothing extraordinary to provoke these events, yet possibly the gods will now pity us for our suffering, for enduring these catastrophes that have humbled us. Perhaps this is their wish." Nikias drew a deep breath. His lips quivered, as he fought off a bout of pain. "In a few days you will be in Katana. Save some wine for the rest of us." He winked then trotted his horse off the road, allowing the column to trudge ahead, spears rattling and armor clanging, individual figures merging into jumbled shadows until the stream of infantry snaked into the night.

Nikias, still wracked by pain, traced up and down the column, ignoring his own discomfort to offer encouragements to the men. He saw most men devoid of spirit; men prepared and willing to accept any fate, no matter how cruel. He worried how much fight was left in any of them, and he worked now to summon what he could. "Heads up boys," he said as he cantered along. "With this army we will fashion our own city—anywhere we please." He kicked his horse, accelerating to a gallop, each hoof-beat a signal to his battered kidneys to unleash new agony. But he ignored it. "In a few days we'll be dining in Katana." This he repeated over and over like a chant to ward off his pain.

*****

"But you must sleep," protested the nurse as she was again rejected. Dianthe cradled the infant in her arms as she sat at the open window, her eyes focused on the brightening horizon to the east. Below, in the courtyard, servants hustled about in anticipation of Agatharkhos. He soon burst through an open doorway fully appareled in his cavalry armor, his short chalmys cloak swirling behind and he bounded to and

Nemesis

fro, chastising one servant then another for not having everything properly prepared.

"This is the one battle which I can predict the outcome, and I shan't miss a moment of it." He yelled to Krios to hustle after him as he jogged to the stables. From her vantage she could no longer see him, but heard clearly the horse as it snorted disapprovingly. Hoof-beats followed. Agatharkhos bellowed out commands to hurry. She sat there straining to catch sight of others as they too dashed down the alleyways and streets with uncommon enthusiasm. They all could sense it, as she could. The Athenians were finished. The war was finished. Now she thought of the implications, both good and bad. She shuddered a bit, thinking of her husband and how his visits to her chambers would, without doubt, increase in frequency with no battle to distract and exhaust him. For a moment she wished him to perish in this last encounter with the Athenians but quickly tried to submerse the thought by attending to her baby. The sun spilled over the courtyard wall now and struck the window, its warmth caressing her face. She began to nod off as she rocked slowly to quiet the infant. Both soon fell into slumber.

"Sister."

Dianthe felt a tug on her peplos gown. She blinked away the sleep and found Elpida staring at her. She smiled. "Come to see your niece?"

"And my sister." Elpida gently pressed back the swath of linen that covered the infant's face. "What shall you name her?"

"I have not thought much on it yet. Besides, I am sure Agatharkhos has a name in mind already." She puckered her face in jest. Elpida laughed. "Do you have a name you would prefer?"

"Of course I do—Elpida. It would be so very easy to remember."

Dianthe grinned. "And do you not think this would be confusing? Two Elpidas!" She stretched out a hand and stroked her sister's face. "One is enough, I would think."

"You look so very tired. Let me tend to her so you can take to bed." Elpida slipped her hands around the infant and lifted her tenderly.

"How are Hermokrates and Phaidra?"

"In moment you can ask Phaidra herself. She brought me to your house and is the kitchen ordering your servants around like they are hers. But only in your best interest, of course." Elpida, with the infant snug in her arms, sat on the edge of the sleeping pallet next to her sister. "Hermokrates is fine, but what you really want to know is about Gylippos." She smiled broadly.

Dianthe blushed then stared at the ceiling. "Of course I am concerned about the welfare of such a close friend of Hermokrates, as I am about Dionysos, and Kalli."

"You love him still." Elpida began humming to soothe the infant, knowing that as long as she held her, she would be safe from Dianthe's wrath.

"I do not. I cannot. I am married to Agatharkhos, and that is that." Dianthe turned away as though she meant to sleep. Her eyes stayed wide open.

"I know what I say is true, whether you admit it or not." Elpida hummed louder now.

Dianthe tugged the blanket to her chin. "It does not matter. War will soon quit Syrakuse, and so will he." Now she repeated those words over in her mind, for although she uttered them, their meaning only now became apparent. He would leave. Without war there was nothing to keep him here.

The door creaked open slowly. "Is she awake?" asked Phaidra as she crept into the room.

Dianthe turned around to greet her. "I am so very happy to see you," said Dianthe as she struggled to prop herself up with a cushion.

Phaidra rushed to her. "Lay back, my dear." She pressed her gently down and stuffed a cushion under her head then pushed away the hair from Dianthe's forehead. "You must rest."

"Do I appear so tired? This is the identical sentiment my sister greeted me with."

"We are all most tired: tired of war, of scant rations, and of funeral pyres lighting the sky." Phaidra smiled "But soon we shall all rest and rejoice. I am sure of it."

"How is Father?" Dianthe, despite the protest of Phaidra, stood and walked to the open window.

"Most importantly he is alive. That is saying very much indeed considering his countless attempts at courting peril." She laughed a bit. "Our Spartan friend, called on him yesterday, in the dark of night, no less. Poor Hermokrates. Gylippos asks much of him. This Spartan should blunt his enthusiasm for battle. Neither Hermokrates nor the Council can tolerate him much longer."

Dianthe turned to face Phaidra. "How can they be so ungrateful? He is the one who delivered them from the Athenians." Her face flushed so she quickly spun round to the window again and stared down to the empty courtyard.

Phaidra sighed. "Yes, he has done much for our city, but he is single-minded in his hatred towards the Athenians and is unrelenting in his designs of their destruction."

Dianthe could only grin surreptitiously. She, too, shared his hatred of the Athenians, and would, if she could, prosecute their destruction. But now she worried for him. She knew these Syrakusans would discard him and Hermokrates too, once danger had passed them by. She wished for the war to continue somehow, to keep him here and a necessity to the city.

*****

Gylippos sat in the shadows of a sun-parched plane tree using the trunk as a back rest as he nibbled on piece of wine-soaked bread. They were loud, and so certain as they poured out of the city in pursuit of the Athenians. A horse snorted. He looked up. "Good day to you Hermokrates."

Hermokrates cantered his horse close to Gylippos. "I do not believe my eyes. A battle is waiting out there and you sit in leisure eating bread."

"Ha! There is no battle out there, only banditry, for that is all that is left to

Nemesis

accomplish against them." He crossed his ankles and stretched his arms overhead as though he prepared to nap.

"No battle? Do you not think there is any fight left in them?"

"Fight, why yes. But it will do them no good. There is only one pass they can negotiate with an army that large, and my Peloponnesians are blocking it. They will be as a wave crashing against a rocky shore. And when all is done only the rocks will be standing." He yawned.

"With final victory at hand, you wish to remain here?"

Gylippos smiled and slowly rose. "You are most correct. I should not remain while you and your citizens risk so much?"

"Then you will join me?" Hermokrates tugged on the reins moving his horse toward the double gate.

"No, I will leave the glorious task of delivering this final victory to Syrakusans. But I shall ride with you for a bit." Gylippos called to Kanthos for his horse. He followed Hermokrates just for less than a stade, parting ways at the road that led to the causeway near the marsh. "Stay safe, my friend. I am curious as to what they have left behind." Hermokrates stared at Gylippos as he departed, watching him take the road that would bring him into the abandoned Athenian camp. Once out of sight he resumed his ride north toward Katana and the fleeing invaders.

Gylippos let his horse meander along the road, allowing Kanthos and his small squad of Peloponnesians to easily keep pace on foot. They came upon the scene of his battle at the causeway where bloated corpses of Athenian rowers and marines scattered across the strand, swaying back and forth with the ebb and flow of the stunted waves in the harbor. A gull screeched. Gylippos spun around, catching sight of one of his hoplites skewering the corpse-scavenging bird. It flailed wildly until a second man loped off its head with a single stroke of his sword. Still more gulls hopped and fed amongst the dead, only reluctantly abandoning their gruesome feast at their approach. The gates on the stockade were closed so he dismounted and tried to shoulder the right gate open but the bolt appeared secured. Kanthos, even at his age found it easy to scramble up and over the timber wall. Soon Gylippos heard the clang of metal upon metal mixed with a bevy of curses from Kathos. Silence. Now the heavy gate groaned open. He led his horse through the gateway, past Kanthos and around piles of corpses that the Athenians had apparently stacked near the gate to keep them as far from the heart of their camp as possible. Kites circled overhead while vultures peered down from the stockade patiently ready to resume their place at the feast. The smoke of dying fires swept by him, nudged along by the breeze. He turned to his men. "Two parties. One patrol to the north gate. One to the gate near Daskon. Survivors are to be taken alive."

Abrias, one of the enomotarchs, jammed his spear into the dust. "We won't kill them, but they might." He motioned to the open gate and the mob of scavengers dispatched from Syrakuse to pick clean any loot.

Gylippos shook his head. "Do what you can," he said, but added grinning, "'but try not to injure them either,"

From here he spotted a scanty array of tents and a lone figure moving about them. Instinctively he reached for the hilt of his sword then grinned, releasing his grip. "Here." He shoved the reins of his horse into Kanthos' hand and began to jog toward the tents. As he drew closer he could hear moaning and men chanting to the gods. One soul dragged his limp body along the pathway by digging his elbows into the hard earth, his hands quivering and misshapen by wounds. He peered up at Gylippos. "Kill me, sir," he implored.

"Kanthos—give him drink," commanded Gylippos. He moved on. Now he could see clearly the figure as it bent over, scooping a handful of water from a pitcher to the mouth of a crumpled man. It was not until he was quite close did he realize this was an ancient man, his chiton blotched with grim and splattered dark with blood. He glanced sideways at him for only a moment then returned to his ministration. Gylippos stood over him, stunned by his actions and lack of concern for himself.

"Spartan, there is no one left to kill here, except me. These other poor souls will not see the sun set today." He moved to another, wetting the dying man's lips.

"Why prolong it if they are certain to die?"

"What else can I do? I am an Iatros, and as a physician I have sworn an oath to Asklepios and Apollo to do no harm. More yet, I am compelled to comfort them. It is more for my sake then for theirs."

"Athenian?"

The iatros shook his head. "I am from the island of Kos. You, sir, are undoubtedly from Sparta."

"And you are called?"

"My name, sir, is Polybos."

Now Kanthos returned with two other slaves hauling bulging skins of water. Gylippos waved them forward. "See to them." The trio began weaving amongst the suffering, offering drink and some words, although few responded.

"What shall be done with me?" Polybos knelt, dropped his head in fatigue.

"That, physician, is up to you. You may remain here and tend to your patients and most likely perish with them, for once I depart I cannot guarantee your safety. Or you may take to the hills before the Syrakusan cavalry runs you down." Gylippos paused. Polybos sighed then cast his eyes down at the earth. "Or you might accompany me. I fear their will be much need of your skills in the coming days."

Polybos stared long and hard at the sprawl of death.

"My men will stay with them until they cross the river," assured Gylippos. "And allow to them a peaceful journey."

Polybos shuffled to Kanthos and presented him with his last skin of water. "You leave scant opportunity for debate, Spartan. Mercy is a trait not often associated with you Lakedaimonians."

"Perhaps, but we are exceedingly practical also." Gylippos led his horse, walking along with Polybos toward the north gate of the camp, passing remnants of tents, discarded armor and the bodies of men and of beasts. As the pair neared the

Nemesis

outer precincts they heard high pitched yelps emanating from beneath a collapsed tent. Polybos flung back a section of the hefty cloth exposing a bitch with four pups of which only one moved about, nuzzling its motionless mother. Again it whined. Polybos gently lifted the squinty-eyed pup, carefully inspecting it. He hesitated before bending over to place it with its dead siblings once again.

"Take him with us," commanded Gylippos, "You two are a most rare commodity in this encampment of the dead." He grabbed the pup by the scruff, smiling. "You shall be called Syotheros—Boar-Hunter. Live up to the name." Gylippos dropped the pup into Polybos' hands.

Polybos, in turn, snatched up an abandoned petasos hat, snuggling the puppy in its upturned crown, and ambled after Gylippos. For a while the two walked along in silence, finally passing through the outer gate where the road appeared chewed up from hoofed beasts and littered with their dung. Polybos shrugged while studying the Spartan. "You are, no doubt, the architect of this destruction. It confounds me that you possess such a tender heart now."

Gylippos laughed. "A tender heart! Something I never have been accused of. It is not so tender, physician. Besides being practical, we Spartans are most certainly pious, and it is the gods who have placed you both in my hands. I dare not oppose their will. I am certain there will be many others to slay."

Here, outside the stockade, the trail of the Athenian retreat appeared quite obvious to him, but to the south, in opposition to it, dust rose over a distant grove. Now hoof-beats pounded louder and louder. Gylippos stared at the commotion of sight and sound, waiting for the horsemen to break across the ridge crest. "Syrakusans," he whispered under breath. Polybos heard him: he said nothing.

A small squadron of cavalry, most likely epheboi. It shall be good to see Dionysos once more, thought Gylippos. And sure enough Dionysos led the small band of riders. They crossed the once verdant expanse of orchards, now barren and studded with hacked tree trunks and trampled earth. Gylippos could easily see the smile on his face as he reined up.

"Good day to you, sir." Dionysos dipped his head quickly as a mannerism of respect. "The countryside between here and the Olympeion is quite empty."

Gylippos pointed to the north. "Ride that way and I think you will find a few of them. Maybe more than a few," he added,

Dionysos slid from his horse. "We have been ordered here to collect any survivors."

Gylippos smiled. "I have already done that."

Dionysos face puckered in bewilderment. He spun around scanning the area. "I see none."

"These two are the only ones left alive." Gylippos unfurled the hat in Polybos' hand, exposing the frisky pup.

"Still, we must scout out the camp," Dionysos insisted.

"Only the slaves of your countrymen scavenge about in there. Oh, and a squad of my Peloponnesians are searching for prisoners, but not to sell or dispatch, but merely to question."

Dionysos, curious, approached Polybos, but ignored the man, drawn as he was to the small dog cradled in the hat. "Large paws. Will make a good hunter, I think." He rubbed the pups head briskly. "Men, I say, are not much better than dogs. They fear the powerful and attack the weak. The strongest of their pack they place above all—and because of this their pack flourishes." He paused in thought. "I misstated it. They are superior to men."

"My boy, you speak more like a tyrant than a citizen of so fanatical a democracy. In Sparta we lean in neither direction, but have perfected a precarious balance between these two extremes."

"I would not presume to argue the merits and foibles of Spartan government with you, nor of the variety of democracy that we pretend to practice here in Syrakuse. But if dogs or wolves or any beasts were as fickle as men are in a democracy, they would surely perish."

Chapter 37
Syrakuse – Autumn 413 BC

Sling bullets pattered off his shield like hail while arrows flitted by, tearing the thick, humid air. Endymion hunkered down low, shield rim scraping the stony road of the ravine. Above and silhouetted by the late afternoon sky, he spotted multitudes of enemy archers and slingers, standing fearlessly in the open, flinging death upon his men. Centered in the narrow defile, a glistening shield wall of Peloponnesians awaited them. In three hours they had managed to advance barely a hundred meters. His men, battered from exhaustion, could barely hold up their weapons. Each step burned the muscles of their legs. Still, they trudged upward until the bodies of their comrades impeded further progress, Slaves rushed forward to remove the fallen, and they pushed on.

He turned around to peer down the funnel-like ravine to the broad meadows they had just traversed this morning. In those wide spaces Syrakusan cavalry nipped at their rear guard, dust marking out the cycle of attack and withdrawal. One of his men stumbled into him. "They must be running out of things to hurl at us." An arrow glanced off his shield. He grinned. Now, with a smile still on his face, a sling bullet tore through his helmet releasing a gush of blood. Endymion pulled him by the shoulder to reveal his comrade's face. The man's eye's quivered in their sockets before locking frozen with a sigh; Endymion pulled his arm away letting the man's limp body strike the road with a thud then stood up, neglectful of the danger, imbued with a new ferocity. He charged forward yelling at his men. "Up! Up!. Better to die up there than down here. Move up!" Here and there an Argive sprang to his feet and tried to advance up the steep ravine, but most fell, stricken by arrows, bullets and hefty stones.

Endymion found himself alone, crouched and shuffling against the torrent of missiles, but somehow remained unharmed. An arrow pierced his shield. Others sprouted like poppies from the turf around him. Suddenly he lost his footing, seemingly lifted from the very ground by an unseen force, a god, or demon. His spear slipped from his grasp. Next his shield. Now a different shield slammed down in front eclipsing him from the barrage.

"Argive, keep your head down!" A strong hand pushed him earthward. "We are withdrawing."

Endymion turned back. Demosthenes continued to brace his shield before the pair, waiting for his men to surround them with cover. Soon a squad of Athenian hoplites ringed them. Carefully and with newfound caution, Endymion retreated down the path and away from the petering salvo of missiles. Once out of range Demosthenes stood and grabbed a wine-skin from one of his men, gulping drink enthusiastically before handing it to Endymion. He too drank sprawled upon the ground near an entangled pile of corpses. The roar of battle had dissipated, now replaced by the incessant buzz of carrion flies. Normally repulsed by this he sat there, dazed and staring up the ravine at the litter of death. Cheers rang out from the top. He had no response, not even a thought, but continued to gaze up at the tiny forms of the enemy poking into the bright sky.

Demosthenes cursed. Endymion turned quickly, his trance seemingly shattered by the coarse string of oratory. "Is there a way out?"

Demosthenes snatched back the wine-skin, sipping more slowly now. "My Argive friend, they have been in the shit for three years. We've only had to deal with it for a few days. I think, only the men of our own army can defeat us."

Endymion drew no comfort from these words. He knew, as did most that the balance had tipped. Life held much less allure than death, and only by death would they escape Syrakuse.

*****

Xenias stood atop a flat-topped boulder peering down into the ravine, watching the Athenians drain away like water after a storm. They trickled out into the fields below, emerging from the shadows of the defile, struck by the steeply angled light of late afternoon. Movement, if any appeared tedious. No tents. Cook-fires numbered few. After more than an hour a group of slaves trudged away from the Athenian camp and back up the ravine and commenced dragging away the bodies of the dead. Xenias slipped a piece of flatbread into his mouth and sat, all the while mesmerized by the morbid activity below. As darkness seeped into the sky, the gloom of the ravine veiled his sight until several torches flickered alight, floating in the black.

"Any wounded?"

Xenias twisted around. Gylippos stood there, steadying his horse by the bridle, his face devoid of emotion.

None. No chance for them, but they kept on coming. No closer than that pile of stones. He pointed to a spot nearly fifty meters from their wall.

Gylippos began to focus on the bouncing light of the torches. He knew what gruesome business took place, the same inglorious but necessary task that followed every battle. "Any count of the Athenians?"

Xenias shook his head. "Hundreds perhaps? Hard to tell in the shadows and dust down there. But they were at it for hours, and so were we." He looked around at the barren plot. "I do not think there is a loose stone atop this ridge, or a surplus arrow or sling bullet." The breeze shifted, drawing the perfume of wood-smoke from the plain below. Even in the dim light, Xenias could make out the listless movements of the Athenians as they ambled about. "Where will they go next?"

Gylippos drew a long breath. "Not far. Perhaps they will test you once more. Or march further inland toward Katana. We have men posted at all the passes, bridges and fords between here and Katana." He rubbed the muzzle of his horse while staring out at the Athenian camp. "They are dead men—not by my hand or yours, or the suddenly invigorated Syrakusans but by their own. This trek they undertake leads straight to Hades." He began to walk away from the ridgeline toward Kanthos. "Take her, will you." He shoved the reins into his servant's hand and disappeared into the

Nemesis

night.

    Kanthos tied the horse to a nearby stump and moved to the wall of rocks and timber. "Are they beaten?"

    Xenias shrugged. "I think not. There may be thousands of them yet alive and being Athenians they certainly would not submit to reality."

    Kanthos stared at Xenias. "By the god you do resemble him—or should I say resemble what he would have looked like if he had lived." Xenias, always uncomfortable with these comparisons to Brasidas, did not reply. "And our commander thinks much like him." Kanthos chuckled a bit. "And do you? Can you tell me what he will do next?"

    Xenias squeezed the knuckles of his right hand, working away the pain. "This is work to him. A task plain and simple. It is his job to defeat them and he will not relent until that task is done."

    "Oh my friend, I had hoped he would simply let them slip away. The Syrakusans would prefer that. So very few still have the appetite for battle. Gylippos may have more enemies in Syrakuse than out there," he said fingering the darkness. "He constantly reminds them of their lack of enterprise in concluding this affair. With security close at hand they grow contemptuous—and supremely ungrateful."

    Xenias grinned. "And you would expect something else? Something more noble?" He shook his head. "They are no different than their Spartan cousins. They fear success. They will discard him as I was discarded. As was my brother. Neither kings, nor warriors, nor even slaves are immune from this reaction to their anxiety."

    "The Syrakusans are indeed ungrateful, and I would expect nothing else, but you lump them in with is very own countrymen. Men of his blood and his land. I refuse to believe that jealousy would move them toward their own destruction." Kanthos waited for Xenias to rebut his comments, but received only silence, allowing him to mull over his own words. His master's actions deserved nothing but praise from the Syrakusans. He had received none. Sparta, too, should undoubtedly heap a full measure of honor upon him, but a voice deep within him whispered otherwise. He knelt and began snapping twigs, sculpting them into a cone. He pulled a small earthenware pot from his satchel, extracting smoldering ember from it. "Time for something hot to eat." He poked the kindling then blew softly, summoning a modest flame. The evening breeze took over now as he carefully laid ever thicker branches upon the growing fire. Within minutes he had his tripod erected and a bronze pot hanging from it, and began to rummage through his bag. An onion, then a fist full of leeks fell into the pot. Now he scooped pearls of barley into the stew, stirring the concoction with a crooked stick he had reclaimed from the dirt. "I wonder what they are dining upon tonight?"

        "What was that?" Xenias snapped out of his night-induced trance.

        "The Athenians. I said: I wonder what they are eating? They can't have much."

Chapter 38
North-West of Syrakuse – Autumn 413 BC

Nikias hobbled from one camp-fire to the next, suppressing his discomfort and doubt while trying to lift the spirits of others. "Two more days and we'll be free of them," he assured a battered squad of Arkadian peltasts. Not a one had the energy to respond or even a crane a neck to look up from their despair. At the next cluster of men—some Argives—he smiled broadly as he watched them scrape their bowls clean of food. "Leave some room in your bellies. Good eating in Katana, and we will all be there soon enough." They stared back at him in silence. Endymion, too, could summon no response. He swabbed his fingers across the surface of his bowl then licked them clean. Nikias walked on. Only Hiero could look beyond Nikias' banter to realize the pain he suffered. Another man would have surrendered to it by now and still would be considered courageous, but Nikias, trying desperately to buoy his men's spirits, pushed himself evermore. Hiero could see his body twitch and quiver with each bolt of pain; Nikias did not let on. Hiero began to weep. He had seen Nikias in deep peril in battle, and crippled with sickness. He had displayed undaunted mettle, but this was different. Nikias' words—earnest, genuine and most desperate—he summoned from deep within. And by this supreme effort only could he keep the embers of hope alight and move the army to safety.

Not far from the Argives and in an area vacant of activity his head began to spin. He wobbled, one leg going limp, the other wavering. Hiero rushed to his side. "Sit here and rest." He eased Nikias to the earth, watching his master's head bob then snap upright as though he had been roused from a midday nap. "You must sleep. I will take you back now." He wrapped an arm around Nikias, lifting him and taking most of his weight. A few steps and Nikias collapsed. Hiero, himself worked beyond fatigue, could not lift him. "Help us!" He yelled several times. Some men turned a glance their way while others moved not at all. A lone figure stood and began walking toward them.

"Come on," whispered Endymion. "We must get him away from the men. This is no sight for them to see."

For a moment anger rose in Hiero. This Argive cared not for Nikias, and it struck him hard to experience this cool indifference to Nikias' pain, but he quickly realized only he truly knew of how his master suffered, He realized also that this man's energy and sympathy belonged to his fellow Argives. They braced Nikias upon his feet, flanking him then hustled off, at times dragging him, at other times slowing to allow him to step along with them. They burst into the tent and dropped Nikias onto his couch, both panting, breathless. Hiero, not looking to Endymion, tossed a fleece over Nikias and finally turned. "Thank you, Argive." Endymion had already departed. No sooner had Hiero planted himself upon a stool then Demosthenes strode into the tent.

"Wake him." Demosthenes rubbed his wounded leg, but did not sit. Hiero

Nemesis

stared back blankly. "Wake him now, or I shall."

"For all I know, sir, he may be dead." He bent over Nikias and shook him gently. Nikias growled, clearing his throat then winked his eyes open. "Demosthenes is here."

Nikias sat up, braced by his left arm and a stack of pillows. "Well?"

"Scouts are back. They do confirm what I had feared—all the passes and bridges have been blocked by the Syrakusans."

Nikias squeezed his eyes with the thumb and fore-finger of his right hand. "Think on what you have said. Is it truly *all* the passes and bridges?" Nikias wiggled the fingers on his open hand and Hiero presented him with a cup of wine,

"All the bridges between us and Katana. Any others mean nothing." Demosthenes impatience grew with the throbbing in his leg.

"It seems to me the Syrakusans possess no infinite number of men. And since the bridges and passes to the north are all so heavily populated by them as you suggest, perhaps the road to the south should be open." Nikias sipped his wine.

"Are you serious? Reverse our march? Head back toward Syrakuse?"

"Our chances might be better if we can make it to the coast and the Helorine Road, especially if the bulk of their forces are here. Once there we can march to Gela and send word to our allies to dispatch supplies. We will find none here. That Spartan has seen to it."

Demosthenes' first instinct was to rail against this scheme, but he looked at Nikias and realized that the old man had endured more than anyone—if he could attempt this grueling countermarch then no other soul had preeminence to complain. "This shall be a bitter command for them to execute. The men are beyond their limits." Then he added as he hobbled out of the tent. "But I will see to it."

Nikias emptied his cup and smiled as his eyes fell upon Hiero. "My dear, loyal friend, do you think they can hold on for at least a few more days?"

Hiero swallowed hard. "After some sleep, and some food, they shall move on. In this I have no doubt. But you, sir—can you carry on?"

Nikias, his pain temporarily subdued by the wine answered serenely, "I shall be leading them to the very end of our journey, no matter where that end may be."

"You too, need rest—and food." Hiero departed searching for the cook, only to find a smoldering, untended fire surrounded by upturned pots and broken vessels. He yelled to the farrier attending to Nikias' horse, "Where is he?"

The farrier shrugged. "Who knows? He bolted from here hours ago." He bent back the horse's leg to reveal its hoof and began an intense inspection. "He's not the only one to desert this day."

Hiero ignored him and began poking through the detritus that surrounded the cook-fire, uncovering a half-loaf of bread and a tiny pot of honey—nothing hot but it may fill the hole in Nikias' belly. As he strode toward the tent he plucked up a wine-skin and slipped in. Nikias slept. Hiero did not disturb him. He tore a small fraction of the loaf and stuffed it into his own mouth before placing the far larger portion on a table adjacent to Nikias and chewed the morsel over and over, until eventually he too succumbed to sleep.

Well before daybreak Nikias had forced himself up and had made his way outside where Medon awaited, clutching a scrawny rooster—normally a meager sacrifice, but the most extravagant one left to him. Finally Hiero emerged and watched as Nikias tipped out a portion of wine from his cup as Medon chanted. The scene took him back to the Piraios years passed, when the fleet sparkled in the harbor and every man, woman and child crammed along the docks or hung from the roof tops that cascaded down the hill towards the sea, their expectations lifted beyond reason by this spectacle of the city's wealth and military power. The anticipated expedition would conclude swiftly and most profitably. How could it not? Now the gaily colored banners were gone. So the cheering crowd. No tripods of incense smudged the clear Attic air. Mud, grime and tarnished armor replaced the ubiquitous garlands that had been draped everywhere on that singular day. Never has so great a power been brought so low. Hiero's despair now transformed to hatred as he watched Medon complete the sacrifice. This man had caused Nikias to squander an entire month with his divinations. He was no seer. He had no divine connections, but proved only a trickster hiding behind a cloak of piety. "Damn you, Nikias," he mumbled. "Damn you for listening to him."

It did not take long for the army to assemble for they had little in the way of burden left. All provender had been devoured and what little water sloshed in half-empty flasks strung around a few men's necks. Once more the hoplites formed a rectangular perimeter containing the slaves, women, cooks and carpenters within. Hiero quickly surmised the reduced size of the formation in comparison to the expansive one of their departure from their encampment near Syrakuse.

The darkness, at least for now, appeared to provide some respite from the relentless Syrakusan cavalry. Nikias may have indeed managed to out-fox them. They trudged on southward for hours unmolested, the cliffs of Epipolai growing larger, stirring uneasiness in him and virtual panic in many of the men. Now well past noon and yet no enemy cavalry had been seen. Even with Epipolai looming nearer his spirits lifted—the first day with no attack. *Perhaps Nikias has gotten us away*, thought Hiero, grinning.

*****

"You, Spartan, allowed them to escape," Athenagoras yanked on the reins of his horse, trying to hold it steady so he could deliver his tirade at Gylippos. "How can so many thousands of men just disappear?" Other Syrakusans, stirred by this accusation, added their displeasure. "You are your father's son," shouted another. "Did he not let the Athenians escape their destruction at the hands of a Spartan army? How much silver did it cost them this time?"

Gylippos until now had endured these insults to him, but would not stand for such toward his father. He reached up and pulled the Syrakusan to the ground, beating him with his command staff until it broke. The Syrakusan did not retaliate, but cowered, his face gray with dust, the only trace of color, a trickle of red running from

Nemesis

his lip to his chin. "You have only contended with these Athenians for a short three years. My country has had to vie with them for a century. There is no amount of silver or coin that could purchase my complicity, nor my father's in such a scheme." He picked up the two broken pieces of his t-shaped staff and strode to Athenagoras. "You, I think would have more to fear than most if any of them were left alive. They might have an interesting story to tell your countrymen," He turned away. "No matter. If the Athenians are not on the roads to Katana then they are moving south. Scouts have been dispatched." Gylippos mounted his horse. `

Gylippos calmly walked away from the Syrakusans for his rage had subsided. Xenias, his face marked by concern said, "I would not turn my back on them. They are men filled with their own importance and forget so very quickly what has been done for them."

Gylippos laughed a bit. "Oh, it is hardly all their fault. I have the uncanny predilection for discovering in others the very attributes I despise in myself. That is how easy it is for me to create enemies where there are none." He walked them both far away from the others. "Xenias, leave a garrison of one-hundred and bring the remainder of your men back toward Syrakuse." He leaned close to Xenias so only he could hear."I do not trust these Syrakusans even in so certain a victory. War is an art for men, not of animals. We must keep these Syrakusans from becoming beasts."

*****

Strange how his mind worked. With no enemy to fight, no terrain to contend with, despair now multiplied. Endymion trudged along the road blindly stepping forward, following the man ahead compelled merely by sound and inertia. The dust hung thick, stinging his eyes and parching his throat. The pangs of hunger, so ever present during the first few days of their trek had become blunted by his thirst. They had had no ration of water since before their attack upon the ravine and the blistering sun hammered at them on this open plain. Here and there, where a meager copse of trees offered shade, men hugged the shadows, refusing to move on. If he discovered some refuge unclaimed he too would cling to it, gladly abandoning this futile march. Only the dry plain stretched out before them.

Ahead he heard yelling. Men poured forward disappearing over a small ridge, most discarding their weapons as they sprinted or stumbled forward. Endymion, too, was drawn forward. Within the roar of indistinct shouts he heard, "Water!" Now he ran, cresting the ridge. Below he saw the vast spectacle of the army wallowing in a shallow river. Behind him more men tumbled and crashed toward it. The Asinaros, more a stream than a river, lured them beyond reason. They splashed and gulped furiously, some collapsing, others vomiting, all mindless of discipline or caution. The Asinaros lie low in the land—the banks rose up like walls. Endymion skidded down the slope, a dust biillowing behind him. He stumbled, rolling into the silted water and began scooping handfuls into his mouth. He gagged, coughed out the grit and gulped some more. Never in his life could he imagine a mere swallow of water to be so precious and incite such pleasure.

Men screamed. An arrow flitted by him, thudding into the chest of another who had just descended the bank. Endymion swung his head side to side and caught sight of scores of men dropping into the water, their blood staining the Asinaros. Above them the opposite bank seethed with enemy archers and javelineers, all hurling murder upon them. Only a few of his men had the will to retreat up the near bank. Most continued to drink, compelled by their thirst. Others stood up straight and motionless offering clear and distinct targets, eliciting what they hoped would be a quick death. An arrow sliced through his thigh; it ripped open a gash that sent blood coursing over his knee and down his shin. His leg buckled so he began crawling up the steep bank away from the fusillade. Men tumbled around him struck down by arrows and javelins. He dragged on, trying to dodge the avalanche of bodies that tumbled down the bank choking the river.

Once over the crest he could see what remained of their army trying, in futility, to repel three wings of Syrakusan cavalry that pressed them against the river. In the center of it all he spotted Nikias, his triple-crested helmet flashing in the bright sunlight as his horse reared up in panic. He scanned the ground for a sword, a spear, dagger, shield even a stone—anything he could employ as a weapon against this onslaught, for he would not perish defenseless. He grasped at what he thought was a spear shaft, but his hand came up filled with bone-dry earth. "Foul Sikelian dirt," he mumbled as he shook his hand empty. He hobbled toward Nikias and the center of the collapsing Athenian formation; the further he moved the thicker the press of men became until he jostled in amongst the few that still possessed both spear and shield. He would not make it so easy for the enemy.

Suddenly a salphinx bleated out a signal. The Syrakusans wheeled their horses away from them. The clamor of battle receded. He could distinguish individual voices, the snorting of horses and the moans of the dying. The Syrakusans had, for the moment, withdrawn. Endymion coolly peered down at his leg, detached somehow, watching the blood sheet out of the wound as though he looked upon the plight of another. He felt nothing as he limped closer to Nikias and the front rankers. Through the forest of bobbing heads and swaying spears, he spied a lone figure calmly walking toward them from the Syrakusan line. By his scarlet chiton he knew him to be a Spartan. The man carried no weapon in his hand and no body guard attended him, only a sword hung in its scabbard at his side. As he approached he lifted his Pilos helmet from his head then cradled it smartly in the crook of his left arm. With the back of his hand he wiped his brow and stepped forward to within a few meters of the Athenian line.

Nikias did not wait for him to speak but slipped from his horse and walked out to meet him. Endymion, meanwhile, had shouldered his way through the silent ranks, following in Nikias' wake. He strained to listen.

The Spartan spoke first. "Nikias, once more I offer you an opportunity to surrender, as I did more than two years past." The Spartan looked back over his shoulder. "I cannot hold them back for long."

Nikias lifted his chin, almost looking down now at his adversary. "Gylippos,

Nemesis

would you surrender? This is only a portion of our army you see here."

Gylippos nodded. "Hmm. Oh yes, your rearguard led by Demosthenes." He paused and shook his head. "They surrendered to me hours ago. What you have here is all that remains of your army."

Nikias' chin dropped. His head hung from his shoulders now. He did not speak. He could not speak. After a long while he drew a deep breath and looked directly at Gylippos. "What if I can guarantee Athens will pay for this. Many times over what this enterprise has cost to both you and the Syrakusans. Allow the men to depart and my officers and I will remain as hostages, a surety to this promise."

"Bargaining to the very end, Athenian. You negotiate like a merchant and not a soldier." Gylippos began to pace deliberately, back and forth seemingly studying the ground at his feet. Suddenly he snapped his head up. "I shall make this counter proposal and I shall make it only once. Surrender now and we shall kill no more of you—at least today."

Nikias looked away. "And the rest of your proposal?"

Gylippos stepped closer. "That is all of it."

You will guarantee that neither you nor the Syrakusans will inflict further harm upon my men?"

Gylippos shook his head. "I can only assure you that no more will die here and now. But I do give you my word I will endeavor to do everything possible to ensure you will be treated well. I do not rejoice in your misfortunes, only in my victory."

Nikias drew his sword from its scabbard, his hand shaking as he presented it to Gylippos. All around the clatter and clang of spears and sword striking the dry earth rang out as the Athenians discarded their weapons. Endymion edged forward, ignoring his wound. His head grew light but he continued to stare at the Spartan until the memory of Mantinea flashed in his mind. This Spartan he had seen briefly on the field that day. Their eyes met as they did back then. Gylippos dipped his head in recognition.

*****

Dianthe sat in the shade behind a column in the women's courtyard gently rocking her baby. She hummed softy, trying to enchant a bout of sleep when the door creaked open to reveal the grinning face of her sister Elpida. Dianthe pressed a finger to her lips. "Shhh. She is finally asleep."

Elpida crept ever closer, getting near enough to catch sight of her niece's serene face. "Would you like me to take her?"

Dianthe shook her head. "I dare not wake her. She has slept so little today because of the commotion out there. The crowd has at long last departed."

Elpida slid upon the bench next to her sister. "Athenian prisoners, so I am told. And there are more to come."

"They march them through the city? To where?" Dianthe continued to sway back and forth in rhythm to her lullaby.

"Not certain," said Elpida with a shrug. "Some say to the quarries." Distant yelling, like the rumbling of a far off storm, began to grow louder, until the uproar spilled over the walls from the street beyond startling the baby. She began to wail. Dianthe rocked all the quicker, but this did nothing to quell the upset for now the clamor grew so loud she could not even hear the cries of her daughter. "Come." Dianthe hustled up the stairs to her bedroom with Elpida close behind. She moved to the window that overlooked the street, a street heaving with people. From the alley leading to the agora a company of infantry appeared, spears bristling skyward and leading them were Hermokrates, Gylippos and Sikanos. The mob cheered them, calling out their names, while some stretched out their hands to touch them as they passed. Behind the last of the infantrymen staggered captives barely capable of walking. Many were bloodied. Most hunkered over, covering their heads with their arms to protect themselves from the stones, mud-bricks, and spit that were hurled their way. Dianthe felt scant pity for the prisoners. The scene only dredged up memories of these once haughty Athenians as they obliterated her world.

Elpida leaned out of the window. "Look. It is Dionysos!"

Dianthe edged close to her sister and gently placed her daughter into her arms. "Dionysos," she yelled out. The young man craned his neck and caught sight of her. "Please come in."

He nodded and spun his horse around disappearing behind the corner of the house. Elpida hurried down the stairs and into the outer courtyard to greet him. A servant ushered him in from the stable. Dianthe though, remained at her window unable to abandon the spectacle. She watched as the townsfolk continued to pelt the Athenians—they ducked and cowered, the weaker stumbling. These poor unfortunates made for easy targets. Unable to rise they curled up on the ground while stones, fists and feet thudded off their failing bodies until they sprawled unconscious. Some of the stronger ones tried to help their comrades but they were fended off by deluges of missiles when they ceased moving forward. The boys in the crowd carried on as though this were some variation in sport, each calling out a particular Athenian and body part before taking aim, cheering exuberantly when they hit their mark. They were indeed violent, but impersonal. To them it proved only a game. But the women exacted murderous revenge upon these prisoners, striking the fallen with brooms, kitchen ladles or shattered pottery, even bare fists in rages that were satiated only by death, all the while unleashing torrents of curses.

Dianthe looked upon this for more than an hour. Her eyes filled. She began to cry. Elpida pushed open the door and burst in. "Aren't you coming to see Dionysos? He's been waiting—." She paused, staring at her sister. "Why do you cry?"

Dianthe wiped the tears from her cheeks with the back of her hand as she sniffled. "I cry for Mother and Father. I cry for those wretched souls down there that are more dead than alive. More so, I cry for myself because my heart is broken and it can contain neither love nor hate."

Elpida turned away in silence and pulled the door shut as she departed.

Chapter 39
Syrakuse – Autumn 413 BC

    Nikias, along with Demosthenes and the other strategoi, stood at the rim of the quarry watching as the survivors of their army scrambled down an array of rickety ladders to the belly of their prison. Some, too weakened by days without food and water, slipped and fell, hitting the hard limestone, their blood staining the gray dust in pools of crimson; most of these failed to rise up. The Syrakusans that had tormented them while they were paraded through the city now ringed the edge of the quarry, continuing indefatigably with their harangues. Nikias turned around. There atop horses lingered the Syrakusan generals. He discerned by his bearing and reputation Hermokrates, and the Spartan Gylippos easily stood apart from the others, while the rest he did not know—that is except for one very familiar to him. He now looked upon Athenagoras, who turned away uncomfortably when their eyes met. Hiero, nearby as ever and ready to assist, whispered, "he does not wish to know you."
    Nikias, with his attention on the descending stream of men, spoke without turning to look at Hiero. "I would surmise I am much like the odd uncle—an embarrassment to Athenagoras."
    Hiero shuffled his feet and readjusted his grip on the wobbly Nikias. "If he possessed the least bit of honor he would petition the assembly on your behalf. After all, it was you who clung to false hopes and promises conjured by him to end this war. Did your money buy nothing?"
    "Money buys much, but it can never purchase honor. Their assembly shall on no account ever learn of what a close and long lasting bond Athenagoras enjoyed with the Athenians. More so, I would venture a guess that he will epitomize the most vigorous of enemies."
    Hiero peered into the seething mass of prisoners in the basin of the quarry. "What will become of us?"
    Nikias' legs buckled as he fought off a bolt of pain. Hiero braced him by tucking a shoulder under Nikias' arm. The episode passed. Finally, after all the prisoners had descended along with Demosthenes and the other officers. Hiero wrapped a hemp grass rope around Nikias' waist then led him to the edge. "I would think the ladder to be overly difficult." Slowly, with the help of a trio of Syrakusan slaves, he lowered Nikias. As soon as his master's feet hit the floor of the quarry the guard browbeat Hiero to retrieve the rope quickly. Once accomplished, they shoved Hiero toward a solitary ladder forcing him down.
    The quarry itself was by now deep in gloom and the night sky above provided a murky back drop for the flickering torches at each of the several guard stations on the rim. The wind raked across the jagged cliffs, muffling the groans and cries of the sick and dying. Incongruous laughter erupted from one of the guard posts. Hiero looked up to spot one of the guards pissing down onto a sleeping prisoner and quickly pulled Nikias up from the quarry wall and moved him into a large cave at the far end of the pit and away from any such humiliation. No thought had been given to

providing fire, cloaks, or blankets for warmth. Most of the men wore only tattered chitons and some had even this scant clothing torn from them by the Syrakusans on their parade through the city. Cold settled over them all. Nikias began to shiver.

"I shall fetch a blanket," Hiero said as he rose up. The men around him shook their heads. "A blanket, he says," mocked one of them. "Bring back one for me while you're at it."

Hiero kept walking. Once out of the cave he stood in the center of the quarry and commenced to study the walls, their height and the distance between guard stations.

"Looking for a way out?" Endymion asked as nudged Hiero. Hiero did not answer but continued to survey expanse of the pit. Endymion pointed to a small ledge near the mouth of the cave. "If a man were to reach that, he might have a chance."

Hiero stared long at the narrow ledge that jutted out from the sheer walls more than five meters high. "Without a ladder I cannot hope to reach it."

"Ah, but if you were to stand on my shoulders—." Endymion grinned. "But of course if you happened to make it that far, the top would still be out of reach. I think you will need my shoulders at least twice."

"You have a wound," remarked Hiero as he glanced at Endymion's bound and bloodied thigh.

Endymion shrugged "And who doesn't?"

The two men drifted apart, strolling aimlessly around the quarry floor, every now and then glancing up at the guard posts. As the night deepened chatter and movement decreased; the cold forced the guards to huddle over their small fires, wrapped in their cloaks. By now most of the prisoners had fallen asleep so Hiero and Endymion meandered to the base of the wall near the cave entrance.

"I'll climb up a bit then you follow," instructed Endymion. "When I motion for you to climb, move on by me." Hiero nodded. Endymion shuffled to the wall, feeling in the dark for gouges left in the scarred limestone by the quarrymen. After a few minutes of groping he planted his right foot on the wall at waist level then scrambled up smoothly exchanging foot and hand holds until he was well up over the height of a man. He dared not speak but instead pointed to the best spot for purchase on the brittle stone. Hiero moved up tentatively, pausing to rest after each step, until he finally squeezed past Endymion.

"Here," whispered Endymion as he braced Hiero's ankles steady upon his shoulders. "Grab a hold on the ledge then pull me up." He stood up cautiously lifting Hiero. His legs wobbled. The wound throbbed. Hiero stretched but his grip fell short. Endymion heaved upward pushing until he teetered on the tips of his feet. Suddenly the weight vanished, relieving the pain in his thigh.

"Come on." Hiero reached back down and pulled his companion to the ledge. After almost half an hour and with careful pauses whenever they heard a guard talk or move about they had secured a perch near the top. Endymion peeked over the rim. The nearest guard post, by his estimate, appeared twenty meters or so from him.

Nemesis

He leaned back and whispered, "Some trees over there. " He sliced the clear direction though the air with the edge of his hand. With both arms over the rim he rolled up and out of the quarry, stopping once clear to listen and scan the area. Satisfied they had not been detected, he waved Hiero on. Crouching all the while the pair waddled across an open expanse to the safety of the grove. Again he paused, listening as he pressed his body against an olive trunk. With Endymion leading, they scampered from tree to bush, to stone outcrop, using every feature of the landscape to conceal their movement. With the guard post fires glowing faintly behind them and his heart slowing to a more normal rhythm, Endymion stood and began to walk. Hiero, at first, continued to crouch, but finally relaxed and stood also. It took a while but the shaking in their limbs subsided and their breathing slowed. The pair strolled almost leisurely now over the rocky expanse, putting distance between them and the quarry. Endymion stared at Hiero. ""You are with the general Nikias, are you not? When I have seen him, you have always been nearby."

"Yes, I serve Nikias."

"Then he still lives?"

Hiero stopped walking. "Yes, though barely. Only his love for the army keeps him alive."

Endymion laughed. "Love for the army!" What an odd comment. He uses us up like fodder for his horses, in this doomed enterprise."

"I will tell you this, so that someone may know the truth. He knew war with Syrakuse was doomed at the start. He argued against it. Other, more ambitious men forced this expedition upon him."

"So in turn did you Athenians force this upon me and my countrymen, most of which lie dead upon this island."

Hiero nodded. "To that I have no reply. But still *you* may live to see your home again." Hiero began walking again then turned to Endymion. "Where is your home?"

"Argos," replied Endymion with a slight smile. "But I fear it is a long way off and I shall never see my home or my family again." Endymion slowed upon seeing a scattering of houses ahead. "And you sir? Does your family wait for you in Athens?"

"What remains of my family is back there in the quarry, and I shall return to him very soon."

Endymion halted, grabbing Hiero by the arm. "Did I hear you rightly? You plan to go back?"

"Why of course."

Endymion shook him. "You cannot. Nikias is dead. They are all dead. I have been convinced since the battle on the Heights that I am dead. If you return you will only confirm this."

"But I must." Hiero crouched to a knee and drew a long breath. "I shall not abandon him."

"Then why escape?"

"To fetch a blanket and some water. A token comfort for a dying man." Endymion reached out to Hiero, lifting him up. He said nothing more.

Eventually, they found themselves moving from a field to a smattering of buildings that funneled into a narrow lane. They bounded from one side to the other of the tapering street, trying to keep out of the foul water that sliced through the center-cut gutter, keeping silent.

Ahead, at a torch-lit intersection they heard several men talking, so they approached with caution, brushing against the walls, hugging the shadows. Not but a few feet from the corner three men, each armed with battle-spears and shields stepped into the alley. They laughed and joked with each other until one of them glanced at the pair. "What are you up to?" The others snapped their shields to the front, sealing off any exit.

"Run!" Endymion shoved Hiero back the way they had come. Hiero hesitated for a moment before instinct took control, sending him into a headlong sprint back through the alley and into the dark, broken countryside beyond. Endymion flung himself at the patrol. A spear-point sliced through his side below the ribs, curling him over just as a shield slammed into his neck .Now upon the ground they kicked him until he passed out, his twisted, bleeding body cradled by the gutter. "Stick him!" shouted one of the Syrakusans. Another raised his spear up, aiming its bronze butt-spike for Endymion's forehead.

"Wait!" The trio spun around. Gylippos slid from his horse and snatched a torch from one of the patrol, moving quickly to Endymion. He slowly moved it back and forth, coaxing as much light as possible from its sputtering flames.

"He's either a thief or war prisoner. Either way he's dead," barked out one of the Syrakusans.

Gylippos continued to study Endymion. "Three times I have come across you Argive, and three times the gods have compelled me to spare you." He rose up to face the Syrakusan patrol. "I will take charge of this man now. I have questions for him."

The leader of the patrol stepped forward and slammed the bloodless butt-spike of his spear into the ground. "He's a criminal. What would a Spartan general want with such a man?"

Gylippos fumbled for his coin purse. "Here." He tossed an obol to the leader. "Some wine and you shall forget all about him." He lifted Endymion's face out of the trickling gutter. "Kanthos!" Gylippos handed the torch to his servant. "Can you manage him?" Kanthos nodded. In an instant Gylippos had remounted his horse to continue his rounds. Meanwhile the Syrakusan patrol moved on, loud, raucous and anxious to employ their newfound coin for a portion of wine.

Kanthos dragged Endymion to nearby wall and propped him up, looking into his fading eyes. Blood soaked his chiton and began pooling on the ground near his hip. Kanthos unslung his cloak and pressed it into wound. Endymion winced.

"Friend, do you have water?" Endymion asked with crisp articulation that

Nemesis

caught Kanthos by surprise. His eyes widened as a bout of pain struck. He coughed, dry at first but soon blood gurgled up into his throat. Kanthos retrieved a wine-skin from his horse, unstoppered it then tipped it slowly allowing Endymion to drink—within a few gulps he commenced to cough again.

"We must stop this bleeding or this will be the full extent of your escape," said Kanthos as he plucked up the torch. When he peeled away the cloak and with the aid of the torch he could now see clearly the long gash in Endymion's side that continued to pulse blood. He shoved an end of the cloak into Endymion's mouth. "Bite on it," he commanded before thrusting the torch into the wound. It sizzled. Smoke sputtered carrying the smell of roasting flesh with it. Endymion twisted in pain. Kanthos withdrew the torch barely enough to inspect the wound. "Bite again." Once more he daubed the seeping wound with flames and repeated this several times until the bleeding had been stanched. "Can you stand?"

Endymion spit the end of the cloak out of his mouth. "Yes." With Kanthos' help he got to his feet but almost immediately fell back again, only Kanthos quick reaction and support keeping him upright. Slowly he gathered enough strength to move.

"Got to get us out of here before the patrol returns." Straining to his limit he managed to get Endymion upon his horse then led him through the maze of streets and alleyways to Gylippos' house. "We'll get you to a couch, my friend."

*****

Nikias had snatched fragments of sleep between his bouts of shivering, enduring the night and his pain in silence. Now he woke once more, scanning the faces of the men adjacent; Hiero was not amongst them. *My dear Hiero, even you have deserted me*, he thought while his eyes grew heavy as the pain and convulsions subsided.

"I am here."

The voice was that of Hiero, but Nikias knew it must be a fantasy conjured by his sickness. He leaned back.

"Nikias, I am here."

He opened his eyes. Above him stood Hiero, unfurling a long cloak which he draped over Nikias' shoulders. Nikias clenched the cloak tight to his chin. "Thank you," he whispered.

From within the deep blackness of the cave the two watched as the new day stroked the rim of the quarry with sunlight. Stirred by dawn, others moved about and found that many amongst them had died this night prior. Men who were able drew upon their reserves of strength, walked or crawled away, creating distance from these gruesome discoveries while others too wracked by fatigue pushed and kicked the corpses away, creating a buffer from ubiquitous death. Nikias struggled to rise. "We must move them."

Hiero had barely the energy to get to his feet, but still he followed Nikias as he inspected the bodies around them. "This one." Nikias grabbed the corpse by one arm. Hiero reluctantly pulled with both hands on the other and they dragged it to the far end of the quarry, a precinct that had by chance become a make-shift latrine. The pair had pulled out several bodies from the piles of the still living before others began to assist. This grisly chore took more than an hour and had attracted a small audience of Syrakusans above.

Whether by prearrangement or sympathy invoked by this scene, the Syrakusans lowered skins of water and a few meager baskets filled with loaves. Hiero managed to filch a hunk during a tussle but could not retrieve even a drop of water. The pair sat in the shade of the cave chewing so very slowly on their scant ration of bread.

Now several ladders slipped over the quarry rim and down the cliff. Soon guards descended, a squad of a dozen or more and they zig-zagged amongst the prisoners while shouting and peering into their faces. When their search brought them to the cave, the leader looked around then barked out, "Nikias, leader of the Athenians."

Nikias was unable to stand straightaway so he yelled in reply, "Over here." Hiero helped him to his feet.

The squad marched directly to him. "Nikias, son of Nikeratos, general of the Athenians?"

"I am Nikias."

"Come with us." Two guards bracketed him then clasped his arms before leading him out of the cave. Hiero trotted after them. While still within the cave he saw a solitary prisoner climbing one of the ladders. "Demosthenes," he mumbled.

Nikias paused as he placed his right foot upon the lowest rung, turning to look back at Hiero. "My friend must accompany me."

The commander of the guards shook his head. "He asked for you and Demosthenes only."

Nikias removed his foot from the rung and faced the guard. "Who asked for me?"

"The Spartan."

Nikias, for the first time since the battle in the river felt a flicker of optimism cross his thoughts. "Please sir, allow my friend to go with me. I am ill and cannot stand alone."

Hiero, not waiting for permission, moved next to Nikias, He peered up at the men leaning over top of the quarry. "Drop a line." In a few moments a coil of grass rope tumbled down. Hiero looped it around Nikias then quickly scrambled up the ladder to the party of slaves that had already begun to heave his master up the cliff face. Once at the top Nikias flung off the rope and stood straight while dusting himself off. He hardly looked the part of a general; his hair sprung wildly from his head while his face, arms and legs were mottled with blood and grime. Still he carried himself proudly, marching toward Gylippos and Ekritos.

Gylippos nodded to Kanthos who at this signal presented a cup of wine to Nikias. Nikias, with thirst kicking at him, refused at first to accept it. "I will think no

Nemesis

less of you if you drink," said Gylippos.

Nikias dipped his head in salute then took the cup. After a long gulp he handed it to Hiero, who also drank. "What service can I be to you, sir?" Nikias glanced to his left, to Demosthenes, who braced himself on an improvised crutch of olive wood. He could smell the stench of the festering wound on his leg even at this distance. Neglected, it had turned septic and was rotting his body.

"You two shall be my guests," said Gylippos with the trace of a smile. "I depart soon for Sparta, and you shall accompany me."

Nikias fought back tears. He had resigned himself to death in the quarry. He knew death for certain awaited him and any other failed commander at Athens at the hands of their fickle democracy. He had never expected such a reprieve. "And what lies in store for them?" He pointed down into the quarry.

Ekritos stepped forward. "They live or die at the pleasure of Syrakuse. It is the fate of the defeated."

Gylippos looked sideways at Ekritos. "If the Syrakusans are smart and if they are both civilized and thrifty, they shall ransom them back to Athens. That, after all, is what Sparta shall do with you."

"Are you certain that the Syrakusans will agree to this?" Nikias asked.

"Certain—no. But there is a payment due Sparta and to me. Two out of thousands would be a small concession."

"There may be some here in Syrakuse that might find it a bit uncomfortable if Demosthenes and I were to enlighten your fellow Spartans as to the internal politics of this city."

Gylippos smiled. "I have more than a vague inclination of whom you speak. I think it a safe wager that the men I stake my faith in hold more sway. At least we should both hope so."

Nikias shook his head ever so slightly. "What do you fear?"

Gylippos, caught off guard by this odd question, did not answer straightaway.

"Well?" prodded Nikias.

Gylippos answered quickly. "Defeat."

"Is that true? Do you fear it so much that you would do anything to avoid it?" Nikias stared up at the cloudless sky. "Think on your reply. Think on it hard."

Gylippos did. No, he would not do anything to avoid defeat. His answer was one of reflex, an answer that he was conditioned to deliver. "I suspect I fear our Law more than anything."

"Ah, now I know we have something in common." Nikias grinned a bit. "I too fear laws of a sort. Not ones such as yours, Spartan, that are as solid and unchanging as stone. Athenian laws are not so immutable. They are fashioned by men and men change. Change is our strength. It allows us to adapt."

"To be flexible is an admirable trait," said Gylippos, "but I have seen first-hand this Athenian fashion of suppleness and adaptability. Like everything you do, it is taken to an extreme, distorted and stretched beyond recognizing."

"And you Spartans are so straightforward?"

"Nikias, if you mean to say something then do so. I am no mood for a bout of nuanced words with couched meaning."

"You fear the law and that is why you carry out your battle orders. It is why you remained here in Sikilia, far from home for so many years." Nikias, exhausted, dropped to a knee.

"It seems you have been dispatched to Sikilia with similar orders."

Nikias craned his neck to peer up at the Spartan. "Clearly no. No such orders were given. That is the issue, and why I lingered here so long when I had ample opportunities to depart. Our Assembly dispensed vague instruction, with the expectation of very specific achievements."

"So being obscure is the Athenian way of being flexible? I prefer Spartan frankness."

"Your Spartan frankness is an illusion. I remained here in Sikilia because I feared how a capricious Assembly would react to a defeat. In Athens thousands govern our city. But these thousands are manipulated by a handful. Your city is governed by a fraction, and I suspect controlled by even fewer."

"Still, Nikias, we do not refashion the law to suit us, no matter how many govern."

"Laws are enforced and interpreted by men. As far as I know, your city too, is ruled by men."

"You will see for yourself when we return to Sparta. There is no circumstance that would have me in such fear of returning to my city, as you are to yours. We do not devour our own."

Nikias slowly rose up and extended a hand to Gylippos. "I pray, Gylippos that you are correct. I think that men are more similar then they like to admit. Do not outlive your usefulness as I have."

Demosthenes hobbled forward. "Sir, I request a sword. Consider it a brief loan. It shall be returned to you shortly."

"No, Demosthenes, you shall not be afforded such a swift and honorable escape from your predicament." Gylippos' tone grew sterner, retaining none of the cordiality directed at Nikias. "You are a demon that must be exorcised, but not here. Sparta will see you in chains." Gylippos turned to walk away, halted and turned. "You must endure only a single day down there before we depart."

*****

Gylippos stood in the courtyard of his borrowed house staring up at the rectangle of sky—Syrakusan sky—that would soon be only a memory. To him it appeared different, more tranquil and frozen in silence. He had grown accustomed to this foreign land and the distraction of war, and contemplated little joy in his return to Sparta. Until now, and for the most part, his adversaries stood out clearly across the field of battle; these distinctions would become muddled again in the politics of his home. Nikias had stumbled upon more truth than he cared to admit to the Athenian.

Nemesis

And then there was his wife. Any brief oasis of pleasant reflection was snuffed out by thoughts of her. As an antidote to these thoughts, his mind conjured visions of Dianthe and in circles one notion chased away the other. Kanthos shuffled past him with a yoke balancing a pair of baskets across his bony shoulders as he headed for the stable. "Leave behind all but my armor."

Kanthos nodded. "This is for the Argive."

Gylippos had forgotten entirely about his ailing prisoner. "How fares he?"

"Still breathing—and eating!"

Gylippos crossed the courtyard and strolled into the servants' quarters to a room so very dark and stifling. Syotheros nipped at his heels in a play act of hunting. Gylippos ignored him. Endymion, upon hearing him approach pushed himself up on his pallet.

"Strong enough to travel?" Gylippos stood just inside the doorway; Syotheros curled up at his feet, snatching a quick nap.

Endymion, peering down at the bandage that wrapped his side replied, "I have asked myself that very question every day for weeks. But to answer you sir, yes."

"Rest now. The tide will not be with us again until late afternoon."

Gylippos turned to leave.

"Am I to go to Sparta?"

Gylippos stopped at the threshold. "Either there or the quarry. The choice is yours." He stepped through a short narrow corridor into the courtyard where he could hear Kanthos cursing the donkey as he struggled to load it. The gate to the courtyard swung open revealing Hermokrates. Syotheros bounded ahead to greet the visitor. "Hermokrates, my friend, enter. I'll send for some wine," said Gylippos smiling.

Hermokrates did not return the greeting or the smile. "I bring urgent news. Athenagoras has persuaded the council to execute Nikias and Demosthenes."

"How could this happen?" snapped Gylippos as he made for the stable, the gate slamming shut with Syotheros whining, shut within the courtyard.

Hermokrates caught up with him and tugged on his arm. "Athenagoras had Ekritos attend the council session, ostensibly speaking on your behalf. Once he agreed to the execution, no more was said. Athenagoras had so worked them to a frenzy with hatred for the Athenians and a lust for vengeance that no one could hear me."

"And when shall this deed be done?"

"A messenger is one the way to the quarry. It is to happen without delay. It may have already happened." Hermokrates kept his hand clamped on Gylippos' shoulder.

Gylippos looked straight into his friend's eyes. "I must try." He pulled his horse out of its stall then mounted quickly and in no time galloped through the streets with Hermokrates in pursuit. Townsfolk cursed him as he waved them from the road, or bumped them as he passed, stirring up a great commotion in his wake that prevented Hermokrates from catching up. As he turned the last building, the expanse atop the quarry came into view. A contingent of guards with spears leveled across their thighs fenced off a small crowd that pressed upon them. Near the edge of the quarry lay one man. Not far off another held a limp body in his arms as he knelt. Gylippos slipped from his horse and ran to the first body, slowing as he approached. Demosthenes lie there, the knotted executioner's rope still wrapped around his neck, hollow eyes staring at the perfect blue sky.

Hiero sobbed, cradling Nikias, talking to his friend and master as though he still lived. "You cannot do this," he scolded. "I did not desert you."

Gylippos drew near, and as he stepped closer he could easily see the purple crease upon Nikias' throat. His shadow covered Nikias' body causing Hiero to peer up through tear-clouded eyes. "I grieve with you," said Gylippos.

"You grieve?" he looked back at Nikias' serene face. *He is finally without pain*, he thought. "He is dead and by your word, Spartan."

"Not by my word, Athenian. I take no pleasure in murder, even of a most despised enemy." He pointed to Demosthenes' corpse. For a while he stood silently over them, staring down. Nikias, pale in death, appeared much older than his years—hair white and his face etched with deep lines "My time here is fading as is my influence. Before I depart, is there service, no matter how slight, that I may render?"

Hiero gently lowered Nikias' head to the earth and stood slowly, his knees shaking and his back bent. "I would ask but two things from you: water, to wash his body and a small sharp knife."

*****

Dianthe sat in the cool shade near the spring of Arethusa, close enough to see the ship but far enough from it not to be seen. Up until now only the nautai and a single platoon of Peloponnesian mercenaries had boarded. Very few lingered about the quays and even fewer gave much attention to Gylippos as he strode up the brow-plank. Syrakuse, no longer in need of his service, had all but forgotten him—that is except for Hermokrates. Dianthe easily spotted him as he rode up to the Spartan's trireme. From here she could not hear the words but saw them exchanging banter, laughing and smiling. Hermokrates slid from his horse and hurried up the brow-plank. He wrapped his arms around Gylippos, pushed him back momentarily with hands clamped on his arm, said something more before embracing his friend one final time before scurrying down the plank to the quay. Men shouted at one another while tossing lines from the ship. Others heaved their shoulders into it, forcing it away from the quay. For a few moments it drifted quietly away. Gylippos stood motionless at the balustrade, never taking his eyes off of Hermokrates.

"Oars!" Even at this distance the command skimmed over the water loudly. The trireme lurched forward, its oars glistening in the late afternoon sun as they rose and plunged in cadence with the kaleustes' hammer strokes.

Dianthe now stared across to the beaches once occupied by the Athenian army, to where petering columns of smoke still spiraled up, marking the incineration of the last of the enemy dead. Her mind flew back to Melos and the pyres of her own relatives and family tended on that day by the once victorious Athenians. In only

Nemesis

several short years these invaders had been brought low. She had not only been rescued from them, but after all, witnessed their final destruction but she felt scant satisfaction. The Syrakusans, on the other hand, reveled in their victory. Teams of slaves carved up the derelict enemy warships, hacking off their bronze rams. She marveled at the long stream of wagons, heavy with these trophies, heading inland to the Olympeion.

"Dianthe!" Elpida tugged on her sister's shoulder "What are you doing here?" Elpida paused, her hand still resting on Dianthe as she leaned forward peering into the harbor. "That is his ship, isn't it?"

Dianthe, with a carefully crafted look of puzzlement, turned around. "Whose ship do you mean?"

Elpida laughed out loud then covered her mouth sheepishly, embarrassed at her outburst. "I am sorry. I should not laugh, for I know you must be distressed."

Dianthe clasped her sister's hand, pressing it firmly to her. "How can I be upset over something that has never happened?"

Voices rumbled from beyond, drawing her attention to the agora. The roar grew and became laced with the screams of women, causing passers-by to pause and stare back at the source of commotion. Without thinking Dianthe and Elpida walked toward the agora drawn along with the others. Young boys sprinted past them—compelled, as boys are by the prospects of the extraordinary. As the two sisters approached the corner of the Long Stoa they saw a crowd pressing forward: people shouting; arms flailing. A squad of hoplites charged into the marketplace, buffeting the mob with their shields as they edged toward the center of attraction. Dianthe picked out Dionysos' friend Philistos from the crowd and shouldered her way to him. "What has happened?"

Philistos turned and smiled upon recognizing her. Athenagoras is dead. Slain by an Athenian prisoner." Dianthe, shocked to silence did not respond. Philistos continued. "He escaped from the quarries. Didn't even try to run." he shrugged.

Dianthe stepped closer to the squad of hoplites, who had by now formed a cordon around the crumpled body of a man. Two of them flanked another man, a thin, sickly looking fellow whose blood-stained arms quivered like saplings in a storm. Now Hermokrates appeared, followed closely by Sikanos. He glanced at Athenagoras' corpse then bent over and retrieved a curve-bladed knife from the pool of blood. "Where did you get this?" He held the knife before the prisoner. The man's knees wobbled. He swallowed hard but said nothing. One of the guards clubbed him with a fist. The prisoner collapsed. "Enough!" shouted Hermokrates. He held the knife up, turning it slowly in examination. Now he looked straight at the prisoner as he waved the guards away and knelt, bringing his ear close to the man's mouth. "What do you wish?" he whispered.

Hiero gazed up, baffled by the question, but composed himself enough to cough out an answer. "To die." He smiled meekly.

Hermokrates rose up quickly and addressed the commander of the squad. "Kill him." Without waiting for the command to be carried out Hermokrates walked away.

The commander hesitated for a moment before waving one of the hoplites forward. He strode ahead, handing his shield to the commander so he could grasp the weapon with both hands. The hoplite reared back and with an underhand thrust drove the spear through Hiero's chest. He perished instantly.

Hermokrates did not turn around but kept walking, brushing past Dianthe without acknowledgement as he headed for the street leading to the Fountain of Arethusa and the sea wall. Dianthe, Elpida and Philistos hurried after him. Upon reaching the wall he braced his left hand on a cap stone and flung the curved knife out into the harbor.

Chapter 40
Thurii – Autumn 413 BC

In two days they had landed in Thurii where Gylippos went ashore only long enough to visit his father's grave, perform the sacrifice, and speak with Alexios as to the condition of his estate. Although he had invited Xenias to accompany him, his servant declined, instead preferring to linger at the wharf near the emporeion watching the freighters unload, stevedores hustling about and merchants squabbling. It seemed to him that these people—no all people—knew nothing of the war, a war that had consumed his life for three years. He envied them. As the sun swung high into the flawless sky he sought shade and went below to check on the Argive. As soon as his left foot slid from the bottom rung to the deck, Gylippos' dog Syotheros ran up to him sniffing, jumping and bowing in play. "You are the only good thing to come out of all of this," he said to the pup as he rubbed its bobbing head. *Except for that purse of Syrakusan silver,* he thought after reconsidering. Indeed his pay as a mercenary captain proved generous enough, even by Syrakusan standards. It would enable him to hire at least three more hands for the harvest each year and still leave enough for a new plough and ox. "And of course a new peplos for Temo," he added, addressing the whirling puppy at his feet. He knew this would be his last campaign outside of Lakonia; he was in his fifty-second year, one of the oldest of the surviving Brasideioi, and more than willing to hand his command over to a younger man.

"Argive," he growled as he ducked low beneath a beam. "Healing well?"

Endymion slapped the wound on his side. "Good as new." He tried to turn away slightly, to hide the look of pain upon his face but it did no good.

"Oh most certainly," said Xenias, laughing. He knelt beside the sleeping pallet in the cool darkness studying Endymion's face that was illuminated by a single shaft of sunlight that spilled through an upper oar-port. Syotheros jumped onto Endymion and began licking his face.

"Argive, there must be some good in you. This pup is able judge of men. After all he found Gylippos." Xenias pulled the dog from Endymion and shooed him away. "Fetch a rat." Syotheros bolted, his excited panting fading as he scurried into the shadows of the hold.

"What will he do with me?"

Xenias shrugged. "With that wound you'll be no good as a shield-bearer. No ransom for you either, unless you are related to an Argive aristocrat, but I doubt that a commoner like you is."

Endymion sighed. "What would it take to purchase my freedom?"

"Manumission?" I don't think a charcoal-burner would have the coin for that. But do not worry. He would not have delivered you from the Syrakusans to recoup only a few obols."

Endymion thought on his words. He was of no value. He owned no rich estate, no wealthy relatives who could ransom him, or any with influence in Argive affairs. He certainly possessed no special skill that would be valuable to a Spartan officer. "He should have killed me back there."

Xenias arched his eyebrows. "It may not have been up to him, my friend. The gods, I think, have intervened in your affairs. How else could you have survived when many other more skilled did not?" Xenias rose, smiling. "Relax Argive, and enjoy your convalescence. It shall be at least ten more days until we reach Gytheion." Xenias made his way to the ladder. Syotheros sat there with his tail wagging and a dead rat clamped in his jaws, waiting for approval. Xenias grinned then bounded up the ladder, through the three levels of rowers' benches to the battle deck and into the searing light of midday. Overhead seabirds spiraled above the stench of the exposed salt flats; the tide was fully out revealing helpless and stranded pickings for the gulls.

Kanthos burst out of the deck-house with Gylippos' battle pack then slid to his knees and began to dump out the contents. "His knife! I cannot find his knife!"

Xenias trotted over to him. "What is this all about?"

"My master's xuele knife is gone missing."

Xenias face puckered as though he were struck by a bolt of pain. "His knife from the Agoge? The gift from Brasidas?"

"Yes, yes, yes," he stammered. I thought I had packed it in Syrakuse, but I cannot be certain."

"One thing that is certain; you will be flogged."

"What are you two up to?" bellowed Gylippos as he strode aboard the battle deck of the trireme.

Xenias, in silence, retreated slowly, leaving Kanthos, still kneeling to answer his master. "Sir, I have misplaced your knife." He winced and looked away, preparing for a blow. A hand clamped down on his arm and pulled him up.

"You have not lost it." Gylippos looked directly at him, but his gaze seemed to penetrate through him and beyond. "I loaned it to a friend."

*****

Ahead the horizon began to darken to violet, but the breeze remained constant and gentle, enough to fill their sail without stirring up the swells. After a while a long strip of black marked out the boundary between sky and sea, growing larger, the detail of tree tops and tower roofs becoming distinct in the fading evening light. Like stars fallen to earth torch lights sparkled across the bending harbor and up the slopes of the town of Gytheion. The sighting of their destination spread quickly amongst the crew, inciting renewed vigor in their rowing and stirring others to climb to the battle-deck from the depths of the ship. Endymion, braced by the iatros Polybos, climbed up into the cool breeze and began to scan the harbor and the hills beyond. He was so very close to home and yet would never see it again. His thoughts flew to his wife but in particular his son. He prayed to the gods that no war would steal *his* life. That instead he could grow old in Argos and care for his family.

"Argive, I see you have made much progress in your recuperation." Gylippos helped him to the balustrade. "It is a marvelous sight." Endymion stared blankly at the Spartan. "Oh, not the harbor or our warships. I speak of the

Nemesis
Peloponnesos—I speak of home."

Endymion had to agree. "It is a sight I thought forever lost. Although I must admit I have never seen it from such a vantage."

"And although I am no seer, I would predict no Argive will ever have such a picturesque view of Lakonia." Gylippos paused in silence to listen to the sweet cadence of the oars plunging through the swells in perfect time with the flute. It was a soothing rhythm reminiscent of a lullaby from his early youth. "Are you able to walk?'

Endymion nodded. "Polybos is to be commended. My strength has more than doubled these past few days. I will be a burden to you no longer."

Gylippos' unseen smile was masked by the darkness. Now voices flew over the water from the shore, provoking an explosion of chatter aboard as crewmen hustled to their lines while the kaluestes barked out orders. Oars knifed deep and shuddered in the water as the rowers' arms flexed to brake the warship. With momentum in check three banks of oars rattled inboard from the port side as the trireme slid alongside the quay. Ropes squealed as they stretched. In a few moments dockmen hopped aboard securing the trireme. From beneath the battle-deck the rowdy conversations of the rowers bubbled up. They laughed and shouted as they worked to snatch their rowing cushions, flasks and satchels. By their talk each one had already planned out in what kapeleion they would drink and with which porne they would frolic. Gylippos disembarked first and stood on the quay surveying the men as they exited down the brow-plank. Endymion and Polybos moved next to him awaiting orders. Finally Kanthos made his way onto the quay leading a single mule laden with Gylippos panoplia. "Kanthos fetch a pair of donkeys." He handed his servant a pouch that clinked distinctively of coins. "The beasts are for you two."

Endymion was more than surprised by such a gesture. As a slave and prisoner he expected no such accommodation. Certainly no Athenian would expend a single obol for a Lakonian prisoner's comfort. "Sir, I mean no ingratitude, but I am more than capable of walking to your city from here."

Polybos looked sideways at the Argive. Pride would certainly not preclude him from accepting this token.

Gylippos stared off into the darkness in anticipation of Kanthos' return, saying nothing in response. Now the rowers began to move raucously off the trireme, oozing noisily into the alleyways of the busy port. Kanthos finally appeared with a pair of donkeys in tow. "Kanthos." Gylippos single word initiated a command previously established. The servant handed a heavy basket to Endymion and to Polybos. "You both have long journeys ahead."

Polybos spoke up immediately. "We are free?"

"That remains to be seen," quipped Gylippos. "You are for the moment at liberty and released from Spartan custody. Whether that is freedom or not, only time will tell."

Endymion's eyes began to well up. "Why?" The single word cracked weakly from his throat. He fell to a knee.

Gylippos approached him. "The gods have protected you, and I will not offend them." He reached down and pulled the Argive to his feet. "But do not think I offer mercy out of weakness or naïve goodness. You live to be my messenger. Tell your Argives what has happened to Sparta's enemies. Tell them what will happen to Argos if they foolishly stand by the Athenians. Such an alliance can only lead to your destruction. Remain quietly in your city and Sparta will ignore you."

Endymion extended a hand. Gylippos hesitated before clasping it. "Whatever your reason, sir, I thank you for your mercy."

The Spartan stared at him coolly. "Never set eyes on me again."

*****

As he descended the foothills that separated Gytheion from the interior, the expanse of the Eurotas Valley spread out before him, guarded for all time by the snowy peaks of Taygetos to his left and the less formidable Mount Parnon to his right—indeed Sparta required no walls for the gods had erected these massive barriers of stone unequaled by any constructed by mere mortal men. Icy wind swept in from the north, biting the exposed flesh of his face and arms. He tugged at his himation cloak, dipping his head as errant drops of frozen rain battered him. Traffic along the Gytheion Way proved light, although on occasion a wagon or two would pass, laden with firewood heading for Sparta.

He turned back, surveying his small caravan of loot wagons and the two enomotai of guards that escorted Sparta's trove of payment from Syrakuse. In his mind he played out his reception. This treasure along with so decisive a victory so favorable to his city and its allies would deserve, at least, a command of a mora. As the day wore on heavy clouds sunk lower, smothering the peaks and veiling the already diminished winter sun. He had hoped to make Amyklai easily by nightfall, but the wagons, slowed by the gouged and muddy road, hindered progress.

"Kanthos, ride ahead to the inn and secure us lodging." He pointed up the road to a faint pair of torches sputtering in the wind that lit the facade of a large mud-brick building. His servant galloped off returning in less than half an hour.

"It's all but empty, sir. No problem with beds or a warm dinner, and the inn-keeper seemed more than pleased to see me."

With the gloom pressing down the column spilled around the inn. A stable boy jogged out from the mews directly to Gylippos, taking his horse first to a sheltered stall uncannily aware of the Spartan's rank and understanding the station of each man in the party, attending to their horses accordingly.

Gylippos flipped his cloak over his shoulder to free his arm as he strode into the dimly lit inn. The hearth glowed invitingly as servants hustled about positioning kraters of wine and several steaming cauldrons of stew.

"Sir, the seat near the fire is for you," announced the inn-keeper as he led Gylippos by the arm. A young, trembling servant-girl, approached, eyes downcast, holding a large kothon that she presented curtly before shuffling away.

Gylippos smiled. The inn-keeper frowned. "She is new to serving, sir. I

Nemesis
apologize."

"Apologize for nothing, man. Were we all so sure of ourselves at that age?'

Gylippos nodded as he sipped the warm, spiced wine. Xenias stepped through the doorway pausing for a moment. Gylippos, for that precise moment, saw not Xenias, but Brasidas standing on the threshold. He blinked his eyes clear then waved him in. "Get all the men in here. A hot meal will do them good."

Soon the two enomotai of Neodameidois crammed into the inn, chattering, laughing, and stomping away the chill from their bones. Gylippos snatched a loaf of bread from a platter and tore off a hunk then handed it to Xenias. "I am certain your wife will be happy to see you."

Xenias nodded. "If she will let me into the house," he said with a chuckle. He dipped the bread into his bowl of stew and before stuffing the morsel into his mouth added, "She was not much happy when I left it."

Gylippos grinned and thought, *quite the opposite with me, my friend.* He watched as Xenias contentedly mopped up his stew with the bread. The man appeared, as always, tranquil. He looked the same before battle as he did during a warm meal, and this again reminded him of Brasidas. He envied Xenias for his companion would return home to a welcoming household and a loving wife with the cares and concerns of only a farmer while he, even in victory, would need to navigate the treacherous dealings of his enemies and his wife. But at least his prospects for divorce had improved, for with his share of the Syrakusans' payment he should be able to repay the dowry. This would, no doubt, offend her family and add to the ranks of his enemies. No, he must wait on this and press for a command first, before executing this plan of release.

"Sir, the horses are fed and the wagons secure," announced Kanthos as he shook the frozen rain from his cloak.

"Warm yourself," said Gylippos as he waved him toward the hearth.

Hunched over by the weight of the brim-full pitcher, the inn-keeper filled Gylippos' kothon. "Are you the man from Syrakuse? From the fighting there, I mean." He tipped the pitcher up, moving next to Xenias and began filling his cup also, studying both their faces. "You sir, must be Gylippos, son of Kleandridas? There has been much talk that you would be returning to Sparta soon."

"Much talk?" Gylippos barely touched the kothon to his lips before laughing.

"Sir, you are quite famous. Every traveler passing through has spoken of the great war at Syrakuse, and of you and your victory."

Xenias perked up. "Someone, at least, seems to have acknowledged that you had a part in this victory, sir. The Syrakusans offered no such reflections."

Gylippos waved at him to continue filling their cups. "It is only human nature to exaggerate peril when first confronted with it, and more quickly deny it once the peril has passed. Fear, like glory, is fleeting"

The inn-keeper paused in front of Xenias. Suddenly the blood drained from his face.

"Well, man what is it?" Gylippos snapped.

The inn-keeper stared now at Xenias. "I would seem to recognize you also sir, but it cannot be so." He reached for a charm that hung around his neck. "But the man I recognize has been dead many years. That man would be the son of Tellis—the hero Brasidas."

"Well he is not Brasidas," replied Gylippos. "But he is every bit the hero." Now he stood up, flexing his stiff back. "Gentlemen, I leave the evening to you. I am tired." He leaned over the fire, rubbing his hands together. "Good night." Instead of following the inn's attendant to his sleeping quarters, he stepped outside. The frigid air slapped him hard, stiffing his muscles again. From here he could see the stable boy wrapped in fleece, squatting near the stable door. As he approached the boy blinked open his eyes and began to rise.

"Stay there son. Keep warm and rest." He pulled the squeaking door open and stepped into the stables. Three of the Neodamodeis snapped to attention as he entered. His dog, Syotheros, bounded over to him, tail swaying exuberantly.

"All secure, sir," barked out the guard in charge of the detail.

Gylippos pulled back the canvas, revealing the neatly positioned sacks laden with silver and coins then ran his fingers over the lead seals that secured each one of them "So this is our victory?" he mumbled.

"Sir?" A guard stepped closer. "Did you say something, sir?"

Gylippos smiled and shook his head. "Have you men eaten?"

"Yes, sir. The boy out there brought us food, sir."

"Come," commanded Gylippos as he departed the stables with his dog. This time the boy failed to move, buried as he was in the bulky fleece cloak and sound asleep.

Chapter 41
Sparta – Autumn 413 BC

Gylippos felt like a youth in the Agoge summoned to the office of the Paidonomos to explain some transgression. He had delivered Sparta's payment from the Syrakusans and was received most cordially by the ephors and the two kings. His mess-mates had congratulated him on both his victorious and profitable campaign, but Likhas seemed withdrawn, detached and almost somber during this celebration. Likhas knew something but said nothing and he mulled over what offense could instigate this summons; he had only been home for less than three days. He sat there outside, chilled by the shade in the courtyard and the anxiety, waiting to be called in the Council chamber. From here he could hear the hawkers in the agora, the chatter of shoppers and the clucking of fowl, an almost pleasant symphony of plenty that his city provided.

The door cracked open and Tellis stepped out, his face void of expression and motioned to Gylippos. It took a few moments for his eyes to adjust to the gloom of the chamber, silhouettes gradually forming into full-featured and recognizable individuals of the Gerousia. Only Tellis did he know intimately. The two kings, Agis and Pleistoanax, sat uncomfortably together as Pharax the Gerousia president stood up. "Gylippos, son of Kleandridas, you have been accused by our allies, the Syrakusans, of misconduct toward their citizens and abusing the power of your command."

Gylippos stared blankly at Pharax. He heard the words, but could not believe them. He and his men had fought and bled for Syrakuse—and for Sparta—and he would be rewarded like this? This must be a nightmare or an hallucination. He sat dumbfounded.

"These charges surprise you?" asked Pharax.

Gylippos refocused then laughed. "Nothing should surprise me, particularly here in Sparta. What species of misconduct am I being accused of? Is victory an indiscretion?" Now his eyes moved to a lone figure standing apart from the twenty-eight seated Gerontes and two kings. Ekritos refused to return his glance.

"Ekritos returned from Syrakuse, but a few hours after you with a sealed letter of complaint from the Syrakusan council. It recounts, in detail, your hubris, harsh disregard for the lives of our allies, and abusive treatment of their citizens. The man described here," said Pharax as he glanced at the tablet, "is nothing less than a tyrant."

"And you accept this fiction?" challenged Gylippos. "I suppose, contained in this document, are glowing accounts of Ekritos' behavior? I would assume also that Athenagoras is signatory to it, and that Hermokrates' name is absent?"

Pharax shook his head. "Athenagoras is dead, so neither his name nor Hermokrates appears on this dispatch." He handed the tablet to Gylippos, and Gylippos scanned it, finding only two names of the accusers—*Agatharkhos* and *Diokles*.

Gylippos looked up. "I know both these men: one is a demagogue and the other a brute. You accept this?" He flipped the tablet onto the floor.

"Two signed, but they represent their entire council," snapped Agis.

Tellis picked up the discarded tablet and walked to Ekritos. "So you say you knew nothing of its contents? You say you were asked by their council to deliver this unread by you?"

Ekritos cleared his throat. "The tablet had the seal of their council upon it when I handed it to Pharax."

"That does not answer the question," stated Tellis.

"That is *my* answer," insisted Ekritos.

Pharax drew a deep breath. "Gylippos, son of Kleandridas, you are dismissed."

Gylippos marched out of the chamber into the bright afternoon. Across the road he caught sight of Kallikratidas kneeling and in a playful bout of boxing with his dog Syotheros.

A hand lighted on his shoulder. "There will be no command for you now," said Tellis. "But Pleistoanax and old Pharax pushed back at them, as did I. How will captaining a trireme fancy you?" Gylippos grinned, almost painfully, disappointed but not wanting to appear ungrateful. "Anyway, the army is marching to Attika under the command of Agis where he will become superintendent of the fortress of Dekelea. That posting, I think, would be most unpleasant. We, you and I, know that to vanquish the Athenians, we must defeat them at sea, and that is where you shall be."

Gylippos nodded and left Tellis at the steps to the Council house as he approached Kallikratidas. "My only two friends," announced Gylippos. In awkward leaps Syotheros ran to his master then rolled onto his back waiting for his belly to be scratched. Gylippos obliged.

"What did they want?"

Gylippos shrugged. "What do they always want? It was surely not to thank me."

"My friend, you have a knack for turning even honey bitter. What did you do now?"

"Win a battle." Gylippos snatched up Syotheros and began walking. "Come, my two friends. I am hungry."

Chapter 42
The Hellespont – 405 BC

Cruising gulls availed themselves of the stiff breeze from the north as they patrolled the sky above the Hellespont, spiraling downward ever slowly until one or more managed to snatch up an unlucky fish. From a hill rising up near the harbor of Lampsakos, Gylippos could see the triremes of the Athenian fleet being drawn upon the beaches near the Goat-Rivers on the distant side of the straight. Day upon day the Athenians formed up, challenging the Spartan fleet to battle and upon these same days Lysandros refused, and the Athenians, frustrated, hauled their vessels ashore more casually with each passing day. Unlike his own men, Gylippos exhibited a similar patience to his commander, enjoying this interlude between the inevitable bouts of combat that had afflicted his world for over a quarter century. His dog Syotheros stretched out at his feet, warming himself in the late afternoon sun.

"Seems no one will disturb your nap today, my friend." He rubbed the dog's side affectionately. Syotheros lifted his drowsy head and flicked open an eye to acknowledge his master then dropped upon the grass with a snort.

Slowly Kanthos trudged up the steep slope, a skin of water slung across his back as he hummed. Syotheros' tail began to beat the earth as he heard the servant's familiar footsteps. "Something for your thirst, sir" He peeled the flagon off his back and handed it to Gylippos.

"Sit down with me." Kanthos planted himself with Syotheros between them. "Strange. We watch them every day and they watch us." Gylippos took a swig then handed the skin back to Kanthos. "Our fleet and our armies have fought across the breadth of the world and now we—the Athenians and us—insist on crowding into these narrow waters. We are like two lions in a single den. There is no avoiding a fight."

"Seems Lysandros has been avoiding it all along," offered Kanthos

"Oh my old friend, he is more than cunning. He will attack—when it suits him."

"Is cunning a proper substitute for courage?" asked his servant. "The advantage gained by his cleverness may be fleeting. I prefer a direct stratagem, one that is more substantial and certainly more reliable."

Gylippos scratched Syotheros' head. "Your words echo those of Brasidas and Xenias. I would not have guessed they would have influenced you so? You may be the only courageous one remaining." His mind wandered now in reflection, to Kallikratidas, to Hermokrates, Tellis and Likhas: all courageous; all dead. This war had out-lived them all.

The quiet harbor of Lampsakos suddenly erupted with activity. From here he could see the crews of the Spartan triremes streaming aboard their vessels and hear the blare of salphinxes. Across the Hellespont he spied the Athenian warships drawn up on their beach helter-skelter and smoke from their cook-fires twirling skyward sky from further inland. Gylippos smacked his dog on the haunches. "Get up, boy. Time to earn our pay."

Lysandros' plan, conceived with patient deceit, had lured the Athenians to utter complacency. Even Gylippos was duly impressed. After reaching his quarters on the waterfront, he donned his armor and scrambled aboard his trireme, the *Ariste,* and formed up with the other vessels of his squadron. Eteonikos and his warships would sail with Gylippos straightaway for the Athenian encampment while Lysandros and the swiftest squadrons would steer south to cut off any retreat by the Athenians. Gylippos stood now at the bow, savoring the dousing that served as a momentary reprieve from onerous heat trapped by his armor. Kanthos, kneeling by the balustrade, clutched his master's shield while sucking air with a labored cadence, working to abate his nausea. Gylippos smiled at his servant's distress—he, on the other hand, had grown accustomed to the sea, inured to the rolling waters of the Hellespont. He enjoyed a remarkable, if unusual contentment at the prospects ahead. Still, he had never taken victory as a certainty, not wanting to exhibit the least amount of hubris that Far-Seeing Zeus would easily discern and so swiftly punish. But in his mind he had already played out the upcoming battle and there was nothing on the horizon or the beach ahead that could disrupt this vision. Here and there an enemy trireme managed to launch and tear southward away from the Goat Rivers. His squadron ignored these fugitives, continuing to slice through the dark and tossing water toward the beach. Men scurried about, most heading inland while some hurriedly snatched up weapons in a pathetic attempt to repel his landing force. One after another, his squadron of warships ground their keels into the shingle, the moan of gravel and sand sounding like a Titan clearing his throat. In seconds the brow plank had been lowered and his marines poured onto the shore. He looked left then right and saw platoon after platoon of marines forming up below the tide-line near their beached triremes, all moving swiftly, purposefully and with confidence for it seemed more like a drill, a casual rehearsal, and not the prelude to vast murder. Once all were ashore the salphinx blasted out the order to advance. They marched slowly—methodically—up past the high tide line and into the scanty pockets of defenders. Metal clanged. Men shouted. Some screamed. Many died. These brief encounters terminated quickly. The advance continued. In less than an hour they had captured thousands of Athenian paid rowers and slaughtered their dispirited bands of defending marines. A war that had been fought now over an entire generation had been brought to a conclusion in so short a time. Once gathered up from their hiding places in the coastal scrub, orchards and beached warships, the prisoners were herded to the open portions of the beach and ringed by light troops. The victors shoved them to their knees or prodded them with spears into tight packs all the while hurling insults and vivid descriptions of their upcoming fate and the joy of dispensing it to these once haughty Athenians.

With the battle over, Gylippos' instincts withdrew allowing thought and reflection to emerge. His mind felt detached somehow, as though this brief and violent event had been experienced by someone else and he had stumbled in, after the fact, as a witness to the result. He tossed his helmet to Kanthos but retained his spear

Nemesis

and body armor as he began strolling the beach. Unlike the harbor at Syrakuse, here there were no feeble, no sickly, no abandoned to evoke pity. He looked at them all dispassionately, content that the gods, in their own time, had enabled Sparta and punished the proud and impious. The faces seemed no different than in the aftermath of other battles—the smiles of relief of the victorious, the sullen resignation of the defeated, and the haunting serenity of the dead.

*****

For two days they had scoured the area around Goat-Rivers, capturing a few Athenian stragglers, but their real task was to recover every bit of silver and coin. By now and at Lysandros' order all the bronze rams of the enemy's vessels had been sawn off and their hulls. These vast skeletons of timber and planking were now used to fuel the hundreds of celebratory bonfires—conflagrations used also to incinerate the dead. Captured weapons and armor had been piled into a huge trophy. Sacks of coin many times over the weight of scores of men had been counted, sealed, and stowed aboard the *Ariste*.

"You shall have the privilege of delivering the yield of our victory to Sparta," announced Lysandros. "Seems they anticipate and value this as much as any returning hero. They should, I suspect, be doubly glad to see you."

Gylippos, although honored, was in little hurry to return home, for the larger portion of his life had mercifully been spent abroad, away from his wife and the corrosive politics of Sparta. Now, in reflection, he regretted their victory somewhat.

"Smile, Gylippos and at least feign a bit of appreciation for this distinction I have bestowed upon you."

Gylippos nodded. "I ask for your indulgence and mean no slight at your gesture but there must be others here more suited to this task."

Lysandros laughed. "Who? Klearkhos there? Or maybe Thorax?" The pair he pointed out knelt in the sand, imbedded in a ring of allied marines, wagering their share of loot in a game of knuckle bones. "No, you are the perfect candidate."

"Since you have had my ship loaded, it appears I must accept." Gylippos turned to his servant Kanthos. "Return to Lampsakos with the ship and make ready for the voyage." Now he scanned the chunky form of a fortress that was perched on a hill overlooking the strait. "I would have enjoyed this victory more so if *he* had been on this beach with his former countrymen."

Lysandros chuckled. "Alkibiades? We should have nothing to fear from him. He has managed to turn every friend and ally into a fervent enemy. Someone will indeed finish him." Lysandros studied the departing squadron. "In no hurry to see Lampsakos one final time?"

"I shall take a patrol cutter across later and for now enjoy this bit of dry land," replied Gylippos. He continued to stare at Alkibiades' castle.

"You want to go up there, don't you?"

"Gylippos shook his head. "I could do with a holiday from battle—at least for a few days, but doesn't it fascinate you that men like him, the very ones that ignite war and continue stoking its flames hardly get scorched by it?"

Jon Edward Martin

"Trust me Gylippos. The gods will tend to him. Now I must tend to my men. Take care of your cargo and perhaps the gods will allow us a reunion at Athens."

Gylippos watched as Kanthos boarded the *Ariste*. In no time the ship had been pushed off the shingle heading for Lampsakos. Kanthos, still unsettled at the prospect of fending off another bout of sea-sickness, scrambled below and wedged himself in between two bundles of fleece, hoping sleep would inure him. Mercifully, he dozed swiftly and for the entire crossing. Even with the raucous shipping of oars upon their arrival he barely opened his eyes, preferring instead to keep to his dreams. Finally once the trireme had been emptied of its crew and silence had prevailed for hours, did he hesitatingly begin to awaken. He heard voices. Not of crewmen at their tasks or boisterous rowers settling into their benches, but of a few men, talking in whispers. He winked his eyes open. At the far end of the hold he spied three men lit by a single oil lamp as they wrestled with the sacks of coin and silver. One of the men he recognized immediately as the servant of Eteonikos. Another was a Spartan officer and the third he had seen previously but could, like the officer, put no name to him.

"Cut the sack on the bottom and leave the seals untouched," instructed the officer. Eteonikos' servant sliced open the stitching on the bottom of one sack and scooped out several handfuls of coin then handed it to another who began re-stitching the open bottom. Kanthos watched them, terror-stricken, for he knew if he was found out they would kill him without compunction. After tampering with a dozen of the bags, they finally dragged themselves up the ladder and out of the hold along with two bulging sacks of pilfered silver. He listened for their footsteps, first across the planking of the deck then upon the thicker beams of the quay until there was silence. Now he crept up the ladder, peering across the deck with his eyes breaching the opening. Satisfied that he was alone he stood straight up in the cool breeze of night but before he could draw a deep breath a voice yelled out, "Stop!" A pair of men—one the Spartan officer and the other Eteonikos' servant barreled at him across the open deck of the trireme. They blocked his path to the brow-plank and the quay. He spun around toward the bow. A sputtering torch marked the tip of the vessel, beyond only blackness and the sound of lapping waves. He sprinted toward the bow and without thinking vaulted over the balustrade and into the water. Quickly overcoming his initial shock, he bobbed up for air. Arrows and javelins poured around him—the archers and acontists guarding the quays had responded with supreme efficiency to the alarm and filled the rails of the warship and the adjacent sections of the docks. He sucked a deep breath and plunged under the swells, clawing at the water trying to descend out of range of the missiles. His lungs burned and the barrage continued. An arrow struck his shoulder. His arm went numb.

"Keep to it, boys!" barked one of the archers. "Send him to Poseidon."

They all hovered over the dark water, some flailing torches to and fro, trying to catch any sight of the fugitive, but after an hour had passed they had sighted nothing. Not even the scant flotilla of row-boats that had launched could find anything, No body. No other vessels. Only the gloomy, tossing waters of the

Nemesis
Hellespont.

*****

Gylippos, forced into a hunch by the low timbers of the warship, rifled through his servants meager satchel of possessions. It made no sense. If Kanthos did decide to run off, after all these years and so many other better opportunities, why leave everything behind? He turned to the commander of the watch-guard. "He ran from you and jumped into the sea?"

"Why yes, well partially, sir."

Gylippos stepped to within an inch of the man. "Partially! Explain yourself."

"Well sir, he was on board sir and others—marines—chased after him. Once he leapt into the harbor they ordered us to stop him. We flung arrows and javelins. He never surfaced."

"Can you point out these marines to me?" Gylippos fought back the impulse to take hold of the guardsman.

He shook his head violently. "It was chaos sir. I did not recognize them."

"And I suppose they are gone?"

The guardsman dipped his head in silence, "Do you wish a patrol sent out for them?"

"Do not waste your time," barked Gylippos. "You and your men seemed more intent on killing a fugitive then stopping to ask why. I would hardly think you could recall these marines, if this is what they are in fact." He shoved the guardsman aside and barreled up the ladder onto the deck. He scanned the warship and the dark water beyond before turning back to confront the guardsman as he ascended the ladder. "Check all the seals." The guardsman called to his squad to descend into the ship. They chattered away as they grappled with the cargo of loot. Meanwhile Gylippos paced the deck, finally halting at the bow. He leaned upon the balustrade, arms spread wide, and stared into the blackness. *What have you done, my friend?* He repeated this over in his mind until interrupted by the guardsman.

"All intact sir."

Gylippos felt a surge of relief that quickly vanished as he thought of Kanthos. *No thief. No deserter. But what did he see?*

"Gylippos!" Someone shouted out his name. Up the brow plank came Lysandros. "Some excitement tonight?"

"More so for my servant. Seems that he drowned." Gylippos motioned to the unseen waters of the harbor.

"Your servant? I heard it was a thief they chased off the *Ariste*."

"Hardly a thief. The seals are intact and my servant is missing, but his belongings are stowed below. And no one can seem to locate the marines that were supposedly onboard when this commotion started."

"Your man, Kanthos? He has been with you how many years? Fifteen? Sixteen?"

"Sixteen years. Why would he bolt?" Gylippos sighed. "He belongs to Poseidon now."

Lysandros rested his hand on Gylippos' shoulder. "I shall keep a watch out for him once you depart. As I have come to know him, he is tough and he is smart. With luck we may find him asleep on the beach at daybreak."

"I pray so," replied Gylippos, half-heartedly. In truth they may, with luck, find only his body. Kanthos could not swim, and he had seen during the last battle, with what enthusiasm these marines could dispatch men. "The tide shall be turning at sunrise and with it we shall be under sail. Have you the dispatches?"

Lysandros handed him the hide sack containing several skytale message strips along with more conventional correspondence. "Be sure to give my regards to Agesilaos —and the Council, of course."

"And Agis?"

"Why certainly," said Lysandros with a grin. "How could I forget?"

Nemesis

Chapter 43
Sparta – 405 BC

"The seals were intact?" asked Pausanias, although he already knew the answer. The question, in and of itself, was a reminder to all that the treasure was returned properly and secure.

Ekhestratos, the magistrate of finance, nodded. "All the seals were intact and the count of sacks reconciled with the lading tally."

"And how do we know that this is truly a discrepancy?" Again Pausanias quizzed the magistrate,

"Each and every sack contained a ticket of its contents."

Again Pausanias interrogated vigorously. "How do we, for certain indeed, know that these tickets are correct? Could they not have been altered? Could the scribe be in error?"

The magistrate cleared his throat. He paused before answering, for he held no desire to implicate so distinguished a Peer. "Gylippos' name, as a confirmation, appears on all the tickets." His answer incited a hum of muffled conversation amongst the Gerontes. Gylippos looked to Pausanias. The king returned a glance of resignation.

Polyakes, the eldest of the Gerontes and president of the Gerousia stood up. "Gylippos, we shall now deliberate. You are dismissed. Return here at sunrise tomorrow."

Gylippos nodded then retreated from the chamber. *Could Polyakes be counted on to be fair? He had been a friend to Brasidas, but his own son, Ekritos, had been a witness against him on his return from Syrakuse. Are our very families so divided?*

Lingering just outside the Gerousia stood Klearkhos. "Well?"

Gylippos peered up at the dimming clouds. "I pray the gods impart to them a vision of the truth. I am no thief. More so, I am no witless dolt. Why would I mark the accounts with my name then pilfer the contents?"

"Your servant then? That is what many say. He conveniently disappeared the very evening before your departure." Klearkhos shrugged.

"Kanthos! Why no." Gylippos shook his head. "This I cannot accept. He had numerous opportunities to bolt. Why then, with the war at an end?"

Klearkhos stared at him. "Precisely, my friend. Think on this. Was he in love with Sparta any more than you? Did he relish returning here with the war at an end? Furthermore Gylippos, Lampsakos is much closer to his home in Makedonia, than Sparta."

"And if what you say is true, what of it? He was my servant and my responsibility. His actions cannot be separated from mine. This fantasy of yours changes nothing." Gylippos embraced Klearkhos. "But I thank you just the same. I know what you are trying to do. Kanthos is dead and my memories of him shall remain unchanged. He was a loyal, selfless companion and this is how I shall remember him."

"Gylippos, I shall not continue this debate, but defer." He walked a few steps away then turned back. "So tell me, what is their decision?"

"None yet. I am to return tomorrow." He paused and smiled at Klearkhos. "This may indeed be my final evening in Sparta."

"Then you will be at your home and not at your phidition?"

"My wife—my loyal wife—has petitioned for divorce, so I shall avoid that place until she has returned to her family."

"Try to stay in good cheer. They may only fine you. So you sell a plot of land and retire to your kleros near Gytheion. You must prefer the sea by now?"

"You know Klearkhos, I should have jettisoned all the silver As a sacrifice to Poseidon!" He laughed out loud. Now his face grew dark and grim. "That loot shall inflict more harm to our country than any enemy."

"Maybe so, but as Arkhidamos said, wars are won with money. Maybe it can also prevent them?"

Gylippos embraced his friend one final time before leaving him. He crossed the agora, but instead of heading toward the Hyakinthia Way took a path toward the Aphetaid Road which wound its way to the Eurotas. Just as the sun dipped below the peaks of Taygetos he arrived at the groves surrounding sanctuary of Artemis Orthia. Sadness fell upon him as memories of the rituals stirred—shouts of the crowds that spurred on the boys as they sprinted through the gauntlet of their older peers, fighting to hold onto their prize of cheese. He lamented the fact that he had no sons, no heir to endure this competition, but still savored his own victory. As he sat there in the stilled sanctuary, the echoes of others lost to him, drifted through his thoughts. Never in his life had self-pity manifested itself, but now, overwhelmed, it crept over him. He tried to fight it back, to push under his thoughts, telling himself that through struggle he would prevail, but now he wept.

"They would have done the same to Brasidas."

Startled Gylippos looked up. Near the temple door stood a tall, broad-shouldered figured, a form most familiar. He trembled now. Was this a vision? A spectre? It had been many years since the shade of his mentor had appeared to him. "Brasidas?" His heart drummed wildly. The figure strode closer, his face still in shadows until he moved to within a few feet of Gylippos.

"Xenias, sir."

Gylippos sucked in a deep breath, as though life itself had rushed back into his vacated body. "Why are you here?"

"Sir, Polyakes asked me to come."

"For what reason? Your service to Sparta and to me, as exemplary as it was, is over."

"Sir, he did not make mention, other than to say I should seek you out. I thought that you required me?"

Gylippos' spirit lifted. "Xenias, I have never said this to you, and I have no

Nemesis

excuse for this neglect, but you and your brother have been my strength. Throughout my life I have exerted all effort to act piously and with honor…"

Xenias interrupted, "But sir it is I who has been honored to have fought alongside you. Why do you speak as though honor and piety are mistaken actions?"

"Because, it seems, I have been abandoned by both the gods and my country. These attributes have done me little good."

"Sir, my brother died a hero, to Sparta and to many Hellenes that he freed from Athens' empire. You, by your deeds, have done no less. Your error, if one must be cited, is that you have survived. Do not out-live your friends."

Gylippos rubbed his eyes clear. "Death is your advice?"

"Why n-no," stammered Xenias. "I give no advice but state only the why of things. Any man without friends, whether in battle or in his home, is without protection and must be vigilant. Although the cloth the Fates have woven for you may seem tattered, it is far preferable than a shroud of death. And to be sure, you possess many friends even if they are not Spartans."

Gylippos wrapped his arm around Xenias' shoulder. "Old Polyakes is a wise man, as are you. I thank you for this visit—but by Zeus and Hades, you almost scared the very life from me. The resemblance is unmistakable."

*****

He rode up the twisting path to the temple of Apollo at Amyklai to the crest of the hill and the groomed meadow that ringed the sanctuary, his dog Syotheros patrolling ahead as always. From here he could see the imposing wall of the Taygetos range and the clouds snagged in its lofty peaks. He gazed north back at Sparta. It was a vantage he enjoyed many times in his life, but never did he imagine the day would come when his final view of home would be from this sacred hill. He dismounted then walked slowly to the temple. No flames burned in the scorched tripods that flanked the entrance. Inside the faint light of an oil lamp bounced shadows off the inner columns as drafts nudged the flame about. Now he uncurled his fist and held up a small bronze figurine of Hyakinthos, his votive offering to the god before his journey. His thoughts drifted back to this past morning and the subtle hopes that he clung to before the session at the Gerousia. He had entered the chamber of the Gerontes in silence. Polyakes read the sentence and in less than a minute he exited still in silence and no longer a Spartan.

By evening he had arrived at the Gytheion docks and the island of Kranai where in the murky past, Paris had taken Helen before they had fled Sparta. Torches marked out the sweeping crescent of the harbor. Activity all along the waterfront proved surprising at this time of day. Warships slipped into berths near the arsenal sheds while wide, sail topped merchant vessels cast off with the tide. Before he could climb aboard his ship someone shouted his name. A messenger waving a scroll approached.

"Sir, a message from Polyakes." Gylippos breath left him. Was this a reprieve? Did the Gerousia reverse its decision?" He fumbled with the cord that secured the scroll. The messenger clamped his hand over Gylippos". "The request that

I am to convey sir is, do not break the seal until you are at sea."

Gylippos shuffled up the brow-plank, uncharacteristically though Syotheros hesitated, allowing his master to the fore. "Come on. You've been to sea before." He slapped his hip and the dog bounded up the plank, tail wagging, as he followed his master to the balustrade near the pilot. The kaluestes shouted orders simultaneously with the captain, stirring the rowers into action. Gylippos picked up an oil lamp then snapped the seal on the scroll as he leaned comfortably against the railing. The note appeared brief.

Gylippos, there are those here in Sparta that do indeed know of your service to your country, and they thank you. But there are also others, who knowing of this service fear and despise you for it. With Pleistoanax, Tellis, Likhas and the rest dead, few along with me could argue the truth. Even Pausanias has sided with Agis against any confederate of Lysandros. These two kings are burdened with jealousies laden upon them by the victories of others. Their own triumphs are all but forgotten. Without war they have no prospects.

Do not be bitter. The gods have plans for every man and I think there is more in store for you.

Polyakes

Gylippos laughed. *Confederate of Lysandros indeed!* He gazed back at the cascading hills of Gytheion where flickering dots of lamp light marked out, here and there, the houses that littered the tilting slopes while torches along the docks outlined the shore with repetitive definition. Throughout his life he had returned and departed through this familiar harbor, but this would be his final view of Spartan soil. It proved a hard and difficult concept to grasp and truly accept; Gylippos had always drawn on the hope fate was not immutable and that circumstances could, through effort, be reformed. His mood alternated between anger and self-pity, but he staved off the sickly feeling of resignation.

Soon the evening mist seeped in, embracing his vessel and obscuring the last fading bit of torch light from the harbor island of Kranai. He wrapped himself in his cloak then sat near the balustrade, moving between dreams and the soothing consciousness of the rhythm of the sea.

Chapter 44
Thurii – 405 BC

The harbor here appeared so very different from Gytheion: hills withdrew imperceptibly, almost serenely, from the shore while the dockyard spread out broadly, protected by only an elbow of land with dozens of grain-lighters, freighters, and fishing skiffs cramming its precincts. Gylippos strained to pick out a single warship but could find none. To the north the beach beyond stretched to the horizon. Inland fields, orchards, and vineyards fanned out in contrast to the fortress-like hills of the Spartan home port, evoking a tranquility he had not felt in years, if ever. Expertly, the pilot threaded his way through the jammed harbor, inviting shouts, whistles and at times curses, from the smaller craft that thumped against the trireme's hull as it glided toward a berth; the boisterous response to their entrance shook him from his trance.

Gylippos scanned the docks and quickly spotted his father's servant as he jogged along, anticipating the ship's final destination on the quay. Alexios, accompanied by two workers from the olive groves, stood dock-side, waiting for the brow-plank to be lowered. He pointed back over his shoulder to a cart teamed up to a pair of plough horses, and tethered to the cart an ink-dark steed with a scarlet caparison nervously pranced in the commotion. "Sir, you have your choice of cart or horse." He shooed his companions up the brow-plank. "Your master's baggage," he commanded.

Gylippos directed them below-decks to locate his servant then descended to the dock led by Syotheros. "Alexios, it is so reassuring to see you again."

Alexios allowed himself a scant and modest smile. I am honored to be of service to the son of Kleandridas," He smiled at the dog. "Kastorian?"

Gylippos shook his head as he studied Syotheros approvingly. "No, although he exhibits the good behavior of a Spartan hound. I found him in the Athenian camp near Syrakuse." Gylippos now turned his attention to Alexios "The estate? I trust you have continued on with your efficient stewardship?"

Alexios' smile broadened. "An excellent olive harvest. And we have managed to sell more than five hundred khoinikes of wine. The pair strolled leisurely toward the cart with Alexios contributing the larger portion of conversation as he apprised Gylippos of the particulars of the finances of his oikos. "Oh sir, I apologize for not mentioning this at first but you have several visitors. They also seemed to have anticipated your arrival here in Thurii."

"Hmm, visitors you say. From where?"

"Syrakuse. Their ship docked three days ago."

Gylippos' thoughts immediately flew to memories of Dionysos. The young clerk and protégé of Hermokrates was now First Man in Syrakuse and at war with Karthage. No doubt he would be inclined to hire an unemployed captain of mercenaries. "Messenger from Dionysos?"

"One most certainly is not. He is your battle-servant. The man named Kanthos."

"Impossible! He is dead."

Alexios eyebrows arched. "Impossible it may be, but this is the very servant that accompanied you nigh on ten years past."

"Wait for my baggage." Gylippos vaulted upon his horse then galloped off, away from the broad harbor through the arrow-straight streets of Thurii proper until he broke into open country beyond the city walls, a landscape swathed in verdant orchards and luxuriant fields. He stopped only once to rest and water his horse before racing the final few stades to his estate. The gate had been left open, so he trotted through where a stable boy ran up to him anxiously snatching the reins to secure the horse. Gylippos failed to acknowledge any of the assembled household staff as he blew by them and into the main courtyard. He stopped mid-stride as he caught sight of his servant hunched over and sitting upon a bench within the shadows of the columns. He stared, working to confirm his vision, all the while wondering if, like Brasidas, this was a shade or phantom of his once lost servant. Kanthos began to rise to his feet, his movements hesitant and his legs unsteady. Gylippos did indeed discover the impossible. But Kanthos, like himself, seemed to have suffered much in the months since Lampsakos. The pair faced each other. Kanthos trembled as tears squeezed out of the corners of his eyes. Gylippos embraced him "I thought you dead?"

Kanthos drew a deep breath. "Oh, sir, they tried. Indeed they tried."

"Sit," insisted Gylippos as he gently guided Kanthos back to the bench.

Before he could ask, Kanthos answered. "Yes sir, Alexios has been the exceptional host. Without any request from me he had fetched the iatros to attend me."

"Alexios is a good man. And you Kanthos are also a good man. That may be the simplest and most important accolade for anyone. And more, you are my only true friend."

"Sir, there are other friends here. Friends that made it possible for me to journey here from Syrakuse, for it was a Syrakusan trireme that had fished me out of the drink and brought me to their city on their return."

"And what other friends? Gylippos asked, expecting to see a lieutenant of Dionysos.

Kanthos, with a great smile on his face, directed Gylippos with a tilt of his head to a darkened portal from where Dianthe emerged. Gylippos felt his body sway as his legs weakened. He stared at her, bereft of words, his mind swirling with fragments of memories, memories that disrupted his current state of tranquil melancholy. She moved toward him, hesitatingly, until falling into his arms. He awkwardly embraced her until she pushed away to look up at his face. "I spun in my mind the words I would speak to you, but now that I am here they are lost to me," she whispered.

He smiled. "Hello might be a good start." He wrapped his arms around her again. "This is something I have imagined and longed for, but never thought

Nemesis

possible."

Dianthe again pushed him away to look at him. Her smile had disappeared while her eyes had gone glassy with tears. She turned around and called to her daughter. "Eurynike."

"By Kastor and Polydeukes, she could be Elpida's twin," said Gylippos as the young girl approached. Behind her, from a shaded doorway, another woman emerged. "Elpida?" Eurynike and Elpida appeared as duplicate reflections in a slightly tarnished mirror.

The young woman smiled and nodded while moving into the light of the courtyard. A young man in his twenties followed her and with restrained eagerness extended a hand to Gylippos. "My name, sir, is Philistos." Elpida grabbed onto his arm and tugged him closer. "He is my husband."

Gylippos turned to Dianthe and without a word a word from him she answered. "Agatharkhos is dead. Killed along with Hermokrates."

Gylippos felt ashamed. This news of her husband's death conjured no sympathy in him, but instead a guilty sort joy. "I am sorry," he answered, pausing before he continued. "How long have you been here?"

Philistos spoke up. "Several days and by good fortune and the help of the gods, your servant Kanthos turned up. But with less good fortune the news of your exile also arrived in Syrakuse. Dionysos, upon hearing of this assumed you would come here to Thurii to claim your property and rights. And so he dispatched me to present his offer." Dianthe now stepped back, withdrawing from the conversation and retreating a distance to stand between her sister and her daughter. Gylippos' watched her with concern. Philistos cleared his throat. "Dionysos offers a commission in his army in the war against Karthage."

Gylippos thought it odd that while Philistos delivered the message with enthusiasm, Dianthe grew more sullen until she turned away from him and walked to the far end of the courtyard. Gylippos nodded to Philistos. "Excuse me for a moment." He approached Dianthe in her isolation. "Is this not a good thing? Do you not wish it that I return to Syrakuse with you?"

She crossed her arms and peered at the ground, refusing to look at him. "Oh Gylippos, are you not tired of war? Elpida and Philistos are returning to Syrakuse. I am not."

"Where will you go?"

Finally she looked up at him again. "As far from war as I can, if only for her sake. With victory, Sparta has restored our island to us. We two are not the only survivors. My cousins have already resettled upon our family's land. They have sent for us."

"Is Thurii not far enough?" he asked.

"For me it is, but is it for you?" she asked. "How long could you fend off the allure of war?"

"For just a moment pretend we are happy and unconcerned." Gylippos clasped her hand and led her back to the company of the others. "For tonight, at least, we may only speak of pleasant and precious memories. There are many days ahead when we can return to our burdens and obligations."

And for that night and several others they thought nothing of the past or the future, preferring the sweet intoxication of the moment. They spent the days touring the vineyards and orchards, Alexios as their proud guide. With true enthusiasm, he detailed the efforts required to produce the many successful harvests of the estate and pointed out the preparations already underway to ensure future ones. During these tours, Gylippos and Dianthe would take what opportunities they could to stroll together and apart from the others. Eurynike seemed content to venture off on the pony given to her by Gylippos. Elpida and Philistos would disappear on these excursions too, reappearing with uncanny timing just as Alexios had missed them.

Each and every night they all dined together. Philistos, being Syrakusan, held no inhibitions in meting out his wine, although once or twice Gylippos' dogged moderation did seem to unsettle him, for to him at least it was a moderation that bordered on abstinence, a self- inflicted torture that neither improved his character or his health. "Do you Spartans never get thirsty?" he would ask before finishing off the last of the wine at each dinner.

On their last evening together in Thurii, Gylippos lay on his sleeping pallet, Dianthe beside him as he gazed out the window at the waxing moon. *It took a lifetime*, he thought, *to finally achieve a bit of happiness.*
*****

Elpida and Philistos lead the way through the harbor town followed by Dianthe, Gylippos, Eurynike and Kanthos. Not far behind Alexios herded the procession of wagons, carts, porters and baggage animals all laden with the paraphernalia of travel. They moved at a casual pace, slowed by their burdens and the rising heat of midday. The docks bustled with slaves loading vessels preparing to take advantage of the tide, while fishermen heaved their catch from the bellies of their boats into barrows and buckets that congested the quays. The two ships were moored adjacent, one a trireme bound for Syrakuse and the other a freighter heading west to the Aegean.

Elpida and Dianthe stood on the wharf embracing each other as Eurynike held both their hands. They cried little, although their eyes were wet with sorrow for they knew this might well be the last time they would see each other. Elpida asked one final time, "Please come with us?"

"Perhaps someday, dear sister." She squeezed Elpida tightly now. "Perhaps."

Gylippos stood back as the two sisters exchanged farewells. Syotheros sat patiently against his master's leg, confirming his presence by touch alone while staring up at the ubiquitous gulls. Elpida stepped away from Dianthe then knelt to hug Eurynike before turning away to follow her husband. Dianthe looked at Gylippos, her expression an invitation to join her now that her sister had departed.

As soon as he took a step, Syotheros, as always, pranced ahead, leading the way. The dog approached Dianthe and sat while she rubbed his head; his tail wagged

Nemesis

with satisfaction. Suddenly the dog got up on all fours and sauntered directly for Elpida's ship, planting himself at the bottom of the brow-plank.

"I think your dog prefers a different voyage," she said, along with a faint laugh. She looked up at Gylippos. His face, so unlike these past days, bore an expression of concern and certainly not one of amusement at his dog's seemingly confused action. Not until this very moment was he certain, but Syotheros knew which ship they would board,

"No, no," she whispered under her breath.

He stepped forward and embraced her. "Dianthe, I truly did not know which journey would be mine, but I do know that the one I choose, I could not ask you to take with me."

"Oh Gylippos, is peace so toxic that you would choose war over us?"

"Dianthe, I may have learned little in my life, but one thing I have come to know is what person is here." He tapped his chest. "I am a Spartan, reared since birth to seek conflict—to embrace destruction. It is my nature to do so. I have no less choice in it this than a bird does to fly or a fish to swim. Spurning our nature would be futile. The only real choice I have is to spare you from this destruction. You have suffered enough. " He slid his hand out of hers and walked to the trireme, refusing to look back for he knew, in truth why he decided so. It was for his sake and not hers that he journeyed alone to Syrakuse.

Glossary

***Agiad**s* – one of the two royal houses of Sparta. Leonidas, Kleomenes and Pleistoanax were all Agiad kings

Agoge – the state sponsored education system of Sparta, focusing primarily on military development, thought to begin at age seven, continuing to age eighteen.

Akratisma – breakfast.

Andreion – the men's dining hall in a Greek home.

Aspis – A shield; the hoplite shield was constructed of a bowl shape wooden core with an offset rim, and was often covered with a thin facing of bronze, although leather was also used; it was held with the left arm by a central armband that moved the weight from the wrist to the forearm, while the left arm gripped a handle just inside the rim.

Bouleterion – the council house in a Greek city.

Chiton – a tunic made from two rectangles of cloth pinned at the shoulders.

Daimon – a spirit.

Deipnon – Supper.

Ekthesis – the act of exposing an unwanted infant.

Embaterion March – a quick-paced march of the Spartan army, often accompanied by the singing of the paian.

Eurypontids – one of the two royal Spartan houses.

Himation – a long cloak.

Histion – the large, square main sail of ancient Greek ships.

Hoplite – a Greek heavy-infantryman equipped with a bronze helmet, an aspis, bronze or linen composite body armor, greaves, a sword and his primary weapon, an eight foot long spear.

Iatros – a physician.

Kaleustes – the seaman in charge of the rowers on a Greek ship.

Kopis – a thick-tipped chopping sword.

Kylix – a shallow wine cup, often fashioned with a stem.

Lokhagos – in the Athenian army, the commander of a unit (***lokhos***) of one-hundred hoplites. In the Spartan army, a commander of a unit (lokhos) of 512 hoplites.

Nemesis

Mora – a division in the Spartan army consisting of two lokhoi (1024 hoplites)

Nautai – rowers on Greek ships.

Omphalotomos – a mid-wife.

Penteconter – an ancient warship with twenty-five rowers per side on a single level.

Periokoi – literally "dwellers about". Non Spartan free citizens of Lakonia. They controlled their local land and politics but were subject to Spartan decisions of foreign policy and war.

Petasos – a broad-brimmed felt hat.

Pynx – the hill in Athens where the people assembled to vote and debate proposals.

Spartiate – a male citizen of Sparta.

Sphagia – the blood sacrifice carried out before battle.

Stadion – a distance of approximately 185 meters.

Stoa – a long building with a series of exterior columns on one side and a wall on the other.

Strategos – in the Athenian army, a commander of one of the ten divisions based on the ten tribes of Athens.

Symposion - a drinking party, usually hosted by the affluent.

Trireme – a square-sailed warship propelled by oarsmen (nautai) positioned in three banks per side; the crew consisted of 170 nautai, 20 epibatai (marines) and several officers.

Xenagos – a captain of mercenary soldiers

Xiphidion – a short sword or dagger

Xiphos – a sword.

Jon Edward Martin

Printed in Great Britain
by Amazon.co.uk, Ltd.,
Marston Gate.